LIVING
IN THE OFFBEAT

PATRICIA HOPKINS

Living In The Offbeat

http://www.wanderlustbooksllc.com

Edited by Paul Alexander Rancier

Published in the United States by Wanderlust Books, LLC
Cover art photo Shutterstock / Blend Images / 94701595

ISBN-10: 0985761326
ISBN-13: 978-0-9857613-2-5

Also by Patricia Hopkins

More Than A Notion

I Am The Shadowman

In Loving Memory of Fran

The Road Less Traveled

Zooming down the smooth sleek surface of the highway,
the vast nothingness of the countryside
makes the miles magically disappear.
Don't remember where I've been or know where I'm headed,
but going to get there fast!

Today I veered off the highway to take the road less traveled.
Filled with potholes and weeds coming through the cracks,
crumbling concrete forces me to slow way down.
Taking a look at what I've been missing
mindlessly rushing my way through life.

Slowing down to appreciate this journey;
Opening my eyes to the wonderfulness
of my family, my friends, of it all.
Realizing this journey is to be savored
for the destination arrives much too soon.

~ ~ ~ Patricia Hopkins

Part One...
Living

Prologue

"Derek? How could you?" She clenched her teeth so tightly, her jaw muscles ached. "Who is she?"

"I didn't mean to hurt you. It just happened... You don't know her."

"Sonofabitch! You have the nerve—the gall, to come to my job and tell me you want a divorce because you've gotten some bitch pregnant? That you're leaving me for her?"

"Ronnie, calm down. There is no need to get overly excited about this. I love her and she loves me. That's all there is to it. I've moved my things out of the house and contacted a realtor to put the house up for sale. Everything is already taken care of."

"Say what? You put the house up for sale? Moved out already? Everything is taken care of? So that's it, huh? After eleven years of marriage, this is all you think I deserve? I gave you the best years of my life... Gave up my chance to have children...Gave you all my love, and now you say you're leaving me?"

"I'm sorry," he whispered. "It's done."

"Yeah, you're sorry all right. Sorry assed good for nothing sonofabitch! That's exactly what you are—sorry! And I'm sorry I ever laid eyes on your sorry ass...."

Chapter 1

Veronica Indigo Pierce's morning began just like every other day. Just like that dreadful day four years earlier when her husband unexpectedly asked for a divorce and sent her world into a harrowing tailspin. She recalled their last conversation and was astonished how one person's decision could affect another's life is such a profound way.

And today when she laced up her jogging shoes to take her daily 20-minute jaunt around the neighborhood, she had no inkling how another seemingly innocent decision would change the course of her life. Someone, somewhere, had dropped a metaphorical pebble in the pond of her life, setting in motion a chain of events whose waves would eventually touch Veronica and upset the comfortable balance she worked so hard to achieve. As she'd soon discover, the ripple effect was very real.

* * *

"Hey lady! Looking good!" shouted out her next door neighbor.

Ronnie waved and picked up her pace. The couple she bought the house from believed the woman practiced voodoo because she was from New Orleans by way of Haiti. Just because her neighbor smoked a cornhusk pipe and wore a charm necklace filled with talismans didn't mean she was a voodoo witch. The sellers also told her the neighbor didn't like them because she wasn't fond of their *auras*. She chuckled to herself.

At 41, Ronnie, as her friends called her, was in excellent shape—physically, emotionally, and financially. It took awhile to get back on her feet after Derek Jordan, her husband of eleven years, left her for a younger woman. Their long marriage didn't produce any children because Derek had already fathered three from a previous relationship. He always told her that three was enough.

Ronnie honored his decision and willingly accepted his children as her own. Despite the fact that she always wanted babies, especially a little girl, she hoped a life spent with her husband would make up for her choice. In the beginning life with Derek seemed to be enough and his children were with them so often, it felt like his kids *were* hers. Nevertheless, once the divorce was final, she rarely saw any of his children. What was the point? They already had mothers.

With the money she received from the divorce settlement, she bought a cute little bungalow in a section of town where Black urban professionals flocked. The locals affectionately nicknamed their neighborhood Beverly Hills East. Jogging through her solidly middle-class neighborhood, she appreciated how her neighbors took pride in landscaping their yards.

It was hard keeping up her home, and not having anyone to pick up the slack, she maintained it herself. At first it seemed like the 30-year old house was nothing more than a money pit. Week after week, something was always breaking down, needing to be repaired or replaced. Ultimately after surviving numerous setbacks, the house was finally at a stage of completion where she could come home after a

2

stressful day and relax. Though it remained difficult paying all the bills on her own, it was worth it because the house belonged solely to her.

Ronnie was a self-proclaimed *fashionista*. Her coworkers teased that they never saw her wear the same outfit twice. Several women looked to her for fashion advice, though at times it became tiresome maintaining the look of a diva. Good or bad, she'd built this image and couldn't retreat without losing credibility. She joked that the weekly appointment with her hair stylist to maintain her natural hair was like having another utility bill. Looking good was expensive as hell, but a true diva didn't care how much it cost.

Because of her high maintenance lifestyle, Ronnie didn't have much money left at the end of the month, but somehow she managed to meet her obligations. Bottom line was as long as she looked good, it didn't really matter how much it cost.

Parked in the garage of her ranch style home was her baby, a brand new "straight off the showroom floor" silver *Infiniti IPL G Coupe*. The car was a gift to herself after receiving her latest promotion. The monthly payments were outrageous, but she was so worth it. Yes, she was living the life so many women envied, yet few in her circle achieved.

Feeling refreshed after her run, she switched gears and got ready for work. Getting dressed was a breeze. She had it down to a science and could be pulled together in less than thirty minutes. Her tight schedule didn't allow room for a real breakfast, so picking up a cup of McDonald's coffee along the way would suffice.

As Ronnie pulled out of the garage, she made a mental note to call the gardener to tidy up the flowerbed. She couldn't stand to have weeds sprouting through the mulch. Another expense, but there was no way she would ever push a lawnmower or get down on her hands and knees to pull weeds. Manual labor was meant to be hired out—not performed by a diva.

From out of nowhere, two large dogs charged her car, causing her to brake abruptly. The dogs stopped at the driver's door, snarling. Their owner ran out of his house yelling, "Daffy! Blazer! Get back here! Now!"

Ronnie waved at her neighbor, trying hard to not be irritated at the dogs that always seemed to get out of the back yard. She was usually able to tolerate other people's animals, but in this case, she hated those dogs. If they weren't out chasing kids on bikes, they were barking at all times of the day and night—disturbing the peace of virtually every neighbor within 100 yards.

"People...would you please control your dogs?" she yelled. *You're lucky I don't call animal control and report your ass.*

The iPhone automatically connected through the car's speakers, distracting her from the barking dogs. She accepted the incoming call and watched her neighbor drag the dogs back into the house. She sped down the street.

"Hey lady, how ya doing this morning?" asked her best friend Joie Parker.

Joie and Ronnie met several years ago at a leadership conference in LA. Assigned to the same work group, they instantly connected, which was unusual in itself because their friendship grew during a point in life where grown women didn't usually make new friends—which is any age after 20. After discovering they lived mere blocks apart, the women established a friendship that continued to grow over the years.

"Hey girl, I'm doing what I do. Almost ran over my neighbor's dogs. Again. Now, I'm picking up some Micky D's java before tackling this traffic." She placed her order and picked up the coffee at the drive thru window.

"I hear ya. I'm sittin' in it already, but at least I only have to do it twice a week. Your office let ya'll do teleworking yet?" Boney James' latest CD played in the background.

"Are you kidding? You know my company isn't about to let us telework from home. They don't trust us to put in a full 8 hours as it is. Can you imagine what would happen if we were out of their sight? Anyway, don't get me started. How was your weekend?" Ronnie merged into the heavy traffic heading towards the freeway.

"It was aw'right. Me and Cedric worked in the garden, planted summer veggies, and then caught an early movie. My mother kept the kids so we did our usual Saturday night role-playing."

"Oh yeah? What was it this time? Pizza delivery guy? Pool boy? Cable repairman? Or was it your turn to play the helpless sexy woman who shows up at the house when wifey's not home?"

"Girl you know us too well." Joie laughed. "Actually, it wasn't any of those scenarios. Check this out. We went to the Chinese restaurant to order dinner. It wasn't in our neighborhood 'cause we didn't want nobody to recognize us. We even drove there in separate cars. Well, while we was standing in line pretending not to know each other,

4

Cedric came up behind me and said loud enough for the customers to hear that he had a huge eggroll back at his place and asked me if I wanted to try it."

"Really? Didn't know you guys were exhibitionists. What did you say?"

"I told him I only like supersized eggrolls. So I asked what did he have—a spring roll or an eggroll? Girl, you should've seen that old man behind the counter. He was grinning like we told him he won the lottery. Anyway, I wore a skirt and wasn't wearing no panties and I pretended to drop something on the floor. I bent over and gave Cedric a sneak preview. He didn't know I wasn't wearing underwear. He almost lost his mind."

"No you didn't... What about the other customers? Weren't you worried they were going to see you?"

"When I bent over, I made sure wasn't nobody but Cedric behind me. That old Chinese man couldn't see nothing."

"Girl, y'all are crazy. And you are a straight up freak. What happened then?" Ronnie enjoyed living vicariously through Joie's antics.

"While we was waiting on our food, we sat towards the back of the restaurant in this little booth—real close like. It was kind of private so Cedric slipped his hand under my skirt. Girlfriend, I was squirming all over the place. I had a mini orgasm in that Chinese restaurant. He tried so hard to hide his erection, but couldn't. It was so funny. Anyway, we never did make it to the house. We left the restaurant, parked in back of that shopping center, and did it right there in the backseat of his car. Cedric had to go back and pick up our food later."

"Umh, umh, umh. Y'all going to get caught one day. Joie, you are so nasty. Sitting in a public booth with no panties on. Just let me know which restaurant it was so I'll remember to not sit in that booth." Ronnie laughed.

"Whatever. My ass wasn't touching nothin' but my skirt and my husband's big ole fingers. Oh girl, that was so much fun. Anyway, that was my latest sexual escapade. Me and Cedric been together so long, we have to do crazy stuff to keep it exciting—you know, keep things fresh. What about you? Don't you and Ike have wild crazy sex?"

"Sorry to say, no. Me and Ike rarely have sex...hardly ever anymore. In fact, it's been so long, I've pulled Big Blue out of retirement." Ronnie sipped her hot coffee.

"I'm sorry too, girlfriend."

"Seriously though, I didn't even see Ike this weekend. He kept his son, so it was pretty much my hanging out alone again. But I picked up a few more outfits for our cruise. Sexy momma is ready for this! Girl, I doubt if we make it out of the cabin. I'm going lay it on him."

"I heard that... What good is having a man if he can't stroke you every now and then?" she chuckled. "So, when ya leaving?"

Ronnie loved how Joie could talk down and dirty one minute, then flip the switch to become Ms. Prim and Proper the next.

"Week after next and I cannot wait to get to the Bahamas. It's my first cruise and I am so excited. Those folks at work are working my last nerve and like I said, me and Ike haven't spent much quality time together lately. He always seems to be so busy." She tried sipping the hot liquid and exclaimed, "Damn it!"

"What's up? Everything okay?" Joie inched along at a snail's pace.

"Yeah, I just scalded my tongue on this hot coffee." She returned the cup to the cup holder and focused on the road. "What's up with this awful traffic? Seems like I-64 gets worse every day. Dang! These people drive like idiots—as if they're the only ones on the road."

"Okay lady, take a deep breath and relax. You ain't gonna get there any faster by stressing. Hey, I have an idea. Let's get a drink after work today, there's something I want to talk to you about."

"Everything all right between you and Cedric?" Ronnie knew something had to be up because Joie never wanted to get together after work.

"Yeah, we're cool. Nothing like that. I just wanna run some ideas by you, that's all. Well, anyway, hope you have a good day and I'll catch up with you after work."

"All right girlfriend, that sounds good. Talk to you later." Ronnie honked at a car that cut her off. The driver held the cell phone in her left hand and texted with her right, oblivious to other cars on the road. "If it's that serious, girlfriend, pull your ass off the road and make a phone call instead!" she mouthed as she sped by.

* * *

Ronnie pulled into the office parking lot a few minutes before 8. *Looks like I'm not the only one just getting here.* Ralph, her boss, pulled into the spot next to hers. He waved. She waved back. She sat in her car pretending to look for something in the glove compartment, avoiding going inside.

She prayed, *Lord, please help me to get through this day. Give me the strength to not curse out these people. I know you're teaching me patience by placing me in an office filled with fools, but I need a break today.* She grabbed the briefcase from the backseat and headed towards the old dilapidated building her company had the nerve to call an office. The building was supposedly temporary until the new office space was ready, but temporary was going on two years. She sarcastically dubbed it the trailer park.

"Good morning Veronica," Ralph said with a smirk. "You have a good weekend?"

He was younger than her by at least 15 years in age and 10 in experience. He'd risen up through the ranks, recently promoted over her, thanks to the good ole' boy network that supposedly ceased to exist with the nomination of the first Black president.

"Yes I did. Thanks for asking," Ronnie replied, not being big on office small talk. She didn't want to have a superficial conversation with Ralph and any reason to get away from him was a good one. She plopped down into her tiny cubicle outside his office, booted up her computer and opened her email.

"Great. Good to hear. Well, me and my friends hung out, did a bit of surfing….." Ralph droned on in the background in an annoying nasally voice.

Oh, no he didn't! Ronnie thought as she read an email about an upcoming conference Ralph had scheduled. *What the hell! I'm supposed to be on vacation that week.* She took a deep breath, printed out the approved vacation request and marched right into Ralph's office.

He held up a finger signifying she wait until he finished his phone call, "Yep, yep, two o'clock sounds great. I'll see you then, honey. Bye-bye. Love you too." He hung up the phone and addressed his employee. "That was my wife; she's learning how to play golf and wants me there for her first lesson. It's going to be so great having her out there with me on Saturday mornings. Now, what can I do for you Veronica?" Ralph sounded as if he had no idea what Ronnie wanted. *What's with her anyway? Always holding on to all that repressed anger...*

"Ralph, um, do you remember approving my time off for the week after next? For my vacation?" Ronnie showed him the papers. "Yes, I am aware of your previously approved time off, but this workshop has been scheduled for months and we really need for you to be there. It's a wonderful opportunity and I think it will be great for you to meet the corporate team. If I were you, I'd jump at this. Your becoming acquainted with the A-list players will only help you succeed. It did for me. What do you think Veronica? Is it going to be a problem?"

"Ralph, this is the first I'm hearing about this workshop *and* I've made plans for week after next. I really can't go. Isn't there someone else who can take my place?" Ronnie tried her best to remain professional and not go off on his ass.

"Veronica, I told corporate all about you and how you were recently promoted based on your outstanding work ethic. The team is flying in to meet the top hitters and I need you to represent our division and stand in for me. I was offered a chance to attend an important conference in Vegas. Unfortunately, it's the same week as the workshop and I've already paid the conference fees and made my travel arrangements."

"So what are you saying?" she asked.

"I'm sorry Veronica, but I hoped you would be more understanding about this. It's too late for corporate to reshuffle their schedules and I didn't think it would be a problem for you to reschedule your vacation because this is a very, very important workshop. You really should mingle with the higher-ups if you want to succeed in this organization." Ralph pasted a phony smile on his face.

"That's not fair Ralph. You know how hard I work. Why didn't I know about this workshop earlier? And more importantly why wasn't I invited to attend in the first place? I would not have made vacation plans if I knew about this sooner. If it's so important to schmooze with corporate, why don't you go?"

Ralph looked at her as if she was on the verge of losing her mind. He smugly replied, "Well if it's going to be a problem... I suppose I can try to get someone else."

She took a deep breath trying to calm her growing rage. "I've come in early and stayed late every day for weeks just to make sure all the work is done so I'll have this time off. Fine. If that's how it's going to be, I'll see what I can do."

She raised her hands in defeat and returned to her cubicle, trying her best to maintain her composure.

Ralph stuck his head out his office door. "Veronica, be a dear and reserve at least 4 hotel rooms and arrange transportation from the airport for the corporate people. Maybe a limousine or couple of rental cars? Okay? I've included their secretary's information in the email to help you out. By the way, they'll probably want to go out to dinner the first night, so check out a few nice restaurants and make reservations. Thanks."

Ronnie gave him the middle finger as she sat in her cubicle fuming.

He shut the door and murmured under his breath, "Those people are always talking about equal opportunities, but when it's finally offered to them, all they think can about on is going off somewhere to party. Humph! And she thinks she should have my job. What a joke..."

Ronnie focused on her computer, sucking her teeth, trying her best to calm down. Her heart pounded in synch to the beat of an ancient drum. *Ancient African war drums played by her ancestors when the enemy was near.* She was not going to let him win. He may have won the battle, but she was going to win the war. She knew her promotion came with a price, just didn't realize it was going to be so high.

Ralph has known about this workshop for months and never once did he mention it to me. Since he made other plans, he expects me to drop everything and brownnose with corporate. He knew about my vacation. But none of that matters because he isn't concerned about providing opportunities--he's only concerned with Ralph and what he can get out of it. Selfish bastard. And on top of everything, this sucker expects me to do secretarial work. I ain't his secretary. I possess more education and experience in my little finger than this prick has in his entire body. Just because he's one level above me, I'm expected to comply with his every demand? I don't think so. What I should do is walk in his office and say, "Screw you, you little weasel. Screw you and this job!

"Hey Veronica? How you doing today? You got a minute?" asked Sam as he took a seat in one of the empty chairs in her cubicle.

Her daydreaming was rudely interrupted and she was immediately reminded that she meant to get rid of these extra chairs. People automatically assumed an empty chair was an open invitation to stop by and chat any old time they wanted. Didn't matter if she was busy or not, because most people didn't notice or they chose not to. Despite her growing anger with Ralph, she wouldn't let her employees know how pissed off she was.

"Sure Sam, what's up?" she asked, trying to put on a happy face. It was difficult switching gears so quickly, but in the months since she received a promotion to supervisor, pretending to care was a trick she quickly mastered.

"Well, I've got a few things going on at home. My daughter got laid off from her job and needs to move back....." Sam's lips moved, however, in her mind no sounds came from his mouth.

9

She tried to pretend to care about his latest problem, but in reality, she was more concerned about her own. She studied the man in front of her. He couldn't have been a day over 55, but looked every bit of 75.

He took no care in his appearance, coming to work in what looked like the clothes he slept in. Most days he didn't bother to shave. She overheard his conversations with other employees that he was just milking the system until he could retire. Every bit of motivation and professionalism left his body years ago.

Ronnie acted as if she was listening, but her mind was a million miles away. *What am I doing here? How did I end up in this dreadful job working for an asshole, listening to other people go on and on about their problems as if I didn't have any of my own? This is not the life I am meant to live, not the life I dreamt of when I was younger with the world at my fingertips.*

She had become part of the establishment, drank the kool-aid and unconsciously dived headfirst into the corporate world—deep into the world she despised as a 20-something year old. Unwittingly, she had changed into someone she neither recognized nor wanted to be.

With this realization, something deep inside her psyche shifted—an imperceptible transformation that took a fraction of a second to occur. Yes indeed. As surely as the hands on the clock ticked off the minutes of the day, a dramatic change had taken place. The cloak of darkness was lifted from her soul and she became acutely aware of who she was. Her throat began to constrict like she was suffocating. She needed to get out of there.

"Um, Sam, uh, I don't mean to cut you off, but I've got to take care of something urgent. I'll talk to you later." Ronnie grabbed her purse and ran out the door.

"Well, I'll be. Where in the world is she going in such a hurry?" Sam asked, as he watched his supervisor abruptly leave the office. "To hell with this... I can't do this anymore. Can't hold my tongue and let this asshole run all over me. I don't belong here. Forget Ralph and this damn job... I quit." Ronnie quietly murmured under her breath.

She rushed out the door, jumped into her car, put it in gear, and peeled out of the parking lot. With no idea of where she was going, she just knew she had to get away and headed towards the freeway.

An hour later, she sat inside her car at the beach, parked next to another vehicle filled with city workers having their morning cups of coffee. She observed the men laughing and telling jokes and realized she and they lived in two very different worlds. Any other time, she would have dismissed the men without a thought, but not today. Today she envied their carefree attitudes. The men nodded good morning. She did the same.

Ronnie plucked her phone from her bag and got out of the car. She exhaled this morning's stress away, locked the car door, kicked off her pumps, and pulled out her spare set of sneakers from the trunk. She took off in a full sprint. Ten minutes later, breathless and sides splitting with pain, she was bent over attempting to catch her breath.

"You okay, ma'am?" asked a young bike cop who stopped by to see what caused a nicely dressed, middle-aged woman to take off in a full sprint on the beach.

"Yeah, I'm fine. Just needed to get rid of some of this stress. I'm okay, officer. Really, I am. Thanks." She straightened up to convince him.

"Well, alright then. I hope whatever's bothering you takes care of itself. You have yourself a good day ma'am," he replied and continued his patrol of the boardwalk.

Ronnie found a seat on an empty bench facing the water. She needed to speak to her man and let him know what was up. She dialed Ike's cell.

"Yo baby, good morning. You a little late calling, huh? Hold on, *why* are you calling from your cell?" Ike was on his way to work after dropping his son off at school. He felt guilty about not spending the weekend with Ronnie, but he only had his son twice a month.

"Ike, I, uh, I'm not at work. I'm at Buckroe beach."

"Buckroe beach? What in the world are you doing out there? And why aren't you at work? Everything okay?" Concern filled his voice. She exhaled and said, "I had to get out of that office—away from that stuffy-assed building. The walls were closing in on me and I just left. I didn't say a word to anyone. Just grabbed my purse and left Hold on a sec, got another call coming in. Never mind, it's just that asshole Ralph."

"What's going on? Did he do something to you?" Ike turned into a convenience store parking lot to give her his full concentration.

"Yeah. No. Well, Ralph didn't *do* anything other than be the prick he always is. He has me filling in for him on some workshop that was scheduled months ago. I didn't know anything about this damned workshop until this morning. He already approved my vacation and knew I made plans. Baby, I'm supposed to be at work when we're scheduled to be in the Bahamas," Ronnie explained while hot angry tears rolled down her cheeks.

"Oh, well, my love that's okay. We can reschedule the cruise for another week. I was gonna tell you later today that I'll have Ike Jr. that week anyway. So if you need to cover your boss at that workshop, don't sweat it." Ike secretly prayed a silent "thank you" for an easy out from their planned cruise. "Ike Jr.'s mother has an important business trip that week and really needs me to keep him. So you see it works out anyway."

"What? You were going to tell me *today* that we need to cancel the cruise? A cruise that's been planned for months? A cruise to celebrate our one-year anniversary and you act like it's no big deal. Uh, what the hell?" The day kept getting better and better and it was only 9:15.

"I'm sorry baby, but it can't be helped. I just found out a couple days ago. He is my son and I am responsible for him too. I can't leave him with a babysitter just so we can go on the cruise. I didn't want to tell you this way. I planned on us having a nice dinner and my breaking the news to you gently. But since you have to work anyway, it shouldn't be a problem. Right?"

"Shouldn't be a problem? I walked out on my job today because I thought this little asshole ruined our trip. Now you're telling me that you were going to cancel anyway because of your baby momma's schedule?" Ronnie looked at the phone, very tempted to toss it in the ocean. "Un-fucking-believable! Uh, I've got to go. I'll talk to you later."

"Ronnie, wait…." The connection was broken before he could say anything more. Ike thought aloud, "As far as I'm concerned, it's a win-win for everybody. I don't know what she's tripping off of. Women… I'll never be able to figure them out."

Ike tried calling Ronnie back several times. When she didn't pick up, he eventually gave up and headed to work at the construction site. He was the lead and couldn't afford to be late.

Ronnie stared off into the horizon. The cell phone rang incessantly, irritating her, so she switched it to vibrate. While watching the birds play in the surf, she reflected back on her life and the choices she had made. Nothing ever goes the way you think it will and even the best made plans go astray. Her failed marriage to Derek; not having children; working in a job she hated; and her shaky relationship with Ike, all proved no matter how much you give of yourself, in the end you only get rewarded with disappointment.

She walked towards the ocean, reached towards the sky, and raised her head to acknowledge the transformation taking hold. *What would happen if I simply walked away from it all? Away from that awful job, from the mounting debt, from the materialism, and away from relationships that leave me feeling emptier than fulfilled? At what cost? What price must I pay to discover my authentic life?*

Ronnie prayed aloud, "Lord, if you're trying to tell me something, my eyes and ears are wide open. So is my heart. What is going on? Has the world gone crazy or is it just me? I've been working all my life, trying my best to do the right thing, staying in bad situations longer than any sane woman would, just to be treated like dirt? I poured my heart and soul into that job and my marriage. Look where it's gotten me." She searched the sky for answers.

"Lord, today I vow to live my life on purpose—to live my life as it's meant to be lived. No more doing what's expected and no more saying yes when I really mean no. No more following the crowd because it's the in thing to do. My uniqueness and my desire to march to the beat of a different drummer--to find the path I'm supposed to be on, all comes from You. You made me this way, I know that now. So with Your blessing I intend to find that path and make it my own."

Chapter 2

"Sam, did she say anything before she left?" Ralph asked and replaced the telephone on its cradle. He'd try again later. Veronica was a lot of things, irresponsible wasn't one.

"No, she mumbled something then just took off. Don't know much more than that." Sam shuffled his massive body back to his workspace.

Ralph muttered, "She better have a darned good explanation for running out of here like that. Who does she think she is anyway?" He tried dialing her number again. Still no response. "What the heck? The final report on our project is due first thing this morning... How am I going to explain to my boss why I don't have that report completed? I'm sure he'd love to hear that it's because Veronica walked out. What am I going to do?"

Meanwhile, sitting at his desk waiting for something to do, Sam pulled out a bag of *Nacho Cheese Doritos* and noisily crunched away. Bright orange crumbs covered his chin and settled upon his sweat stained shirt.

"Hey Sam? Come here would you?" Ralph reverted to plan B. Well, actually there was no plan B, he was just thinking on the fly. The truth was he had less confidence in Sam than he did Veronica. At least Veronica took pride in her appearance. This joker looked like he slept in his clothes and never met a bag of chips he didn't like.

"Be right there," Sam answered.

The old man hoisted himself from the chair and unsuccessfully brushed crumbs from his face. The artificially colored cheese tinged his fingers an unnatural shade of fluorescent orange. He had no napkins so he sucked the flavor from his fingertips and wiped them dry on his pants.

Ralph heard Sam before he saw him. On good days the old black guy wheezed loudly and on his bad days, which seemed to be most, he incessantly filled the office space with sickening sounding, phlegm filled coughs. He'd rather not have to deal with Sam, but he was Veronica's alternate. Sure, he was a nice enough guy, but what a slob.

"Sam, I need a favor. I have a project for you to work on. Please, take a seat." He didn't have a choice. Veronica's exit left him in a bind, so Sam would have to do.

* * *

Ronnie drove home in a daze and contemplated her next move. She would not—no, could not go back to that office to kiss her boss' ass and allow that job to suck the life out of her. The time had come to make a change and shake things up.

The cell phone continued to blow up with calls from her supervisor, Ike, and Joie. Too many questions swarmed in her head each begging to be answered. They all wanted to talk, but she didn't feel the need to speak to anyone.

With the push of a button she silenced the phone, causing the screen to go black. Quitting that job was long overdue. There were no regrets about her actions or decision. The stress-induced headaches; the tell-tale beginnings of an ulcer; the premature gray hair; and her dreading Monday mornings, all of that would soon go away. *Well*, she thought, *time to get this show on the road...*

The house was cool, as the programmed thermostat was doing its job to conserve energy. She wasn't supposed to be home mid-morning on a workday; consequently, everything seemed a little bit off. In a matter of hours, her entire world had changed into one she no longer recognized. By walking away from her job, she unwittingly gave up her identity, not to mention her only means of income. Yet, despite the obvious, Ronnie felt overwhelmingly at peace. That job caused her to be miserable for so long, that leaving it was a welcome relief.

I need a drink. It's early, but so what? If I'm going to start living life on my terms, why not begin by throwing the rules out the window? Today is the first day of the rest of my life and cause for a celebration. The liquor cabinet was fully stocked with Tanqueray gin, Cuervo tequila, Bacardi rum, Hennessy and Alize cognac, even a bottle of Crown Royal for the fellas. None of it looked appealing. Maybe wine would be better.

She perused the wine rack trying to decide upon red or white when the gold foil on the bottom rack caught her attention. Champagne? Why not? Champagne would be perfect! She usually didn't drink the bubbly except for special occasions. A coworker had given Ronnie the bottle for her last promotion and she absent mindedly tucked it away in the wine rack. That's where it remained until now.

She reached into the kitchen cabinet for a glass and before she popped the cork, she held the bottle close to her chest. Then she allowed the hot tears to finally come. For the first time in my life, I am finally free...

15

After all that drama of dealing with a bunch of grown-assed children pretending to be adults, walking away was a lot easier than she ever imagined it would be.

It was also time to kick her close friend, *Fear*, to the curb. For all of her adult years, she lived her life with fear and fear paralyzed her into staying in a job she hated. Fear kept her trapped in a net of safety and security. Do what society says, take the easy way out and don't think for yourself. Get the right job and live in a cookie cutter neighborhood like everyone else. It was easier to follow the path of least resistance and go along with the other sheep. Fear eventually crept into her soul and brought torment instead of power. Fear convinced her to not chase her passions or dreams, but to instead remain in the status quo.

Today Ronnie chose to close the door on fear and let victory take its place. The tears were replaced by a huge smile, followed by a giggle, and ended in a fit of laughter that dropped her to her knees.

Ronnie recovered and surveyed the bottle of champagne lying on the floor. *A Mimosa would be perfect about now,* she thought. She stood and went to the refrigerator for orange juice. The last time she drank a Mimosa was a couple years ago when she vacationed in the Dominican Republic with a few girlfriends.

With her hand on the fridge handle, her eyes settled upon a magnet from Puerto Azul. That magnet had been there for so long, it blended into the background, but right now it stood out like a shining beacon of hope. She poured the juice, popped the champagne cork and topped off the glass. In a toast to her new life, the drink went down quickly.

The house was way too quiet for a celebration to be going on. She needed music to liven things up. Chris Botti was always nice, but way too mellow and might bring her mood down. The only requisite at this point was for the music to be upbeat and loud.

After her second or third Mimosa, she scanned the radio and settled upon a generic rock station. The music was obnoxiously loud and fast and almost impossible to dance to. In fact, it was so fast she wasn't able to catch the beat. So instead of dancing, she listened, nodding her head trying to catch the music between the beats. And that's when it hit her. *Wow! It is all about the music between the beats. Most people can't hear it because they're focused on the entire song. The music between the beats is the offbeat—a realm where only a few lucky folks can hear and even less understand. That's where I want to live my life—in the offbeat.*

16

Listening to the likes of Guns n' Roses, Van Halen, and Motley Crue, she was able to draw a correlation between the frenzied pace of the music and her rapidly spiraling out of control life. Despite the songs sounding as if they were thrown together haphazardly by strung out musicians, a simple beautiful truth came through with each strum of their guitar strings. Even when things seemed totally out of control, they weren't because there was a sense of order to everything. Those big hair bands from the 1980's helped her understand there was a message behind the music and it was there for those who really paid attention.

With the music blasting on high, she barely heard the doorbell ring. The mailman slipped a bundle of letters into the mail slot. Peeking through the curtain, she waited until he made it to the sidewalk before opening the door.

Most of her personal business, including paying bills was done online, so the pile was mostly junk mail. Flyers of businesses pushing monthly specials, grocery stores advertising weekly sales, and letters to 'current resident' made up the majority of the bundle. In the jumble of papers, she almost missed the overstuffed blue envelope addressed to her. The return address was Caribbean Tropics vacation club. *Caribbean Tropics? I haven't thought about that company in forever.*

On the spur of the moment and pumped full of free drinks, Ronnie and her girlfriends combined their resources and joined the club during that trip to the DR. As far as she knew, only a few took advantage of the club's benefits, returning with stories of relaxation and fun. Though she received regular correspondence from the vacation club, usually it went straight in the trash because she had no time for such things.

Today the packet from the vacation club was received with an entirely new perspective. Time was no longer an issue; money would be eventually, but not today. In her excitement, she ripped the envelope apart with her teeth. Brochures for island getaways to the Bahamas, Jamaica, Puerto Rico, and the Dominican Republic fluttered to the floor.

"Lord, are you trying to tell me something?" Ronnie asked again for the second time this morning.

She picked up the colorful pamphlets and took her sweet time to read. The letter went over the vacation club's terms, beckoning her to take advantage of the benefits before they expired. Until today, there was no time for an extended vacation. When she did have time, there

17

was never anyone to vacation with, and the thought of vacationing alone was never appealing. And when she did have time, her money was short. Anyway, Ike was always too busy to go anywhere for any length of time—money or not. At this point, there was absolutely no reason not to go.

Using the vacation club for a couple of weeks in the DR during the off-season would only set her back a grand or so, including airfare. She rationalized that she needed the vacation to clear her mind, to give her some well-needed time to plan out her future. The seed was planted and the plan began to take root.

"All right, I get it. I can take a hint." She shouted.

The decision was made. She was going on a two-week getaway to the city of Puerto Azul in the Dominican Republic. A quick phone call to the Caribbean Tropics vacation representative was all it took to make the arrangements for the flight and resort accommodations. Thirty minutes and $1076 later, she was booked on Friday's flight to Puerto Azul. Why wait? The way she figured, nothing ventured, nothing gained.

The bottle of champagne, combined with the intense emotions from earlier, proved to be too much. She dozed off in her chair with the music blaring loudly in the background and vacation package brochures in her lap.

A couple of hours later she awoke with a start. The memory of this morning's events came back with a vengeance. The conversation with her boss and her walking out of the madness reverberated in her mind. She smiled as she imagined the shocked expression on Ralph's face when he realized she wasn't coming back.

Her head pounded and her stomach churned. Maybe it wasn't such a good idea to drink an entire bottle of champagne on an empty stomach. After popping a couple of aspirin to ward off the throbbing in her temples, Ronnie found her cell phone and turned it on. It listed over 50 missed calls with about half as many messages. She deleted all the messages without listening to any. In time she would return the calls, but not today. Besides, she knew without listening to her messages that the concern was not for her well-being, but about how her actions specifically impacted them. Her supervisor was concerned about how her leaving would affect his production status. Ike wants to know what was up and if they were still on for the weekend. Joie probably *was* concerned. She'd call her back in a few.

Ronnie made a sandwich, grabbed a bottle of water and took her laptop into the serenity of her garden. She listed all her assets including savings, checking, IRA's, and retirement accounts on a spreadsheet. Seeing it in black and white was depressing. The bottom line revealed she wouldn't be debt free, including having her house paid off, for at least 27 years. Twenty-seven years? If she were lucky, she could retire by the time she was 70 and live off her retirement account.

No matter how many times she crunched the numbers, she came up with the same conclusion. Her assets were totally out of synch with her liabilities. "What the hell am I working so hard for? I am in debt to my eyeballs and barely keeping my head above water. I'm living paycheck to paycheck."

Although she made six figures, she didn't have enough money to sustain her standard of living. Her income was enough to survive—barely. Because her promotion came with a raise and a new title, she was supposed to look successful. The expensive car, a nice house in the right neighborhood, the designer suits and shoes, all helped add to her angst. The more she made, the more she spent, the more she owed. Her lifestyle had become an illusion and maintaining an illusion of wealth was slowly suffocating the life out of her.

Ronnie's coworkers with children often expressed envy towards her lifestyle. They thought since she didn't have kids, she had all kinds of money to burn. Truth be told, she did have a little bit of money saved, but not enough to stop working. Ronnie knew she was in a vicious cycle. She made no time to enjoy life, and the less she enjoyed her life, the more depressed she became. The more depressed she became, the less she wanted to work. And so on, and so on, and so on…

She studied the spreadsheet. It was the first time she consciously looked at her finances from an entirely different perspective. Here it was all spelled out—crystal clear. She worked at a job she hated so she could appear to be successful to people who didn't matter. If that wasn't the definition of crazy, she didn't know what was.

"What the hell am I working so hard for?" she asked aloud. Shaking her head in disgust, she pulled up the website for the Caribbean Tropics to review the resort's accommodations.

Her cell phone vibrated with Joie's name appearing on caller ID. Ronnie decided to put her friend out of her misery and take the call. "Hello? What's up?"

"I've been calling you all day. Ike called and said you quit your job this morning. Is everything all right? Where are you?" Joie asked in true concern.

"Hey girl, I'm sorry I worried you. Ike told you right. I couldn't take it anymore. I didn't feel like talking and just needed some time to think and clear my head. I'm okay. Been at home all day."

"I'll be leaving work in a few minutes. Is it okay if I stop by?"

"As long as you don't try to change my mind or talk me out of this. Yeah, you can stop by."

"Okay, I'll be there in an hour. Need me to bring anything?"

"Just a smile and your congratulations. See you soon." Ronnie hung up and continued to research Puerto Azul. Her flight was leaving Friday morning and she only had a few days to get ready.

Chapter 3

Joie needed to talk to Ronnie. A few days ago, she received a phone call from a private investigator looking for Veronica Pierce. It was something about a child searching for its mother. The caller ID didn't give any clues to her identity, as it was a private number. Joie didn't take the bait because she knew Ronnie didn't have any children, she told the caller she didn't know what she was talking about and hung up. Although she dismissed the call as a prank, the call bothered her and she wanted to discuss it with her girl.

She tackled the evening traffic to get to their neighborhood. She had known Ronnie for several years and never seen her friend like this before. Both went through some stuff, but always managed to tackle it together. Was she having a mid-life crisis? Had she lost her mind? Did she have an incurable disease and didn't want to tell anyone? Obviously, there was something up, and as her closest friend it was up to her to get to the bottom of it. She pulled into Ronnie's driveway and prepared to cross examine her.

After what seemed like an eternity of ringing the doorbell and alternatively knocking on the door, Ronnie finally answered and let her inside.

"What in the world are you listening to? No wonder you couldn't hear me knocking. You need to turn this crap down." Joie went directly to the stereo and quieted the noise blaring from the speakers.

"Well, hello to you too, girlfriend," replied Ronnie, stepping aside out of her way. "I have to keep the music turned up loud so I don't have to hear that incessant barking."

Joie heard the dogs barking, but didn't think they were the problem. She looked her friend up and down. Twice for good measure. She didn't look like she was having a mental breakdown. She wasn't drunk or drugged. In fact, except for a little puffiness around her eyes, she looked perfectly fine.

"Okay... Now that I know you're still alive, let's get out of here and go somewhere for a drink. We need to talk," stated Joie.

Ronnie complied by retreating to the bedroom to change. Minutes later, she returned fully dressed and said, "Girlfriend, let's roll."

Joie drove. Although Ronnie looked physically alright, she wasn't sure what was going on inside her head. After all, it's not every day that you up and quit your job. She knew about a little hole-in-the wall that served up good drinks and afforded privacy for intimate conversation.

"Girl, what have you been doing? Your hair is all messed up. Didn't you just get it done a couple days ago?" Joie sipped on a brightly colored blue cocktail while her friend took the empty bar stool next to her. "Hey bartender, get my friend one of these please."

"It's been one of those days." Ronnie straddled the barstool. "Let's see if there's an open booth. This stool is so uncomfortable, plus I feel like I'm going to fall off this rickety thing."

They trailed behind the waiter to a booth near the window. This area gave them a bit more privacy than sitting at the bar.

"Okay girlfriend, spit it out. What is going on with you?" Joie made herself comfortable.

"I quit my job. Something snapped inside me and I walked out."

"I don't get it. You been bitchin' about your job for years, just like I have. Just like everyone else we know has." Joie motioned for the waiter. She needed food in her stomach to help soak up the liquor.

"You are correct. I have been bitching about my job for years because I absolutely hated it. Girl, I reached my breaking point this morning when Ralph told me to cancel my vacation."

"What? Why? I thought you planned your trip months ago. How he gonna cancel your time off like that?" Joie took the menu from the waiter and shooed him away.

"He didn't actually cancel it—just advised me to postpone it. Ain't that some shit? He expected me to rearrange my vacation around his plans. Told me he needed me to fill in for him so he could go to some other conference. I kept my cool in the office and didn't go *there*, but I was this close to snatching his smug ass by the throat."

"I know you was pissed. So what did you do?"

"Oh, I was pissed off all right. I went back to my desk and tried to calm down. I couldn't. It was like old Kizzy crept up in my soul and told me it was time to go."

"Kizzy?" Joie laughed.

"Yeah girl," Ronnie joined in the laughter. "Kizzy, Jane Pittman, and even ole' Harriet Tubman made me gather my things and leave the ole' plantation. You should've seen the look on old Sam's face when I left." Ronnie decided upon a seafood appetizer plate.

"That is too funny. What did Ike say when you told him?" Joie waved back the waiter and placed their order. "And bring us another round, please."

Ronnie sucked her teeth before answering, "Ike said not to sweat it. We could take the trip another time."

"I thought he would be just as upset as you. You mean he was okay with rescheduling your vacation cruise? I had no idea he was so….understanding."

"Understanding my ass... Ike planned to tell me this evening that he planned to cancel anyway. His ex has a business trip that week and he feels obligated to keep his son. So, it turns out I got angry over nothing...no, that's not true--it was over something. But I'm all right now. The reason behind my quitting was messed up, but the quitting part was way overdue." Ronnie shook her head in disgust.

"Ouch! That's gotta sting. I'm sorry Ronnie. That is fucked up!"

"Girl, I don't want to talk about this anymore. You said you wanted to talk to me about something. What's up?" Hot angry tears rolled down Ronnie's face. She brushed them aside, annoyed by their impromptu appearance.

"I don't even feel right about telling you my news after what you been through." Joie reached for her friend's hand and held it momentarily. "What cha gonna do now?"

"I'm taking a well-deserved trip to Puerto Azul in the Dominican Republic. I already made my reservations to leave this Friday."

The waiter brought out their food and another round of drinks. He took away the empty glasses to make room. Joie took a huge gulp from her glass.

"Uh, if you plan on driving, you'd better make that your last one." Ronnie gently reprimanded her friend.

"Don't worry 'bout me girlfriend. This drink is mostly sugar and ice. I don't feel nothin' yet. I am fine. So you're going to the DR?"

"Yes, I had so much fun the last time; I know it's going to be wonderful going back. I'd ask you, but I know you probably can't get a kitchen pass on such short notice. You would love it there. It's so beautiful."

"What you talking about? I *have* been down to the Dominican Republic. Don't you remember when I told you about when me and Derek went down there a few years ago? That was an amazing time…" Joie realized her mistake just as soon as the words left her mouth.

The look on Joie's face told Ronnie it was more than a Freudian slip of the tongue. "Derek? Don't you mean Cedric?"

Joie momentarily froze. "Uh yeah, of course I meant Cedric. Dang,

I don't know where Derek's name came from." Her nervousness was evident as she spilled the drink down her shirt. She reached for napkins and knocked the silverware on the floor. She looked up at Ronnie. Guilt and sorrow were written all over her face.

Ronnie stared at Joie and it was as if someone had finally lifted away the veil of fog. She could see clearly now, yet was unable to comprehend what she heard. "Joie? You and D-D-Derek?"

Joie looked away. Ashamed and embarrassed.

Ronnie sat back in her seat and allowed the revelation to slap her straight sober. She remained silent as she watched her best friend in the world try to cover up the fact that she had an affair with Derek—when he was still her husband.

Without having to ask, Ronnie remembered when it happened, because she felt abandoned that week. Derek was supposed to be away on a business trip. Joie told her that she and Cedric were taking a vacation to an island getaway. Joie returned suntanned and full of happiness. Cedric on the other hand, seemed distraught, but never spoke of it. To this day, he never spoke about that trip. Maybe Cedric didn't know it was with Derek, but he probably suspected something was off.

Suddenly everything made perfect sense. Hindsight can be an unkind bitch. When she and Derek split, Joie seemed more upset than a normal friend should. She embraced Ronnie's grief and even shared a bottle of brown liquor to ease away the pain. They cried buckets of tears together and Ronnie had no idea Joie was also soothing her own sense of loss. Derek not only left Ronnie, but he also walked out on Joie.

"My girl…" Ronnie stood, dropped a $20 bill on the table and headed for the door.

"Ronnie! Wait up! It ain't what you think. Let me explain!" Joie dropped another couple of $20's on the table and ran to catch up.

Ronnie realized she didn't have her car. She had no way home. She pulled out her cell and dialed Ike's number. He didn't answer so she left a message. "Hey baby, I need a ride home. Call me."

Joie finally caught up and blurted out, "Girl, slow down! Let me explain. Please!"

Ronnie turned to face Joie. "All right, explain to me how my best friend can screw my husband and have the nerve to say she's still my friend. I'm listening."

"I'm sorry. It just kinda happened. A few years ago, early in our marriage, me and Cedric was going through some stuff and I needed someone to talk to. I dropped by your house, but you were gone shopping. Derek saw that I was a mess and offered his ear. He consoled me and ended up giving me a hug. It started out innocently. Nothing happened that day, but he offered to listen anytime I needed someone to talk to. At first, it was just phone calls and texts about me and Cedric's issues."

"Did he also talk to you about me?" Ronnie couldn't bear to look at her.

"Yeah, sometimes we talked about you guys. But mostly it was me complaining about Cedric."

"Humph! Keep going. What else?"

"Well, uh, this is really difficult to talk about. I put it all behind me because the situation was so wrong." She wiped her nose on her sleeve and kept speaking. "Anyway, one day Cedric was out fishing. I was really messed up about something—don't even remember what it was now. I asked Derek to stop by on his way home from work. The garage door was stuck open and I couldn't close it. At first he didn't want to, but said since you were working late, he'd drop by for a few minutes. I poured him a drink and one led to another. Before I knew it, we kissed. That kiss ignited something between the two of us. We both knew it was wrong and we tried to stay away from each other. I am so sorry. Please forgive me."

Ronnie narrowed her eyes and asked, "How long did it last? How often did you screw my husband?"

"Um, uh, well...actually, it lasted about a year." Joie winced in embarrassment.

"So you're telling me you had an affair with my husband right under my nose? And you took a vacation with him to the DR when he was supposed to be away on business?" She shook her head in disbelief. "I confided in you about our problems. Even took your advice about my marriage."

Joie remained silent, unable to think of anything to say.

"Damn Joie, it's not only messed up that you cheated on Cedric, but to do it with Derek? I don't know what to say to that. Gotta admit though, I didn't have a clue. You are one slick bitch. Now get the hell out of my face!" She began walking away in the opposite direction from the restaurant.

"Ronnie, I'm sorry…." Joie knew it was no use pleading for forgiveness. She turned and headed towards her car.

"How could you do some hurtful shit like that to *me*?! You are supposed to be my girl! My best friend!" Ronnie shouted out and headed towards the corner 7-eleven. With the day she was having, that little tidbit of information was the last thing she needed to hear. It didn't matter that she was now divorced from Derek. She felt betrayed. She didn't know what hurt more. She suspected her husband of cheating during their marriage. She thought Tequitta was the only one. But to discover he was also with Joie was too much to bear.

The lounge Joie selected was not in the best part of town, not to mention it was getting late. As Ronnie approached the store, she spied a group of young brothers hanging around the side. *Probably dealing drugs*, she thought. She didn't have any more cash on her and Ike still hadn't returned her call. A car beeped its horn. She jumped before looking back. It was Joie.

"Girlfriend, please get in the car. I am not leaving your ass down here to get raped or murdered. At least let me take you home," she pleaded.

The thugs were looking at her, no they were leering—like a pack of wolves that spotted a lone sheep. This was not a difficult choice. Hang out at the store and hopefully catch up with Ike or get in the car and deal with her lying, cheating-assed, ex-best friend Joie. A car pulled up to the group of thugs and the driver stuck his hand out the window. One of the young men approached the car, looked around suspiciously, then pulled something out of his pocket and handed it to the driver. The exchange took place in all of 30 seconds. A police cruiser suddenly appeared and turned into the parking lot. The group dispersed as if by magic.

"Okay, but only because I need a ride." Ronnie got in without looking in her direction.

They rode in silence before Joie built up the nerve to speak. "Listen Ronnie, I know what I did—what Derek and I did was wrong on so many levels. After that trip to the DR, we decided to end the cheating for good. Neither one of us meant for it to happen nor did we mean to hurt you. Lord knows I didn't intend to hurt Cedric. He knew I was involved with someone, but I never told him who. We never spoke of it again. And I put it behind me and totally forgot about it until today.

You were right back then when you suspected Derek was being unfaithful to you. He might have been with me, but he ended up marrying that trick he kept on the side. What was her name? Tequila?"

"Tequitta."

"Whatever. It's still ghetto."

"Yeah, you're right about that." Ronnie laughed in spite of herself.

"Look, you have every right to be angry with me and I understand if you never want to speak to me again. I struggled with telling you for so long, but every time I did, Derek convinced me it wouldn't serve any purpose. So we kept the secret—all this time." Joie turned in Ronnie's drive, leaving the car running.

Ronnie stared ahead, filled with a burning rage. "Don't you know that everything done in the dark will eventually come out in the light? You put this behind you years ago as if it never happened. For me, this shit is raw. Like it just happened..."

"What more can I say? I'm sorry," Joie's eyes filled with tears.

"All those years when Derek and I were having problems, a lot of that was because of you. So whatever you choose to believe, do not expect me to shake this off like its nothing. For all I know, if he hadn't left me for Tequitta, he may have left me for you. On top of everything I've gone through today, I find out my best friend...." Ronnie wasn't able to finish her thoughts as she got out the car. The betrayal was a searing knife stabbed deep into her gut.

*   *   *

Ronnie crawled into bed still wearing her clothes and mercifully fell sound asleep. But she didn't stay that way for long. Her dreams tormented her with images of Derek making love to Joie—images that caused her to wake up in a cold sweat. Early the next morning, after a fitful sleep, she awoke with a mind-numbing headache.

She checked her phone for missed calls. *Ike didn't call me back last night. That isn't like him at all. He's usually so reliable and considering my state of mind yesterday, Ike should've been running to check on me. Something isn't right.*

Despite the throbbing of her temples, she reached for her sneakers and simultaneously popped a couple of aspirin. She was halfway out the door when the remembrance of yesterday's events hit her like a ton of bricks. It was no wonder she had a headache, but since she was already up and ready to run, she continued with her routine.

The mindless run through the neighborhood was a welcome relief from her rapidly spiraling out of control life. The cool morning air and the muscle burn that crept up her shins and into her calves, took her mind off the headache. Neighbors were out walking dogs or jogging, just like every other morning. In spite of how awful she felt, the world had not ended.

Thirty minutes later she was back in her kitchen—hot and sweaty. She checked her phone again—still no word from Ike. However, there were three missed calls from Ralph probably wondering if she was coming in. She didn't care because there were more important issues to address. Ike's whereabouts being foremost in her mind.

She dialed Ike's cell. It rang several times before his voicemail kicked in. She called twice more—still no answer. She became worried when he didn't pick up. Without thinking, she grabbed her purse and headed out the door to his house, which was less than ten minutes away.

Ronnie realized she was probably overreacting, but she needed to see Ike, her man—the last friend she had left in the world. Needed to rest her head on his chest and hear him say that everything was going to be alright.

She turned into his cul de sac and came to a complete stop when she saw the familiar red SUV parked out front. As if on cue, the front door opened and Taylor, Ike's ex-wife, exited the door holding her son's hand. Ike followed wearing pajama bottoms and nothing else. First he hugged and kissed his son, then did the same to Taylor. Ronnie watched Ike strap his son into his seat in the back of the SUV before retuning inside. Adding insult to injury, Taylor threw a kiss as she backed out the driveway. They looked like the happy family they once were. No one noticed Ronnie quietly watching the remaining shreds of her old life unravel right before her eyes.

"This cannot be happening. Not Ike too…" she said aloud. "God, please don't let this be happening. I can't take no more. What did I do to deserve this?" Unfortunately, at this point, there was nothing left to do but drive away.

*   *   *

Joie felt awful beyond belief by the time she made it home. Cedric was sitting on the sofa snacking on a bag of potato chips, sipping from a bottle of beer, watching a basketball game. He seemed surprised when

Joie pulled off her pumps, threw her purse on the sofa, and snuggled up next to him.

"You okay?" asked Cedric. He could count the number of times Joie watched any type of sports with him on one hand.

"Yeah, I'm all right. I just left Ronnie. Where's the kids?"

"In their rooms doing homework. How is she doing?"

"Not too good. She quit her job today." Joie took a sip of his beer.

"She did what?! Why? Is she okay?" Cedric hit the mute button and provided her with his full attention.

"She said she got pissed because her boss told her to cancel her vacation. You remember she and Ike are supposed to go on a cruise? Well, turns out her boss decided he needed her to cover for him on a conference. Guess that was enough and she walked out."

"Who in the world just ups and quits their job? Sounds like she's got a screw loose if you ask me." He returned his attention to the game.

"Well good thing nobody asked you. Is that all you're having for dinner?" Joie looked at his bag of chips.

"Naw, I picked up some Chinese food earlier. There's leftovers on the stove if you're hungry. Oh yeah, I almost forgot to tell you. You had a phone call earlier from some woman. She left a message—said her name was Lexi McCray."

"I don't know anyone by that name. Used to know a Lexi from college, but can't imagine it could be her. Probably just another telemarketer." Joie picked up her things and headed towards the bathroom. She needed a bath to relax and take her mind off Ronnie.

"Hey…"

"Hmmm, what's up?" Cedric answered, barely taking his eyes off the game.

"I love you."

"I love you, too. Does this mean I'm gonna get some tonight?" He started to rise off the sofa.

Maya and Trey chose that very moment to come running down the hall. They were laughing and chasing each other—two very happy children in a loving family. She wanted to make sure it stayed that way.

Joie looked with longing at Cedric and shrugged. "Hey, you two come here and give your Mommy some love." She kissed the 5-year old twins with such vigor they decided enough was enough and went to play with their daddy.

Cedric sat down defeated. He knew once the children were up and about, chances of him spending quality intimate time alone with his wife were slim to none. Oh well, back to normal. Normal is good.

Joie finally got the kids settled down and drew her bath. She reminisced about her year-long affair with Derek, all too aware of what she'd given up by being with him.

Joie wasn't lying to Ronnie when she said it had started out innocently. After all, isn't that how most affairs begin? Innocent phone calls, secret text messages, followed by chance encounters at familiar hangouts, all culminated in spending time alone at out-of-the-way motels. Yes, it all started out innocent but didn't stay that way once she admitted she was sneaking around on her husband *with* her best friend's husband. It wasn't so innocent when she was honest with herself. But she wasn't honest. She tried to rationalize it every which way she could. Convinced her conscience what she was doing wasn't wrong. For the longest time, she managed to maintain the charade.

She and Cedric had been married for a few years and were having the usual problems most new couples experience. Their marriage was stale and needed some excitement. They rarely made love and spent even less time together. And as that stupid country song proclaimed, she went looking for love in all the wrong places.

Joie had known Ronnie for about a year and met Derek shortly thereafter. She considered them both as friends. When she needed someone to talk to and Ronnie wasn't around, Derek was right there— an all too willing ear to listen. There was no physical attraction. Not at first. He was Ronnie's husband and strictly off limits. Too bad she didn't stick to her convictions. She reprimanded herself; if only she went home that day when Derek told her Ronnie was out shopping, none of it would've happened.

Truth was, she had every opportunity to stop the affair from progressing, but she didn't. Derek's off-hand flirtatious remarks made Joie feel sexy, wanted, desired. The way he complimented her on how she looked, smelled, even spoke was too irresistible to ignore. She craved the attention—the affection Cedric failed to provide.

Gradually the innocent flirtations turned physical, then sexual. Very sexual. It all started with a simple caress of a hand. A momentary touching of flesh as they brushed against one another while passing in a narrow space set them on fire. An innocent kiss on the cheek to say hello or good-bye, lingered on their lips. Their sexual desire for each other grew to the point that it was impossible to resist.

The affair caused irreparable damage to both marriages and they knew it couldn't continue that way for long. After a year of sneaking around and meeting behind their spouse's backs, they went on a trip to the Dominican Republic to celebrate their "one-year anniversary" and to make final plans for their future together. They had a wonderful fun-filled vacation and fell in love for real, or so Joie thought. To end their adulterous affair and seal their relationship, they hatched a plan. The plan was for Joie to ask Cedric for a divorce and Derek would ask Ronnie just as soon as they returned.

Joie came back from her vacation as happy as could be, ready to start over with her new found love. All she needed was the go-ahead from Derek to coordinate their mutual divorce requests. Weeks went by and he never brought it up. In fact, she didn't hear from him at all. He avoided all contact with her when she stopped by to visit Ronnie.

Finally after months of waiting, Ronnie told Joie that Derek had asked for a divorce because he was in love with someone else. Joie was confused. Derek hadn't coordinated this with her, and yet he'd told Ronnie he wanted a divorce. When Ronnie told Joie the name of Derek's new love was Tequitta, she nearly passed out. Derek was not only cheating on Ronnie, but he was cheating on Joie as well. She was heartbroken but couldn't reveal her true feelings to anyone. The gut-wrenching tears she shared with Ronnie weren't for the breakup of her friend's marriage, but were for the life she would never have with a man she loved deeply—the family they would never be.

The twins were born seven months later. She never revealed her pregnancy to Derek. And her husband never suspected the children were not his.

Cedric startled her back to reality when he stuck his head around the door and interrupted her thoughts about Derek.

"The kids are asleep. You want some company?" he asked exposing his nakedness.

"Come here sexy." She pushed all thoughts of Ronnie and Derek aside. *Umm, now that's what I'm talking about.* Cedric sank down into the warm water with his wife, and there they made passionate, sensual, married love.

Chapter 4

Ronnie didn't know what to do and there was no one she could call who understood. There was no way in hell she would tell Joie about Taylor leaving Ike's house at 6:30 in the morning. Ike never mentioned anything about getting back together with his ex. If he had, this would all be a moot point. *This* problem was one she'd have to tackle on her own.

Her cell phone rang. It was Ralph, so she didn't answer. He was the last person she wanted to speak to. It was his fault her life was falling apart. If it hadn't been for his rescheduling his conference, she would never have quit her job, wouldn't know anything about Joie and Derek messing around, and had no reason to stop by Ike's house to witness his little family reunion. *Ralph is responsible for everything because he started this chain of events in motion. Damn him!*

She changed directions and headed towards the office. It didn't occur to her how she would look showing up in her jogging clothes, hair uncombed, no makeup, and mad as hell. She wanted to give the little jerk a piece of her mind for screwing up her life.

Her cell phone rang again, but this time it *was* Ike calling. She wondered what kind of lies would spill from his mouth. She answered, anticipating another round of deceit from a supposed loved one.

"Hello Ike. See you finally got my message."

"Good morning Ronnie. I'm sorry I didn't get a hold of you yesterday, but I had kind of a family emergency and turned my phone off. Is everything okay? Why did you need a ride?"

"Family emergency, huh? Obviously everything turned out alright and I made my way home. It doesn't matter now anyway."

"Don't be mad at me. I know you had an awful day and probably needed a shoulder to cry on. Look, my son hurt himself at school yesterday and I ended up taking him to the emergency room," he explained.

"Oh, I'm sorry. The poor baby. What happened?' Ronnie felt foolish.

"He fell during recess and hit his head. He needed a few stitches, but thankfully it wasn't life-threatening."

"You must have been worried sick," she replied, waiting for the rest of the story.

"I stayed up with him all night to make sure he didn't have a concussion. Baby, last night was rough."

Still no mention of Taylor's early morning visit. "So you stayed up with him all night? Just you and him?"

"Of course it was just us. I dropped him off at his mother's house before I called you. He seems fine now. Uh, why do you ask?" Knowing Ronnie extremely well, he heard the unspoken accusation in her voice.

"I was worried when you didn't return my call last night. When I wasn't able to get a hold of you this morning, I got worried and drove by your house to see you." Ronnie hoped Ike would be man enough to tell her the truth.

"Um, uh, I didn't see you this morning. Uh, when did you stop by?" He thought about Taylor. *It was nice hooking up with her, even it if was probably just for a minute.*

"Well Ike, I pulled up just in time to see your ex leave. Seems like you weren't alone after all; looked a little cozy to me. I didn't want to intrude so I left. It's obvious you two still have loose ends to tie up."

"You're stalking me? Damn it Ronnie! What do you expect me to do? She *is* the mother of my child and there's always going to be some kind of feelings between us. When we were in the emergency room together with our son, old feelings were rekindled. One thing led to another and she ended up spending the night. I'm sorry baby; it just happened," Ike explained.

Ronnie sighed wearily, "Ike, go back to your wife and son. It's obvious you still feel something for her, so you need to make up your mind about what you want."

"Baby, you know I love you. I just need a little more time to straighten a few issues out. Let's get together after work today. We need to talk."

"No, that isn't going to happen. I am too old to be playing games with you. I just saw you kiss your ex-wife not even two hours ago. I'll bet you told her the same thing, didn't you? That you need a little time? I don't need, nor do I want your baby-mama-drama in my life. I am not doing this with you."

Ike remained silent on the other end.

"Good-bye Ike. Have a nice life," she said before breaking the connection.

Ike held the phone in his hand in disbelief. "I know this heifer didn't just hang up on me." He shrugged. "Oh well, sometimes it's better to stay with the devil you know…"

Men… They're all just a bunch of grown assed little boys. Ronnie didn't feel upset, angry, or sad. No…what she felt was relief. Relieved to be free from the drama filled life Ike continued to bring. She wasted a year of her life trying to make a relationship work that wasn't meant to be. Ike was her first serious relationship after her divorce and she really wanted to make it work. Unfortunately, making it work became more important than the relationship itself. Ike was a nice enough man who should've stayed with his wife and raised their son. In essence, he was a single man who was still married. Half in, half out. Ugh! Not the best person to be involved with. She wanted no further part of it.

Joie, on the other hand, now that was a different story. To be betrayed by her best friend, the one she shared her thoughts, dreams, and secrets with; that really hurt. Little by little, she recalled weird conversations they'd shared over the years. Joie seemed preoccupied with Derek and his new life. She asked seemingly innocent questions about him and dropped off-hand remarks about his wife.

In hindsight, Joie's preoccupation with Derek bordered on obsession. At the time Ronnie thought it was because her friend felt sorry for her; now she knew the real reason. The only explanation Ronnie had for never suspecting Joie cheating with her husband was it was too unbelievable. Things like that don't happen to women like her, so she never even considered it.

To her credit, Joie taught her one thing; never underestimate anyone. Not your husband and especially those you call *friend*.

Ronnie exited the highway and turned into the office's parking lot. Ralph's car wasn't there which meant he was either running late or not coming in at all. It was still fairly early, so most employees wouldn't arrive for another hour. She decided to wait a little longer for him to show, anticipating cursing him straight to hell for ruining her life.

As she gathered her thoughts, a beautiful purple butterfly appeared out of nowhere. She watched the butterfly take off and land, over and over again, flitting about effortlessly fluttering its wings. It looked like it was trying to find a way in through an open window, but finally gave up and landed on her windshield—silently watching her.

When she was a child, she used to be very afraid of butterflies. She remembered what her father told her to allay her fears. *Daddy used to say God sends butterflies as a reminder of the beauty that exists in this world. He said that butterflies symbolize how something ugly and unsightly can transition into a beautifully unique creature, and no matter what you're going through, as long as you get through the difficult part, you will always be better on the other side. And whenever you see a butterfly, you're supposed to say a prayer.* So she prayed for peace.

A car turned into the parking lot and parked next to hers. It wasn't Ralph, it was Sam.

"Good morning Veronica," said Sam, as he stood next to Ronnie's car, speaking to her through the window. He looked at his supervisor, noticing her messy hair and unmade face. She looked like she had a rough night.

"Morning Sam," replied Ronnie. She got out of her car and stood beside him. "I uh, was just waiting to see Ralph. He's usually here by now." She checked her sports watch.

"He's coming in late this morning. He stopped by the corporate office first before coming in. So what's going on with you? Are you alright? You left pretty abruptly yesterday." He was genuinely concerned.

She looked at the disheveled man standing before her and wondered, *how can this joker possibly offer me any advice? He can barely put two sentences together.* But wouldn't you know it, that purple butterfly flew straight to Sam and landed on his shoulder.

"Look, I've got a few things going on in my life right now. Because of Ralph, I cancelled my vacation, which led to a whole bunch of other stuff popping up. I just wanted to share a few of my thoughts with him and tell him to kiss my ass while I'm at it."

"Listen, I know you probably don't want to hear what I've got to say, but I'm going to say it anyway. I've been with this company for over thirty years now. I've watched these young hotshot white boys come in, quickly move up the ladder, then leave for better opportunities—over and over again. I've also seen my fair share of young black professionals, just like you, come here and work their asses off trying to climb that same ladder. I used to be one of them, believe it or not. Truth of the matter is, no matter how hard you work or how many long hours you put in, you're never going to get any higher than you are now."

She crossed her arms impatiently waiting for him to finish. He didn't have a clue what he was talking about as far as she was concerned. *Will you hurry up so I can go?* she thought.

35

"Face it Veronica, how many black women do you see in the corporate office? That's right, none. And there's only three minorities, one brother, one Latino and one Asian. The quota has been met. So if I were you, I'd turn around and forget about giving Ralph a piece of your mind. It'll make you feel good for a minute, but it won't change anything. He'll just crap on you more."

He observed her doubt filled expression and continued, "Have you looked in the mirror this morning? Pardon me for saying so, but you're a mess. You're usually dressed impeccably. You have your stuff together more than anyone else I've seen walk through these doors. Now look at you! You're about to stoop to a level you should never consider. If you don't want to work here, that's fine. But leave here with your dignity intact. Think about your parents. How would your mother feel if she knew you'd sunk to Ralph's level? Don't end up like me—beat down and not giving a damn anymore." He shuffled away, leaving Ronnie to contemplate his words.

His words caught her off guard and cut like a knife, especially the comment about her parents. She wasn't expecting to receive insight from Sam. She watched the purple butterfly lift off from the old man's shoulder. It fluttered above his head for a moment then took flight, soaring high on the breeze. Mulling over his Sam's comments, she got into her car and headed back to the highway.

Daddy sent down a message to remind me of the strength that runs through my veins. As she drove past her building, an overwhelming sense of calm soothed away the irritation. A blue car stopped just short of where she was. It was Ralph. She waved in his direction, leaving him with his mouth wide open in surprise. She would call and explain eventually, but for now, the confused look on his face was priceless.

* * *

Joie was too busy getting busy with her man to even think about checking messages last night. It wasn't often that she and Cedric made love on the spur of the moment like that, and any way you sliced it, making love to her husband was more important than fretting over Ronnie kicking her to the curb.

On her way out the door, she grabbed the note pad where Cedric wrote that woman's info. She didn't know any Lexi McCray, so returning her call didn't seem urgent. It could wait until she got to work.

She hit up Ronnie on speed dial before remembering their now defunct friendship. Joie knew she was wrong for what she did, yet she rationalized; *Ronnie ain't even married to Derek no more. So why is she trippin' so hard?* Then the reality of the situation kicked in. *Hmm, well considering Ronnie does know about the situation, maybe it's best if I kept my distance. I don't know what my girl will do next. Stability of the mind is not her strong suit at the moment.* Maybe she'd tell Cedric about her affair with Derek. *Naw!* She tossed her phone back in her purse and turned up the radio. Life goes on.

Joie spent the good part of the morning in her office reviewing the previous month's financial reports. Being an accountant was not her ideal job, but it paid the bills and allowed her to live a relatively decent life. The Excel spreadsheet was displayed on both monitors. She was almost done when the phone rang. Most of the time when she was heavily involved in work, she'd let voicemail pickup to avoid losing her spot. This time something made her take the call.

"Joie speaking, how may I help you?"

"Hello? Am I speaking to Ms. Joie Parker?"

"Yes, this is Joie Parker. How can I help you?

"Ms. Parker, please don't hang up. You don't know me, but my name is Lexi McCray. I'm a private investigator who specializes in locating parents of children put up for adoption. Do you have a few minutes?"

Joie's attention was piqued. She swiveled her chair around and closed the office door with her bare foot. "Uh, I don't understand. Didn't I tell you the last time you called I can't help you? Who hired you and why are you calling me again?"

"Ms. Parker, I would prefer not to discuss this very sensitive matter over the phone. Can we please meet somewhere? Maybe over a cup of coffee?"

"Listen, I don't know what this has to do with me. I am a very busy woman and I don't have no time for clandestine operations. As far as I'm concerned, we really don't have anything to talk about." Joie was put off by the woman's presumptuous attitude.

"I understand your hesitation, but I promise to only take about 20 minutes of your time. I can meet you today if you're available."

"Look, you've got to give me something here. Why should I leave work to meet a stranger to talk about something I know nothing about?" Joie was this close to hanging up.

"Uh, well, I usually don't mention client's names over the phone, but it has to do with your friend, Veronica Pierce."

Joie could have been knocked over with a feather. "Veronica? You want to talk to me about Ronnie Pierce? Oh shit-t-t!"

"Yes and that is all I can say for now. Can we meet?" asked Lexi.

"Yeah, okay Ms. McCray, I will meet you. Be at the Starbucks in the Richtowne Coliseum Shopping Center at 11."

"Thank you Ms. Parker, I'll see you then."

"How will I know you?" asked Joie.

"Don't worry. I'll find you," replied Lexi.

Joie hung up the phone and wondered why a private investigator would be asking about Ronnie. As far as she knew, Ronnie wasn't adopted—her mother was her real mother. Maybe it had to do with Derek's kids. She knew guessing was futile, but not knowing was killing her.

For the second time that day, she hit Ronnie's number on speed dial without thinking. *Damn!* Before the phone connected, she again remembered they were not speaking. First she'd find out what was going on and then maybe—just maybe, she'd clue her girl in on this new development. It was ten o'clock. There was just enough time to finish her financial review before going to meet the mysterious P.I. Lexi McCray. She laughed. *Lexi McCray? Even her name sounds like a fictional character from some badly written mystery novel.*

Chapter 5

After leaving the office and getting a kick out of seeing Ralph's shocked expression, Ronnie made her way home. It was still early and she realized there was absolutely nowhere she needed to be. Minus work, family, and friends, her day ahead lay stretched out—as blank as the canvas of an artist without a vision. She understood it was up to her to decide how to paint her picture, what to do with her free time, and how she would live her new life.

In her 40 something years on this earth, Ronnie had survived and overcome most obstacles placed in her path. The hurt feelings springing from the betrayal by the people closest to her would also pass; this she understood. Until that time arrived, it was her choice whether to shrivel up in defeat or blossom under her own strength. Her trip to the DR was only a few days away, yet the pressure to succumb to a debilitating depression was a powerful force to be reckoned with.

She pushed all negative thoughts aside and declared, "I will not let this mess take away my joy. I am strong and I will get through this because I am truly blessed."

Over the next couple of days Ronnie took control of her situation. If she was going to revamp her life, all the material possessions holding her back would have to go. She contacted a realtor, put her house on the market, and advertised the *Infiniti* for sale on *Craigslist*. Without having a full understanding of *what* she was doing, getting rid of all the excess baggage felt like something she needed to do. It just felt right. She surveyed her house and made note of all the items purchased during a time when she was upset, depressed, or merely bored.

The spare bedroom that served as a second closet overflowed with clothes, shoes and accessories—some still with the price tag attached. The excess clothing bordered on the edge of being obscene, so she began pulling out old outfits from the closets to get rid of. Clothes that patiently awaited those fifteen pounds to disappear went first. Then she got rid of the shoes that pinched her feet. Dresses meant for those special occasions that never seemed to come were tossed aside in another heap. Shoeboxes full of belts and extra buttons stacked on the top shelf were next to go.

In reaching for the boxes, one toppled open spilling old love letters from Derek to the floor, surrounding her in painful memories. She stopped cleaning and sat on the floor. She picked up a letter, still fragrant with the scent of his favorite cologne and read. The words of his everlasting, undying love used to put a song in her heart; now they only made her sad. He promised to love, cherish, and spend all his waking moments making her happy. Sadly, all the promises made when they were in love lay scattered at her feet, broken and empty.

"Guess your promises weren't worth a damn, were they Derek?"

She balled up the letter and scooped the rest in the trashcan. Hot angry tears sprang forth. The tears that flowed were for the loss of her marriage, the chance for babies she sacrificed for his worthless ass, having to finally walk away from a job she hated, breaking up with Ike, but most of all the betrayal of her best friend Joie. She let the emotions overtake her and cried until there were no more tears left.

Finally she picked herself up and pulled the woman she knew back together. There was only so much time she would allow herself to have a pity party and that time was almost up.

Several hours and four overstuffed trash bags later, she surveyed the result of her efforts. Her donation to the Goodwill was going to make quite a few sisters out there very happy. And she didn't even want to think about the value of all that stuff—all that time and money wasted on clothes she never wore. But it felt good to declutter her life and enrich someone else's at the same time.

A small sheet of paper caught her eye. She bent over to pick it up. It wasn't paper, it was a photo turned upside down. She flipped it over and gasped. *I haven't seen this picture in almost twenty years. It must have been in the box with the letters.* It was one of those four-framed black and white pictures taken in a photo booth. The picture showed a very young couple happily in love.

* * *

Ronnie and Travis first met during their freshman year of college. Both were eighteen years old and like most of the other students, it was their first time living away from home. The University of Illinois at North Pointe was close enough to Oklahoma City if she ever needed her parents, but far enough away to feel like she was on her own. Her major was business and his was in liberal arts.

It was during the first couple weeks of the term when they first took notice of one another. They recognized they were in several of the same core classes. At first, they only spoke to say hello. Then they began hanging out during breaks, discussing the previous class or reviewing assignments. They were friendly, but that's about it. Ronnie had her friends and Travis had his. Popular and pretty, she was considered to be "the bomb" by the young brothers who unsuccessfully pursued her.

Ronnie made up her mind early on, encouraged by her mother's insistence, to stay away from boys and focus primarily on her studies. As her mother liked to point out to her family, *my child has a future, unlike her cousins who always manage to get in some kind of trouble.* Ronnie was the first in the Pierce family to go to college and she didn't want to ruin it by getting distracted.

Travis was a quiet, shy, nerdy guy who only opened up during class discussions or with Ronnie after class. They were as different as night and day. Travis Mitchell Bradford was white *and* he was from California, the bastion of liberal thinking. Though it was the 90's, the conservative people of Illinois unfortunately continued to perpetuate that, 'What you doing with him?' attitude, thus they kept their developing friendship at arm's length. At times, it seemed the disapproval came more from her friends than his.

Their platonic relationship changed during sophomore year when Travis returned from summer break taller, more muscular, and with a deep sexy voice. He stood a little over 6 feet, with curly black hair, and dark brown—almost black eyes. His lips were nice and plump, just like she liked them and instead of his usual old black plastic frames, he took to wearing wire-framed glasses with funky blue-tinted lenses. He was no longer the nerdy artsy guy who was fun to talk to, but he now turned heads wherever he went. Ronnie thought he was actually very handsome.

In spite of it all, Travis didn't let his newly found popularity ruin his charming personality. Ronnie discovered he had grown in the confidence department along with everything else. Yes, Travis had finally come into his own. Although, they had fewer classes together that year, they started hanging out more often. The occasional lunch soon turned into real dates and before Ronnie realized it, she and Travis had become an official campus couple.

Outside of class they were inseparable. They no longer cared what other people thought and to their true friends, race didn't matter. Over time their differences drew them closer together and made them grow stronger as a couple. Young and deeply in love, they started thinking about what it would be like to have a life together after college.

During their junior year, Travis took Ronnie home to Santa Elena, California to meet his parents. His family immediately loved and accepted Ronnie, even going so far as to invite her to spend the upcoming holidays with them.

Unfortunately, that was something she could never do—take Travis home to meet her family. Ronnie's mother would have killed her if she came home with him. She made it known to everyone who'd listen that they were not spending their hard earned money sending their daughter to college to bring home a white man. Ronnie could either abide by her parent's strict rules, or find another way to pay for college. Her father's feelings weren't as set in stone as his wife's were, but he realized early on that it was best to let her have her way.

Travis grudgingly accepted the many excuses she provided whenever the subject came up about meeting her family. For many years, Ronnie managed to keep him *and* their relationship a secret. She rationalized what her parents didn't know wouldn't hurt them.

Ronnie defied her parent's wishes for the first time in her young life when she and Travis moved from their respective dorms and rented a cozy little apartment off campus. The apartment wasn't anything special, as it resembled more of a hotel suite than anything else. But it was close to campus with all the amenities they needed—a bed and a kitchen. Nothing else mattered. They were together—young, happy and in love. Problem was Ronnie never told her parents she moved out of the dormitory.

Everything fell apart Thanksgiving weekend of her senior year. Her parents invited Ronnie home to spend the weekend with her family. She rarely made it home anymore and they missed her. When she told them she couldn't make it because she had a major project to complete, they seemed to understand. And as far as Ronnie was concerned, that was that.

The truth was she and Travis wanted to spend a long weekend together and cook their own Thanksgiving meal. Just the two of them. She reminisced at the memories of her first attempt at cooking a turkey and smiled. It was only partially thawed and she unwittingly left the plastic wrapped innards stuffed deep inside the turkey's cavity. When all was prepared, they set the table with a small turkey and all the sides. Travis discovered the innards when he was cutting the bird. He pulled out the steaming plastic bag of gizzards, heart, and liver. When they realized what it was, both fell out laughing. Dinner turned out okay. It didn't taste like either of their mom's cooking, but that didn't matter. Ronnie remembered they were just about to have dessert when an unexpected knock at the door changed everything.

Because they were a very popular couple, she imagined it was one of their friends dropping by to say 'hello'. But of course it wasn't. Their unexpected visitors turned out to be her parents. Ronnie recalled hearing her mother's voice when Travis answered the door.

"Pardon me young man; I'm looking for Veronica Pierce. Do you know where I can find her?" asked her mother in a proper Midwestern voice.

"You mean Ronnie? She's in the kitchen. Can I help you?" responded Travis.

"Oh? We're Veronica's parents, Vernon and Dianna Pierce. Will you please go get her?" Her mother's annoyance and impatience were evident in her tone.

"You're Ronnie's parents? Well, it's nice to meet you both. I'm Travis, Ronnie's boyfriend."

Ronnie remained in the tiny kitchen, holding her breath, waiting for the other shoe to drop. When the awkward silence continued without letting up, it was time for her to make an appearance. She willed her feet to make the few steps to face her parent's wrath. Heart pounding, palms sweating, and hands jittery, she summoned her courage as she came from the kitchen.

"Mama? Daddy? What are you guys doing here?" She went to her parents and hugged and kissed them. In spite of the circumstances, she was genuinely happy to see them.

Travis stood back and wrapped his arm around her shoulder. He was surprised when she stepped away. "Honey, are you going to introduce us?" he asked, confused.

"Uh, of course. Mama, Daddy, this is Travis." She watched her mother's reaction. It wasn't good so she focused on her father. "Hey Daddy, what are you guys doing here?" she asked again.

"We, uh, felt real bad you were spending Thanksgiving alone, so your mother and I decided to drive up and surprise you. We wanted to take you out to dinner to give you a break from your big project..." He hesitated, looking Travis over.

By then Travis had figured out the situation and turned three shades of bright red. "Well, Mr. and Mrs. Pierce it was nice to finally meet you. I'm going to excuse myself and let you have some time with Ronnie." Feeling hurt and confused, he looked to Ronnie for an explanation. When she didn't say anything, Travis grabbed his jacket and walked out the front door.

"What in the world is going on here? Since when did you move out of your dorm? And who is this 'Travis' person? Does he live here?" asked her mother, looking around the tidy, small room with obvious disapproval.

Ronnie knew it was time to grow up. "Mother, Travis is my boyfriend. We met a few years ago. We've been living together since August—the beginning of this semester," she explained, nervously shifting from foot to foot.

"You mean to tell me you and *that* boy are living together? Have you lost your mind? You know how I feel about *those* people!"

"Mama please, he's not like that and neither is his family. We love each other and plan on being together. I knew how you feel about white people so I was afraid to tell you about him. About us."

"Child, you know how your mother feels about Caucasians. What they did to her family back in Georgia when she was a child was despicable. Remember she told you about how they burned a cross on her yard? How they tied up her sixteen-year old brother and tossed him in the back of that pickup truck, took him out in the woods, and nearly beat him to death? Sweetheart, I know you think you love him, but something like this will never work," her daddy gently explained.

"Daddy, you know you don't feel that way. Those are Mama's feelings, not yours. You taught me that we're all God's children. That we're supposed to love our neighbors. Doesn't that include white people?"

"Yes dear, that is what I've taught you," he sighed. "Veronica, try to see it from your mother's perspective. She was only 5 years old when she first got called a *nigger*. We understand all white folks aren't hateful. We just never expected our own daughter to lie to us, nor that you'd be involved with one of them."

Vernon stopped speaking when he realized neither woman would listen. Both were stubborn as mules and there was no way to pacify one without hurting the other, so he remained stuck in his usual place—in the middle.

"Listen to me, Veronica Indigo Pierce! If you want us to continue paying your tuition and other expenses so you can finish college, do what I say! End this, whatever it is with that boy, and move back into your dorm. I've already spoken with your dormitory manager about your moving out. That's how we found out where you lived. She said your room is still vacant. I don't care how you do it, but take care of this situation. C'mon Vernon, let's go. I feel one of my migraines coming on," her mother said, massaging her temples.

Tears ran down Ronnie's face. She dropped her head in shame and said, "I'm sorry. I never meant to hurt you guys. I didn't experience any of what you or Mama went through. All that racial stuff didn't happen to me. You raised me to accept everyone—well everyone except white people. I love him, but I'll take care of it. I promise."

"Well, since you've already eaten your Thanksgiving dinner, we're going to head back home before it gets dark. You let me know if you need anything. Remember we love you and just want what's best for you. Now come here and give me some sugar."

Ronnie fell into to her father's loving embrace, feeling safe in his arms, she absorbed his strength. Despite how she felt, she loved her parents and her father was her rock. He kissed her on her forehead and slipped a hundred dollars in her hand. Her mother gave her a perfunctory hug before leaving. Sadly, that visit was the last time she would see her father alive.

On the way home, their car hit a patch of black ice and slid off the road. The car flipped over and her father was thrown out. He was killed instantly.

Soon after returning from the funeral, Ronnie kept her promise and quickly ended her relationship with Travis. She moved out of the apartment and back into her dorm room. She never explained her actions to Travis. Thus, as a result of her silence, he neither understood nor did he agree with the breakup. However, when Ronnie told him that her moving back into the dormitory was the last promise she made to her late father, he had no choice but to acquiesce.

Ever since that day eighteen years ago, she and her mother were estranged. It seemed to Ronnie that her father was what kept his wife from crossing that line of hatred for white people and without him she displayed no restraint.

Although most people said Ronnie was just like her mother, the interesting thing was she did not share her mother's prejudices. Yes, she understood what those people did to her mother's family was beyond wrong and those involved would all pay for their sins. Maybe punishment wouldn't come from the court system, but make no mistake they would all get what they deserved. Unable to tolerate the hateful spiteful words that continued to spew from her mother's mouth, she made the difficult decision to cut all ties.

Ronnie tossed the faded picture of her and Travis into the trash along with Derek's old love letters. Might as well, because that part of her life was over—over and done with and buried deep in the past where it belonged. No sense dredging up old memories she could do nothing about. She gathered the bags of donations, dumped them in the trunk of her car and dropped them off at the nearest Goodwill.

* * *

Joie parked in front of Starbucks. It was almost eleven. With a few minutes to spare, she ordered grande lowfat mocha and a turkey-bacon roll.

"Excuse me, are you Ms. Joie Parker?" asked a tall bespectacled blonde woman.

Joie looked at the woman and almost choked on her food. She was probably in her early 30's and looked more like a model than a private investigator. Joie had fully expected Lexi to black. No particular reason, but she sounded like a sister on the phone.

"Yes, I'm Joie. You Lexi?" she asked as she started to put her food away.

She nodded and sat opposite Joie. "Please, eat." I'm just going to pull out my *iPad* to take a few notes. You don't mind do you?"

"Your show. Now, what's this about Ronnie?"

"First, if you don't mind I'd like to ask you a few questions. Here's my business card and credentials, in case you're curious."

Joie studied the card while Lexi spoke.

"Okay, well, let's begin. As I said on the phone, my client hired me to locate her biological parent. All my leads have directed me to a Veronica Pierce. The woman I'm looking for is an African-American

46

woman in her early 40's, originally from Oklahoma City. Do you know her? Is it possible the woman I'm looking for is your friend?"

"Whoa! Hold up! How do I know you're who you say you are? There's all kinds of crazy people running around looking for personal information. You could be one of those nuts for all I know."

"I assure you Ms. Parker, I am legitimate. Here's the number to the Santa Elena police department. I work closely with the police as a freelance P.I. Give them a call and ask for Detective Barber. Go ahead, I'll wait."

Joie dialed the out-of-state number and was immediately connected to the Santa Elena police. The desk sergeant transferred her call. She spoke with the detective for a few minutes and was apparently satisfied with his response. "You come all the way out here to Virginia from California and you're not even sure you got the right person? Your client must be loaded."

"Ms. Parker if you don't mind, how about we stick to the business at hand? I don't want to waste anymore of your time than necessary." She checked her watch.

"All right. Yeah, I know Veronica Pierce. We've been friends for years and I know Ronnie don't have no kids. Hey, how did you end up with my number anyway?"

"Um, well, let's just say I have friends in law enforcement and you were actually quite easy to track down. You would be shocked to know how much a determined stranger can learn from a *facebook* page, random posts on the internet, *linkedin* and such. I called your house a few times, and when you got upset I suspected you were the right person. Normally in these situations, it's easier to contact a close friend to confirm the identity of the potential parent before contacting the actual individual. This way if there are spouses or other children involved, I can be as discreet as possible. I never know how much a person shares with their loved ones. You would think husbands and wives don't keep secrets from one another, but you'd be surprised what doesn't get said."

Joie thought about her life and the secrets she kept. She pushed those thoughts aside. "You're right about that, but Ronnie never mentioned having any kids. You mean to tell me she has a baby out there somewhere that she gave up for adoption?"

"Well, I'm not one hundred percent certain yet, but with your help, I'll soon know. Look, I have an old picture of my client's mother.

Can you take a look and tell me if it's your friend? Is this Veronica Pierce?"

"Let me see…" Joie studied the photograph lying on the table before her. There was no denying it. It was a picture of a much younger, happier Ronnie.

"Well, is it her?" Lexi leaned forward, excited.

"Yeah, it's her all right. My, my, my… Ain't that a bitch? Ronnie gave up her kid for adoption? When? How old is he? Or she? Is it a boy or girl? How old…"

"I'm sorry. I can't give you any information about my client. Do you know where I can find Ms. Pierce?"

"Yeah, but if you don't mind, I want to talk to her first. This is not the kind of information you want to be blindsided with. Give me a couple of days and I'll get back with you."

"Thank you, this news will make my client extremely happy. Can I expect to hear from you by Friday?" she asked, standing.

"Friday should be good. I'll give you a call. Is this a good number?" She fingered the card and stuffed her turkey wrap into the paper bag. This unexpected news took away her appetite.

"Yes, that's my cell number. I'll be in the area until Friday awaiting your call. It was a pleasure meeting you Ms. Parker and thank you for all your help." Lexi shook hands then bopped out the door looking extremely pleased. She pulled out her cell phone and gestured elatedly as she walked to her car.

"Well I'll be blessed. My girl has a child out there somewhere. All those years she used to tell me how she regretted not having any. Well, I guess I'm not the only one keeping secrets around here," Joie muttered to herself. On impulse, she pulled out her cell phone and started to dial Ronnie's number. "I'm sorry, but this shit is too juicy to pass up." She hit her number on speed dial. As expected, voicemail picked up. She left a message. "Ronnie, I know you're still angry with me, but girl we need to talk. Call me when you get this message. It's urgent."

*   *   *

Ronnie checked her phone. There were two messages from Ralph and one from Joie. Enough time had passed where she could finally speak civilly to her ex-boss so she returned his call. "Hello Ralph, its Veronica."

"Veronica, well it's about time you called. Do you realize I've had to reschedule a week's worth of appointments because of you? What the heck is going on? Where are you and when are you coming back to work?"

"Ralph, I've taken the past few days to contemplate my present job situation. I'm telling you, something has got to change." She swallowed the lump in her throat. Officially quitting her job without a backup plan wasn't as easy as she initially imagined.

"What are you saying?"

"I'm telling you *this* isn't working. I'm not cut out to be an assistant compliance director for a sports management firm. I've been working my ass off for the last nine years and all I got was some fake promotion to be your assistant. Without my input, this section would go under in a heartbeat."

"Veronica, you *are* one of our most valuable employees and have saved this company more times than I can count. Let's try to work this out. If this outburst is about your vacation, I can try to reshuffle my plans so you won't have to go. I'm sure my superiors will understand when I explain. What do you say?" Ralph pleaded.

"Tell you what, I'm taking a couple of weeks off—taking some time to clear my head. I'll let you know my plans when I return. How's that?" Ronnie knew she had him by the balls, because there was no way Ralph could keep this department running smoothly without her. Yes, it was a man's job, but it took a woman to get the job done.

"I suppose if you need the time off then you should take it. I'll submit your paperwork to personnel to make sure you get paid. But if you ever pull something like this again, you're through. We have a business to run and I can't have my employees walking out during critical moments. I will see you in two weeks."

On the off chance that she would have a change-of-heart in the DR about quitting her job, she felt better having a backup plan. Stringing Ralph along for a couple of weeks wasn't so bad. In fact, it was a well-deserved guilty pleasure. With that little bit of business taken care of, she cleared the remaining missed calls. She noticed the message envelope. She listened to Joie's voice on the other end and it pissed her off all over again. So she deleted the message without responding.

Chapter 6

Friday finally rolled around and it was time for her vacation to begin. Ronnie took a taxi to the airport because it was cheaper than leaving her car in long-term parking. Since she wasn't speaking to Ike or Joie, she had no one to drop her off anyway. *Oh well, in no time at all I will be soaking up sunshine and sipping mojitos on the beach.*

As she walked through security, she noticed practically everyone was saying good-bye to a loved one. Expressions of love, prayers to have a safe flight, and comments similar to and including, can't wait to see you again, bounced around throughout the crowd. And in that moment, surrounded by strangers, she felt totally, absolutely, and sadly all alone. She pulled herself together, sucked it up, and went to locate her gate.

The first leg of the flight landed at the Miami International airport. After clearing customs, she found her gate in the international concourse. The area was a virtual microcosm of the United Nations with people from all different nationalities. She had never heard so many different languages spoken in such a small space.

"May I have your attention please?" announced the gate attendant over the intercom. "Flight 3499 for Santo Domingo is now boarding. We are now seating rows..."

Ronnie listened for her section and quickly found her seat on the packed airplane. Unfortunately, she had the middle seat with two big burly men on either side. *If either of these goons moves an inch in either direction, I'll be sharing more than just an arm rest,* she thought. Because there were no other seats available, she sat back and tried her best to get comfortable.

* * *

The pilot announced their descent to the island. Flying over the mountainous terrain, she got the impression that the jungle was trying to reclaim its land. The island's vegetation was plush, green and represented various tropical species of trees, plants, and flowers. In fact the foliage was so over abundant; it reminded her of the setting in *Jurassic Park.*

Ninety minutes after takeoff, the flight touched down on the tropical island of the Dominican Republic. The pilot landed the plane with practiced precision on a runway that began and ended at the water's edge. Any slight miscalculation may have resulted in the airplane skidding off into the ocean.

She felt the humid tropical breeze as soon as the plane's door opened. The air was heavy with the sweet intoxicating scents of tropical flowers. It was the type of fragrance those artificial air fresheners always touted, but never managed to meet.

When they were allowed to deplane, the passengers trailed each other across the tarmac, following red arrows pointing to the terminal. Walking through the narrow breezeway to the terminal, she was greeted by Dominicans offering their most popular island drink—rum.

"*Hola* cousin. Welcome to the Dominican Republic!" shouted a man holding a tambourine. He was part of a three piece band, playing native music, welcoming visitors to their country. She tossed a couple of dollars in the donation bucket.

The men who looked like her relatives back in the states, shouted out, "*Gracias!*"

Clearing customs was a relatively painless process that only took a few minutes. Once outside the baggage claim area, a young man who resembled a distant cousin held up a sign for the Puerto Azul vacation resort.

"Excuse me. Are you the driver for Puerto Azul?" she asked the young man.

"*No hablo ingles.*" He shrugged.

She pointed to her reservation containing the name of the resort.

"*Si, si, vamonos!*" He nodded and motioned for her to follow him to a very much appreciated air-conditioned tour bus.

The ride to the opulent resort took its passengers past shanty towns with structures held precariously together by rusty nails, thick rope, duct tape, or whatever its inhabitants could find. Little brown children ran barefoot up and down the streets playing like only children can. Mopeds and motorcycles, many with up to three riders, zigged and zagged effortlessly between traffic. Heavily guarded gated communities, filled with expensive homes painted in tropical colors dotted the landscape for as far as the eye could see. Those houses were obviously for very wealthy locals or foreigners who fell in love with the island and decided to make it their home.

She felt sorry for the multitudes of homeless kids who ran alongside the bus trying to sell trinkets whenever the bus stopped at traffic lights. The bus driver, obviously used to the kids, honked his horn to scatter the children before he pulled back into traffic. Perhaps the children were being groomed by unscrupulous businessman who relied upon the pity of tourists to buy useless junk from wide-eyed tykes. She hoped at least they were being cared for properly.

Due to traffic congestion and ongoing construction, it took a little over an hour to travel the short distance from the airport. When they finally arrived at the resort, Ronnie marveled at the spectacular entrance. Magnificent palm trees lined the meticulously clean roadway and an army of gardeners tended the landscape, hosing down walkways and pulling stray weeds that dared to pop up between cracks in the sidewalk.

"Welcome to Puerto Azul. Please go inside and have a cool drink of fresh fruit juice. Your bags will be waiting for you after you check-in." The driver opened the door and held his hat out for tips. Numerous bellhops unloaded the bus while the guests went inside.

The open-air lobby was covered by a thatched leaf roof. Large fans hanging from wooden beams circulated a refreshing breeze. Despite the stifling high heat and humidity, it was surprisingly cool inside.

After she checked in, a bellhop walked her up to her room and provided a quick tour along the way.

"You are in building four, second floor, room 228. We have five restaurants with every type of food imaginable. The bus to the casino runs hourly beginning at six o'clock. The beaches are that way and the swimming pools are everywhere. Everything is included so please enjoy all the amenities you wish." He spoke in heavily accented English, yet Ronnie understood him perfectly.

She surveyed her surroundings and was amazed how the very tropical plants kept tame by her flower pots at home, could grow to monstrous proportions when left unchecked.

"Thank you so much. Here's something for you." She handed him a generous tip.

The spacious suite was decorated tastefully with no detail overlooked. In the separate bedroom, a king-size bed took up most of the space. The bathroom was wonderful as it contained a steam shower. *I can't wait to try that.* The *cypertine* ceramic tiled floors, the expensive high-end quality furniture, and attention to detail exceeded the high standards of the resort's guests. There was even a compact kitchenette with a fully stocked refrigerator and bar. The large balcony provided an unobstructed view of the aqua blue ocean. She grabbed a bottle of cold water, eased down unto the lounge chair and finally exhaled. Two weeks of uninterrupted fun, sun, and pleasure await my indulgence.

After taking it all in, Ronnie proclaimed to the world, "Today is the first day of the rest of my life. Here's to finally being able to live my authentic life—one day at a time!"

She felt slightly out of her comfort zone sitting in the massive dining room alone. Practically everyone was paired off as couples. Single women traveling without a man vacationed with girlfriends—like she did last time. She wished she were with someone special, too. In that moment, she missed her best friend Joie, but right behind that thought was the memory of what Joie had done.

To distract her attention from feeling lonely, she just decided to sit back and enjoy the show. Ronnie observed her fellow diners piling their plates high with all sorts of food—truly a gluttonous sight. She watched friendly Dominican waitresses busily tending to their customers—refilling coffee cups and offering glasses of water.

¿Perdóneme señorita, se sienta alguien aquí?" asked a very fine brother who seemed to come from nowhere. He was extremely handsome with a smile that quickly melted the ice built up around Ronnie's heart.

"I'm sorry... Uh, *no hablo espanol*," replied Ronnie, recalling the little bit of Spanish she learned in high school.

"I see. I asked if someone is sitting here—in this chair." He continued to smile.

Ronnie blushed and stammered, "No, n-no one's sitting there." *Lord have mercy. This man is too fine.* She managed to display her favorite come hither look, pushed a loose strand of hair behind her ear, and gave him a toothy grin. She thought *I can't believe my luck. The first night and I'm already being hit on. Maybe I won't be alone on this trip after all...*

"Oh good, do you mind if I take this chair? We're one short." He pointed in the direction of a table full of laughing children.

She felt foolish. "Oh, please. Go ahead. Take it. Looks like you need it more than I do," she replied, hoping he missed her flirtatious gestures.

"*Gracias!*" He picked up the chair and carried it to his table.

Ronnie regained her composure, returning her attention to the kindle she brought to catch up on reading. In between bites she thought, *At least my meal is tasty.*

After dinner, she took a short walk around the grounds before returning to her room. Ronnie hadn't realized how absolutely worn out she was from traveling; she ended up falling into bed before nine.

Faint daylight streaming through a break in the blackout drapes awoke her. Ronnie threw back the heavy curtains and took in the beautiful view of the surf breaking against the shore. The sun just barely peeked over the horizon. *It's going to be a perfect day,* she thought. Wanting to take full advantage of the early morning serenity on the beach, she changed into a swimming suit, grabbed a towel, and made her way down to the water's edge. She prepared to experience a lovely sunrise.

The water was cool at first, but as her body got used to the temperature, she gradually waded into the clear water until she was waist deep. Ocean water usually freaked her out because she never knew what lurked underneath. She tried to keep images of sharks, sea snakes, and jellyfish from her mind. As if on cue, a snorkeler appeared just a few feet from her. She jumped in surprise. The man stood, spit out water and began coughing through his mask and snorkel.

"Hey, are you okay?" Ronnie shouted.

The snorkeler continued to cough even after removing the mouthpiece. He nodded to signify 'yes'. Yet, he continued to cough up water.

She waded to where the man stood and stated, "You don't look so good. Let me help you back to the beach." Ronnie held the man by the arm as he continued to be wracked by dreadful sounding coughs. They made it to the beach where she spread out her towel and motioned for him to sit. The coughing had subsided, but he still seemed out of it.

He managed to say, *"Gracias"* before whipping off his mask. *She's the woman I borrowed the chair from in the dining room.*

"Hey, I remember you... Aren't you the guy from last night?"

The man blinked several times trying to clear his vision.

"Remember me? You took my extra chair." Ronnie was surprised at the coincidence, but it didn't matter. From what she saw last night at dinner, this man was taken and had several children to seal her fate to stay far, far away.

"Sí, I remember you now. What are you doing out here by yourself? A beautiful woman should not be alone on the beach at this hour. It's

not safe." He was finally able to speak without coughing—a good sign. He pulled the floppy fins from his feet.

"Looks like I was doing a lot better than you were," she laughed. "What were you doing out there, alone, snorkeling at this time of morning?" *Umm... Nice body.*

"Well, you do have a point and you're absolutely right. It probably wasn't the best idea for me to be out here alone. Snorkeling is so much better during the early morning hours. The fish tend to rise to the surface because it's cooler and the sunrise provides me with just enough light to see. I'm here alone because I have no one willing to snorkel with me."

Ronnie checked out the stranger wiping his face dry with her towel. He wasn't from the states, his accent proved that. His mocha skin didn't provide any clues as to his ethnicity. He was fit, but not overly muscular which meant he only worked out occasionally. He wasn't pretty but was very handsome. She felt an instant attraction.

"Thanks for helping me out of the water. I lost my bearings and guess I swallowed too much water. By the way, my name is Luis." He extended his hand and presented her with a huge smile.

"I'm Ronnie. Pleased to meet you, Luis. Glad I was there to help. Well, I'd better be going. I've got a lot going on today." She saw no need to continue this conversation any further.

"Oh, well then, let me give you your towel. Maybe I'll see you later?"

"Thanks. Yeah, I'll see you around." She knew she needed to get away fast because she found him very attractive. He seemed to give off vibes that he may be interested in her as well. The last thing she needed was to spoil her vacation getting caught up in some mess with a married man.

Ronnie was intent on not letting her singlehood get in the way of having a great time. She went to the DR for fun and that's exactly what she intended to have. Over the next few days, she went on sightseeing excursions of the city, toured local factories, shopped at one of Puerto Azul's largest outdoor markets, ate, lounged by the pool reading her kindle, ate lots of good food, and slept. By the fourth day she was bored out of her mind and needed something exciting to shake things up.

* * *

"Miss, the next horseback riding excursion leaves at eight. If you hurry you can probably make it." The young clerk patiently explained different options to his indecisive customer.

"Hmm, I don't know. It's been a long time since I've ridden a horse. I don't know." Ronnie shifted from foot to foot.

"They're going to leave in a few minutes. If you'd like, I can have the driver wait, but I need to know right away. And just so you know, the next excursion is next week."

"Well, maybe I shouldn't. I don't want to get hurt." She turned and started to walk away, but bumped right into someone's chest. It was Luis.

"C'mon, live a little. The horses they use are old and very tame. I'd even put my mother on the back of one," replied Luis.

"Hey, what a nice surprise. What are you doing here?"

"I'm going on this excursion. How about you?"

Ronnie looked for his wife and kids. He appeared to be alone. Again. "Uh, you traveling solo? Where's the family?"

"My sister and her kids are at the pool. They're afraid of horses, so I'm taking this trip on my own."

What?! Did he say sister and her kids? But she still didn't want to get too excited before she knew the real deal, so she asked, "What about your wife? Does she ride?"

"I'm not married. Just got divorced. That's why I came down here on this trip with my sister and her family. Needed some time to get away from it all." His face clouded over.

"Oh, I'm sorry. When I saw you at dinner last night I naturally thought those children were yours." *Thank you Jesus!*

"Um, excuse me, I don't mean to interrupt, but are you going or not? The driver is about to leave," interrupted the clerk.

"I'm sorry. Yes, I'm going. Put me down for one."

"So you're traveling solo as well?" asked Luis.

"Yeah, not only on this excursion but for the entire vacation."

"Very brave of you. I don't know many women who would travel alone, not to mention take a vacation at a romantic destination such as this." *I'm kinda digging on this sister and she is so pretty.*

"Call me brave then. I needed this getaway, so I treated myself. Anything wrong with that?"

"No, not at all."

"Good response." She laughed. "Now, we'd better hurry before we get left behind."

"Well then, shall we?" Luis motioned for her to go ahead of him.

* * *

They sat next to each other on the ride up the mountain. The riding stables were midway to the top—just a few more miles away. Every so often she caught a whiff of masculine smelling soap and aftershave when Luis shifted in his seat. He smelled clean and fresh.

"All right Luis, what's your story?" she asked point blankly. He laughed at her boldness, but happily obliged. "My full name is Luis Eduardo Duarte and I am the first generation of my family to live in the states. The majority of my family remains on the island and lives in the city of Santo Domingo. I return at least once a year for a mini reunion and we stay at the resort. I try to visit often because it is a wonderful opportunity to stay in touch with my family and my heritage."

"Very admirable. I *live* in the states and haven't been home for years," she joked.

He took note of her off-hand remark but chose not to respond to it. Instead he asked, "Ronnie, so tell me what brings *you* to *my* beautiful country?"

"Let's see. Well, a few years back me and a few coworkers took a trip with this vacation club. One step on the island convinced me I wanted come back often. We had such a wonderful time, we ended up joining a vacation club, but I never used the program. I would've come back sooner, but you know how it is… Life always gets in the way."

"I hear you. And it always will, *if* you let it. Like I said, I've returned to the DR at least once a year to visit—sometimes more." He laughed. "My mother wouldn't have it any other way."

"That sounds so cool. This time when I decided to come down, I didn't let work, family or anything else stand in my way. Not even the fact that I didn't have anyone to travel with. This trip is all about me."

"You have no one special who could have accompanied you? Not even a girlfriend?"

Ronnie didn't want to discuss Ike, nor did she want to talk about Joie. But what the hell? "Since you asked, I just broke up with my boyfriend, and my best friend and I are going through some drama at the moment. That's why I'm traveling alone. I needed to inhale some different air, get a fresh perspective. You know what I mean?"

"Yes, I do know. Like I told you earlier, my divorce became official a few weeks ago. I'm used to traveling here alone, though. My ex-wife didn't like the DR because she said it was too *uncivilized.*"

"Oh really?" Ronnie didn't know what else to say. She watched Luis staring at something out the window and thought, *There is no way in hell I would let a man as fine as this be alone for a month in the DR. His wife must not have taken a good look at the women down here, or else she didn't care. Obviously she did neither.*

"Yeah, being apart was not a good way to spend a vacation. Anyway, that's over now because I'm a free man."

"Congratulations to getting your freedom back."

Luis pulled two bottles of water from his backpack and offered one to Ronnie. "And here's to your having a wonderful vacation."

The rickety bus finally stopped. By the time Ronnie stepped off the bus, she felt like she had already ridden a horse. The tourists unloaded their things and followed the guide to a fenced in area of the stables.

"May I have your attention, please? How many of you have ever ridden a horse? How many within the last couple of years? Who has never ridden at all? The reason I'm asking is because we want you to be comfortable and at ease. It's better for you and better for the horse if we match you with a horse based on your experience level," he explained.

"Uh, it's been over twenty years since I've ridden," Ronnie answered. Naturally, her comfort level was the lowest of the low.

"*Señora*, Charley horse will be very good for you," said a young stable hand. He brought out an old, broken down horse named Charley. Charley looked as if he'd seen better days and was on his last leg—to the glue factory.

"*Primo*, this horse is for you." Luis' horse was an energetic young stallion, only wanting to romp and play.

The ten riders mounted their horses and followed the lead guide up the trail. Old Charley horse took his dear time catching up with the others, because he seemed more interested in munching grass. When Luis noticed Ronnie's predicament of handling a lazy horse, he paced his horse to remain by her side. When Luis's horse wanted to run, he let him. Then they'd backtrack to Ronnie and Charley slowly making it up the mountain at their own pace. At one point, Charley actually stopped to eat fruit off the bushes.

"What's wrong with this horse?" Ronnie laughed. "All it wants to do is eat. It even tried to take me over there in the meadow. Probably wants to take a nap."

Instructed by the lead to keep the group fairly close, a stable hand came from behind and unexpectedly gave Charley a whack on the rump. The old horse immediately took off in a trot proving it could run if it wanted to. The problem was it *didn't* want to.

"Whoa, that was quite a run," Luis teased when he caught up.

"Luis, why did they give me this old broken down horse? I came up here to ride not wrestle with Charley."

He laughed, "I don't want to hurt your feelings Ronnie, but one of the stable hands said you reminded him of his mother and he didn't want you to get hurt. So they gave you the safest, most gentle horse in the stable. Old Charley wouldn't hurt a flea."

"Since you put it like that, I suppose I should feel flattered they cared. But to say I remind him of his mother. Ouch! At the very least, I hope he was one of the younger ones. Resembling someone's mother can really hurt a woman's self-esteem."

"Take it as a compliment, I've seen his mother. She's not half bad," Luis teased. "He wasn't trying to put you down or anything. Trust me; I think you look beautiful sitting atop that horse. Want me to take your picture?"

"Yes and thank you for the compliment. You know, it really is breathtaking up here. What a magnificent view."

The city of Puerto Azul laid spread out in the distance. From their vantage point on the mountain, the city appeared to be surrounded by water on three sides—in a crescent shape. Houses with tin roofs popped up through the vegetation from the valley below. Ronnie imagined not much had changed during the last fifty years or so.

She dismounted Charley and tied him to a tree where the rest of the group had gathered. Luis did the same with his. He plucked a small fruit off a tree and took a bite, then picked another one and offered it to Ronnie.

She turned her nose up in disgust. "What is that?"

"It's a guava fruit. Take a bite," Luis insisted.

"But you picked it straight off the tree. It hasn't even been washed yet. Isn't it dirty?"

"This is most likely the cleanest, freshest fruit you will ever eat. It's untouched by human hands—well, except for mine. No pesticides, no pollution, no bad stuff. It rains up here practically every day. You won't find fruit anywhere that is as pure as this. Try it."

"You do have a point. At least I know where this fruit came from." She took a bite. The inside was soft and filled with sweet and sour little seeds. "Mmm, it's delicious, except for the seeds." She spit the hard bits into the brush.

"Now we will walk to my uncle's farm," stated the lead guide in broken English. "It is right over the hill. The horses will stay here to rest. Follow me." The guide stepped in horse shit along the way like it was nothing.

Ronnie followed the group navigating between horse droppings. Luis trailed closely behind speaking in Spanish to one of the guides. Although they weren't together, he unofficially appointed himself as her partner for the day. Everyone else was coupled up, so why not?

The guide pointed to several chairs set up under an overhang. The "farm" was not what Ronnie expected. Unlike previous farms she had visited in the states, this was in no particular order—it had no rhyme, nor reason. It was as if, whatever will be, was.

Chickens ran freely around the yard. Pigs roamed unrestrained behind a wire fence that needed mending. Banana trees sprouting green bananas grew wild everywhere. Avocado trees, heavy with ripened fruit, draped against the overhang, and Guava trees lined a large garden. The makeshift garden was filled with row after row of spiky stalks topped off by green pineapples. Tall sugarcane stalks jutted from the ground like weeds all over the property. She counted at least five massive buckets used to catch rainwater. And huge horse flies were everywhere.

In Ronnie's eyes, the family possessed virtually nothing. Yet despite the lack of basic necessities, the families' behavior indicated the opposite was true. Coming from inside the small house were the unmistakable sounds of music and laughter. They sounded happy, but mostly they sounded content. Witnessing how the locals lived caused her to reevaluate her life and appreciate that what she did have *was* more than enough.

"Water and *Cokes* are one American dollar each and *Presidente* beer is five dollars. Let me know what you want and please try to have the correct change," the guide said.

Ronnie overheard some in the group balk at the prices. What she realized and others obviously didn't, was the little money gained from these daily tours kept the farm running and this family fed. Her fellow tourists would probably waste hundreds of dollars on overpriced souvenirs during their stay. Spending a few dollars for water was the least she could do to show her appreciation for her host's hospitality.

Luis sat back in his chair, interlocked his fingers behind his head and exclaimed, "I love it up here. One day I'm moving back, going to buy some land and live out the rest of my life smoking cigars and drinking rum."

"That sounds nice. Really nice." Ronnie agreed.

"Ronnie, come here. I want to show you something." He reached for Ronnie's hand and signaled the guide who acknowledged their departure.

No one else in the group paid much attention to either of them because they were too busy complaining about the heat, bugs, smells, you name it. Ronnie accepted Luis's hand and followed his path. They walked through a break in the trees and came upon a clearing.

"Oh my! Luis, it's absolutely beautiful! What is it? What *was* it?" A group of five buildings in various stages of disrepair filled the vast space. The surrounding crumbling walls made of rocks and mortar indicated years of abuse and neglect. The largest building appeared to be the main house and the others were probably once guest cottages or servant quarters. The jungle had reclaimed large segments of the lot, but one could still make out the grandeur that once existed.

"Many, many years ago, a very wealthy family owned this villa. They abandoned it when the family lost their wealth and could no longer afford to maintain it. The people you met today, the tour guide and the family who owns this farm are my relatives—my cousins. They care for the villa as much as they can, but it is very expensive and takes so much time."

"If they don't own it, who does? Why are they still taking care of it when no one lives there?"

"The state owns the property and pays my cousins a very small pittance to keep the jungle at bay. The villa has been up for sale for years."

Ronnie took in the panoramic view. "I love it up here. This is the perfect setting to write that novel I've kept pent up inside all these years. Up here on a mountaintop, in the clouds, away from it all... Perfect."

Luis smiled at her enthusiasm. "You write?"

"Not really, but one day I'd like to. Just seems like I don't have time for anything I really want to do. Too busy working and all."

"I understand. We all get busy making a living and forget how to live. I make a point to live each day of my life well. That way I have no regrets."

"That's great if you can pull it off."

"Don't underestimate me because one day this will all be mine. I'm going to buy it so it will belong to me and my family. Live here and raise a family."

"Well, I hope your dream comes true because this looks like it used to be a beautiful villa."

"And it shall be again," proclaimed Luis. "Just have to find that one special lady to share it with." He added off-handedly.

Ronnie didn't know how to respond to that last comment, so she let it slide.

On the return trip down the trail, Charley was just as slow as before, but this time Ronnie was in no hurry. She was too busy enjoying the scenery and the company of men speaking their native language.

A little boy, around four and a half years old, sat on the back of a donkey a few feet from the trail. He watched the tourists and hoped to one day be able to ride.

The guide yelled, "*Ramone, va a casa!*" Telling the boy to go home.

The boy replied back that he wanted to ride a big horse like the one Luis rode. His response made all who understood Spanish burst out in laughter.

On the last leg of the return trip to the stables, one of the guides gave Charley a firm smack on the butt to hurry the old horse along. "Charley *va manos!*"

Ronnie held on for dear life as Charley took off in a full trot. She heard Luis and the rest of the guides encourage the old horse on and eventually fell into the bumpy ride with ease, laughing all the way back. Back at the stables, everyone praised the old horse for showing his spunk.

Ronnie dismounted Charley and gushed, "Oh my God! I can't remember the last time I laughed so hard. Charley, you did good." Ronnie lovingly rubbed the old horse's neck.

To show her appreciation for the tour, she dropped an extra $20 bill in the tip hat held by a young boy.

"*Gracias senora!*"

From the boy's reaction, you would have thought she left $100, but she supposed it was all relative. She watched with irritation as the rest of the group walked by without so much as a glance in his direction.

Luis silently admired Ronnie. It had been a while since he observed an attractive woman enjoy something as simple as horseback riding. Although he tried hard to remain nonchalant about Ronnie, he had to admit he was impressed. *She isn't pretentious like most black Americans who visit my island. She isn't ghetto, high maintenance, or trying to impress anyone. This lady respects my culture, my people, and our way of life. Thank goodness she doesn't have that awful attitude so many women seem to have nowadays. What a refreshing change.*

The tour guide explained that an authentic Dominican lunch was included in the excursion's price, and they were going to stop at a local restaurant before returning to the resort. By now it was late afternoon and Ronnie was hot, sweaty, and in definite need of a shower. But she was also famished.

The buffet included roasted chicken, local fish sautéed with fresh vegetables, red beans and rice, salad, sweet plantains, fresh lemonade, and flan and fresh fruit for dessert. The food smelled delicious and whet her appetite.

The group of ten shared a large dinner table and enjoyed a family style meal on the outdoor patio. As they broke bread, shared stories, and got to know one another, all barriers of race and nationality were broken. By the time they returned to the resort, Ronnie felt like she had made nine new friends.

"Luis thanks for hanging out with me today. I had so much fun!" Ronnie didn't want to admit how lonely she felt before meeting him. Now, the thought of spending the remainder of her vacation alone no longer seemed appealing.

"No need to thank me, I had a great time as well." He hesitated momentarily and asked, "Will you please have dinner with me? After three weeks of listening to my niece's and nephew's nonstop chatter, it sure would be nice to have some intelligent adult conversation." Luis stepped in closer. He was nervous, because it had been a while since he asked a woman on a date. He felt out of practice.

Ronnie considered his invitation and what it really meant. She knew all about holiday romances because it was the stuff sugary-sweet romance novels were made of. Boy meets girl, they fall in love, have a torrid romance, and ended up going their separate ways when the vacation was over. Yeah, it always started out hot and heavy but quickly fizzled when the realities of everyday living set in. She contemplated hanging out with Luis. *He is kinda cute and I had fun with him today. I'm not looking for anything serious, just having broken up with Ike. And since he is recently divorced, I seriously doubt if he's looking for anything permanent. Why not have a good time?*

"Okay, I'd love to have dinner with you. Where should we meet?"

"Be in the main lobby at seven. There's a nice little jazz bistro in town I'd like to take you to. They serve fresh seafood. Is that all right with you?"

"Sounds perfect, and by the way… I love seafood. See you then."

Chapter 7

Joie tried calling Ronnie several times with no success. *Probably screening her calls again,* she thought. She recalled Ronnie mentioning something about going out of town, but Joie didn't think she was serious. Ronnie didn't do anything on the spur of the moment. She was as reliable and predictable as an old pair of broken in sneakers. Methodical to a fault, she never strayed outside the perfect little box she created for her life. Well, she hadn't until recently.

"Hey honey, I'm gonna swing by Ronnie's before coming home. I haven't heard from her in days and I'm starting to get worried," she explained to Cedric.

"Let me know how she's doing. I already got the kids. We just left the park so I'll pick up a couple of pizzas on the way home. Thin crust combo good for you?"

"Yes, and cheese for the kids. Thanks love. You're such a good father. I love you."

"Not a problem. I promised them if they did well on their writing tests, we'd make a day of it. They did, so we are. Anyway, I'll see you at home. Love you, too." Cedric hung up.

Cedric wasn't privy to the drama unfolding between the two women, nor why they hadn't spoken. Joie didn't know how to explain their rift without going into the tawdry details. It was better if she kept things to herself for now, so she let him assume Ronnie's issues were related to quitting her job.

Joie knew she had destroyed her friendship with Ronnie. It was bad enough she slept with Derek, but the fact it was her best friend's husband made it one hundred times worse. She didn't blame Ronnie for not speaking to her. In fact, had the situation been reversed, she probably would've kicked her ass *and* told her husband about the affair. She had to hand it to her girl; she kept it together and stayed cool. Probably helped that Derek left both of them for that hoodrat Tequila, Tequitta, whatever the hell her name was. She loved her friend dearly and wanted only to make amends, if that was possible.

Joie thought she was on the wrong street and drove right past Ronnie's house. She turned around when she realized her mistake because she *was* on the right street. She rolled to a stop in front of her girlfriend's home. A huge For Sale sign was planted squarely in the

65

middle of the lawn.

"What the hell? Ronnie's selling her house? I knew she was upset, but to go and do something like this?" She dialed Ronnie's number again. The call went straight to voicemail.

"Where the hell are you Ronnie?" she asked herself. And while sitting in front of Ronnie's house worrying about her friend's fragile state of mind, she considered calling the police, but thought better of it. Ronnie was a grown assed woman and wasn't missing. She just didn't bother telling Joie her plans.

Her phone rang. "Ronnie? Is that you?" asked Joie.

"No, sorry, it's Lexi. Lexi McCray."

"Oh, I was expecting someone else."

"Ms. Parker, I haven't heard back from you so I was just checking in to see if you've made contact with Ms. Pierce yet?"

"No, no I haven't. I've been trying to catch up with her myself. She mentioned something about going out of town earlier this week. As soon as I hear from her, I'll let you know. Okay?"

"That's too bad. I hoped I'd be able to meet her before I left. Look, I've got to get back to California tonight. I have a very urgent meeting to attend tomorrow; otherwise I'd stick around for a few more days. Do you have any idea when she's due to return?"

"No, unfortunately, I don't."

"I see. Well, if you don't mind, is it possible for you to give me her direct cell phone number? Perhaps I will have better luck." Lexi suspected a rift between the ladies. *What girlfriend leaves town without telling her best friend when she's going to return?* There was more to this story between Veronica and Joie Parker, but she left it alone. It wasn't any of her business unless it affected her client's chance of locating her mother.

"Sorry. You understand I can't do that. I'll tell her what's going on when I speak to her again. Until then, please be patient."

"I'll give you a week. If I don't hear from you by then, I'll track her down and contact her directly."

"You mean to tell me you're willing to potentially wreck her life by bringing this person who claims to be Ronnie's child straight to her front door?" Ronnie looked at the sign on the lawn and inwardly fell to pieces.

"Yes, that is precisely what I intend to do. It is much simpler for all involved when I go through a close friend or loved one, but when neither is possible, I do what I have to for my client's sake. It is business ma'am, strictly business. Nothing personal about this at all," explained Lexi.

"Honey, it may be business for you, but it is extremely personal to Ronnie. What if it is her kid? Then what? Is she supposed to drop everything and suddenly become Mommy to this child? People need to stop stirring up mess when they should let the past stay buried where it should be. In the past."

"That may very well be true. Do you have children, Ms. Parker?" asked Lexi.

"Yeah, I got kids. Twins as a matter-of-fact—a boy and a girl. Five and a half years old."

"Do you believe all children should know who their parents are?"

"Of course I do. Why do you ask?'

"Because only a parent, especially a mother, can understand the importance of a child knowing their roots—their heritage. Would you ever deny your children knowing who their father is?" she asked rhetorically.

Joie didn't respond.

"Of course you wouldn't. Look, there's no guarantee Veronica and her child will have a relationship, but don't you think they should at least have the opportunity?"

Joie pondered her words. If she didn't know better, she would've thought this P.I. McCray had delved into her private life and uncovered a few skeletons in her closet. That was impossible because there was only one person who knew the truth about her twin's father. And if Joie had anything to do with it, she vowed to carry that secret to her grave.

"You do what you must. In the meantime, I'm gonna keep on trying to reach Ronnie. I'd rather she hear this news from me, instead of some stranger knocking on her door screaming out 'Surprise!'"

"Fine. I'll be back in one week whether I hear from you or not. Good-bye Ms. Parker."

Joie clicked off and turned towards home. She wanted—no, she *needed* to see her little family.

Joie pulled in the driveway just as Cedric and the kids were arriving home. He parked first. She pulled in after him and retrieved the mail from the mailbox while he helped get the kids out of the backseat. The twins ran to their mother and gave her the hugs and kisses she so desperately needed.

"Hey baby, I didn't expect you back so soon. How's Ronnie?" Cedric asked, as he balanced two pizzas with one hand and hugged her with the other.

"I don't know. I still couldn't get in touch with her. Guess what else?" She kissed his scruffy bearded cheek.

"What now?"

"There's a For Sale sign on her lawn."

"What? She's selling the house? Well, I guess she would since she don't have no job no more." Cedric laughed.

He never cared much for Ronnie. She was stuck up and thought she was too good for them, especially since she and Derek split. He preferred that his wife not spend so much time around Ronnie, lest her high and mighty bourgeois ways rub off on Joie.

"Don't talk about my best friend like that. She's just going through some things right now."

"She ain't going through nothing worse than the rest of us." Cedric replied in a dismissive tone. "Maya? Trey?"

The children bounded into the kitchen. "Sir?" they answered in unison.

"Did you guys wash up like I told you to?"

"Yes sir. We even used soap. Wanna smell?" Maya presented her freshly scrubbed hands for inspection. She poked Trey to do the same. He did.

"You are so mean. Here's the mail. I'ma go change."

"I'm just saying that her troubles ain't no bigger than ours or anyone else's." He furrowed his brow. "And here you are, crazy enough to call her your best friend. What kind of a best friend puts her house up for sale without saying a word? And why hasn't she returned your calls? What's up with that?" He playfully grabbed his wife's rear as she wiggled away.

Joie lovingly swatted his hand away and headed for the shower. All that drama with Ronnie was getting to her. She loved her husband so much and after they got over those rough patches in the early years, she knew without a doubt Cedric was her one and only true love. All that mess with Derek was just the devil trying to mess up her life. She thought about taking a weekend away. Just the two of them. Maybe her mother would watch the kids for a couple of days.

When she returned to the kitchen fifteen minutes later, the children were nowhere in sight. Cedric stood over the kitchen sink with a drink in one hand and a letter in the other. He was furious.

"Hey honey, where are the kids? They finished eating already?" Joie was still in a playful mood as she bopped into the kitchen.

"I sent them to their rooms," he replied in a tightly controlled voice.

Joie witnessed an expression on Cedric's face she'd never seen before. His eyes were bloodshot like he'd been crying. The set of his jaw let her know he was angry. Angrier than she'd ever seen him before.

"Baby, what's wrong? What is it?" Joie asked, gently touching his arm.

He pulled away. "What the fuck is this?!" He tossed the papers at her. They fluttered to the floor.

Joie bent down to pick up the letter. "What do you mean? What is it? What are these papers?"

"They're DNA results for the twins. About a month ago the police came to the school and did DNA test kits on all the children. You know, in case they ever came up missing. The twins thought it was fun having their mouths swabbed. Remember I told you I was having it done?"

"What are you talking about? DNA tests? You had the kids tested?" She stared at the letter.

"Yes Joie. That is exactly what I am saying. The kids were tested and so was I. They needed to test at least one parent for comparison purposes. So guess what I learned in this goddamn letter?!"

Joie feigned innocence, praying that her husband wasn't about to say what she had feared for years.

"According to the test results, there is no way I am the father of the twins! Joie? What the fuck did you do?!" Cedric asked, as angry tears streamed down his face.

Joie felt her world come crashing down all around her. She prayed for the floor to open and swallow her up. She wished a tornado would materialize and pull her through the open window. She willed fast-moving floodwaters to sweep her away. She waited for a bolt of lightning to come from the sky and strike her down. Sadly, all that came was the silent fury from her devastated husband.

Unable to move, she stood her ground and accepted his wrath. Then she sank to the floor on her knees and quietly begged, "Baby, I am so sorry... I messed up... Please, please, please forgive me."

Chapter 8

Ronnie was more excited than she'd been in a long time. Luis had actually asked her out. Thoughts of Ike momentarily surfaced. She was surprised she wasn't more upset at their breakup. Although she held great affection for Ike, he wasn't ready for a serious relationship yet. He still had unresolved issues concerning his ex-wife and son.

After a year of sacrificing her life trying to make things work, she finally figured out that pursuing a relationship with Ike wasn't worth the effort. Ronnie felt second string when it came to Ike's son and ex-wife. She felt Ike was emotionally attached to his ex and Ronnie only got what was left, which wasn't very much. And in that moment, she vowed to never allow any man to put his needs before hers ever again. *Either I come first, or not at all!*

She looked in the mirror, putting on her makeup and held a conversation with her reflection. "Girlfriend, tonight you are going out on a real grown up date. Not to Chuck E. Cheese's or an early matinee to see a G-rated movie, or to hang out at the playground in the local park. No ma'am! This time the date is all about you. You're being selfish you say? So what? It is your right to be a little selfish sometimes." For once, Ronnie chose to focus on her happiness and damn if it didn't feel good!

When Luis arrived at his family's vacation villa, he told his sister all about Ronnie. She was happy for him. Happy he finally met someone he *wanted* to spend time with. Although his divorce was fairly recent, the separation had dragged on for what felt like an eternity. It drained Luis emotionally and financially. Since then, every woman he met was flawed. His sister always said in time he would meet the right woman and he would know it immediately. Until now, he never believed her. Perhaps this time she was right.

When his sister discovered his new lady friend wasn't Dominican, she was disappointed. Slightly more so because his friend didn't speak Spanish, but he vowed to fix the language barrier if anything more developed between them. His sister accepted his choice and that was that.

Luis finished dressing and nervously watched the hands of the clock tick by. When the clock hit six forty-five, he made his way down to the lobby. Ronnie was already there waiting.

"You look beautiful!" exclaimed Luis.

"Thank you. You don't look half bad yourself. I love that shirt."

"Thanks, its traditional Dominican menswear—perfect for this climate. I've called a taxi to take us to dinner. It should be out front. Ready?"

*   *   *

The waiter seated the couple at a small table towards the back of the room. The club was small, intimate, and filled with tourists. Mostly white, black, and Latino. They fit right in.

"What is this place? It doesn't look like any of the jazz clubs I'm used to."

"Well, actually it's not like your typical state-side jazz club. The drinks are cheaper, the food is more delicious, and the music is unlike any other." Luis ordered a bottle of *Brugal Anejo* rum with two glasses.

"Um, Luis, actually I don't like rum. I think I'll have something else," Ronnie replied, slightly taken aback by his arrogance in ordering for her.

"Oh, I'm sorry. I hope I didn't offend you. This is what we Dominicans drink and I naturally assumed it would be fine with you. What else would you like?" He hoped he hadn't overstepped his boundary.

"No, no you're right. That's okay. I'll try the rum. Hey, when in Rome, or in this case the DR... Right?" She acquiesced. *I've got to chill. He's just trying to be nice.*

Luis filled two small glasses with the amber colored liquid. Ronnie sipped. Then she sipped again, this time without the hesitancy.

"Yummy. That's very good. What kind of rum is this? It goes down so smoothly."

"So, you like it? I thought you might. It's made here on the island."

"Yeah, surprisingly I do. Very tasty," she replied. "Okay, tell me. Why did you really leave this wonderful country for the states? It's positively beautiful here. I can't imagine leaving all this to live somewhere else."

"You know the old saying about the grass being greener...? Anyway, I left primarily because of a lack of opportunity in the DR. I moved to New York when I was eighteen to attend college. After graduate school, I returned home with plans to start a graphic design business in Santo Domingo. I tried but could never get the capital I

71

needed. As you can probably tell, my country is very poor and was more so fifteen years ago. After years of never getting anywhere, a former classmate told me how hot the job market in California was for graphic artists. So with his help, I found a job, learned the market, and eventually started my own business."

"Interesting story... I'd love to hear more about your business sometime. That must have been quite a change going from the DR to New York and then to California?"

"You have no idea how much of a cultural change it was. New Yorkers tend to be edgier and you know exactly where you stand with them. Californians are different. Overall, they give the impression of being laid back, but that's only because they're self-absorbed, if you know what I mean."

Ronnie nodded in agreement, even though she had no idea if what he said was accurate.

"I live in Montverde; it's an exclusive enclave tucked off the beaten path. My business is in the city of Logeta, a few miles north of Santa Elena; a small beach town near the ocean famous for strawberries and avocados."

The waiter returned to take their orders and informed them the band would be setting up soon. Ronnie motioned for Luis to order for her, so he did.

"I actually visited Santa Elena many, many years ago. What I remember is the buildings were beautifully designed in old Spanish style type of architecture. I've only been to NYC once so I can't relate to the edginess."

"Oh yeah? So you've been to California? That's pretty cool." Luis replied.

"Yep and believe it or not, I didn't even know there was a country called the Dominican Republic until a few years ago. Call it my own ignorance, but the only Latinos I knew were from Mexico."

"Yes, I've heard that from a lot of Americans. Anyone who isn't white or Black must be Mexican." He laughed at the absurdity. "Where did you say you're from?"

"Actually I don't believe I did. I live in Hampton, Virginia, but am originally from Oklahoma City. Are you familiar with either area?"

"Not really. Can't say I've met anyone from Virginia and definitely not Oklahoma. Is everyone from Oklahoma as nice as you?"

"Well, probably not as nice as me, but pretty close." She teased. "Oklahoma City was a pleasant enough city, but I needed to get out of there."

"Why?"

"Boredom mostly. I was eighteen when I first left for college. I had the choice of going to a local state school or one in Illinois. I chose the latter because I wanted to see the big city, and after I graduated, I moved to the east coast—to Virginia. Also, I left because there were too many freakin' tornadoes. I've never been through one—had a few close calls, but thank God I never actually experienced an actual tornado. The way they drop out of the sky out of nowhere... Whew! Gives me chills just thinking about it."

"Tornadoes, huh? For me, it was hurricanes. Unfortunately, I have lived through a few and those things are nothing to play with. Can't hide from a hurricane either!"

"So we agree that tornadoes and hurricanes literally suck!" exclaimed Ronnie.

"Uh, yes, I think we can both agree on that." He laughed. "So what do you do back there? In Hampton? You work or have a family? What keeps you occupied?"

"Until last week I worked for a sports management company. We primarily drafted contracts for athletes fresh out of college. Sometimes high school. My job was to negotiate terms that benefited the management more than the athlete. I quit because it wasn't what I wanted to do with my life. One day I got fed up and walked out. No family... I'm divorced. No kids."

"Sounds like your job was quite interesting... What are your plans now that you've given up your career?"

"Right now, the only plan I have is to enjoy my time here in the DR. I'll figure out the rest when I get back. I'm going through some pretty heavy stuff and just needed a break."

Luis attempted to figure out Ronnie. She was a single woman vacationing alone in the DR after recently walking away from what sounded like a very lucrative career. He thought she was fascinating and wanted to know more. "If you don't mind, I'd like to share some of that time with you. I'm here for another week before having to return to California. What do you say?"

"Luis, I'd like that." She was pleased.

He refilled both their glasses with more rum.

Ronnie was uncharacteristically relaxed and very open, which was a departure from her usual personality. Normally, she was guarded and kept her personal life very private, but there was something about Luis that made her feel safe and comfortable. She felt that she could trust him.

"Want to hear something that's messed up?" She slurred her speech slightly. The smoothness of the tasty rum was deceptive and its effect snuck up on her.

"What do you mean? Messed up?"

"About me. My life. My world."

"Sure. Why do you say it's messed up?"

The rum loosened her tongue, giving her permission to speak freely. Good thing because she needed to release the words and let go of the angst. "Before I left, I found out my best friend had an affair with my husband, my now ex-husband, a long time ago. She didn't mean to tell me. It accidently just slipped out in casual conversation."

"That's awful! What did you do?"

"Not much I could do. Shit happened over five years ago. My husband left me for another woman and it wasn't even my best friend. He got the other girl pregnant and felt marrying her was the 'right thing to do'. Him being an upstanding citizen and all."

"Ronnie, I'm sorry."

"Told ya it was and that ain't all. My boyfriend and I broke up because he's still hung up on his ex-wife. I caught her coming out of his house early one morning. He didn't even try to deny it. Said she needed him and everything he did for her was because of his son."

"Sounds like he didn't cut that tie all the way. That was his fault. Either you're in, or you're out. Sounds like he was still in. Didn't matter what that piece of paper said." Luis emptied his glass.

"Yeah, my life is pretty messed up right now. I quit my job, put my house up for sale, and gave away most of my clothes. Got no family. Got no man, and now got no friends. I'm all alone in this world." Ronnie didn't drink brown liquor often because it tended to bring out the pity party, the sadness, and all the stuff she didn't want to talk about out loud.

"You say you have no family… *¿Qué pasa con su madre y su padre?*"

"My parents?"

"*Sí.*"

"Well, my father passed away eighteen years ago. God rest his soul. My mother lives by herself in Oklahoma City. I haven't spoken to her in several years. We have issues we need to work on."

"You do have a lot going on. But you seem like a strong woman who can handle it. Hang on sister; everything is going work out fine. Promise." Luis covered her hands with his own strong ones.

"Oh yeah, how do you know?" Ronnie enjoyed his masculine touch. It was comforting.

"Just do. That's how."

"I am strong, but you know what? I'm tired of being strong. I need a strong man to take care of me." She exhaled. "Don't you find it interesting how life never seems to work out how we plan? I thought I'd be in a totally different place at this stage of my life, not starting over again. Life can be a bitch."

"I know what you mean. Plans don't always work out the way we think. Look at me. I made all kinds of plans for my life. I wanted to get married, settle down and have lots of children."

"I know what you mean because I wanted the same thing with my husband. Too bad it didn't work out that way. What happened with your wife?"

Luis didn't normally talk about his ex-wife on a first date, but Ronnie was different—she seemed to genuinely care about his life. He took another swig of rum and started talking. "My wife was a black woman—a sister. She referred to herself as a high maintenance diva queen. She never wore the same outfit twice in one month. Her life revolved around hair appointments, getting her nails and feet done, shopping, and working out. The woman didn't even have a job because she loved to say that a real man wouldn't allow his wife to work. I quickly discovered she wasn't interested in having children. She didn't like them."

"Didn't you know all that when you married her? Did she flip the script or something?" asked Ronnie, feeling guilty. Up until this trip, many would have called her a high maintenance diva queen.

"Yes and no. She was a model when I met her and at the time it was cool. My ex was a beautiful woman—on the outside. I fell for her external looks. We went to Vegas and tied the knot. Only knew her for a week before we got married. I thought she was the perfect woman for me."

"So what happened?"

75

"Once we got out of the bedroom, I really got to know her and we discovered just how different we were. We tried to work on the marriage, but mostly I worked and she pampered herself. No one wanted to hire her because she was considered "difficult to work with". I kept busy trying to build up my company and she spent my money as quickly as it came in."

"That's really messed up." Ronnie sat back in her chair. It never surprised her how stupid men were. As long as they paraded around with a stereotypical "beauty queen" on their arm, they foolishly thought they had it made. Luis was just another sucker as far as she was concerned. A fine sucker, but a sucker all the same.

"After a few years of supporting her habits, I finally came to my senses, cut off the money supply, and told her to go out and find a real job. Any job. She refused. Guess when I stopped giving her money, she found some other man who would. She walked out on me and went to live with some Hollywood producer. I filed for divorce and it took a couple of years to get finalized because she refused to sign the papers."

"Sounds like you haven't had an easy time with relationships either."

"That's okay, because I never really loved her—didn't even *know* her. She used me to provide her with a standard of living she had become accustomed to. Found out a year into the marriage that I was her fourth husband. Thank God we didn't have children."

"Sounds pretty messed up."

"I'll never make that mistake again."

"What's that?"

"Marry someone I haven't taken the time to get to know. I'm too old to go through that again."

"I hear ya. Me too. So what happened to your ex?"

"Last I heard she was in Hollywood working in the porn industry. She finally got the fame she always craved."

Ronnie laughed, "I'm sorry; I don't mean to laugh, but are you telling me she's making porn movies?"

Luis joined in her laughter, "Yep, she went from beauty queen to porn queen."

They continued to laugh at the irony of each hooking up with the wrong person. A look passed between them. Both realized they both wanted the same thing, but had foolishly married the wrong people. If they had met at another time in another place; it would be the two of them sitting in the DR enjoying an anniversary celebration, instead of bemoaning failed relationships.

The conversation became too heavy with what-ifs and coulda beens. It was serious talk that quickly turned into a buzz killer. Ronnie never meant for their chat to go down that road so she abruptly changed the subject.

"Look, the band is setting up."

"Are you a fan of Dominican *merengue?*" He appreciated the distraction from the conversation, as well.

"Um, I don't really know. I've heard it before, but I never really thought about it. I suppose I do, especially when it has a funky beat. I first heard it during my trip here and haven't heard it since. I thought this was a jazz club? By the way, this food is wonderful."

Luis laughed. "That's good. I like to see a woman enjoy her food. As for this being a jazz club, the band performs a fusion of *merengue* and jazz. If you're strictly a fan of jazz, I promise you, you will not be disappointed."

"Considering you've been right about everything so far, I'll take your word for it. I love live music. Watching musicians connect with their instruments to make something out of nothing is fascinating. I think they're really cool."

"I agree. Musicians are a different breed. So tell me, who is your favorite?"

"That's easy. I absolutely love Prince. I honestly believe he is the greatest performer I've ever seen live in concert. I saw him twice and both times he gave an amazing performance. He didn't need any special props; just the artist and his guitar. It was spectacular and beyond description. There are no words that can describe his amazing talent. You ever been to one of his concerts?"

"No, I haven't. I'm not a big fan, but I understand what you mean because I'm into jazz. When I listen to music, and I mean *extremely* good music, it transcends the ordinary and takes me to a different place. It doesn't matter if it's guitar, piano, trumpet, sax, drums… Like you said, the way a musician connects with his instrument is what makes him an artist. Anyone can blow a horn, but if there is no love, no soul, no passion, you may as well be listening to a computer streaming together 0's and 1's. Watching a true artist perform effortlessly takes me to another dimension."

Ronnie and Luis finished their dinner, grooving along with the band. They didn't speak much, mainly just listened. For the next hour or so, they sat back and watched the band perform their craft in the small intimate jazz club.

The band played a popular song and the floor quickly filled up with couples dancing the *merengue*. Men and women of all ages kept time with the quick beat of the music. Simply watching the dancers made Ronnie tired.

All of a sudden Luis jumped up and reached for Ronnie's hand. He said, "Come on. Let's dance." He moved his feet and hips in time to the rhythm.

"I can't move like that. I'll look stupid."

"No, you won't. I'll show you. It's easy and its fun!" He pulled her to the dance floor.

Luis placed Ronnie's left hand on his shoulder. He took her right hand in his and showed her how to move her feet in time to the quick beat. After she nailed the dance step, he twirled her around in a circle. When the music was over, he dipped her backwards and planted a great big kiss on her lips.

"Oh my! That was fun, but I need to sit down. Oh my goodness, I'm in pretty good shape but I don't know how they can go so long without stopping." Ronnie gulped down a cold glass of water, hoping the liquid would not only cool her down, but also stop the tingling in her lips from that kiss.

"You did great. You must have Dominican blood in you because you moved like you've been doing this dance all your life."

"I had a good teacher. By the way, what was that kiss about?" she asked off-handedly.

"You danced so well, I simply got caught up in the moment. Hope you didn't mind…" Luis fought the urge to kiss her all evening, but couldn't resist after the sexy dance.

"Not really. It was just a surprise, that's all. Anyway, I love that song. It was perfect to dance to. That's how I managed to keep up with you. I followed your lead and listened to the music. After a while, I didn't have to think about how to move my feet."

"Exactly! You shouldn't have to think about the actual dance—just feel the beat and let the music take you where you need to go."

She laughed. "Easy for you to say, but I have to admit, the music sure did make it easy to keep step."

"Now that's what I'm talking about! Did you hear how they made each note count? How well each note meshed together? The melody was fluid and the harmony perfect. But it's not just the music we hear that makes the song; it's what happens when the music isn't playing. In that minute tiny little pause between the notes, there is an unmistakable harmony. A coming together of a beautiful creative process. That space is just as crucial as the actual notes themselves."

"Yeah, it's the space between the notes. The sound you can't hear—what's leftover between the beats. You're telling me you hear it too?"

"Yes, of course. It's only for a split second, but if you listen, really listen; it's something you *feel* in your soul more so than what you hear with your ears."

"Wow... You do realize you have just blown my mind with all this philosophical talk, right?"

Luis was pleased that she understood.

"You mean to tell me you can also hear the offbeat?"

He nodded.

"The very first time I experienced that quietness was after I quit my job--before coming on this trip. I thought I was crazy when I first heard the offbeat. Or didn't hear it... You know what I mean."

"I don't think it's that unusual. Possibly, the reason you didn't hear it before is you weren't listening. Your life was too busy and you managed to fill every tiny bit of space with useless things. An actual space between musical beats does exist. It's also called the offbeat. Music isn't just the sounds you hear, but it is also the space between the notes. The quiet, the pause, the white noise. Any musician knows where that place is and so do most creative types. For others, it is a concept and a way they choose to live."

"Go on, I'm feeling you…"

"People have different names for the same thing: Marching to the beat of a different drummer; decluttering your life; living in the offbeat. They basically all mean the same thing. You cut out the background noise and make whatever you're doing your own. It's what happens when you step out of the crowd and into your own space."

"Hmm, that's definitely something to reflect upon. Luis, I have already decided that is how I intend to live my life—in the offbeat!" declared Ronnie.

Luis poured their final drinks for the evening. "Here's a toast to Ronnie finding that space between the beats and making it her own."

After a couple more songs, they watched the band pack it up, and call it a night. They were quiet on the taxi ride back to the resort, each lost in their own private thoughts. When all was said and done, the evening was a huge success.

"I had such a wonderful time. Thank you for inviting me to dinner." Ronnie momentarily hesitated before adding, "Um, I have another excursion planned tomorrow morning on a catamaran. They're taking us to a little island off the coast to snorkel. I know you like snorkeling. Want to come?"

"First of all, I also enjoyed our evening. You're lots of fun to be with and about going snorkeling, I'd love to join you. I'll see you downstairs first thing tomorrow morning," replied Luis checking his watch. He discovered the more time he spent with Ronnie, the more intrigued he became. He really liked her. *And* to meet a Black woman who wasn't afraid to get her hair wet *and* go snorkeling? He had to see that with his own two eyes.

"Okay, I'll see you around eight." *I wonder if he's going to kiss me good night. I sure hope he does,* she thought.

Maldito ella tiene buena pinta! I really want to kiss her again. "Eight o'clock it is. Well, goodnight." Luis awkwardly kissed her cheek and quickly left.

"Goodnight." Ronnie watched Luis descend the stairs. She touched her cheek and wondered if that was how Dominican men courted their women.

* * *

Over the remaining days, Ronnie and Luis became inseparable. Where you saw one, the other was never far behind. He even went as far as suggesting extending his trip by a couple of days to spend more time together. They didn't restrict themselves to the resort, nor to tourist traps.

Luis taught her Spanish phrases and gradually introduced her to his culture. Not having the opportunity to provide a private tour to anyone before, he was absolutely thrilled to show off his homeland. Luis borrowed a motorcycle and took her to places no tourist would ever see. They rode up mountains, visited secluded beaches, and ventured through back alleys of ancient cities. He showed her isolated hillside villages where the people lived only off the land they farmed. Ronnie was intrigued and dismayed at the same time. His country appeared to be at opposite ends of two spectrums. The people were either extremely wealthy or otherwise destitute. Very little existed in between. Poverty was more rampant than she initially suspected among the locals. And yet, fabulous ritzy resorts were popping up along the most highly desired coastlines.

"Luis, what's going on here? Why can't we get to the beach?" she asked when they rode by a large construction site for another resort. Signs were posted everywhere restricting access to the private beach.

"It's foreign money coming in—mostly European. They develop these vacation resorts and restrict access to some of the best beaches from the citizens. Since the economy is so heavily dependent on tourists, very few complain about the outcome of prime land being bought up by non-Dominicans. On the bright side, at least jobs are plentiful. They're low paying service jobs to support a thriving tourist industry, but at least the people are working."

"That's awful!"

"No, that's life in the DR."

A blend of Spanish, Taino, and African ancestors produced a beautiful race of Dominican people with sun kissed skin in various shades of brown. The combination of genes resulted in very handsome men and gorgeous women. The blending of cultures was not only evident in skin tone, but in their music, food, and traditions.

Luis gave Ronnie a walking tour of old Santo Domingo. He pointed out historical landmarks and explained how his country ended up where it was today. The DR held so much promise, yet it hadn't developed as quickly as it could have.

"Luis, you mentioned you wanted to move back here someday. From what I've seen in the short time I've been here, they could use an entrepreneur—a businessman—a Dominican businessman, who will contribute to the economy. Someone who can give the younger generation hopes and dreams and inspire them to reach for the stars. Seems like now would be the perfect time. I don't know. You tell me. Am I wrong?"

"Ah, if it were only that simple. Starting a legitimate business in the DR takes connections and lots and lots of money. Government assistance to start-up companies does not exist here as it does in the United States. The state has extensive control over private citizens and the process is riddled with bureaucracy and legal hurdles. I am working on getting the necessary licenses, filing the correct paperwork, and looking for investors to get this started. It may take years, which is why I'm working on it now."

"Oh, I had no idea. Goes to show you how blessed and spoiled we are in the states."

"I'll agree with you there. Americans do not know how good they have it." Luis, being a proud Dominican, wanted to show Ronnie everything and tell her as much as he could. To share his culture with someone who was truly interested in learning was amazing. She asked relevant questions, pointed out inconsistencies, and made intelligent observations about the conditions of the country and its inhabitants.

Ronnie imagined had she lived under some of the conditions she witnessed, she'd have no reason to sing and be happy. Yet, most of the people she met were quick with a smile and a kind word. *Maybe there is something to living on an island after all...* Compared to some of the people she'd recently met, she had everything she needed and more.

On the way back to the resort, Luis turned the motorcycle onto a dirt road, off the beaten path of the main street. Ronnie didn't know where they were headed and really didn't care. She was just enjoying the ride.

At times the path was blocked by thick vegetation. Luis took it all in stride and pushed the plants away. It appeared they were traveling deep into the jungle.

"Where are we going?" Ronnie asked, after traveling several miles on the road.

"You'll see… It's a special place I used to come when I was a child. We're almost there!" he shouted over the noise of the engine.

Finally the jungle opened up to a secluded beach. Luis left the motorcycle on the dirt path so as not to get sand in the engine. He removed his helmet and helped Ronnie off the bike.

"It's absolutely gorgeous, Luis! Look at how blue the water is." She took in the amazing view of a beach scene so spectacular; photographers would kill for the opportunity to shoot there. The bright sun reflected off the fine white sand. The strong surf of the deep blue ocean pounded against the shore in wave after wave of frothy white water.

"*Si, es muy magnifico!*"

"Look at all those crabs running into the water. There must be thousands of them."

Luis laughed at Ronnie's reaction. "*Mi familia* used to come here all the time to fish. My father and several other men would launch their small fishing boats from that pier over there and bring home enough fish to feed everyone. I loved this place."

Luis shook a palm tree causing a couple of coconuts to fall to the ground. He removed a small machete from a bag hanging on the motorcycle and chopped off the tops.

"Be careful!"

"Don't worry. I could do this with my eyes closed." He made a hole in one coconut and offered it to Ronnie.

"What am I supposed to do with that?" she asked, looking at the hairy object in her hand.

"Drink it; it won't hurt you. Its coconut milk and it's very delicious." He turned his upwards and drank down the liquid inside.

Ronnie watched Luis in awe. She'd never seen anyone so quick to eat and drink food in its natural state. Her food came prepackaged from the supermarket in sanitary cellophane wrappings. However, because she wanted to have a unique experience with Luis, she trusted his judgment and tried the coconut milk. The cloudy liquid dripped from her chin. "Interesting flavor, I expected it would have more of a coconut flavor; it kinda tastes like water."

"That's because most of the flavor comes from the meat—the white part inside, but the milk is good when you're thirsty."

"Dang, you've got me doing all sorts of stuff I never thought I'd do."

"Sometimes it's good to step out of your comfort zone." He absentmindedly tossed small pebbles into the surf.

"You really miss living here, don't you?"

"Yes I miss it, it's my home. But so is California."

"I think I understand. Your heart is here in the Dominican Republic, but your head is in California because of your business. That's quite a dilemma you have Luis. What are you going to do?"

"This is my country—my roots are here and always will be. My business is doing very well and I want it to continue to grow. So, for now, I'll continue to travel back once a year. Maybe next time I come, I'll have a very special lady to accompany me."

Ronnie played around with the thought of being with Luis on a more permanent basis. Wondered how it would be to be with a person she was so acutely in tune with. She pushed the thoughts away because after this trip was over, chances are she'd never see Luis again.

"Hey, it's getting late. We don't want to be caught out here after dark. I just wanted to share this with you—let you see some of my childhood jaunts."

"Thank you for sharing. This truly is a magical place. Who knows, maybe one day I'll have an opportunity to watch you fish off that pier."

"And maybe I'll hold you to that. Come on, let's get out of here." He helped her on the bike and made their way back to the main road.

Dusk had settled upon the country by the time they returned to the resort. Luis returned the motorcycle to the guy he borrowed it from and walked Ronnie to her room.

"I won't be able to see you tomorrow, because I promised my sister we'd go visit our Uncle Nando. He lives a couple hours away. It's a long standing tradition to get together once a year at his villa in the mountains. It's mostly an excuse to eat, drink, dance, and celebrate with *mi familia.*"

"Sounds like fun." She unlocked the door, feeling slightly hurt she wasn't included.

"I hope you understand why I can't invite you. You realize I'd love for you to go with me, but this reunion is strictly for family and mine is very heavy on tradition. It would be awkward to bring someone I've only met just last week. Please try to understand," Luis explained, standing outside Ronnie's suite.

"I understand it's not personal. It's a family *thang*. I'll find something to do until you return. Those covered beach beds look inviting and perfect for reading. You go ahead and enjoy your family. I'll see you when you get back."

"Yes, you will." He hesitated for a moment then stepped inside the room. "Before I go, I need to tell you something. I like you Ronnie. A lot. The short time we've spent together has been great and I've developed feelings for you. This "feeling" is new for me. I dated off and on while I was waiting for my divorce to be finalized, but hadn't met anyone who held my interest for very long. I don't know what it is, but there is something very special about you that pulls me in. I am so attracted to you physically, spiritually, emotionally—sexually... Feel like I've known you all my life. Just in case you were wondering, this isn't some island romance and I'm not trying to get you in bed. Trust me, if sex were the only thing I wanted, it wouldn't be difficult to find. But you..."

Luis took Ronnie by the shoulders and gently pulled her towards him. He gazed into her eyes trying to read her thoughts. His breathing quickened. Unsure how she felt, he waited for her to give an indication that this was what she wanted as well. Her body relaxed and she moved towards him. His strong arms embraced her. They met midway in a long, passionate kiss that went on for minutes. His erection stiffened against her leg. Strong arms encircled her, pulling her closer. Ronnie responded in kind, pushing her hips against his. His kiss was intoxicating and she became lightheaded—felt her knees buckle. By the time they reluctantly pulled apart, both were left breathless.

"I'd better go before I can't. I'll be back the day after tomorrow. Promise." Luis opened the door and quickly left.

"Uh, okay. See you." Ronnie was left speechless. Her fingers touched her lips where his once played. She closed her eyes and imagined making love to Luis. Imagined him taking her to the mountaintop and back. Another couple staggered past her open door, groping each other along the way. How she wished that were her and Luis. She shut the door and sat on her bed.

In all the time they had spent together, tonight was the first time he displayed any sentiment other than friendship. The thought of having a purely sexual island fling had occurred to Ronnie, if only for a moment. After all, Luis was a very sexy man and she hadn't made love in months.

Confused over her recent encounter with Luis and a bit out of sorts, Ronnie needed a distraction. She pulled her eReader from her bag. *I need to think about something besides Luis and wondering what kind of lover he is. I wonder if he is gentle, passionate, enthusiastic, rough, or freaky? Hmm, I've never made love with a foreigner before. Do Dominican men make love differently than American men? I wonder if I'll notice a difference at all.*

She turned on the eReader to help get her mind off Luis. The cell phone slipped from her bag to the floor. Prior to arriving in the DR, she turned off the phone's call receiving function, but left the text messages active. By force of habit, she checked her texts. Several were from Joie. "Call me", "We need to talk", "I'm sorry", and so on were the types of text she sent. Ronnie deleted them one-by-one and turned the phone off.

Her thoughts returned to Luis. *He has feelings for me? What kind of feelings?* Both were just getting out of relationships and the chance of rebounding was too great, especially now. She could not afford to get involved. There was already too much stuff going on in her life. The best she could hope for was a long distance friendship. With all the drama awaiting her back home, getting involved with Luis or anyone else for that matter, was not something she wanted, nor needed.

Ronnie admitted her feelings for Luis were undeniable and if it were any other time in her life, there would be no hesitation on her part. And as much as they both wanted it, she really didn't need another complicated relationship in her life. Luis was handsome, kind, funny, and unattached with no children. In other words, perfect. Except for the fact that he lived on the west coast, they could really have something special. No, she had to stop this before it went any further.

She crawled into bed and fell asleep dreaming about making passionate love to Luis on a wonderful island paradise.

Early the next morning, instead of going to the beach, she took a detour to the travel agency located in the lobby. She cut her vacation short by a couple of days and rescheduled her return trip to the states on the first flight leaving that evening.

After returning to her suite, Ronnie packed up all the souvenirs and mementos she acquired on her trip. *Who am I kidding? If I stay here any longer, I'll just end up having an ill-advised love affair with Luis and leave the island broken-hearted.* The attraction to this man was real and it was intense. In her current emotional state, she was bound to make all kinds of foolish mistakes. When it came to Luis, she couldn't risk the drama.

Before she boarded the bus headed to the airport, she handed an envelope containing a letter explaining her rapid departure, to the concierge to give to Luis. Perhaps he wouldn't understand, but that was a chance she had to take. Luis was a distraction of gigantic proportions. One she couldn't afford to have right now.

The trip had accomplished its goal of easing her stress and clearing her mind. She knew what she had to do, and getting involved with another a man wasn't anywhere on the list. Some other time, some other place, the prospect of a romance would have been a welcome treat. But not today… Today, she would go home to face her demons.

Chapter 9

"Get up off your knees!" yelled Cedric. "Get up Joie! Who did you fuck?! What muthafucka do these kids belong to?!"

Joie remained knelt on the floor, bent over, head touching the cool kitchen tiles. Tears streamed down her face, forming a small puddle at his feet. She rocked back and forth.

The twins heard the commotion and ran into the kitchen.

Trey was the first to speak, "Daddy? Mommy? What's wrong? Why you crying? Mommy? Mommy?"

Maya looked at Cedric and asked, "Daddy, why is Mommy on the floor crying?" Tears formed in the little girls eyes.

Cedric looked at the children he loved with all his heart. The children he raised from babies. His pride and his joy. The children he just found out weren't his. His heart broke in that moment. He grabbed his car keys and without a word walked out; leaving the three of them crying and calling out for him.

The screen door slammed shut. Joie heard the engine start, followed by the squealing of tires as Cedric peeled out the driveway.

She finally raised her head to see her babies crying, trying their best to console her. She grabbed onto the both of them, kissing them, telling them everything was going to be alright. She didn't believe it, but they didn't need to know that. Not yet.

Joie finally managed to calm the children down and get them to bed. They both wanted their daddy, especially Maya. He was the one who read bedtime stories and tickled them until they went to sleep. In fact, he was closer to the twins than she was. Joie believed she subconsciously pushed them closer together to help ease the guilt that never left her mind. If she stepped back and let him be the favorite parent, his not being their natural father wouldn't matter so much.

The quiet sobs coming from her children as they cried for their daddy were almost too much to bear. She tried her best to soothe them by rubbing their backs and singing lullabies, but as Trey so eloquently stated, "Mommy, you're not doing it right. Only Daddy knows how to put us to sleep."

By midnight, she concluded Cedric wasn't coming home. In his haste to leave, he didn't take his cell phone so she had no way to get in touch with him. Not that he wanted her to anyway.

The next morning Joie awoke to a terrible headache. In the midst of tossing and turning, she probably only got a good two or three hours of sleep. She reached over and discovered Cedric's side of the bed was cold. Empty. Yet, hope still remained that Cedric had returned in the middle of the night and slept on the living room couch. She pulled on her robe and went to check. He wasn't there.

She called in sick from work. However, the twins needed to get to school. Normally Cedric dropped them off on his way to work. Today, it was her job. Come to think of it, it may end up being her job for the rest of her life if Cedric didn't come home. She pushed the thought away because it was too painful to consider. Joie knew it was a possibility, but she wasn't ready to face reality yet.

A quick shower helped ease the pounding in her temples. By the time she was dressed and on her way to wake the twins, she heard noise coming from the kitchen. Her heartbeat quickened. "Please let it be Cedric," she prayed.

She hurried to the kitchen to apologize, but she quickly found out it wasn't Cedric. It was the twins all dressed and ready for school. The sight of her children made Joie smile just a little. Maya had picked out their clothes. She was dressed in a church dress and boots, while Trey wore a dirty shirt and pants a couple of sizes too small. He looked miserable. Maya stood on a chair getting a box of cereal from the cabinet. She'd already set the table with a couple of cereal bowls, glasses of orange juice and a box of raisins.

"Baby girl, what are you doing in here?"

"I'm making breakfast," Maya replied. "Mommy, if me and Trey are really good, then will Daddy come home? We promise to be good. Will you tell him that we're sorry for being bad yesterday at the park?"

"Sweetheart, Daddy isn't mad at you or Trey. You didn't do anything wrong. Sometimes adults have arguments and fight. Daddy just needed to have his time alone. Kind of like an adult time-out."

"He's not mad we threw rocks at Nicole's dog?" Trey asked.

"You threw rocks at Nicole's dog? Why?"

"Because it kept barking at us. It wouldn't stop so we threw rocks at it. Daddy told us to stop but we kept on. I think he got mad at us then." Trey sniffed, bravely trying to hold back the tears.

"Well I'm sure Daddy understood why you were throwing rocks. And no, he wasn't mad about that. Come here, let's get you changed."

Joie helped Maya get the cereal box down. She'd let her slide and keep the outfit she selected on. She didn't need another battle this morning. Poor Trey, he was at the mercy of his "big sister by three minutes" clothing whims. There was no way she was going to have her child sit in school in skin tight, high-water jeans.

Joie drove by Cedric's office after dropping the twins off at school; his car still wasn't there. She called and spoke with his supervisor who said that no one had heard from Cedric. Joie was worried. She really needed someone to talk to so she tried Ronnie's number again. When she didn't answer, she left several texts pleading for her to call her back.

Who would have thought one bad decision years ago would come back to haunt me like this? That damned affair ended up costing more than I could ever have imagined. She pounded the steering wheel in frustration. The secret she managed to keep for so long was quickly unraveling. Secrets surface in the most inopportune times and always come back to mess up your entire life. Not only your life, but also the lives of so many people you loved.

Joie never told Cedric that he wasn't the twin's father. She wanted him to believe they were one happy family. Derek didn't know he *was* the father, and for that matter, neither did Ronnie. But in time everyone would know the truth, including her precious, innocent little children. They would soon learn that the life they were living was all one big lie. She'd always heard: *Everything done in darkness will soon be revealed in the light.* It had come to pass.

Joie had no idea what she would do if Cedric didn't return. Even more frightening was wondering what she would do if he did. How could he live with her knowing she had perpetuated such a huge lie? On the other hand, a life without her husband was unimaginable. Everything had changed. Nothing was the same. Hopelessness and despair tried to rear its ugly head and cause her to do something she would surely regret. Joie was no longer herself—no longer the carefree, happy wife and mother. She faced who she was—a woman who cheated on and lied to her husband to cover up some downright lowdown dirty shit. Somehow she had to fix this and make it right; for her sake, as well as her children's.

She wanted to feel numb. Needed something to take her mind off her troubles. Take the sharp edges off her pain. Liquor wasn't strong enough. *I know what I need...* She turned the car in the direction of the convenience store she picked Ronnie up from on that fateful day. Turning into the parking lot, she recognized one young man from that night. He stood outside as if he were on guard duty or something. *Looks like he never left.* It was obvious what he was up to—even at this time of the day.

Every now and then, she and Cedric would smoke a little weed. Nothing much and not very often, just enough to relax. They believed it increased their desire during sex and helped her to reach climax. Normally, Cedric was the one who brought it home, so she had no idea how much weed cost. A dime bag used to cost around ten dollars back in the day. Now there was no telling how much it cost to get high. She looked in her wallet and found fifty dollars. Joie rolled up to the kid and got a good look. He couldn't have been a day over sixteen.

"Hey you! Come here!" Joie called out.

He looked at the woman old enough to be his mother and turned away. Twisted his mouth sideways and spit on the ground.

"Young brotha! Excuse me, I said come here."

"Whatcha want?"

"I don't know. What you got?" Joie felt old and out of practice. But mostly she felt out of place.

"Look lady, I don't know what you talking about. Why you sweatin' me?"

Joie looked at the boy and thought about Trey. In ten years, without a father to raise him right, he could end up in the same place. Doing the same thing. Hanging out at the local convenience store selling drugs to strangers who didn't give a damn about him. She changed her mind. She was not going to contribute to the delinquency of this minor. Of someone else's child.

"I just want to tell you not to throw your life away. You probably don't realize it now, but what you're doing is going to end up hurting you in the long run. Go back to school, get your education and make something of yourself."

"What the fuck you talking about lady?" He spit on the ground again. Turns out he was just spitting out the shells from sunflower seeds.

"I'm talking about you and your life. Your future. Here let me give you my husband's name and number. His name is Cedric Parker. He's a youth counselor for troubled teens. Give him a call. Whenever you want to talk. Okay?"

The boy sauntered over to the car, trying his best to keep his pants from falling down. He looked at her and skeptically asked, "What you wanna help me for? You don't even know me."

"You're wrong, I do know you. You're just like every other sixteen-year old young man I've run into. You just got on the wrong path. Here take his card and here's fifty dollars. Go buy yourself a new pair of shoes or a belt." She handed him the money. "It's not too late to make a change."

"Ain't that some shit?! Thank you. Ain't nobody ever said nuthin' like that to me before. Or never gave me nuthin'. I'ma call him."

"I'll let him know. By the way, what's your name?"

"Name's Fresh D."

"No, I mean your real name. The one your Mama gave you."

"Oh, that name. It's Dwayne, but I don't like it. That's why I call myself Fresh-D."

"Okay Fresh-D, my name is Joie Parker. I'm gonna tell my husband to expect a call from you. Now get your butt off this corner before you get picked up and hauled off to jail."

"Thanks Mrs. Parker. Thank you! You aw'right..."

Joie knew the chance of him giving up the profitable business of selling drugs to go straight was not in her favor. That boy probably didn't have anyone who cared about him; otherwise he wouldn't be hanging out selling drugs instead of in school preparing for his finals.

Chapter 10

Upon landing back in the United States and going through the very efficient customs process at Miami International, Ronnie felt the familiar stress creep back into her neck and shoulders. Everyone was in such a friggin' hurry. She figured the convoluted process was by design—the way customs liked it. Anyone unfamiliar with the frenzied pace attempting to smuggle drugs or contraband in, would surely make some kind of mistake and unknowingly reveal themselves. The agents stood throughout the terminal, watching passengers and patiently waiting for criminals to slip up.

The long taxi ride home afforded her an opportunity to catch up on voicemail and text messages. There were quite a few to go through. Same old stuff, just a different day. She didn't want to lose the good vibes she picked up in the DR. Just wanted to drift on that cloud for as long as she could. The cell phone was a distraction, so she put it away.

Ronnie walked into the stillness of her home. *Looks like the realtor was busy while I was away.* The huge For Sale sign planted squarely in the middle of her front yard brought back the reality of her situation. A lockbox was awkwardly attached to the door handle, containing the keys allowing realtors to show her home while she was away. The tell-tale fragrance of scented candles and freshly baked cookies permeated the air. She suddenly felt like a stranger in her own home.

The blinking red light on the house phone caught her eye. *Probably just a bunch of telemarketers.* She listened to the messages while she fixed herself a drink. With memories of *Brugal Anejo* rum on her mind, a bottle of *Bacardi* rum beckoned her. She poured a straight shot of the *Bacardi*.

"Yuck! This tastes like crap!" she exclaimed and poured the liquor down the drain. "Got to get me some of the good stuff tomorrow. Hope they sell it here. Guess a glass of wine will have to do."

Most of the phone messages were either hang-ups or prerecorded voices touting her good fortune in being selected as a finalist in a sweepstakes or some other type of contest. All she had to do was call the 1-800 number to claim her prize. The very last call made her stop cold in her tracks.

"Hello, my name is Lexi McCray. I'm a private investigator looking for a Veronica Pierce. If you are not her and have received this message in error, please delete without listening any further. Ms. Pierce, when you receive this message, please call me as soon as possible. This is regarding an urgent matter." The woman left an out of state phone number. *I wonder what in the world that was about. If she's selling anything, she has certainly taken an original approach.*

There were also several messages from Derek's brother, Charles. Even though she and his brother were divorced, Ronnie and Charles managed to keep their friendship intact. They talked about their careers, Derek's kids, and general issues of the day. She considered him the older brother she never had. Ronnie made a mental note to call him back.

As expected, Joie had left dozens of voicemails, called and hung up too many times to count, and sent just as many text messages. In time with a whole lot of prayer, she would probably forgive Joie. Maybe. In time. But not today. Today that woman was the very last person she wanted to hear from.

It was well past midnight and all she wanted was a long hot shower and a nice warm bed. Her cell phone rang. It was another out of state number with an 805 area code she didn't recognize. *Who can that be calling me this late?* She wondered.

"Hello?" answered Ronnie.

"*Hola?* Am I speaking to Ronnie? Ronnie Pierce?"

"Yes, this is her. Who is this?" The man's voice wasn't familiar.

"Ronnie? It's me, Luis."

"Luis? Oh, hi." Ronnie hadn't expected his call until tomorrow at the earliest. He was supposed to be at his Uncle Nando's villa.

"Ronnie, the concierge gave me your letter while I was arranging for a rental car. He said you checked out. Why did you leave without telling me? I thought you were here until Saturday. Did I do something wrong? Did I offend you?"

"Luis, I'm sorry. No, it wasn't anything you did and it really was a last minute decision. I really, really like you. Probably more than either of us realize. It's just that I have too much going on in my life at this moment and unfortunately, the last thing I need right now is to get involved." She explained.

"Don't be sorry. I should be the one who's apologizing. I didn't mean to kiss you. I got caught up in the moment. I thought it was what you wanted as well..."

"I did at the moment. Still do. The more I thought about the possibilities that existed for us, the less it made sense for us to continue. I live in Virginia; you in California. Spending a couple more days together in the DR simply didn't make much sense in the long run. I have a lot on my plate right now. Like I said, I'm sorry."

"Guess that takes care of it then. Before I go, I have to tell you; I believe you *think* too much Veronica Pierce. You ever hear of letting go and letting God? Listen, if you ever want to try this again, you have my number. And by the way, California is only a plane ride from Virginia. It's not like we live in two different countries. I believe this could be the beginning of something beautiful and I don't want to let it go yet."

She laughed, "You're right and when I finally decide how I'm going to live my life, I'll give you a call."

"Go take care of your business my friend. I'll give you your space, for now. Be good."

"You do the same. Bye." She sighed and hung up.

Ronnie hoped she wasn't blowing her last chance of ever finding true love. In the span of the week and a half they spent together, Ronnie could see the potential for them becoming so much more. A strong mutual attraction existed. They connected in so many ways, emotionally, mentally, intellectually, and spiritually. A lifetime had passed since she felt that way for any man. However, the problem with Ronnie was she was a realist. She knew vacation romances didn't last. Without the mundane day-to-day routines of life, even the least likely person you could imagine yourself with could magically look better on vacation. She needed to be with Luis in the real world to determine if they had a chance. But for now, they were worlds apart in more ways than one.

She stripped out of her traveling clothes and got into the shower. She allowed the warm water to seduce her with a promise of relaxation and it felt great pounding on her tired aching muscles. Fifteen minutes later, she fell into bed and let sleep take her away.

Chapter 11

Instead of wasting time and energy driving around aimlessly searching for Cedric, Joie went home and waited. And waited. And waited. She put her life on autopilot while she waited. Every morning she got up, went to work, took care of the kids, came home and waited some more. She was resolved in her patience. Either he'd come home or he wouldn't, but she vowed to wait for as long as it took. So she did nothing but wait between the string of events that filled up her life.

Six days later, Cedric came home.

She saw his car in the driveway when she was coming home from work. Various thoughts crossed her mind. *Thank God he's home. Oh shoot! The kids are in the backseat. I can't take them inside because there's no telling what Cedric is going to do or say.* Her emotions vacillated between relief and dread.

"Yay! Daddy came home! I can't wait to see him. Hurry Mommy, park the car!" screamed Maya.

"Yeah Mommy! Hurry up! I want to see my Daddy!" echoed Trey.

Ronnie drove right past the house. She wasn't sure of Cedric's state of mind and didn't want to expose the twins to whatever mess she would walk into. She dialed Ronnie's number then remembered she wasn't home. Just as she was about to hang up, Ronnie answered.

"Hello?"

"Ronnie? Um, hey, it's Joie. Oh, you're back in town?" Joie didn't know which was worse. Asking Ronnie for a favor or dragging the kids into a potentially violent situation. She chose the former.

"Yes, I'm back in town. What's up?"

"Welcome back. We really need to talk. But before we do, I really need your help."

"You need *my* help?! You're calling to ask *me* for a favor? What the hell Joie? Don't you have any dignity?"

Joie sighed wearily and said, "I realize I deserve that and more. Look, I got the kids with me. Me and Cedric are going through some stuff right now..."

"Humph, I'll bet you are... What do you expect me to do about it?"

"Ronnie, it's not what you think. I can't talk about it now because the twins are in the car with me. I was wondering if you could watch 'em for a few minutes so Cedric and I can talk. You know I wouldn't ask you unless it was an emergency, considering we're no longer speaking…

Look if you can't do it, I understand. I can take them across town to my mother's house."

"Joie, got to hand it to you girl, you know my downfall is my Godchildren. Bring them on over. I miss the little angels. You and I will straighten out our mess later."

"Thank you, Ronnie. I'll be right there."

"Awww, we're not gonna see Daddy?" asked the twins in unison.

"No, I'm gonna take you to Aunt Ronnie's house. You'll see Daddy soon. Okay? Me and your Daddy got some grownup stuff to discuss." Joie walked the twins to the door. She had to admit Ronnie looked fabulous. All tanned and relaxed. "Thank you so much. I promise I'll be right back and will fill you in on what's going on."

"Hey twins! Your Auntie Ronnie missed you guys. I went on a trip and brought you back a few goodies. Go on in the living room and turn on the TV. I'll be right there." Ronnie stood in the door with her arms crossed after she gave each of the kids a hug and kiss.

"Thanks for watching the kids." Joie returned to her car and drove the longest drive ever to get to her home.

Ronnie watched Joie drive away, wondering what could be so bad she couldn't take her kids home with her.

"Humph, I wonder if he found out about her cheating? Naw, it couldn't be that. Too many years have gone by, but you never know. The truth always comes out. Eventually," she said to herself and went inside. "Hey Trey, Maya, what you kids been up to?"

* * *

The stereo blared out Miles Davis' bluesy jazz tunes. Cedric sat in the living room sipping on a glass of cognac. A lit cigar sat in the ashtray. Its heavy pungent smoke trailed upwards to the ceiling. Any other time, Joie would have let him have it about smoking a smelly cigar in the house. Today, she decided to let it go.

"Hi," said Joie.

"Hey."

"Where ya been?"

"Driving around. I ended up in Charleston."

"Oh? You drove all the way down to Charleston?"

"Yep, I kept driving until I was tired and couldn't drive anymore. I spent a few days on a friend's couch 'til I was cool enough to come home."

"Well, I'm glad you're back."

"Where are the kids?"

"Um, I dropped them off at Ronnie's house so we could talk. I'll pick 'em up later."

He nodded his head. Usually neat and clean shaven, he appeared unkempt. He wore the same clothes he wore when he left. He needed a shower and a shave, badly.

"Oh, she back? Y'all straight now?"

"Yeah, she's back. Haven't had time to talk to her yet. I'm more concerned about us at the moment."

"Concerned? You're concerned about us? What do you mean? *Us?* You destroyed *us* Joie. There is no *us* left." He slowly exhaled smoke in her direction.

"Uh, what do you mean? Cedric, we can work this out. We still love each other. Right?"

"Love? Are you serious? Joie, don't you realize the extent of what you've done? Tell me, how do you intend for us to *work this out?*" he asked, coolly.

"Baby, we can go to counseling. Talk to our pastor. Maybe we could separate for a little while if you want. Just don't give up on us."

"You got it all worked out, huh? I just found out the worst lie a wife can perpetrate on her husband. You lied to me about our children! My children! All this time, I thought I was their father. It's not just the fact of you fucking around on me, but to betray me—to betray our family?"

Joie crossed her arms and sucked her teeth. This was not going the way she hoped it would. "Cedric, I'm sorry. I made a mistake. I didn't know how to tell you so I didn't say anything. Our family is—was, so happy. I didn't want to ruin anything."

"Who is he?"

"Who is who?"

"Don't be a smartass. You know what I mean. Who is the father of the twins?"

"It don't matter."

"Maybe not to you, but it matters to me. And in time, it will matter to Trey and Maya. They deserve to know who their real father is."

"Cedric, you are their father and their daddy. You're all they know. Who their biological father is don't matter because that is over now."

"Who is he, Joie?!"

The muted sounds of Miles' trumpet wafted in the background. It was the background music to the horrible drama unfolding in the life of the Parker family. Joie poured herself a much needed drink.

"Cedric, can't we get past this? Just put it behind us and go back to the way we used to be? No good will come of you knowing who he is."

"Did you love him?"

Joie wasn't expecting that question. For the briefest of moments, she looked away. Her eyes misted over.

He sighed, "That's what I thought. Who the fuck is it Joie?!"

She moved closer to the door, nervous about the path they were going down. His anger frightened her.

"Don't do this to me, Joie... Don't make me turn into some goddamned animal! At least respect me enough to tell me who the muthafucka is who fathered my children. I deserve to know whose kids I've been raising for the past five years."

"Okay, you're right... It was Derek," she whispered.

"Derek? Derek who?"

"Derek Jordan."

"Derek Jordan? Ronnie's ex-husband?! Oh shit!" He rose to his feet laughing. But it wasn't funny and he wasn't laughing because it was funny.

"It was a mistake. I made a huge mistake. I'm sorry." The tears finally came.

"Does Ronnie know?"

"Yeah, she found out a couple weeks ago."

"So that's why y'all not talking? Now everything makes sense. Sonofabitch! You were fucking Derek behind me *and* Ronnie's back. Damn! All this time I thought *she* was the fucked up one. Turns out it was you all along!"

"I'm sorry. Can't we get past this?" Joie pleaded.

"Not this time baby. We're through. I want you and your kids out of my house first thing tomorrow."

"What a minute. Your house? This is our home. Where we supposed to go?"

"I don't care but y'all ain't going to stay here in this house. The house that is in my name. Remember, years ago when you said you didn't want me to add your name to the title? Well, I didn't. So get the fuck out! I'll be back tomorrow and I want you and your kid's stuff out of here. You'll be hearing from my lawyer soon."

"But the kids...what will I tell them?"

"I don't know. Lie to them. You seem to be really good at that." Cedric walked out the door and potentially out of Joie's life forever.

She stood in the doorway and watched her husband calmly drive away. He was much more composed and restrained than she imagined he would be. She knew he would be upset, but to put her out of her home? Put the kids out of the house too? Cedric couldn't be that heartless. Or could he?

* * *

Joie knocked on the door and waited patiently. Ronnie finally appeared, looking pissed off.

She threw the door open. "What the hell is going on? Maya told me that she hasn't seen her daddy in a long time and she misses him."

"Can I come in? I'll explain everything. It's about time you knew the whole truth anyway." Joie slurred her speech.

Ronnie observed the weariness her ex-best friend wore like an old heavy sweater. Dried mascara circled her eyes giving her the look of a raccoon. She smelled of hard liquor.

"Yeah, come on in." There was no way she was going to give those kids back to Joie in the condition she was in.

"Where are the twins?"

"They're in the family room eating mac n'cheese and watching cartoons. Hope that's all right. Wasn't expecting company and that's all I had."

"No, that's fine... They love macaroni and cheese. Especially the way Cedric used to make it."

Ronnie watched Joie fall apart in front of her eyes. Silent tears turned vicious and wracked her body into near convulsions. Snot dripped from her nose; she wiped it away with her shirt sleeve.

"Hey, hey, hey.... Stop that. C'mon in and tell me what's wrong. It can't be that bad. Sit down." Ronnie steered her to a chair and handed her a box of tissues.

"I messed up. I really messed up this time. Ronnie, I am so sorry. You are my best friend and I screwed you over. I am so sorry." She began to cry again.

"Joie, get over it. Yeah, you did some foul shit by having an affair with my husband. That is some unforgiveable stuff."

"I told Cedric."

"You told Cedric? What do you mean? You're telling me he didn't know?" asked Ronnie.

"No. Not until a few days ago." She sniffed, unsure about how to proceed.

"Well, no wonder he was angry. Men aren't as forgiving as us women are when it comes to affairs. When you first told me, I wanted to kill you. No, really I did. Being betrayed by a loved one is the worst thing in the world. Now don't get it twisted, I'm still dealing with this shit. Taking some time away helped more than you could know."

"I know and I appreciate you watching the kids for me."

"So he didn't take it well, huh? What did he say?"

"Ronnie, that's not all. You may as well know everything since I've told you a little. After I finish, I'll understand if you never want to speak to me again."

"Hold on. This sounds serious. Let me check on the twins first. I'll be right back."

Joie opened the bottle of cognac and poured two glasses. They'd both need a little something to take the edge of the conversation.

Ronnie returned to the living room. "Okay, they're good. I told them you're here. They wanted to watch a movie so I put in a DVD for them. What's up Joie?"

"Here have a drink first."

"All right, I'll drink with you, but looks like you don't need any more after this."

Joie didn't know a good way to deliver bad news so she just blurted it out. "Ronnie, that's not all. Cedric isn't the twin's real father."

"He's not their real father? What do you mean? How do you know?"

"I lied to him. I've known all along he's not their father. He found out by accident a couple of weeks ago. He had the twin's DNA tested for some project at school and they also tested his. We got a letter in the mail with the results. That's how he found out he wasn't the father. By a damned letter. He was devastated and took off for almost a week.

We didn't know where he was or if he was coming back."

"Oh no! That must have been awful for him...and for the kids..."

Ronnie looked at the woman she no longer knew. The woman she called her best friend for almost a decade. Someone she shared her most intimate thoughts and dreams with. The sister she never had, had turned into this drunken lying-assed stranger sitting in front of her.

"Yes, it was kinda messed up. I never intended for him to find out. I didn't want to upset our lives by revealing this secret."

"Wow! You say that like it means nothing. Like you just told me you lied to him about hiding money or wrecking the car. This is some big deal shit! Joie, you have ruined his life. You do realize that, right?"

"Hold on to that anger sister, 'cuz I'm not finished." She turned up the glass until it was empty.

"What else?" Ronnie steadied herself for the final blow.

"It's Derek. Derek is the twin's father." Joie hung her head in shame. She prayed this day would never come, yet here it was and she had to face the truth. The secrets kept hidden in the dark all those years finally made their presence known to all. It usually does.

"Derek got you pregnant? You're telling me he's Maya and Trey's father? You're lying! Joie, please tell me you're making this shit up!" Ronnie stared at Joie in disbelief, shaking her head.

Joie sat on the couch, chewing on her bottom lip, looking pitiful.

"Girl, you are truly despicable! You're a damn snake—lower than the lowest. I can't believe you! Who are you?! And how can you live with yourself?"

"Don't judge me! I made a mistake. I had an affair. So what? People make mistakes all the time. But you wouldn't know that would you? You were too busy trying to "find yourself" and focusing on your career to properly take care of Derek. He wanted a wife. Someone who would be there to take care of him. Make him feel like a man. Treat him like he was the most important person in the world. That's where I came in. He wanted to be treated like a king, yet you treated him like a little boy. You emasculated him! That's why he left you!" Joie's anger turned to indignation.

"You know what? You are the worst kind of human being. You get all up in my face for all those years, pretending to be my friend and then put a damn knife in my back! I can't believe you used me to get to my husband!"

"Humph, it ain't that serious, girlfriend!" Joie stood with her hands on her hips, rolled her neck and said, "Well, I guess he fooled us both, didn't he? Turns out he didn't want neither one of us. And I ended up pregnant. I couldn't tell my husband the truth."

"You are so full of shit! You could have told me. How could you do that to *me*? Lie to me all these years? Pretend to be my friend?"

"Obviously I wasn't thinking about you. I was only thinking about myself. I loved him. He said he loved me. We made plans to be together. To this day, I regret getting involved with Derek. I hurt you. I hurt Cedric and I ruined my family. I've got those two amazing children to raise. Probably on my own now." Joie's tone softened.

"I can't believe what I'm hearing! You made plans to be together? I don't know what to think. Didn't know something from the past could hurt so badly." Ronnie held her head, feeling a headache coming on.

"Haven't you ever done things in your life you regret? Things you weren't proud of?"

Ronnie didn't miss a beat. "No, no I haven't. I've never done some evil shit like this. Never did anything to hurt the people I love." She had enough of Joie and screamed, "Bitch, get the hell out of my house!"

At this point, only the truth mattered and for Joie there was nothing left to lose. It wasn't her intention to throw Ronnie's past in her face, but it was what it was. There may not be another opportunity to get this off her chest.

"Oh really? Is that right? You've never done nothin' you're ashamed of? Well let me tell you something girlfriend, I got a call from a private investigator looking for you. Said you put a baby up for adoption and that child is now looking for its mother. Couldn't be you now, could it? Miss I never-do-anything-wrong! Looks like you got a few skeletons hiding in your closet too!"

Ronnie's heart stopped beating. She felt faint and began to sway. She watched Joie's mouth move in slow motion until she could no longer hear anything. The floor shifted under her feet and the room grew dark.

Joie, seeing Ronnie was about to faint, caught her friend and gently eased her to the floor. She ran to the kitchen, grabbed a bottle of water, and used the cool water to revive her.

"W-w-hat happened?" asked Ronnie when she came to.

"You fainted. Are you okay?"

"Yeah, yes. I'm better."

"I'm sorry Ronnie. I didn't mean to tell you like that. About Derek or that McCray woman. I'm not trying to hurt you anymore than I have already. It's my big assed mouth. My tongue cuts sharper than a razor sometimes."

"Oh yeah, you really caught me off guard with that one. Not sure which one hurts the most. Damn Joie!" She sat up and eased her way to the sofa. If she had the strength, she'd punch Joie in her gut.

"Take your pick. I was surprised by that phone call as well. Lexi McCray contacted me a few weeks ago. She's a private investigator and has been trying to catch up with you for the past couple of weeks."

"Lexi McCray? That name sounds familiar. Why did she call you?" She set aside the fight. For now.

"She said it's usually easier to go through a close friend or family member rather than contacting the individual directly." Joie reached inside her purse. "Here's her card."

Ronnie looked at the card. Memories from eighteen years earlier flooded back.

"You sure you're alright? You don't look so good."

"How do you expect me to look? You've dropped two tons of bricks on me all at once."

"Ronnie, you have a child?" asked Joie, gently.

"I'm sorry. I can't do this right now. This is too much. You. All this..."

"I understand. I'll get the kids and we'll get out of here," Joie said.

"You okay to drive home?"

"It's only around the corner. I'll be fine." Joie wobbled as she stood.

Ronnie looked at Joie. She didn't look fine. "C'mon, I'll drive you guys home. You can get your car tomorrow."

* * *

The twins waved good-bye as they went into their house. Ronnie returned their waves and blew kisses at them both. She took a nice long look at the kids and clearly saw the resemblance of her ex. Trey's nose and Maya's smile were purely Derek's.

She wondered how she could've missed it before. Probably because there was no reason to suspect they were anyone other than Cedric's children. Now she knew differently. Her Godchildren were her ex-husband's biological children. The children she loved so dearly were the result of an adulterous affair between her husband and best friend. Yet Trey and Maya were innocent because they played no part in how they came into this world. In her heart and her mind, she decided none of that mattered. She loved those dear, sweet little children with all her heart. Nothing would ever change that fact.

"Ronnie, if you can find it in your heart to forgive me… Well, anyway, thanks for bringing us home. I'll come get the car in the morning. Don't know what's going to happen after tomorrow or where we'll be living."

"Go take care of those angels. Everything else will work out for the best. It always does. I've got to go."

"Uh, Ronnie?"

"What now Joie?"

"I really do hope it is your child. You would've made a great mom."

Ronnie waved and backed out the driveway. She didn't want to discuss any more of her personal life with Joie.

Ronnie made a pot of coffee. It didn't matter that it was late. She couldn't sleep if she tried. She fingered the card, turning it over and over in her hand. Where had she heard that name before? Lexi McCray?

Could it really be that eighteen years later her daughter had come looking for her? She thought back to that fateful day, eighteen years ago when she made the decision to put her baby girl up for adoption.

* * *

Shortly after the breaking up with Travis, Ronnie discovered she was pregnant and the baby was due in May. Upon notifying her mother of her condition, Dianna took immediate charge as she always did. She made arrangements for Ronnie to move back home, complete her remaining classes online, and receive her degree in the mail.

Her mother also convinced Ronnie giving her child away was the right thing to do. She would be graduating from college in a few weeks with her entire life to look forward to. Said she would eventually marry a nice man, have a few kids of their own, and live a wonderful life. Ronnie's mother told her that if she kept that baby, no decent Black man would ever want to marry her. A biracial child would make her life difficult. Said the baby would be shunned by both black and white alike, only to live a life of confusion not knowing which side it really belonged to.

She missed her father because in tough situations he was the mediator between Ronnie and her very strong-willed mother. Without him, she was left to fight all her battles on her own. More often than not, Ronnie was not the one to come out on top.

About two weeks before the baby was due, she called Travis and told him she was pregnant and had already made plans to put the baby up for adoption. She sent him the proper paperwork and left it at that. On April 29, 1994, a few weeks before she was supposed to walk across the stage to receive her college degree, she gave birth to a baby girl. The nurses took the baby away because she didn't want to see it. It was easier that way. And with everything going on, telling Travis about the baby's birth was not a priority in Ronnie's mind. It was an afterthought. After Travis signed the release papers, she never heard from him again.

She prayed her baby girl would end up in a very loving family with a mother and father who loved her unconditionally. So without the comfort of having her father's perspective, she listened to her mother's dribble and signed away all rights to her child.

* * *

Her thoughts turned to Derek. She married him when she was still in her late 20's, her prime child-bearing years. He already had children and didn't want more. Or so he said. So she did what any young woman in love would do. She pushed that biological urge to have children deep, deep down. Suppressed the urge by taking care of Derek's children. Ronnie convinced herself life with Derek would be enough to keep her happy. Little did she know that eleven years into their marriage, he *would have* more children. Not just one with Tequitta, the woman he left her for, but also twins with Joie. She laughed at the irony of sacrificing her needs for someone who really didn't give a damn about her. How she hated him in that moment.

"Lord, in the past few weeks, it seems that you've been sending me messages. Telling me to find the path you intended for me. I'm just about to start over, to begin a new chapter in my life... Now you're telling me my daughter is searching for me? Gotta admit I don't understand."

Her cell phone beeped with a voicemail message interrupting her prayers. She picked up the phone. The latest call was from Joie, but there were also several messages in her voicemail.

"Hey girl, I wanted to thank you again for watching the kids. And if there is anything I can do for you give me a call." Ronnie deleted Joie's message.

"Veronica? It's Ralph. Your two weeks are up and I'll expect to see you in the office first thing on Monday morning. I've been working on a huge project and need your input. Hope you had a good rest." She also deleted his message.

"Ms. Pierce, its Norma Jean, your realtor. Good news! We have someone interested in buying your house. Call me when you get back in town." Ronnie held mixed emotions that someone was interested in buying her house. She'd call Norma Jean tomorrow.

"Hi Ronnie. It's Luis. I've been thinking. When I get back to the states, I'd really like for us to meet. Get to know each other better. Your place or mine—of course I mean Virginia or California." He laughed. *"But really, I don't want to let this thing we have end. Not yet. Call me."* She smiled thinking of Luis.

"Ronnie, it's Charles, I've left several messages on your house phone. Please call as soon you can. It's urgent. Thanks. Bye." Hmm, wonder what that's about.

She picked up her house phone, scrolled through the missed calls for Charles' number, and dialed her ex brother-in-law.

"Hello?" Charles answered.

"Hey Charles its Ronnie. Sorry I didn't get back to you earlier, but I've been out of town. How you doing? What's up?"

"Hey Ronnie," he replied, sounding tired.

"I'm sorry. Hope I didn't wake you."

"No, I'm up. I'm at the hospital." She heard him tell someone in the background that he'd be right back.

"Hospital? You okay?" She became worried.

"I'm fine. It's Derek."

"Derek? Derek's in the hospital? Is he alright?"

"Well, not really. He had a stroke a few weeks ago and was in a coma for a few days. When he woke up, he kept asking for you. Been asking for you ever since. He said he needs to tell you something."

"Wait a minute Charles. What are you saying? What's wrong with Derek?"

"I'm saying that you need to come to the hospital as soon as you can get here."

"Uh, ok. I'll be there tomorrow morning."

"Ronnie, you're not listening. If you're going to come, make it soon. Like tonight."

"Tonight? Is it that serious?"

"Unfortunately, yes. The doctors say he could go at any minute."

"Where is he? What hospital?"

"DePaul Central. Sixth floor. Room 612.

"I'm on my way."

"Thanks Ronnie. See you soon."

"All right. Bye."

It was already after ten o'clock. If Charles said she needed to hurry, then Derek really was in bad shape, because Charles was not one to exaggerate. She pulled her thick hair into a ponytail, grabbed her purse, and drove the thirty miles to the hospital. When she got there, the receptionist directed her towards the elevator. To the sixth floor.

The first person she saw was Tequitta sitting on a couch in the waiting area. Her eyes were red and swollen, indicating she had been crying. A little girl, who Ronnie assumed was her and Derek's daughter, rested her head on her mother's very pregnant lap. Derek's parents sat on the couch opposite them. They stood when they saw Ronnie, opening their arms for a hug. She also acknowledged Tequitta, though she really didn't want to.

"How is he?" Ronnie asked his mother

"Chile, he won't be with us much longer." Her husband handed his wife a handkerchief to dab away her tears.

"What happened?" asked Ronnie.

"We don't really know," responded his father. "Doctors can't figure it out. All of a sudden he just started feeling sick. He came down with a really high fever a few weeks ago and complained of a headache. The doctor admitted him to the emergency room and he's been here ever since."

"Mr. Jordan, isn't there some kind of medication they can treat him with? What *are* they doing for him?"

"Ronnie, you're asking all the questions we've already asked. There's not much more they can do now, 'cept make him comfortable. Stop fretting and go in and see him. His kids are with him now," explained his mother.

It all felt so surreal. Ronnie walked down the sterile hallway to room 612. With each step, the hallway appeared to get longer. She found his semi-private room and looked inside. His three oldest children surrounded his bed, talking to him, laughing with each other over antics from younger days. Charles stood at the foot of the bed. When Derek's youngest son looked up and saw Ronnie, they motioned for her to join them. Each hugged her when she entered the room, including her into their family once again.

"C'mon kids. Let's give them some privacy," stated Charles.

Charles hugged Ronnie and quietly whispered in her ear, "Thanks for coming."

"Hey Derek." Ronnie really didn't know what more to say. She hadn't seen him since the day the divorce was final. The man lying in bed looked old, weak, and fragile; nothing like the virile young man she married. He was now connected to various wires, tubes, and electronic monitors which displayed his vital signs for all to see. A steady stream of oxygen was pumped into his body though a small tube inserted in his nostrils. The private room smelled of alcohol and urine. He needed a shave and a bath.

"Ronnie," he said in a raspy voice. "Thanks for coming. Have a seat."

"Okay," she replied, trying to keep her true feelings hidden. In all honesty, it was difficult seeing Derek in such obvious pain. She suppressed the urge to leave.

"Hey, how you been? You looking good. Always did know how to take care of yourself." He spoke in a strained, halting voice.

"Thanks, so do you." No need in adding to his suffering by telling the truth.

"I know I am probably the last person on this planet you wanted to see, but I'm glad you came. Listen Ronnie, I want to apologize—*need* to apologize to you. Want to tell you how sorry I am for what I did. You were the best thing that ever happened to me and I messed up in so many ways. Too busy thinking about myself to consider you. I was selfish." He coughed.

"You want some water?" offered Ronnie.

"No, I'm fine," he added weakly. "That's not true. Doctors say I don't have much time left. I'm dying. Organs already started to shut down one at a time. Pretty soon, I won't be able to speak. Can't believe I'm on my way Home." Another wet cough wracked his body.

A nurse came in and adjusted his IV, wrote notes in his chart, and took his pulse. The machine that monitored his heartbeat sounded like a bad imitation of a warped bass drum. Ronnie watched the lines jump up, flat line, then jump up again. Over and over. In between the beats, he momentarily appeared to be at peace. It seemed as if the effort it took for his heart to beat zapped all his strength away. She prayed he found solace in between those beats. Prayed he discovered peace in the offbeat.

"I wanted to see you one last time before I have to leave. Tell you how much I still love you. I did you wrong Ronnie. Did some things I wasn't proud of. Years ago, I asked the Lord for his forgiveness and to help me lead a Christian life. I asked for His guidance to grow spiritually. The Man upstairs helped get me through many a dark day."

"God is good."

"All the time." Derek smiled.

"I saw Tequitta in the waiting room. You have a beautiful little girl. Looks like another one on the way?"

"Yeah, she wanted Laila to have a brother or sister. She didn't want her to be an only child. I'm afraid I won't be around long enough to see this one being born. It's a boy." His eyes misted over speaking about his children.

Ronnie felt the beginnings of anger rise deep within her belly and she fidgeted in her chair to push it away. No use in letting that monster out. It was too late for bitterness.

"I guess congratulations are in order then." Ronnie pushed her hurt feelings aside and wiped away a tear.

Derek noticed Ronnie's discomfort. "Thank you," he paused. "Ronnie, I am so sorry we didn't have children together. I was selfish and thought only about myself. I knew you wanted kids. In the beginning, that's all you ever talked about. You should've had children 'cause you would have been a great mother. Once you stopped talking about 'em, I thought you were cool with your decision. When I found out Tequitta was pregnant...I knew it would hurt you badly."

"Would've been nice to be a real family—with kids and all. Maybe then we might've stayed together."

"Yeah... Never meant anything like that to happen. Tequitta getting pregnant... Hell, I didn't mean to have an affair either. Since it did happen, it was my responsibility to take care of the baby. You feel me?"

"Well Derek, all that is in the past. We've both moved on. I'm happy and looks like you were also. I'm fine, so there's no need to worry about me. Our marriage was good while it lasted and it gave me lots of good memories." She smiled.

"We did have good times together. Right? When we were on that dance floor, we put everybody to shame. All of 'em folks moved to the side to watch us dance."

"That's right. Didn't matter what kind of dance it was. We moved together in perfect synch."

"I'm not going to keep you long. Just wanted you to know that you were—*are* still one heck of a lady. Look, I wanted to do something for you. You know…kind of make up for what I put you through. I took out a small life insurance policy when we were still married. It's not much; just $50,000 and you're the sole beneficiary. I'm leaving it to you because it's the least I can do for your putting up with my mess."

"Derek, I can't take that money. What about your children?"

"My children will be taken care of. I was over insured, come to find out. Lucky for me I stayed current on all the premiums. I want you to take that money and do something good for yourself. Let loose and live a little. Go do something you've always dreamt about doing. Maybe take some time off work and write that great novel you've been talking about all these years."

"That's very kind of you." She studied him. "I can't believe you remembered about my writing. And just so you know, I forgave you a long time ago. Let go of the anger and made it a point to forgive you and everything you did to me. I had to; otherwise I couldn't have made it through my own dark days."

Derek sighed peacefully and smiled. The nurse must have increased the medication in his IV. His eyelids became heavy. "Thank you, Ronnie. Thank you. God bless you. God bless you……" His mouth slacked open as he fell into a quiet slumber. The thin sheet across his frail chest rose and fell. Rose and fell. Rose and fell in perfect rhythm with his heartbeat. She watched him sleep. He looked peaceful. The machine slowed, his pulse rate dropped, but the comforting blips continued to scroll across the monitor.

Ronnie bent down and kissed him on his cool forehead. "Goodbye Derek. Be in peace."

Charles stood outside the room waiting for Ronnie before she left.

"How is he? Really?" She asked.

"Doctors don't know. They ran all sorts of tests and experimented with different medications. They even performed exploratory surgery, but they still don't know what's killing him. We just know his prognosis isn't good. The machines are barely keeping him alive."

"Charles, he doesn't seem that bad to me. Are you sure?"

"He's coherent for now. Goes in and out. Most of the time, he doesn't know where he is. I think he held it together long enough to see you."

"Maybe the doctors are wrong. I'll pray for him. For you. For the family."

"Thanks Ronnie, we all appreciate that. I'm glad you made it. Y'all straight?"

"Yeah, we're good. Our marriage wasn't all that bad. We had good times, too. Lots of good times." She reminisced, smiling at the memories before the relationship turned sour.

"That's good. Well, it's late and I know you want to get home."

"Call me if anything changes. Either way. Okay?"

"I will sis. You take care and drive home safely." Charles added, kissing Ronnie on the cheek.

She returned to the waiting room with the rest of the family. All the people who loved Derek were there, except for Joie. She thought about mentioning Joie's little deception to Derek, but thought better of it. It wasn't her place. Not her concern. At this point, bringing up an old affair would do more harm than good. She gave hugs all around and left the family to comfort each other. She was now outside the circle. No longer part of the Jordan family. No longer belonged in Derek's world.

Charles called early the next morning.

Ronnie was sound asleep when the phone rang. "Hello?" she answered groggily.

"Ronnie, its Charles. He's gone."

"What?"

"Derek passed during the night. In his sleep."

"Charles, I am so sorry."

"Thanks, he's no longer in pain."

"My God, I can't believe he's gone…"

"Neither can I. I'll call later with the funeral arrangements."

"Okay."

Chapter 12

Joie didn't take the news of Derek's passing very well. When Ronnie told her, she was shaken to the very core of her existence, because despite it all, she did indeed love him. Joie knew she couldn't have a life with him, and she ultimately accepted that fact. But that didn't stop her heart from holding him dear. Now, thanks to her, Maya and Trey would never know their real father.

Since returning home to live with her parents, her situation seemed much easier to deal with. The twins loved their grandparents and wanted to share all the events of their five year old lives with the old people. Her mother adored the children and gave Joie as long as it took to get herself together. Their unconditional love was the only thing she could count on nowadays.

Derek's funeral was held four days later. Joie went because she wanted to pay her last respects to the family and say good-bye to Derek. Tell him about his children he never knew. Let his spirit lay eyes on Maya and Trey for the first time.

Ronnie, Joie and her children sat towards the back of the church, conveniently away from the immediate family. The last thing she wanted to be was a distraction. Additionally, because they were so young and this being their first funeral, the twins were naturally uncomfortable and itching to leave. They constantly fidgeted in their seats, alternately tugging at Joie's sweater asking when they could go. To help keep them calm, Joie gave Maya a coloring book with crayons and then produced a couple of action figures for Trey.

"He looks good. Don't he look good Ronnie?" Joie commented on Derek's body.

"Yeah, he looks okay. He was so thin. Guess it was the illness."

Joie pointed towards the front of the church as the family filed past to view the body. "Is that Tequila? Well, I'll be... Her little girl looks just like Maya, don't she Ronnie?"

"Her name is Tequitta. And yes, that's her daughter."

Ronnie took a good look at the little girl. Joie was right. She looked like Maya's sister. Both were the same age, same height, even shared Derek's features. No doubt about it, Maya belonged to Derek.

"What the...? Tequila is p-p-pregnant?" asked Joie in disbelief.

"Listen Joie, if you're going to sit with me, you need to be quiet. Don't you start no mess up in here and ruin Derek's homecoming. Show some respect," she whispered harshly.

"I had no idea he even had a daughter. And she looks like they're around the same age. Why didn't you tell me?"

Ronnie looked over at the pained expression on her ex-friend's face. "What? You didn't know? Of course you wouldn't know. He was my husband..." She allowed her words to trail off, giving Joie ample room to finish the sentence any way she chose, because at that moment, she really didn't care how Joie felt.

Joie disregarded Ronnie's sarcastic comments. She thought about it. Did the math. Put two and two together. Derek was involved not only in one affair, he was having two! And he'd gotten both women pregnant around the same time! *Ain't that some shit?!* She looked at Ronnie and wondered how she could sit there besides her, watch Derek's pregnant wife—his previous mistress, falling all over his casket crying uncontrollably, and maintain her composure. Her girl must be made of steel.

The ushers stood next to their pew with their white-gloved hands extended. It was their turn to say goodbye. Ronnie sat still and shook her head. She didn't want to see him like that. Lying lifeless in a pearl blue casket.

Joie gathered the children and escorted them to the front. They were confused. Neither one knew the man their mother wanted them to see so badly. Maya hung back and hid behind her mother's skirt, gripping the silky fabric in terror. Trey walked bravely ahead, curious to see what all the fuss was about.

They stopped in front of the casket. Joie bent over and whispered quietly, "Derek, I want you to meet your children, Maya and Trey. I'm sorry you never got the chance to know them, but they are great kids. Sorry we never got our chance either. I'll always love you." She said with tears streaming from her eyes.

She straightened and turned around to see Cedric holding unto Maya's hand. She started to speak, but he shook his head "no". In front of the church, at Derek Jordan's funeral, was not the proper place for any kind of discussion they needed to have. She took Trey's hand returned to her seat. That's when she noticed Derek's family staring at her and the twins. Looks of surprise and disbelief were evident on all their faces and in their voices. One look at her children and her secret was secret no more.

113

When Joie returned to her seat, Ronnie was no longer there.

Honestly, who could blame her? Even *she* didn't want to be there. Not like this. Cedric walked Maya back to Joie, kissed her on the cheek, reached over and patted Trey on the head, and walked out of the church without uttering a single word to Joie.

She felt their stares, heard the whispers. "Tsk, tsk, tsk..." "She got some nerve showing up here?" "It's a doggone shame. Can't believe Derek would do something like that!" "Who is she?" "Do you think those are his kids?" "That little girl look just like Tequitta's daughter." "Did you see his first wife sitting back there with her?" On and on it went until Joie could take no more. Coming to his funeral had to be done. She wanted Derek to know about the twins, even if it were too late. She didn't care what his family thought. These kids, her lovable children, belonged to him too.

Joie left the funeral early in order to protect her children from the awful, hateful comments coming from his family. She grabbed her babies by the hand and took them home. Home to her loving family— the only family they had at the moment.

* * *

Ronnie thought she could do it. Thought she could attend Derek's funeral, show up and sit near the back to pay her final respects to the family. But seeing Tequitta—a very pregnant Tequitta, and Derek's family comforting her was too much to handle. She was supposed to be the wife, part of his family. She was married to him longer than that skank knew him. Yet she was the one who sat in the back pew like a guest while his family surrounded and comforted Tequitta in her overly dramatic display of grief. And when Joie went up there with her kids and bent over his casket... She'd seen and heard enough. She was too through.

In her heart, she had already said her final good-bye to Derek in the hospital. In their own private conversation they made peace with one another. A public display of grieving wouldn't make the situation any more tolerable. As she was reminded in the hospital that night, she was no longer Veronica Jordan, Derek's wife. She was the ex. The ex-wife, ex-stepmother, ex-aunt, ex-sister-in-law, and so on and so forth. She needed to let it go—needed to let them go. That part of her life was over forever. No more ties to the Jordan's.

The house phone rang. She was still in no mood to speak to anyone, so she let the answering machine take the call. She listened as the answering machine clicked on to take the message.

"My name is Lexi McCray. I'm looking for Veronica Pierce. Please call when you receive this message. This is urgent. Thank you."

Ronnie stopped and listened. *Lexi McCray? I knew I heard that name before. She left a message on my answering machine when I was in the DR.* She found the card Joie gave to her and re-read it. The card said Lexi was a private investigator. Joie told her she specialized in locating adopted parents.

Her heart started doing flip-flops in her chest and she thought. *Could it be true? Is my daughter really looking for me? Found me?* She picked up the phone and started to dial Ms. McCray's number. She stopped. What was she going to say? What if it was her daughter? What would she do? How should she react? Only one way to find out.

Ronnie poured a glass of wine, gulped it down, and dialed. The phone rang four times before she answered.

"Lexi McCray," the woman answered.

"Ms. McCray, this is Veronica Pierce returning your call."

"Ms. Pierce, can you hold on for a moment? I need to end my call on the other line."

"Yeah, I can hold." Ronnie took a seat in the chair by the window. Her neighbors had recently landscaped their yard in a variety of colorful flowers. The effect was tranquil and very soothing; the perfect setting to place the call that would change her life.

Lexi clicked off the other line. She was in the midst of giving her client an update when Veronica called. Not wanting to get her hopes up, she didn't mention who the caller was on the other line.

"Hello Ms. Pierce, thank you for returning my call. My name is Lexi McCray. How are you doing today?"

"Well, considering I just left my ex-husband's funeral, I'm doing alright. What can I do for you?"

"I'm sorry for your loss. Please accept my condolences," she cleared her throat and continued. "The reason I'm calling is I am looking for my client's birthmother. Do you mind if I ask a few questions to determine if you are the correct Veronica Pierce?"

"Oh, okay. Sure. What do you need?"

"Please excuse me if I sound impersonal, but I must confirm your identify before we go any further. I hope you understand."

115

"It's alright. Go on." Ronnie was just an anxious to find out if it was indeed her daughter searching for her.

"Thanks. Do you know or were you ever involved with a Mr. Travis Mitchell Bradford?"

"Yes, I know Travis. Go on."

"Great! Did you have a child with him who was born on April 29, 1994?"

Ronnie nearly dropped the phone. "Yes, yes I did. Is my daughter looking for me? Is it her?"

"Yes Ms. Pierce, your daughter hired me to locate you. Look, I really prefer to not do this over the phone. I'm currently in town. Is it possible we can meet somewhere? I can drop by if it's more convenient for you."

Ronnie whispered, "Thank you Lord," before answering. "Sure, I would love to meet you. How does 3 o'clock sound? My address is 1201 Clovis Street."

"1201 Clovis? Got it. See you in a couple of hours. And Ms. Pierce, you have just made a young lady extremely happy."

Chapter 13

Ronnie kept close watch on the clock. The five minutes that elapsed since she hung up seemed to take an eternity, and she had another two hours to go. She needed a friend to talk to and share her exciting news. Joie was the only girlfriend she knew well enough to share something so personal. Ike was no longer in her life. She couldn't call her mother. She had no one. And right on time, she thought of her new found friend from the DR.

Ronnie held her breath and dialed his number, unsure if she was going the right thing or not.

"*Hola?*" he answered on the first ring.

"Hi, is this Luis?"

"Yes, this is Luis."

"Hi Luis, its Ronnie. How you doing?" she asked, getting the small talk out of the way.

"Ronnie? *Hola!* So good to hear from you! What's going on beautiful?"

"I, uh, got your message the other night and just wanted to hear your voice. See if you made it back home."

"Yes, I am back in California. I got back last night as a matter of fact."

"Good. Happy you're back. I miss you...." Too many conflicting emotions swirled around in her head. She needed to release them but didn't know where to begin.

"I miss you too," he said, hearing her unspoken angst. "Ronnie, what is it? Sounds like you have something on your mind. You alright?"

"You got a few minutes to talk?"

"Of course, what's going on?"

So for the next hour or so, Ronnie filled Luis in on the past week. Only seven short days elapsed since he last saw her and it felt like decades. They talked about Derek's passing, and the ongoing drama with Joie. She revealed how she'd given up her newborn daughter for adoption. Luis was genuinely concerned and interested in helping out his new friend. He cared about her and knew she needed an impartial ear. The truth was, it was another way to learn more about this mysterious woman who so intrigued him. He listened, asked questions, weighed her decisions, and offered advice.

"What are you going to say to the investigator? Are you ready to meet your daughter? Is this something you want to do? You know you don't have to. There is absolutely nothing that says you have to reveal yourself. Laws do exist to protect you from this kind of thing."

"I thought about all of that. Why does she want to see me? Does she hate me? Want to tell me how awful a person I am for giving her up? Or will she want a relationship with me? Do I have what it takes to be a mother of an eighteen year old, almost grown young woman?"

"Meet with the P.I. See what she has to say. If you don't feel comfortable with the situation—start picking up bad vibes—leave it alone. Nothing says you have to go through with this."

"You're right. It's just so much going on all at once. Too much."

"Ronnie, you wanted to change your life. You're getting what you asked for. No one said changing your life was going to be easy or pretty. Let me share something with you. The pastor of my church explained that keeping God's will in our lives will take us to places we have no intention of going. He explained the best thing we can do is let the will of God control our lives. Stop trying so hard to control every little situation."

"I would love to learn that trick because I can't seem to let go of anything," she sighed.

"I understand, but listen. The pastor used a river stream as a metaphor for God's love. The natural course of a stream is for the water to flow in one direction. Picture the gently flowing currents as a symbol of God's will. When an obstacle, for example a large rock, is placed in the middle of the stream, the current will easily go around or over the obstacle. If it sits there long enough the water will eventually wear the rock down. Sometimes, trash—also known as distractions, gets tossed into the stream. Trash may flow with the water for a while, but eventually it gets pushed aside and washes ashore, meaning that those distractions won't last forever."

Ronnie nodded in agreement. "You're making sense so far..."

"Now consider what happens when you go against the flow and choose to follow your own free will. Swimming upstream against the current can literally make your life very difficult. Going against His will can be manifested in so many ways. Problems at work, trouble at home, relationships that don't seem to work; they are all obstacles or distractions in that stream."

"I get it. So you're saying I haven't been able to get around those obstacles because I've been following my own path—my free will?" asked Ronnie.

"Yes, that's exactly what I'm saying. That stream of water keeps pushing you backwards and you've become tired. When you reach those obstacles in the stream and get tired of swimming against the current, you naturally remove yourself from the stream. Since the obstacle is protecting you from the flow of water, you start to feel safe. However, it's all an illusion because you're not safe, just merely protected by your situation; your obstacle; your distraction. You literally get stuck. Stuck behind that rock and going nowhere fast. It becomes easier and easier to stay stuck in that bad situation, because it requires no effort on your part. But you are not doing what God intended. Just know that His Love will remove that obstacle from your path so you may return back into His stream. Make sense?"

"I like that Luis. Never been explained to me like that before…"

"Now, I'm not saying that your life will always be easy. That stream can take you into rough waters and make you think your world is spinning out of control. Much like the turbulent pattern of white water rapids. I have a feeling this is what it feels like you're going through right now. But if you hang tough—stay faithful, you can make it through these rough waters. And on the other side, He will put you in a place of peace, serenity, tranquility, and joy. Stay in his stream Ronnie. Don't let these distractions take you away from doing God's will."

"Thank you Luis. You have helped me more than you could know. I'll let you know what happens."

"You are welcome, my friend. Take care of yourself and have faith that it will work out."

"Okay, I'll do that. Oh, and by the way, I'm looking forward to seeing you again. Think I'll have some free time to make a visit out that way pretty soon. Once I get my situation straightened out here."

"Sounds great. I look forward to seeing you, too; because we also have a few issues we need to work on. I'll talk to you soon. Take care." Luis hung up.

Norma Jean called again and left another message while Ronnie was at Derek's funeral. With Derek's unexpected passing and everything else going on, she neglected to return the realtor's call. Lexi wasn't expected for another half an hour. She dialed her realtor expecting good news.

"Hey Norma Jean, I received your message. So we've got a buyer already?"

"Hello Veronica. Well, not exactly. When I made that call and left that message, we did have an interested buyer. Turns out they withdrew their offer at the last minute."

"Withdrew? Can they do that?" Ronnie felt a headache coming on.

"Yes, they can, and they did. Gave up $2500 in earnest money though."

"Do you know what happened? Why they changed their mind? Was something wrong with the house? Something I can fix maybe?"

"Uh, well, it's uh, your neighbor."

"My neighbor? That old woman? What could she have possibly done to change their minds?" asked Ronnie.

"Apparently they stopped by the house for one last look before making their final offer. Anyway, the old woman said she wanted to meet her new neighbors. She wanted to feel their spirits, so she pulled out a bundle of herbs and started speaking in some unknown crazy language. They asked her what she was doing. She apparently told them she was looking for evil spirits that may have attached themselves to their souls." Norma Jean laughed.

"And? What did she find out?" Ronnie laughed in spite of herself.

"That woman told the husband his wife has very dark spirits surrounding her. She did offer to get rid of them and gave the wife a charm necklace to wear. The husband said his wife was so upset she burst out in tears. They contacted their realtor immediately and withdrew their offer."

"Oh my! I had no idea my neighbor was like that. She never bothered me."

"Maybe you have good spirits hanging around you." Norma Jean chuckled again. "Don't get discouraged yet. Your house is a relatively new listing. You'll have more offers soon. It's a nice house in a good school district. So, for now relax and let me do my job. I'll call you if anything changes. Otherwise, plan on having an open house next weekend."

"Thanks for the update Norma Jean. I appreciate your honesty," she chuckled. "I think I'll have a chat with my next door neighbor. I can't have her scaring off potential buyers."

* * *

Joie called. And even though she had no intention of ever speaking to Joie again, Ronnie decided to give her another chance. She had Luis' words fresh on her mind and understood it was her time to practice the art of forgiveness.

"Hey," answered Ronnie.

"Hey girl, what happened? Why did you leave the funeral? You aw'right?" As far as Joie was concerned, all was well. In her mind, they had a small disagreement and soon everything would be back to normal.

"Joie, why are you calling me? I saw that performance you gave up there—at Derek's casket. What was that about?"

"Sorry, I didn't mean to hurt you or the family. Derek needed to know about his children. That's all. Everyone's gonna know anyway. Now that the secret's out, it's just a matter of time before they all find out. It may as well be sooner, rather than later."

"I shouldn't have gone to his funeral. I already said good-bye to him at the hospital. He and I worked out our stuff. Cleared the air. Made our peace."

"That's good Ronnie. Really good. He left this world knowing you forgave him. Only wish I had a chance to let him know the truth about the twins. Can't live a lie forever and expect all to go well, can you?"

"You said a mouthful sister. Look, I'm expecting company any minute. I'll catch up with you later."

"Oh really? Who's that stopping by?"

"None of your business, but I do want to talk to you later. We need to clear the air."

"Aw'right. I'm here when you wanna talk. Later."

"Bye."

Lexi McCray rang the doorbell promptly at 3 o'clock. She was smartly, albeit casually dressed in a tailored blue pinstripe pants suit. She carried a brief case in one hand and a bottle of water in the other. Ronnie opened the door.

"Good afternoon Ms. Pierce. It is so good to finally make your acquaintance." She flashed a mouthful of perfectly bleached white teeth. Her dark tan made her smile appear almost florescent. Lexi reminded her of an actress in one of those toothpaste commercials.

"Good to meet you as well, Ms. McCray, please come in."

"Lexi, please call me Lexi."

"Fine. You can call me Ronnie."

"Great. Shall we get started then?" she asked, opening her briefcase. Lexi produced a birth certificate, adoption papers, and a stack of photos of her daughter. She handed them to Ronnie.

"Oh...my...God! She is absolutely gorgeous! What's her name?"

"Her name is Kiara. Kiara Indigo Bradford."

"Wait a minute. Indigo is my middle name. Did you say her last name is Bradford?"

"Yes, she has the last name of her father, Travis. He raised her from a baby," explained Lexi.

Ronnie gasped. Instinctively her hand went to her mouth to stifle her surprise. "Travis raised her? But how? We both signed the adoption papers. We gave up our parental rights. I know because I saw the papers with my own two eyes."

"The story goes, after Travis found out you gave birth to your daughter he drove down to the hospital in Oklahoma. Travis said after one look at his daughter, there was no way he could give her up. Oklahoma's adoption law gives biological parents a three day window to change their minds. Travis requested his rights as the father be reinstated; he petitioned the court for sole custody of his daughter. The state didn't notify you because you had already signed over your parental rights."

"Travis had her all this time? Why didn't he try to contact me sooner?"

"You'll have to ask him that. But considering you put her up for adoption, the natural assumption was you didn't want anything to do with your child. The only reason you've been contacted now is Kiara wanted to meet her biological mother—now that she's over eighteen."

"She must hate me. He must hate me. Travis raised her all this time knowing that I voluntarily gave her up. I don't understand why she would want to meet me. Doesn't she have a new mother?"

"Why don't you save all those questions for Kiara? Obviously she does want to meet you, otherwise I wouldn't be here. Look, if it's alright with you, I'm going to give her your phone number. She wants to talk to you. Maybe meet. Between the two of you—three of you, if Travis gets involved, you should be able to have all your questions answered."

"You're right. It's the least I can do. Please, give her my number. I'm looking forward to speaking with her. Kind of nervous right now, but that's to be expected. Right?"

122

"You'll be fine. Kiara and Travis are wonderful people. They are very loving, understanding and accepting people." Lexi started gathering her things to leave.

"Lexi, where does she live? Where are they?"

"Oh, I thought I mentioned that earlier. They live in Santa Elena, California. She graduates from high school in a few weeks."

"Santa Elena? I can't believe he moved back home. Travis used to always say Santa Elena had the most beautiful beaches and breathtaking sunsets in all of the United States."

"That's it then. My work is done. I'll be going now, but if you need anything, anything at all, please don't hesitate to call. Kiara is my client, but I'm offering my assistance to you as well because I love it when a story has a happy ending." She pulled her *Ray Ban* sunglasses from atop her head and placed them over her eyes.

Ronnie walked Lexi to the door. *Who would've thought a tall, thin, blonde woman could make such an impact in my life in just a matter of moments?*

Lexi waved as she pulled away. She noticed that standing in that doorway, Ronnie appeared hopeful and frightened at the same time. Like a vulnerable little girl. After doing this for so many years, Lexi had developed a feeling for how reunions would go and she knew this one would turn out well. She was all too aware how this revelation would affect the lives of many in a profound way. There were many days when she hated her job. However, today, this wasn't one of them.

Chapter 14

"Joie? Do you mind if I stop by? I need to talk to you." Ronnie momentarily dismissed her anger because she needed her friend.

"Hold on a minute." Joie placed her hand over the phone and yelled out to her mother, "Hey Mom? Can you watch the twins for a little while? I'm going to meet up with Ronnie. I'll be back before you know it. Thank you." She replied back to Ronnie, "My parent's place is no good. Too many people. How about we meet at the seawall?"

"The seawall? What seawall?" asked Ronnie.

"Next to the fishing pier at the old Fort Monroe. Remember where the guys used to fish?"

"Oh yeah, that's a good place. Very peaceful. I'll meet you there in fifteen minutes."

Ronnie parked in the parking lot facing the water. The seawall encompassed the entire post making for a great jogging trail. In happier days, she and Derek used to take long leisurely walks out there. Today the sky was overcast with a slight chill in the air, courtesy of a northern breeze. She sometimes imagined writing her first novel sitting on one of those park benches, watching pelicans dive awkwardly into the water. *Lord knows I have enough material to write a couple of novels, especially with this shit going on now.* Massive cargo laden ships sailed quickly by.

Joie pulled up next to her, speakers loudly blaring out the hypnotic sax played by her favorite musician, Boney James. "Hey lady! So glad we're gonna do this."

"C'mon, let's walk. I need the exercise, plus it'll relieve this tension."

"Ronnie, you've been my girl for many, many years. I can't begin to make up what I did to you. Saying I'm sorry doesn't begin to express my feelings. I was wrong and I ask for your forgiveness."

"You know Joie, what you did has gotten some folks killed, and don't think for a moment that thought didn't cross my mind." Ronnie laughed.

"I deserve that. I can take my lumps. Give 'em to me."

Two large dogs pulled a petite woman behind them. She looked as if she were holding on for dear life. One padded over and sniffed Joie. The woman tugged the dog away.

"Looks like you have a new friend," joked Ronnie.

"Yeah, I do seem to attract dogs."

"You know that is not even close to being true. What about Cedric? He's a great guy."

"Cedric don't want nothin' to do with me. I saw him at the funeral and he didn't even bother to speak. At least he acknowledged the kids. They miss him so much."

"Listen Joie, it took some time and a lot of praying, but I forgive you. I also forgave Derek a long time ago. I've tried living with hatred in my heart and actually did for a long time after Derek left me. I cursed him to hell and back, and wanted him and his sidepiece to fall off the face of the earth. But you know what? I discovered while he was out living his life, I was stuck in a bad place. After awhile, I realized holding on to that stuff was only hurting me. I needed to let it go, for my sake."

"If I were in your position, I don't think I would be so quick to forgive."

"You'd be surprised what you'd do. Girlfriend, you better hope that no one ever betrays you. It is not a good place to be in."

"So we're good then?" Joie chewed her bottom lip. It was a tic leftover from childhood whenever she was anxious.

"We'll never be like we used to be. I forgave you, but I will never forget what you did. Your behavior shows a severe lack of character. And right now, I'm not so sure about how to include you in my life again."

"Ronnie, you're judging me again. If you're going to be so forgiving and God like, you need to hold back on being so damned judgmental."

"You're right. Let's just be natural about this and see where it takes us."

"Cool. Now, tell me. What's going on with you? Who is Lexi McCray and why is she looking for you?"

"Funny you should ask. Lexi stopped by the house today. Told me my daughter hired her to locate me." She stopped walking and looked out over the ocean.

"What? Get outta here… You have a daughter? When did this happen? How old is she?" Joie joined her at the seawall.

"It was a secret. I didn't tell anyone. Only people who knew were my mother and the baby's father, Travis. I gave birth while I was still in college." Ronnie tried to let the vastness of the ocean put her dilemma in perspective.

125

"I'll be blessed! You have a grown daughter? Congratulations... I think."

"This is crazy, right? I'm still getting used to the idea, but her name is Kiara and she lives in California. She recently turned eighteen."

"She must be something else. The child hired a private investigator to find her biological mother. Not too many children would have the presence of mind, or the money to do something so grown up. How do you feel about this?"

"I'm excited. Scared. Happy. Nervous. Terrified. I haven't even spoken to her yet. Lexi is going to give her the news. Kiara will call me in her own time. After we talk, then I'll know more."

"I am so happy for you, girlfriend. Come over here and give me a hug."

"Thanks, I had to tell someone. Needed to share my good news and I couldn't think of anyone else; you've been my best friend for so long."

"If you don't mind me asking, why did you give her up? You love children. I can't imagine why you didn't keep her. Did she have special needs or something?" asked Joie. She stopped and stared before whispering, "Were you raped? Is that why you didn't keep her? If that's the reason, I can understand why meeting her might be kinda hard."

"No, nothing like that. She was perfect and conceived in love. But having a baby didn't fit into my life at the time because I wasn't ready to be a mother. I thought someone else could give her a better home and raise her with love. You know?"

"But *you* are so filled with love. I can't imagine a better mother. What about the daddy? What happened to him?" Joie was full of questions.

Ronnie relayed the entire story about Travis, her parents, and why she felt she couldn't raise a biracial child. Told her that Travis took Kiara and raised her on his own. How he did what she couldn't do.

"He sounds great! However, I'm kinda shocked because I never imagined you were racist. I didn't think you had a prejudiced bone in your body. Guess I didn't know you that well either, huh?"

"Girl, please... You know I am not a racist. Travis and I were in love. I wanted to be with him and only him, but I promised my father—God rest his soul—that I would break it off. And that is what I did. When my mother found out I was pregnant, she convinced my stupid naïve twenty-two year old butt to give my baby up for adoption."

Joie shook her head, "That's awful. But now you have another chance and an opportunity to fix things. You can get to know your daughter. Maybe even her father again. Hmm?"

"Definitely want to get to know my daughter. Travis is another story. That was a long time ago. We've both grown up a lot since then. For all I know, he's happily married. Anyway, I met someone when I was in the DR."

"Oh really? Do tell."

Ronnie glanced at Joie and wondered if she was doing the right thing in telling her so much of her business. In spite of it all, having Joie in her life was a blessing. Her girl stood by her side through thick and thin. Never wavered.

"His name is Luis. Luis Duarte. He's from the Dominican Republic and was home visiting his family. He lives in California."

"Oh really? A Dominican man? I hear they are fine as hell and sexy too! Did you have an island fling that ended up in hot sweaty sex on the beach?"

"He is very handsome and no, we didn't get that far. He's recently divorced... I just broke up with Ike... Neither one of us wanted rebound sex."

"Shoot! Why not? Sometimes sex without commitment is the best. No expectations. No heartbreak. You have a good time, lots of hot sex, and go your separate ways. Probably would've done you some good." She laughed.

"Don't get me wrong now. I thought about it, but too much was going on in my head. Knowing me, I probably would've stopped in the middle of bumping and grinding and started talking about my problems. I'm going to take some time to get to know *me* again."

"I hear ya. Last thing you need is to get involved with somebody who lives in California anyway. Girlfriend, I know you have a lot going on, but it sounds like you have a definite trip to the West Coast in the very near future."

"You're right. As soon as I get everything tied up here, there's no telling."

"So ya still thinking about giving up your job? Also I meant to ask you, what's the deal with the For Sale sign on your lawn? You're really moving?" she asked.

"Joie, I had a revelation. It was as if God Himself had spoken directly to me. He told me I was wasting my life here—in Hampton. I am spinning my wheels because I'm not happy. I work my ass off every day. And for what? I don't have anyone to share my life with. When I saw Derek laid out to rest like that, I knew I was making the right decision."

Joie sighed wearily, "Yeah, I know what you mean.... Derek was too young to die."

"Life is too short to be messing around. Tomorrow is not promised. I vowed to myself and to the Lord that I was going to find my purpose. Grab on to that thing I'm supposed to be doing and make it my own. I am going to follow this thing and see what happens. For now, I have to get rid of all that stuff that's holding me down. If giving up that job and selling my house is going to get me there faster, so be it."

"You are so brave. I'm terrified of being on my own. Scared I can't take care of me and these kids too. Guess that's why I lied to Cedric for so long. I knew I'd lose him if I told him the truth." A lone tear fell from her eye. She wiped it away.

"Girl, I am not brave, I'm just as scared as you are. I just know that I've got to do something or else end up hating my life. I can't do that. This life is precious and not to be wasted. Anyway, God won't let me hide behind my fears."

"I hear that! Well, if there's anything I can do, just ask. Okay? I'm not sure how much longer I'm gonna be at my parent's house. I'm trying to catch up with Cedric and find out what he's gonna do. Guess I've got to give him a little more time. Hope he's as understanding at you were."

"Cedric is a good guy, but don't hold your breath. What you did to him and what you did to me are two different things. Like I said, I forgave you, but he may not be so forgiving. I was betrayed by my girlfriend. He was betrayed by his *wife*. That makes all the difference in the world. If I were you, I'd start working on a backup plan."

"You're right. I made my bed and might have to sleep in it alone from now on. I've got to get back to the kids. Momma has book club tonight. I can't hold her up on that. You take care Ronnie. Don't be a stranger. Please let me know how things work out with your daughter."

"I will and you take care of those beautiful angels for me. I sure wish Derek would've gotten a chance to meet them."

"Me too, Ronnie. Me too."

* * *

Joie headed to her parent's home. When she got there, she walked inside the house to find her mother pacing the floor, arms crossed tightly across her bosom, with a worried expression on her face.

Her mother was dressed in a maid's uniform for her book club meeting. One of the rules of the book club was everyone dressed up like one of the main characters. They were reading some book about black women working as maids in the homes of southern white women in the 1950's. Thus, the maid's uniform. According to Joie's upbringing, it seemed wrong to celebrate maids and play dress-up, but it was her mother's thing. Not hers.

"Mom, what's wrong? You okay?"

"Don't know. Cedric stopped by. He wanted to see the kids. I told him you weren't here." Joie took off down the hallway. "Maya, Trey? Where y'all at?"

"Joie, that's what I'm trying to tell you. He was out there in the front yard talking to 'em. I went in the back to make a phone call. Thought everything was okay. That it was alright leaving 'em with their daddy. When I came back up front, he and the twins was gone."

"He took them? Where did they go? Did he say anything to you? Leave a note? Anything?" Joie started to panic.

"Calm down honey. He is their father. He wouldn't hurt them children. I don't know what's going on between you two, but something ain't right. Why would he just up and take them kids without saying nuthin' to me?"

"Mom, I didn't want to tell you like this, but me and Cedric are going through some dark days. Shoot, I may as well tell you because you're going to find out eventually." She took a deep breath and continued. "Mom, Cedric isn't the twin's father. He just found out last week. That's why we're fighting." Joie sat down and held her head in her hands.

"What do you mean he's not their real father?"

"He found out by accident. Now I'm not sure what he'll do."

"Cedric ain't them kid's father? Well who is then?" Joie's mother stood in front of her daughter.

"Derek Jordan was their father."

"Derek Jordan? Was that the man's funeral you went to today? Wait a minute. Did you say Jordan? As in Veronica Jordan's husband?"

"Yes Mom. He's one and the same. Only her name isn't Jordan anymore. She changed it back to Pierce when they divorced."

"Girl, are you telling me you went an' got yourself pregnant by Ronnie's husband?"

Joie was tired, deflated, defeated. "Yes Mom, I did. But none of that matters now. I need to find my children."

"Lawd have mercy! Wait 'til I tell your father! And you say Cedric just found this out?"

"Yes, that's why I've got to find them. I don't know what he'll do. He's so angry at me."

"Well, whatever you did, I know Cedric and he ain't gonna hurt them kids. Now that I know what's going on, just give him a little time. They were laughing and having a good time when I went in the back, that's why I felt it was okay to leave for a minute. Listen to me, I don't care how mad he is at you, he ain't gonna hurt them kids. He loves them little boogers. He may not be the real father, but he is their Daddy."

"Okay Mom, I'm going to give him the benefit of the doubt. But if he ain't back in an hour, I'm gonna call the police."

"I knew there was something wrong. Cedric ain't never acted funny towards me before. Child, do what you gotta do. Take care of your business. Cedric ain't them kid's real father? Never saw that coming. You seen my feather duster? Well, I gots to go. The book club is waiting." Her mother left the room, shaking her head in disbelief and returned to whatever she was doing before the drama kicked in.

Joie dialed Cedric's number. It rang several times before he answered.

"Hello?" he answered.

"Hey Cedric, Mom told me you stopped by to see the twins. Is everything okay?" Joie tried her very best to speak in a calm voice. *Don't want to piss him off and make him do something drastic.*

"Yeah, we're okay. I missed them so I picked them up. We're at the park. Is that alright with you?"

"Yes, of course it's alright. What time you gonna bring them back? They haven't had dinner yet and they have school tomorrow." Joie grew hopeful. Maybe he was coming around after all.

"Don't worry about dinner. I'll feed them before I bring them back in a couple hours."

"Sounds good. Okay. Well, I'll see you soon."

"Yeah. Bye." He hung up.

Joie took Ronnie's words of advice to heart while she waited for Cedric to bring the children home. *What if Cedric doesn't want to get back together?* She had to face facts and develop a backup plan—a Plan B, if it came to pass. There was no way she could live in her parent's home for much longer. She was used to her own space and her own rules. So were the twins.

She took stock of the balance in her savings account. Over the years she accumulated a good amount of money. Cedric always told her the money she made was their "icing on the cake". As a youth counselor, he made more than enough to take care of his family. Always made it known to all that he was the breadwinner and his wife only worked because she wanted to—not because she had to.

She researched a few apartment complexes and quickly realized she needed a house, not a temporary apartment. Out of the blue, she thought about Ronnie's place. *If things with Cedric don't work things out, maybe I can rent Ronnie's house until she finds a buyer.* She didn't want to think negatively, but if they did get divorced, she would eventually have to find a home. Until that time came, and hopefully it never would, perhaps Ronnie would agree to her Plan B. She realized asking Ronnie for anything at this point was a major imposition, but what other choice did she have? Joie tucked the plan into the back of her mind until she needed it.

Just as he promised, Cedric brought the kids home before dark. She met them at the door and hugged both children as if she hadn't seen them in months.

"Hi Cedric, you want to come in for a few? Have a drink?" asked Joie.

"Sure. I have a few minutes."

"Maya, Trey, go back to your rooms and get ready for your bath." She watched the children obediently do as they were told.

Her mother had left for her reading group so they had the house to themselves. Cedric followed Ronnie into the kitchen. She pulled a couple of beers from the fridge and set them on the table. They took a seat opposite the other.

"What's up?" asked Cedric.

"Thanks for coming over to see the kids. They really missed you. Your stopping by means a lot to me, too."

"I miss them. It's difficult not seeing the children. I've been their father for the past five years, so I am struggling with coming to terms with what's happened. Trying to understand what you did and what I should do. This whole situation is really messed up Joie." Cedric ran his hands over his bald head.

"I don't know how many ways to say I'm sorry. What can I do to make this up to you? Tell me. I'll do anything."

"There is nothing you can do, Joie. After seeing you at Derek's funeral today with the kids... Look, I understand that he was the *sperm donor*—their biological father. But make no mistake Joie; I am their father and the only daddy they have ever known. I love Maya and Trey. They're *my* children."

Joie cried tears of happiness hearing Cedric express his feelings about their kids. Maybe there was hope for them after all.

"Yeah baby, you are their Daddy. Always have been and always will be." She smiled and went to hug him.

Cedric cringed slightly and pulled away. "Oh, I meant to tell you. That boy you gave my card to called. He wanted me to tell you 'thank you'."

Though Joie was hurt Cedric shrugged off her touch, she let it slide. Played if off.

"Oh yeah? Dwayne called? That's great because he looked like he needed direction in his life—someone who cared. How is he, by the way?"

"The kid, Fresh-D is what he likes to be called, called me after he narrowly missed being shot. He was selling drugs in an unfamiliar part of the city. Another drug dealer got upset because Fresh-D was in his territory. So the other kid pulled out a gun and started shooting. He narrowly escaped getting hit by a bullet. After that, he decided to go straight. Called me up that same night and asked how I could help him. Poor kid lives with his grandmother."

"Cedric, that's awful! Is he all right?"

"He will be. Joie, it's the same old tired story I hear all the damn time. Kids don't have a father in the house and most of the time they don't even know who he is. The mother is on welfare with too many mouths to feed. They end up with a man in the house who ain't about shit. Dwayne, being the oldest son, couldn't stand for this man to live there so he turns to the only way he could to make money. He started selling drugs as a way to get out. The boy is only fifteen. His only focus should be school, not worrying about making money to escape from his existence. Anyway, he moved in with his grandmother who is not equipped to handle an angry out-of-control teenager."

"I hope you can make a difference in his life."

Joie looked at the man she married. The same strong man she wanted to spend the rest of her life with. She saw how devastated he was about the entire situation and wondered if any of their marriage could be salvaged.

"That's why I've got to stay involved in Maya and Trey's life. No matter what you did to bring them into this world, I am responsible for them. I will not let Trey end up like Fresh-D and I will not let Maya end up like his mother."

She winced. "Baby, that's great for the twins. But what about us? Is there a chance we can fix this?" Joie pleaded.

Cedric took a step back and dropped his head. He shook it from side to side. Went to the door and looked outside. "Joie, I talked to a divorce lawyer last week. I filed the papers and you should be receiving them soon. I can't be married to you. Every time I look at you, I see you with Derek. I imagine you underneath him, screaming out his name. I hate him and I despise you."

He laughed, "Check this out. Derek is gone. Why should I hate a dead man? He can't hurt me anymore. Right? I went to his funeral to curse him; instead I did nothing and left. What was the point? He's no longer here. But I still hate him and what he did to my family. He impregnated my wife when it should have been me; fathered two wonderful children who should've been mine; and ruined any chance for us to have a normal life. So Joie, to answer your question, there is no chance in hell we can fix this."

"Okay." She stood with her back against the sink, arms crossed, tears streaming down her face. There was absolutely nothing she could do but accept the consequences of her actions and learn to live with them. She watched Cedric leave and knew this time, he would not be back. Ronnie was right; she did need a Plan B after all.

Chapter 15

Ronnie carefully combed through the package Lexi left on the counter. She studied each document as if it were a precious jewel. The folder included letters, photos, and the adoption records. She immediately recognized the signature on the previously state sealed records as her own.

* * *

Memories flooded back to the day she gave birth. The labor pains were so intense they awoke Ronnie from a sound sleep. She waddled to her mother's room and told her something was wrong; her bed was wet, but it wasn't urine.

Dianna went into immediate action and called the doctor to tell him they were on their way to the hospital. She helped Ronnie into the car and drove directly to the hospital in downtown OKC. All the while she coached her on getting through the unbearable labor pains, assuring her child that she'd be fine.

Ronnie was in labor for over nine hours and it was by far the worst pain she ever experienced in her life. With the thought of dying foremost in her mine, she lost control of her bowels right there in the bed. The nurses acted as if this were normal and happened every day. Perhaps in their world, it did.

Dianna remained right by her side in the delivery room encouraging her child to breathe, push, breathe, push, breathe, push; holding Ronnie's hand, wiping her face, and feeding her ice chips. Finally, when she believed she couldn't stand any more pain, the baby came. The nurses were all excited and told her it was a girl. A nurse who didn't know Ronnie was giving the baby up for adoption tried to show it to her. The nurse proclaimed she was the most beautiful new born baby she'd ever seen. Luckily another nurse took charge and quickly rushed the baby from the room. Neither Dianna nor Ronnie ever saw her.

After the delivery, the hospital placed Ronnie in a room with another new mother. Dianna relentlessly tried to get her daughter moved to another floor but was unsuccessful. Reasoning was, she had just given birth and required additional monitoring because of a few complications she had experienced during the delivery. Therefore, the maternity ward was where she would remain.

For two brutally painful days, Ronnie suffered through the other new mother's excitement and joy of experiencing her first child. It was pure torture, that's the only way to describe it. Ronnie almost changed her mind about the adoption several times, but Dianna was there to hold her child true to her decision.

Ronnie was devastated after the birth and succumbed to a serious bout of depression for weeks. She remained in her room and cried for days. In her state of mind, she barely made it through her finals. Yet her mother was there every step of the way and did everything within her power to get her child back to normal. Eventually Ronnie did graduate, but did not attend the ceremony. The college mailed her diploma to her mother's house weeks later.

Once the bout of depression wore off—her doctor said it was a natural postpartum depression that most new mother's experienced— she gradually returned to normal. Only it wasn't the normal she desired. In the span of less than a year, she lost her father in a tragic car accident, broke up with her beloved boyfriend, delivered a baby she later put up for adoption, and barely graduated from college.

In her twenty-two year old mind, it was all her mother's fault for everything bad that happened in her life. As a result, Ronnie blamed her mother's racism for how her life turned out. Her mother's hatred of her white boyfriend—actually for all folks of the Caucasian persuasion, had resulted in a tragic turn of events in the Pierce family. Consequently, she turned her back on her mother, took a job on the east coast, and for almost two decades never looked back. The seed of unforgiveness was planted deep in her soul and she tended that seed daily until it matured into a full blown tree with roots that ran deep.

* * *

Ronnie's cell phone rang. She didn't recognize the number, but answered anyway. Hoping it would be Kiara.

"Um, hello?" she answered in a squeaky voice. She cleared her throat and repeated, "Hello?"

"Hi, I'm looking for Veronica Pierce," replied a soft-spoken, very proper female voice on the other end.

"This is Veronica Pierce."

"Ms. Pierce? Hi, my name is Kiara. Um, uh, Lexi McCray said it was like okay to call you. I hope I'm not like disturbing you or anything," she responded nervously.

"You're not disturbing me. I've been waiting for your call. How are you?"

"I'm fine. Uh, how are you?" Kiara asked, hesitantly.

Ronnie wanted to jump through the phone and embrace this woman-child who shared her genes. It broke her heart to hear the tentativeness in her voice. "Kiara, I'm so happy you called. Please call me Ronnie."

"Ronnie? Okay. Um, I uh… Wow! I had like all kinds of things I wanted to say when I finally heard your voice, but now… I'm sorry. I'm a little nervous." She apologized.

"Don't be nervous. This is hard for both of us. How about we take it a little at a time? Okay? Tell me about your school…"

For the next hour or so, Ronnie discovered how wonderful her newly found daughter was. She was at the top of her graduating class and received a scholarship from Ronnie and Travis' alma mater, though her final decision was yet to be made. Her hobbies included photography and graphic design.

When Ronnie asked about Travis she replied, "Daddy is fine. He was like really nervous when I told him I wanted to find you. I've always known you gave me up for adoption. He was scared you'd reject me so he made me wait until I was like over eighteen before he gave me any information about you. Daddy is very protective of me."

Ronnie felt the tears before she realized she was crying. "Well, it sounds like Travis did a really good job with you. You've turned into quite the young lady."

"Thank you. Sometimes when Daddy got really angry at me, he used to like slip and say 'You are just like your mother. Stubborn!'" She laughed.

Ronnie shared in her laughter. "Unfortunately, that trait is dominant in the Pierce women."

"Umh, Ronnie? Can I like ask you something?" Kiara returned to seriousness.

"Yes, Kiara. What is it?"

"I'd really like to meet you. Like in person. Is that possible?"

"Yes, yes of course. I'd love to meet you, too."

"Really? This means a lot to me. I, uh graduate from high school in like a couple of weeks. Do you think you can make it?"

Ronnie prayed a silent, *Thank you Lord* and answered, "Yes Kiara, I will be there."

"This is so cool! I'm going to send you an invitation with like all the details. What is your address?" she asked.

Ronnie gave her the information and in turn wrote down Kiara's phone number and address.

"I can't wait to meet you. After Daddy finally starting talking about you, he said you were like a really cool person. So, I'll see you in a couple of weeks then?"

"Yes Kiara. I'll be there."

"Awesome! Bye Ronnie."

"Bye Kiara."

Ronnie planned on being in California in two weeks to make the graduation. Since she wasn't there for all the other important events in her daughter's life, she could be there for at least this most important milestone.

* * *

Joie put the twins to bed. They didn't complain too much about sleeping on opposite ends of the same bed anymore. Both understood it was better than sleeping on the floor; which Joie threatened them with when they started fighting. Maya wanted to be in her own room with her dolls. Trey hated the fact he shared a bed with his sister. He explained to his grandfather it was just yucky and little big men didn't sleep in the same room, not to mention the same bed as their sister, even if she were his twin.

"So what are you gonna do now?" asked Joie's father, joining her in the hallway outside the children's room. Her mother had previously filled him in on her situation with Cedric, the twins and Derek.

"Only thing I can do. I've got to find somewhere for us to live. Daddy, I really messed up this time. Didn't I?"

"Child, you did make a few mistakes. I ain't gonna lie. They was some doozies. But don't you dare start feeling sorry for yourself. You got them kids to take care of. They didn't ask to be brought into this world like this, but now that they are here, Maya and Trey are your responsibility. Pull yourself together girl, pray about it, and get your butt moving. This ain't no time to stand around moping."

"You're right Daddy. Cedric has made up his mind. He'll continue to be in the twins' lives, but our marriage is over."

"Come here. Everything is going to be all right. It's gonna hurt like all get out for a long time, but you will get better. This'll all get better. It always does. Now go on to bed. You've got a busy day ahead of you tomorrow."

Joie returned her father's embrace, happy he was still in her life to provide well-needed guidance. She wiped her face and went to her room.

Chapter 16

First thing Monday morning, Ronnie dressed up in her sharpest outfit, one of the few suits she kept. Her intent was to present a smart, professional appearance for this meeting with Ralph. She recalled ole' Sam's advice about not stooping to Ralph's level and took it to heart. But the thought of quitting after telling Ralph about himself sure would feel good.

She was the first to arrive at the office. The parking lot was empty. Just the way she wanted it. No distractions. No problems.

Her cubicle was as she left it; neat and tidy with very few personal mementos. Drawings by Maya and Trey and a couple of pictures with her and Ike in happier times were tacked to the cabinet walls. She abhorred clutter in the workplace and never understood why people brought all kinds of junk from home in a vain attempt to make their cubicles look all comfy. Work was work, home was home. She was never one to confuse the two.

Ronnie removed reams of paper from a box, stacking them neatly on the floor and filled the box halfway with her things. Looking at the few measly items accumulated over almost a decade made her sad. *This is all I'm leaving with? After all these years with this company, I'm walking out with a few pictures, a couple of thumb drives and a small alarm clock?* She thought her personal effects looked pathetic sitting in that cardboard box. So for good measure, she plucked one of Ralph's model cars from a shelf in his office and plopped it on top. For some odd reason, that made her feel better. The box didn't appear as empty when she gently placed it in her trunk.

She patiently awaited Ralph's arrival. Anticipated how their meeting would go. It would probably only take a few minutes of listening to him beg before she dealt the final blow and quit. Ronnie planned to savor his anger. She knew he'd throw a hissy fit and looked forward to it. She heard the door open.

In walked Sam, huffing and puffing, and out of breath from walking across the parking lot.

"Veronica? What are you doing here? I didn't expect to see you this morning. Does Ralph know you're coming?" asked Sam.

"Uh, well, no. Not exactly, but he did leave a message on my voicemail regarding work he wants me to catch up on."

"Huh? Is that right?" Sam appeared surprised and a bit puzzled. He kept rubbing his chin, shaking his head.

"Sam, what's up? Why do you look so confused?" Even though Ronnie planned to inform Ralph officially of her resignation, she wanted to do things on her terms.

"Well, between me and you, he said you weren't coming back. He told everyone that personnel was sending you a letter of dismissal for being absent two weeks without your supervisor's approval. He already hired your replacement. He's supposed to start today."

"What? They were going to fire me? Ralph gave me two weeks of vacation before I left. And you say they already found my replacement?" Ronnie felt that old rage rising.

"That's what I'm trying to tell you. Ralph told his boss you walked out of here without saying a word. He told everyone you got mad because he asked you to cover for him in that conference. Veronica, you should've heard him trying to defend himself. He threw you under the bus, backed up, and drove over you again. So if I were you, I'd just leave now and leave well enough alone."

"Is that right? If you were me you'd just leave well enough alone and let that asshole get away with his lying ass? He knows good and well we talked about me being gone for two weeks because he agreed to it."

"I'm just asking is it worth it? The last time I saw you, you looked like you were ready to tell him off and quit. Now you look almost...happy. Did something happen to change your mind?" Sam looked past her into the empty cubicle. "

Ronnie followed his gaze. "Well, that's beside the point. Ralph did approve my vacation. It doesn't matter what we discussed after that. He lied to cover his own ass."

"So say that is what he did. Is yelling and screaming going to change anything? Is it going to make anything better for you? In the end, you're still fired. You don't want to work here anymore. Do you?"

"You do have a point. I guess I did walk out abruptly and left him in a bind. Didn't I?" she laughed. "I don't know. It would feel so good telling his ass off. Let him know what I think about him. You know?" Ronnie crossed her arms and tapped her right foot.

"I understand. But then what? So you tell him off. What have you accomplished? Listen, my advice to you is to maintain your professionalism. He's expecting you to act a fool and go off. That's what he thinks *we* do. Why don't you come at it from a different angle and blow his mind by taking the high road. Work it like President Obama does—cool and easy."

Ronnie studied the disheveled man giving her fatherly advice. All those years she prejudged Sam by his outward appearance. She looked down on him because he wasn't Mr. GQ and dismissed him because *she* believed he lived way below his potential. Yet here he was offering her advice she so sorely needed. Good advise at that. She vowed to change her attitude immediately.

"Sam, once again you're right. I am going to approach this another way. I think I'll tell Ralph I'll be submitting a letter of resignation explaining my actions leading up to those two weeks. Make his boss aware of the many hours of unpaid overtime I worked to help him complete those tasks to prepare for that conference. Let everyone know most of the ideas Ralph pitched were mine. I have all the research and documentation to substantiate my claim. What does Ralph have? A half-baked story about an angry black woman with a chip on her shoulder? Thanks Sam."

"There you go sister! Now that's what I'm talking about. Be classy. Veronica, I know it was hard being the only woman in this office, but I must say you were the best supervisor I had the pleasure of working with. You're going to go far in this life once you figure out what you want to do."

"You know that's right! I'm on a mission right not and I'm not sure where this is going to take me. I am going to let go and enjoy the ride. Find pleasure in the journey. Not going to let Ralph, this job, anyone or anything steal my Joy."

Ronnie and Sam turned towards the door at the same time when they heard the door open. In walked Ralph, followed by a tall, dark, handsome brother in an expensively tailored Italian suit. They were laughing, like they were old friends. Ralph stopped in his tracks when he saw Ronnie. He let the handsome man in his office and told him to wait.

"Veronica? I'm surprised to see you here," remarked Ralph.

"Hi Ralph, you left a message on my voicemail. Remember? Anyway, I told you two weeks ago I'd be back."

"What gives? You storm out of my office two weeks ago with some veiled threat of not returning. I haven't heard from you at all since then. You never returned any of my calls…and yet here you are this morning acting as if nothing has changed. Well, I am sorry to report that you have been summarily dismissed." Ralph took extreme pleasure in firing Veronica.

"You're firing me after we both agreed I could take time off?"

He shrugged nonchalantly.

"Ralph, you gave me your word!"

He crossed his arms across his chest and exhaled loudly.

"Fine, if that's the way you want to play this, don't bother. I quit! I'll be submitting my letter of resignation to personnel later this week. In that letter, I will include all the details to make sure everyone knows all those great ideas you came up with over the past few months were mine. No more pretending and taking the back seat to let you shine."

"Are you threatening me, Veronica? You know darn well we collaborated on those projects." Ralph turned a rosy shade of red.

"Yes, we collaborated all right. I did all the work and you took all the credit."

"Don't you know that's what assistants do? They make their bosses look good. And don't be so sure I couldn't have done those projects on my own. You may have put in the work, but it was a team effort and in the end, the team is what's important. That is all that matters." Ralph barely managed to contain his growing anger.

The man who walked in with Ralph overheard the conversation. He came out of the office. "You must be Veronica Pierce. I've heard all about you."

Ronnie cleared her throat, crossed her arms and rolled her eyes. She barely contained the *sistah neck roll* that threatened to make its presence known. "And? Who are you?" she asked with an obvious attitude, certain this was one of Ralph's golf buddies.

"My name is Henry, Henry Waters. I'm from the corporate office. It's a pleasure to finally meet you. Ralph told me a bit about your situation. Said you walked out on him without any prior notice. From what I just overheard, that wasn't true."

She relaxed, embarrassed how she accidently let her sistah side make an impromptu appearance. "Um, Mr. Waters, I recognize your name. Sorry about my behavior. It's just that Ralph and I had a major misunderstanding, but I meant what I said. I am going to resign. After ten years of working in this position, I realize this isn't the right place for me." She glanced over at Ralph.

"Mr. Waters, we have a lot to do this morning. This situation with

Veronica has been blown way out of proportion. How about we just let her go and get back to work?" Ralph squirmed uncomfortably.

"Just a moment Ralph." He raised his finger at Ralph. "Ms. Pierce has been a very valuable employee with this company for a long time. She's been very loyal to us and I don't intend to let her leave her with the wrong impression."

Ralph backed off and propped himself up against a file cabinet, looking like a petulant little boy.

"Ms. Pierce, please let me explain what's going on. Corporate has relocated me to run this department. When we discovered you were absent for those weeks, we knew we would be in trouble here. Make no mistake about it; your accomplishments and hard work have not gone unnoticed. But we have a business to run. Two weeks without you was unacceptable. So Ralph has taken over your position and I'll be running the office from now on."

"You're the new boss? Ralph is the person who replaced me? You mean he got demoted?" She burst out laughing. "I'm sorry, this isn't funny. It's just that Ralph has led everyone to believe he was the head honcho. Said you guys at corporate put him in charge because of his great management skills. I knew that was a bunch of bull, but to see him demoted? Well, that's worth getting "fired" over."

"After listening to your conversation, I think we may have acted hastily. I'm going to put a call in now and have you reinstated." He reached for his cell phone.

"Just a moment Mr. Waters, thank you for wanting to bring me back on, but I meant what I said. This office—this position, isn't right for me. I *am* going to submit my resignation. However, I appreciate you clearing my name and letting corporate know I did not go on vacation unauthorized." She replied and gave Ralph a smug look of satisfaction.

"Very well, then. That's that. As soon as I get settled in my office, I'll make that call. In the meantime, on behalf of the company I want to express our extreme gratitude for your loyalty and dedication to us over the past ten years. Whatever you do, wherever you go, I wish you only the best. And by the way, it was very nice meeting you Ms. Pierce," he replied full of charm.

"Likewise Mr. Waters. Well, I'm going to go now. I have lots to do." She waved at Ralph and said to Sam, "Thanks buddy. Thank you for everything." She gave the old man a big hug and walked out the door with her head held high and her dignity still intact.

"Ronnie, open the door! It's Joie! Open it!" she yelled.

Joie continued to pound on the door because ringing the doorbell didn't help. She felt the sound of the heavy bass drum vibrate the large living room window. Boom, boom, boom, boom! Over and over the bass drum thumped loudly keeping time to the song. Joie gave in to the music and subconsciously started nodding her head in rhythm to the beat. The music was turned up so loud there was no way Ronnie heard anything outside her house. Finally a lull came when the CD ended. She quickly rang the doorbell again and again. With all her might, she knocked on the front door as hard as she could.

Ronnie pulled back the sheer curtain and peeked out the window, then opened the door. "Joie? What are you doing here?" she asked, surprised and slightly annoyed at the interruption. She was packing up, getting the house ready for the movers. They were coming tomorrow to put her things in storage. Storing her stuff until she could find a new home in California.

"Ronnie, you were right. Cedric called our marriage quits. He stopped by the house today, took the kids out, came back and told me it was over. We're through…"

"Oh Joie, I'm so sorry. C'mon in." Although Ronnie thought Joie deserved everything she got and more, she still felt compassion for the woman. The end of a marriage was hard on even the most jaded people.

"Thanks, at least he's gonna still be the twins' daddy. He said those kids are his no matter who fathered them."

Ronnie handed a box of tissue to Joie. Her girl looked awful. Eyes red, mascara running down her face, snot coming from her nose and she was dressed in a combination of sweat pants and a pajama top. A comb hadn't touched her hair in days. She looked a hot mess.

"Cedric's a good man Joie. Maybe in time, he'll come around. Don't expect a miracle. Remember he just found out some shit that would destroy the strongest man. Give him time."

Joie looked around the living room piled high with boxes. Trash bags filled with various items took up most of the hallway. "Wait a minute. What's all this? You're really serious about moving, huh?"

"Yes, I am. I'm serious as a heart attack. I didn't tell you about my conversation with my daughter, did I?"

"No, no you didn't, but please go on. It'll take my mind off my worries for a minute. So fill me in. How did it go?"

"Joie, she sounds absolutely amazing! She's smart and well-spoken. Kiara invited me to her high school graduation. That's why I decided to move things up a bit. I'm heading out sooner than I originally expected. Heading to Cali. And you know what? I'm excited! I haven't felt excited in such a long time."

"Whoa! Hold on a minute girlfriend! What do you mean getting out of here? I understand about the downsizing and selling your house and all… But you're actually moving? All the way out there? To California? You're leaving Hampton? Leaving me?" Joie was visibly upset. Shocked by this revelation.

"Yes, that's what I'm saying. I officially resigned from my job today. Going to sell my car, and I'm selling my house. *Although the woman next door scared off my potential buyers with all her voodoo witch doctor mess.* And I am not leaving you; I'm moving there to get to know my daughter."

"Ronnie? What about me? About us? We've been friends forever. What'll I do without you?" Joie sat staring wide-eyed, like a frightened child who just learned she was about to lose her best friend.

"Joie, I understand how you feel. But this ain't about you. Ain't even about me. My daughter—my only child wants to meet me. Wants me in her life. Don't you understand? I have to do this. Not going is *not* an option." She went back to packing boxes. Needed the distraction to avoid cursing this heifer out.

"But why do you have to move? Why can't you just go for a visit and come back? You belong here… This is where your life is. Not out there." Joie pleaded.

Ronnie became angry. "Look Joie! You have everything here. A good job. Family. Your parents. Children. You used to have a good marriage, but you threw that away. This is where *you* belong, not me. I have no reason to stick around. And stop being so damned selfish and think about somebody else for a change. See that's your problem… You're fuckin' selfish! Don't nobody matter in your world except for Joie. As long as Joie gets what she wants, everybody should be cool! That what you think?" She returned her attention to packing.

Joie stood watching her friend. Suddenly, the proverbial light bulb came on. Since she'd known Ronnie, her girl was always doing for everyone else. First it was Derek, then his kids. Anytime Joie needed anything, Ronnie was the first and last person she called. Even Ike had used her for his own personal gain. And those assholes at work took advantage of her kindness at every turn.

"I understand. I get it. I have been a selfish asshole. I am so sorry Ronnie. All this time I have always thought about myself. You've always been so accommodating to everyone. Never saying no. Always willing to help. I get it. You're taking back your power."

Ronnie turned around after rummaging through a box. She stood still and listened to Joie, taking in her explanation. Hearing it out loud made perfect sense. Taking back her power was exactly what she was doing. The two women were on the same page for the first time in their lives. For a few moments in that shared space it all made perfect sense. They didn't speak, just smiled and enjoyed their mutual understanding.

Magically the spell was broken. Without the sound of the stereo or television blaring in the background, the silence was replaced by the obnoxiously loud noise of what seemed like dozens of simultaneously barking dogs.

For the past few years, ever since she bought her house, every morning and most of the evening, her neighbor's dogs barked incessantly.

Before Joie realized what was going on, Ronnie hurried past her and went outside. Joie followed. She watched her friend walk out into the middle of the street and stand in front of the offending neighbor's houses. In one hand she held an air horn—the kind you use in sports stadiums to cheer for your team. In the other, she held up a megaphone.

She raised the can and turned it on. The sound of the air horn in the quiet neighborhood was unmistakable. Every neighbor within earshot came out to see what the commotion was. Ronnie waited for the people with the dogs to come to their doors.

Into the megaphone she yelled out, "Will you please shut up your mutts?! For four years I've listened to your damn dogs barking day and night. Do you think you're the only people on this street?! There are children who live here. Retired folks. Shift workers. We are sick and tired of hearing your friggin' mutts barking! Shut them the hell up! Please!"

Suddenly the neighbors started to cheer and chime in. "Way to go!" "Thank you!" "Yeah, I can't even sit in my backyard anymore cause of your dogs." "That barking wakes up my baby every morning." "This

146

used to be a quiet neighborhood." "It's 'bout time someone said something!" "What you running in there? A kennel?"

The dog people closed their doors on the angry neighbors and retreated into their respective homes. They must have brought their dogs in, because finally the annoying barking stopped. Ronnie almost felt bad for them but it had to be done. She'd put up with the noise long enough. Anyway, now that she was leaving, what could it hurt to make her feelings known? Maybe it would help the rest of the neighbors—the ones that wanted to say something, but feared retaliation.

Ronnie's next door neighbor held up her charm-laden necklace and saluted the ladies. Her husband stood by her side. It was the first time she'd seen them together in awhile. Her neighbor was tickled pink at Ronnie's display. Ronnie waved at all her grateful neighbors and went back inside.

"What was that about?" asked Joie.

"Taking back my power girlfriend… Taking back my power."

"Girl, you are crazy!" Joie broke out in uncontrollable laughter.

"Yeah, so what? Those people know them dogs annoy the hell out of everybody with all that barking. And they don't care. They should be grateful no one did anything more drastic. C'mon, I'll pour you a drink."

"Look at you acting all super hero like and shit! Where's your cape and red boots?" Joie laughed again. It felt good to laugh with a friend.

Ronnie shrugged it off. "Anyway, let's get back to your problem. What are you going to do?"

"That's one of the reasons I wanted to talk to you, but now since I realize I've been dumping my problems on you all this time, I'm not sure…"

"Woman please! Talk to me. I'm cool." She poured two shots of brandy and handed one glass to Joie.

Joie sat back in the overstuffed chair. She placed her hand on her forehead in deep thought. Ronnie was leaving. Cedric was gone. Her two best friends would soon be out of her life. Didn't matter, she had to keep on moving.

"Remember, you told me I needed a Plan B just in case Cedric and me couldn't work this out? Well, I've been thinkin'. I need a place to live and you need somebody to buy your house. I was wondering if you'd consider selling your house to me?"

"You want to buy my house? Why? What if you and Cedric get back together?"

"What if we don't? I can't sit around my parent's house waiting on him to forgive me. They live clear across town. The kids love their school and this neighborhood. It's already hard enough for them without their daddy in the home. I'm trying to make this situation a little easier for my kids. That's all. You know I have always loved this house. You've done such a good job with it. It'll be perfect for us."

"You're for real?"

"Yeah, I am. Cedric was plain as day about not getting back together with me. I've seen him angry before, but this is something else Ronnie. Not only does Cedric not love me anymore, I truly believe he hates me. He told me he cringes when he looks at me." She sniffed and pulled a tissue from the box Ronnie gave her earlier.

"That must've been difficult to hear. Okay, if you're sure about this, I'll put you in touch with my realtor. And just so you know, I'm not trying to get rich off selling this house. I only need enough to pay the realtor and her broker's fees without coming out of pocket."

"Thanks Ronnie and I hope you find whatever it is you're searching for. Your daughter is soon going to find out how powerful her birth mother is. Look, there is a bright side to your moving to California." Joie wiped her eyes dry.

"Oh yeah, what's that?"

"Me and the kids can come out to visit. We can all go to Disneyland, Hollywood and such." She sniffed again. "It's all going to work out fine. For you and for me. I know it will. It has to." Joie rose to leave, but stopped and hugged her friend. "When you leaving?"

"Movers are coming tomorrow. I will probably stay in a motel for a couple of days, and then I'm pulling out."

"So soon? That's pretty quick. Is it okay to bring the twins over before you leave? Let them tell you good-bye before you get on the road? You know how they love them some Auntie Ronnie."

"Joie, everything *is* going to be alright. Trust me. You will get better. And yes, I'd love to see Maya and Trey before I leave. I'll call you to set up a time. In the meantime, here's my realtor's number. Her name is Norma Jean. She's really nice and like I said, I'm not trying to make money off this house."

"Thanks Ronnie. I intend to be fair with this, so I'm not going to take advantage of our friendship either. This is strictly business. Oh yeah, I forgot to tell you, I saw Ike the other day in the supermarket."

"Really? That's nice. Was Ike Jr. with him?"

"Yeah, he was with him. His ex-wife too. Looked like they were back together. He was pushing the cart and his ex was putting stuff in. Girl that *Negro* had the nerve to act like he didn't see me. Stared me straight in the face and turned away without even speaking. I'm glad you're not with him anymore. They might have been divorced on paper, but if you ask me he was *still* married to that woman."

"Good thing I didn't ask you. You're right, though. He was still married to her. Divorced and married at the same time. Well, anyway, I wish him well. Some couples are just meant to stay together."

"Hmmm? I suppose that could be true."

"Hey Joie?"

"What's up?" She stopped at the doorway.

"At least we already know my neighbor likes you." Ronnie relayed the story about the previous interested buyers and her supposedly voodoo practicing neighbor.

"That is too funny!" remarked Joie. "That old woman is as sweet as they come. I ain't worried one bit about her and the twins already love her. Says she's just like another grandmother. Okay girlfriend, I'm a let you go so you can finish packing. One more thing; Ronnie girl, thanks for everything. You have been an amazing friend and I have been truly blessed to have known you. I only wish I had been a better friend to you."

Chapter 17

The movers arrived early in the day and packed up the house's belongings for storage. Eight hours later they were finished. Even after scaling back and getting rid of a ton of stuff, a considerable amount of personal belongs remained to put into storage.

The professional cleaning crew showed up hours later and did an excellent job cleaning the house. It was now ready for its new owners—Joie and her children.

Ronnie realized trying to find a buyer on *Craigslist* for her car wasn't going to be an easy task. Too many callers wanted to either low ball or tried to cheat her by saying they'd pay her by check after she turned the title over to them.

Instead of dealing with all the screwballs that seemed to lurk on that website, she drove to the nearest dealership, haggled over the price and ended up trading in her *Infiniti G Coupe IPL* and driving away in a late model *Hyundai Accent*. It wasn't as luxurious as the *Infiniti*, but it had a good engine and transmission, four decent tires, and could get her cross country. She walked away free and clear having paid off the remaining balance on her car loan.

She called Luis with an update.

"Well, I did it," she announced when he answered the phone.

"*Hola* Ronnie. What did you do?" he laughed at her enthusiasm pouring through the phone.

"I spoke to my daughter and she sounds fantastic. I can't wait to meet her. And guess what else?"

"I'll bite. What?"

"She lives in Santa Elena, California. Her high school graduation is a couple of weeks away and I promised I'd be there to meet her and see her graduate."

"I'm so happy for you..." The rest of her words caught up with him. "Um, did you say she lives in Santa Elena?"

"Yeah, she lives there with her father. His family is from Santa Elena. Why? Do you know where it is?"

"Yes, I do. It's midway between Logeta and Montverde, between my business and where I live."

"Really? Well, I'll look you up when I get there because I'm headed out that way for her graduation. I'm also considering moving to California. I want to be closer to my daughter so I can get a chance to know her. I officially quit my job this morning. I have a couple months severance pay and have a few dollars in the bank. So what better time than now?"

"Did you say you're thinking about moving to California? Why? Isn't this kind of *sudden*? You don't strike me as the type of person to make such a hasty decision."

"I know and a few months ago you would have been exactly right. So much has happened lately, it almost feels like I have no choice in the matter. It feels like something I *have* to do. You know what? After I went to my ex-husband's funeral, I realized how precious life is. Tomorrow is not promised and we can go at any time. I don't want to spend my life with a bunch of regrets. I figure I have a second chance with my daughter and I plan on getting it right."

"I understand. Well, you know I would love to see you when you get here. Show you around and give you a tour of the area. It is quite beautiful here." Luis tried not to get his hopes up high. Ronnie wasn't coming out there to see him. He didn't want to get in the way of her getting reacquainted with her child.

"Luis you know I can't drive all the way out there and not see you. You're the other reason I'm considering moving to California. We really did hit it off, didn't we?"

"I wasn't going to go there, but since you did. Yes, we did hit it off. I really do like you and want to spend more time with you. In fact, I was wondering when I could come out to visit you. I mentioned that to my sister the other day when she asked about you."

"Your sister asked about me? That's cool. Tell her I said *hola* the next time you speak to her," she laughed. "I want to see you just as badly. I haven't stopped thinking about you since I returned. You do realize I'm going to have to learn Spanish if I move out there. I heard half the population of California speaks Spanish. Is that right?"

"Maybe not half, but being bilingual is definitely a plus. Stick with me and you'll pick it up in no time. So when are you leaving and how long of a drive is it?"

"It's a very long drive. About three thousand miles from here to Santa Elena. I'm stopping to visit my mother in OK City. I haven't seen her in a long time. Anyway, a side trip to Oklahoma adds only an extra hundred miles. I plan on taking my time to enjoy the scenery. Make time to see the heartland and embrace the wanderlust I recently discovered I have inside."

"Sounds great, but I thought you two were estranged."

"We were—are, but it's time I put all that to rest. Part of me letting go of the past and trying to move forward."

"I hear ya." He thought about the closeness of his own family. Ronnie's relationship with her mother seemed so foreign.

"Are you ready to see your mother?"

"Yeah, I gotta admit it's been a very strained relationship for quite a few years. But she is my mother and I am her only child. Enough time has passed for both of us to have grown up."

"Must be difficult."

"What's that?"

"Not having a relationship with your mother. I can't imagine not having family in my life—especially my mother."

"It is harder than you think. Family ties are very important, that's why I'm so excited to finally meet my daughter. Maybe there's still time to establish a bond. At least I hope so."

"Since she has your genes, I'm sure she will be an amazingly gifted young lady with a winning personality."

"Thanks Luis, you are so kind. Well, I'd better go. I have a meeting at the mortgage company. Have to finalize a few documents."

"Good luck. I hope all goes well."

"Thanks, me too. It's mostly formality. All the financial stuff has already been taken care of. I have to sign my name on a bunch of paperwork and turn over the keys. Know what?"

"What's that?"

"I forgot to tell you that my friend Joie is buying my house."

"Is that right? How do you feel about selling it to her?"

"I'm happy Joie and her kids will be living in my house. I put so much of my heart and soul into making that house a home, I'd hate to turn it over to a total stranger. At least now I know a loving family will live there. And it's great for the twins to be able to stay in the same neighborhood and not have to change schools. Lord knows, they've lived through enough drama in their short lives already."

"That's great…really great. Hey, I have an idea. Would you like some company on your trip? It's probably not a good idea for you to drive cross country alone," noted Luis.

"No, I'll be okay. And I won't be alone… I'll have my daddy's spirit with me."

"You sure? I can fly out and meet you somewhere. When are you leaving anyway?"

"No, it's okay…really. Anyway, I'm thinking about heading out early Friday morning, Saturday at the latest. It just depends on if I get everything taken care of."

"Fine, but if you change your mind, I'm just a phone call and a plane ride away."

"Thanks, I'll keep that in mind," she replied.

"Everything always works out when you do the right thing. I'll let you go. Call me when you get on the road."

"I will. Talk to you soon. Bye."

Ronnie reflected back on her life and all its irony. Her newly found daughter lived in Santa Elena—less than thirty miles from Luis. And the most ironic part was Kiara's father raised her for all those years. When Travis discovered Ronnie put the baby up for adoption, he stepped in without hesitating and took over.

In all the excitement of planning to leave Virginia, Ronnie overlooked making living arrangements for California. The realization hit that she would soon be homeless.

The first thing she did after hanging up from Luis was search the internet for homes or apartments to rent in Santa Elena. *Goodness! Who can afford to live out there? The amount of money to rent a small cottage or even a small one bedroom apartment is astronomical*, she thought. Not knowing much about the area or where she would be comfortable, she concluded her best bet was to rent a month-to-month efficiency apartment. It still cost an arm and a leg, but at least she would have a place to sleep.

She hurried over to the mortgage company and thought about how things turned out, once again believing that the Lord works in mysterious ways. Days after the previous offer on the house fell through, Joie put in an offer on Ronnie's house. The twins were thrilled to remain in their old neighborhood and even more so to live in Auntie Ronnie's old house. Even though their parent's breakup was hard on them, they were resilient kids. And like most kids, they would bounce back to normal in a matter of weeks.

With the money she received from Derek's insurance policy, Ronnie put away twenty grand in college funds for Trey and Maya. Another ten thousand was used to pay off her credit cards, and after selling her vacation and sick days back to the company, she had a good chunk of change to last until she could find a job in California.

An hour later she left the mortgage broker, free of her house, free of debt, and free of all that held her back. She hummed happy tunes as she made her way to her new downsized *Hyundai*. It was difficult giving up her *Infiniti*, but it felt oh so good to drive off in a fully paid off car.

After saying good-bye to Joie, Maya and Trey, there was no reason to stick around. The agony of living a life meant for someone else was over. The old Veronica Pierce was no more. And the new Ronnie vowed to quit being so accommodating, putting others needs before her own, and saying yes when she really meant no. No longer would she swallow her pride, her thoughts, her dreams... Those days were over.

The time had come to stop planning out every moment of her life and to start living more spontaneously. Today was a brand new day! A day meant for living the life she was meant to live. It was time to start living her life in the offbeat.

Part Two...
In The Offbeat

Chapter 18

Ronnie checked out of the Hampton Inn on the outskirts of the city, noting the coolness of the morning air, and inhaled Virginia's fragrant woodsy aroma for possibly the very last time. It was time to get on the road. The motel's parking lot was partially empty as its temporary residents were in various stages of leaving for their prospective journeys. Some by car, others by airplane.

She merged into the light traffic and headed towards Richmond to catch I-64 going west. The car was stocked with snacks, CDs, and water. Sirius XM radio would probably provide most of her entertainment, but every now and then she wanted to hear just what *she* wanted to hear.

Traffic picked up slightly outside of Richmond, it still wasn't bad though. The talking heads on the local radio kept her laughing in between playing old school music. Sarah Matthews on the Cool Breeze morning show kept everyone up on the latest gossip from Hollywood. And that C. Nelson Black was too funny.

On the western side of Petersburg, she broke free of traffic and was virtually alone on the road. Miles upon miles of monotonous open road invited her to take advantage of the quiet stillness of the countryside. She reflected on the events of the past month. So much had happened in such a short time. Most of it didn't seem real; it mirrored a bad movie on the *Lifetime* channel. Even *she* had trouble coming to terms with the drama that seemingly dropped out of the sky! Who would've thought little ole' boring Veronica Pierce could have such an exciting life? A life filled with adultery, betrayal, lies, deceit, and illegitimate children? She could only laugh about the irony of her life.

Twelve hours later she arrived in Bowling Green, Kentucky exhausted. She located the nearest Holiday Inn off the interstate and checked in.

"Do you know where I can find a good meal?" she asked the desk clerk.

The clerk, who was missing his bottom two front teeth, looked as if Ronnie had asked him to explain the theory of relativity. She watched him cross his arms, furrow his brow and stroke his hairy chin, for what seemed like an eternity before he spoke.

"Uhhh, let's see. Thar's a real good seafood place up yonder—believe it's called Henry's seafood. For barbeque, thar's Smokey Jones a few miles in the other direction. Course TGIF, Wendy's, KFC and the like are also around them same parts. Cain't go wrong either way. You bound to find sumthin' up in thar. Always got the hotel restaurant right hur'. Got some real good burgers 'n fries if you fancy that kind of food," he responded.

"Thank you, burgers and fries sound great. Think I'll have that. Don't really want to drive anywhere now that I've stopped. I'm kind of tired, you know."

"I reckon. Why don't you put your order in now? By time you get situated in your room, food should be ready to go."

"That's a great idea. I think I'm gonna do that. Thanks again," replied Ronnie, already amazed at how helpful people were.

"You welcome ma'am. You in room 413. Elevators down yonder on the left."

Ronnie took a quick shower before going back downstairs to the restaurant. She sat at the counter and ordered a beer to accompany her meal. One bite into the cheeseburger and she was in heaven.

"Mmm, that is good," Ronnie told the bartender, an older white woman with shortly cropped blonde hair.

"That there burger is made with 100% Angus beef. You won't find any of that pink slime in these burgers. No siree!" she declared.

"Good to know." She wrinkled her nose. "I even hate the way that sounds...pink slime."

"So, where you headed?"

"California by way of Oklahoma City. I'm going to see meet my daughter." Ronnie took a swig of beer to wash down the burger. Since releasing the secret about Kiara, she wanted everyone in the world to know she had a child.

"Going to meet her? Is that right?"

"Uh huh, first time in eighteen years."

"You must be excited," stated the bartender.

"Yes I am."

"Got six of 'em little rascals myself. Oldest is thirty, youngest nineteen. Can't seem to get rid of the youngest one," she chuckled. "Guess I spoiled her so much she don't wanna leave home."

"You have six children?" she sighed. "I always wanted a big family but it didn't turn out that way for me."

"How old are you if you don't mind me asking?"

"I don't mind. I just turned 41," replied Ronnie.

"Shoot! What you worried about then? You still got time to have a few. I was 43 when my last child was born."

Ronnie looked at the vivacious bartender. She displayed the energy of a much younger woman with a sunny disposition to match. "Looks like God blessed you, but I don't believe that's in my cards."

"Sugar, you have got to have faith. If it's God's will, you can have a dozen children. You already got one. That's a start."

"Yeah, but she's already grown. And it's kinda tough to have a baby with no man." *Another person talking about God's will. Hmmm....interesting.*

"You still got all your vital womanly plumbing, don't ya?" she whispered.

Ronnie blushed at her boldness, "Yeah, yeah I do. Why?"

"There you go. I'm just telling you what I know. It is still possible."

"Thanks, but I won't hold my breath." Ronnie finished her meal and left the bartender a generous tip.

"You take it easy now Sugar. Remember, until God says it's a no go, anything is possible."

After a good meal and a couple of beers, Ronnie returned to her room. She wanted to get another early start the next morning. So with the television set to a mindless movie, she quickly fell asleep. The next thing she knew, it was time to get up and get back on the road.

Chapter 19

It was early evening—twilight, by the time she finally arrived in Oklahoma City. She checked into a local hotel. She was tired, yet restless and couldn't sit still. The anticipation of seeing her mother was overwhelming. The house was only a fifteen minute drive into town. *Why wait until tomorrow? What would it hurt to do a quick drive-by? I'll take a quick check of the house and the neighborhood and be out of there in no time.*

The tree-lined streets of her childhood home were slightly disconcerting. Not much changed. The houses were older, showing their years, much like its inhabitants. Both required a few nips and tucks here and there to hold it all together.

Ronnie almost drove right past her mother's house. She didn't recognize it because the last time she was home was over eighteen years ago. The house had since been painted a pale shade of grey with the door a deep shade of crimson red to accent the grey siding. The garden filled with brightly colored flowers, made the house stand out from the rest, giving it great curb appeal. The front porch, where she and her father used to sit and tell stories, still contained the lime green metal porch swing built for two.

Ronnie eased the car into an open parking space a few houses down. While she sat in the car, she reminisced about the little girl who grew up in a home filled with love and affection. The family of three was happy and needed nothing more than love to keep them that way.

The front door opened. Ronnie watched an older woman step outside holding a beverage in one hand, a lit cigarette and a magazine in the other. The lady was thin with a slight pot belly. A scarf, that had seen much better days, kept whatever she was hiding on her head out of public sight. She was dressed in a snap-up house dress and wore bright white sneakers on her feet. She sat on the rocker, placing her glass on the side table. Ronnie gasped when she realized the woman was her mother.

The neighbor across the street yelled out, "Hey Dianna, you got any sugar I can borrow? I'm baking a pound cake for church tomorrow. I thought I had enough, but my grandkids must've used the last making kool-aid."

"Yeah, c'mon over. I'll put you some in a baggie."

"I got food on the stove, so I'll send little James over for it. Thank you!"

"That's fine. Hey, put me a slice on the side after you cut it. Your pound cake is delicious with my morning coffee."

"Girl, you know I always saves you a piece. My grandson will be right over for the sugar. See you tomorrow."

"Okay, see you tomorrow," Dianna replied.

As part of the neighborhood watch group, Dianna was always on the lookout for strangers in the neighborhood—people who didn't belong. She studied the person sitting motionless in the unfamiliar car with out of state tags parked on the street. She dropped her cigarette into the flowers, continuing to look. Ronnie remained in her car unable to move. Their eyes locked and for a split second, Ronnie felt like pulling off and never looking back.

Her mother carefully descended the uneven concrete stairs and stood on the crumbling sidewalk. She yelled out towards the parked car, "Who is that in that car?"

On no, I didn't mean for her to see me! Ronnie opened the car door slowly and stepped out. This is not how she pictured her reunion. She kicked herself for stopping and catching her mother off guard. "Hey Mama, it's me. Ronnie."

"Veronica? Is that my daughter? It is you! Well, don't just stand there! Come on over here and give your mother a hug!"

Retreating into the shell of her former childhood identity, she dutifully approached the woman she held in contempt for almost two decades. They stared at one another. The years had not been kind to sixty-eight year old Dianna Pierce. She looked every bit her age and more.

"Hi Mama."

"Oh my God! You finally came home. Finally came to see your old mother. I'm so happy to see you." She embraced her only child and lovingly stroked her hair. Tears of joy flowed from her eyes.

"Mama, how you been. You look good." Ronnie was taken aback when she realized her mother was actually crying.

"Oh, you know. Just trying to make it. You got a minute to come inside?" Dianna couldn't believe it was true. Her baby had finally come home.

"Yeah, yeah, Mama. I got some time."

"Oo wee! Veronica you look great! All grown up and pretty... And look at that beautiful figure! You sho 'nuff got your mother's genes."

Ronnie followed her mother into the small living room. She looked around the room that time had all but forgotten. The sofa she spent so many evenings sitting next to her parents watching TV was the same. Old pictures of family members sat in the same place on the same shelves. An old console stereo system sat against the wall topped with a *Bose* surround sound system—the kind they advertised on the back of *Parade* magazine.

"You want a cup of coffee? You do drink coffee, don't you? I got something stronger if you want it." She pulled out an old dusty bottle of brandy from the bottom shelf of the stereo cabinet and wiped the bottle clean with her housedress.

"No, Mama, I'm fine. Sit down. Relax. It's just me." Ronnie patted the seat next to her on the old couch.

"You're right. I'm treating my own daughter like company. Guess it's been so many years since I've seen you, you feel like company." She snickered.

"It has been quite a few years, hasn't it? How you been doing Mama?"

"Oh, I can't complain. Got old folks aches and pains mostly. But still holding on to my mind and my heart's still strong." She self-consciously tucked her hair under the ratty scarf.

"You look good. You still working in that old flower shop?"

"No, they closed that shop down years ago. Gave me a nice little pension though. With that and the money left over from your Daddy's life insurance, I've managed to get by. I also got a little bit from Social Security coming in too."

"That's good. Real good."

"So how have you been? Tell me about yourself. What brings you out this way? Fill me in on what I've missed. You married? Got any children? Last I heard you were living in Virginia somewhere."

"Actually, I'm between jobs at the moment. No husband; we were divorced a few years back. I just went to his funeral last week before I got on the road. I'm on my way to California and just wanted to stop by for a visit. It's been way too many years since I've last seen you."

"You're right about that. Aw, baby. I'm so sorry to hear about your ex-husband. Never even got a chance to meet him. Damn shame… What was his name? How long were y'all together?"

"His name was Derek Jordan and we were together almost twelve years."

161

"That's too bad. And y'all never had any babies? I remember you used to always talk about how many kids you were going to have. Used to line your baby dolls up and play Mommy. Me and your daddy used to get a kick out of watching you play."

"I was just a kid then. I had the same dreams of all little girls." Ronnie wasn't yet prepared to share the news with her mother about finding her daughter.

"You know, I never meant for so many years to go by without us speaking. Vernon would've never approved of us behaving like this."

"You're right. Mama, I'm sorry. I was angry with you for so long. I blamed you for ruining my life when it wasn't your fault."

"Uh, well we all have our shortcomings. I don't hold it against you. You did what you had to do."

Ronnie used every bit of constraint she could muster to hold her tongue. Either her mother didn't know what she was talking about or she took no responsibility for her role in Ronnie giving up her child.

"It's getting late. How about I come back tomorrow morning? We can catch up then. Maybe go out to brunch or something?" She stood and headed towards the door. She needed fresh air.

"That sounds really nice. You can pick me up for church at 9:30. We'll go eat afterwards."

"Church? I haven't been to church in years... Not since I was married."

"Maybe that's your problem, so be here at 9:30. It's still the same church. Pastor Grant will be happy to see you again."

"I'll be back first thing in the morning."

"Where you staying anyway?"

"In a hotel around the corner."

"Well, when you come back tomorrow bring your things. You're going to stay here with your family. In your home."

"Yes ma'am. See you in the morning. Bye Mama."

"Bye baby. See you tomorrow. And drive carefully!"

When Ronnie made the decision to visit her mother, she vowed to give her the benefit of the doubt. The hurt feelings, disappointment, and anger she held close to her heart for her mother slowly began to dissipate. Both women were stubborn and held on to grudges that should've been let go, a long time ago. Nevertheless, Ronnie was her mother's daughter and the apple didn't fall far from the tree.

This reunion couldn't have been easy for her mother either, especially with her showing up out of the blue. From what she remembered about Dianna Pierce, she would've gone all out when expecting company. Got her hair and nails done and be dressed to kill.

Still she was happy to finally reconnect with her mother, much like she intended to connect with Kiara.

Ronnie realized how good it felt being back in Oklahoma City. She looked up in the big sky and smiled. When she lived there as a teenager, she hated it and couldn't wait to leave. Thought the people were country, backwards, and much too conservative for her tastes. However, having lived on the east coast for the past couple of decades, she welcomed the slower paced life and friendly people without the big city attitude. She developed an appreciation for the small town atmosphere and sense of community larger cities sorely lacked.

* * *

The next morning, Ronnie showed up right on time to take her mother to church. When she saw Mrs. Dianna Pierce open that door, her mouth flew open in surprise. She looked years younger. Now this was the woman she knew. Her mother looked positively radiant, as if a transformation had taken place overnight. Her shoulder length hair framed her face in soft, bouncy curls. She wore a tailored pink suit and vibrant green pumps. Her expertly applied makeup was impeccable and her Sunday best outfit was topped off by a lime-green hat.

"Mama, you look wonderful," she told her. Ronnie didn't pack any special dresses, so she wore a casual blue jean pants suit. Next to her mother, she looked frumpy.

"Thank you daughter. You look good, too. You ready?"

"Yes ma'am. Let's go."

They sat near the front of the sanctuary, one row behind the deacons. Her mother said she wanted everyone to see her daughter sitting in church with her. After going through the announcements, the roll call of sick and shut-ins, and another fifteen minutes of the choir singing inspirational hymns, the visitors were asked to stand.

Dianna stood and pulled Ronnie to her feet. "Everybody, this is my daughter, Veronica Pierce. She is here visiting and I feel so blessed she has finally come home," her mother loudly announced to the congregation.

163

"Welcome back, sister Veronica," replied the woman making announcements. "Church, you know what we do."

The church congregation trailed by to welcome her home as the music ministry played in the background. Ronnie felt the love. She really did.

Pastor Grant took his place behind the podium, propped a pair of glasses on his nose, and opened his Bible. "Today's message is about God's will. When you live your life doing God's will, your life will be changed forever. Try walking in faithfulness, truth, and love. If you are stuck and your life isn't going the way you planned, it is time to do something different. Read your Bible for a start. You may have to give some stuff up, might even have to move to another city, away from the things that are keeping you stuck. We all have free will. God *gave* all us free will. But have you tried doing His will? Stop doing what you do because it *feels* good. Doing only what *you* think is best. I've come to tell you, it ain't always about *you*. It's about Jesus! Halleluiah! Take a moment to Bless God and others. See what He can do in your life. Can I get an Amen?!"

A chorus of "Amen!", "Preach Pastor!" and "Say it!" echoed throughout the congregation.

Pastor Grant delivered an inspirational sermon that morning. The Holy Spirit was in that room touching everyone with His presence. Ronnie felt moved to tears. Her spirit had been neglected for so long, she forgot how good Joy could feel. She hugged her mother and silently thanked the Lord for bringing her to this place.

"Pastor, that was an unforgettable message you delivered this morning. It really touched my soul," Ronnie said.

"Well, well, well…. If it isn't little Veronica Pierce all grown up. It is truly a blessing to have you here with us today. Your mother is so proud of you."

Ronnie looked over at her mother who appeared embarrassed.

"My mother's been keeping you informed about me? That *is* very kind of her."

"Yes, Sister Pierce tells us you're out there in Virginia working at a big time sports company. I just wished you'd make it home more often because she really misses you," replied Pastor Grant.

"I've missed her too. Take care Pastor and thanks again for delivering such a powerful Word today."

"How long you going to be in town?" asked Pastor Grant.

"Probably a couple of days. I'm actually on my way to California."

"Very good. You two ladies have a good time together and try to hold on to the Word you received today."

"I will. Bye now."

Dianna didn't have much to say. She seemed embarrassed to have Ronnie know she was proud of her. They walked back to the car.

"That was a really good service. Thanks for inviting me. Pastor Grant still has it!"

"Yes it was."

"Mama, you've been keeping tabs on me? On my life? You're proud of me? Really?"

"Of course, you're my daughter. Why wouldn't I be proud of you?"

"But how? How do you know what's going on in my life? I don't understand."

"A long time ago I called your office and asked for you. I googled your name on the internet. Anyways, you weren't there so I left a message with this gentleman named Sam. I told him I was your mother and explained that we hadn't spoken in years. He's kept me up to date on you ever since."

"Sam? Old assed Sam from work? You've been talking to him without me knowing it?" Ronnie felt her temper flare.

"When you didn't return my calls, I thought you was still angry and didn't want anything to do with me. I got to talking to Sam and explained our situation. Sam seemed nice enough and agreed to keep in touch with me. He only told me the important stuff about you and your job because he didn't know much about your personal life. What did you expect me to do? You wouldn't talk to me."

Ronnie recalled receiving those messages. She was still married to Derek at the time. She rationalized not returning her mother's calls because then she'd have to explain to Derek why they weren't speaking in the first place. Derek didn't know Ronnie had a child. It was a secret only she and her mother shared. After awhile, it was easier to pretend her mother treated her badly and she didn't want anything to do with her. Everyone bought the story. After awhile, even she believed it.

"Mama, after you convinced me to break up with Travis and give up my baby, I was so angry at you. It took a lot of prayer and learning forgiveness to overcome my anger. It's hard to believe you talked to Sam about me. He never let on. Not even once."

"Listen, I'm sorry for what I put you through. But I did what me and your father believed was best."

"I understand you guys were from a different era and I get that you held different beliefs. But I gotta tell you, to this day I regret giving up my only child. And it was all you, not Daddy. He was gone before I found out I was pregnant. But you know what Mama?"

"What's that?" Dianna hated hurting her child, but despite it all she held on to the belief she'd done the right thing.

"Everything is going to be okay. Just like the pastor preached today, when you do God's will, it all works out in the end."

"Amen daughter!" she laughed.

"Now, where do you want to eat?"

Dianna recommended a local restaurant where the food was supposedly good, portions were generous, and the prices very reasonable. They waited about 20 minutes for a booth and spent the time catching up on each other's lives.

Ronnie watched the waitresses bring out plate after heaping plate of food to their customers. Pancakes, omelets, waffles, steak and eggs... You name it, it was being served. Ronnie ordered eggs, bacon and toast. Her mother wanted steak and eggs with pancakes on the side. The waitress brought out a steaming carafe of hot coffee and set it on the table. Their food soon followed.

Midway through their meal, a young couple with two small children was seated opposite them. Looked like a nice enough family. A biracial family.

"Would you look at that?" sneered her mother.

"What? What's wrong Mama?" Ronnie looked in the direction of her mother's disdain.

"Umph, umph, umph! Would you look at that? Got the nerve to come out in public with those *mulatto* kids... Damn shame..." She shook her head in disapproval.

Ronnie dropped her fork on the table. She couldn't believe her ears. "Mama, you mean to tell me you still have a problem with mixed race couples and biracial children? It's 2012!"

"I don't care what year it is! It ain't right. How could she be with that *white* man? Lay with him? Have his babies?" She stopped eating as if she lost her appetite and starting sucking at her teeth.

"You have got to be kidding me... We just left church! We both received a Word overflowing with love."

"I don't care what year it is. Or what I just heard. It ain't right. Blacks supposed to be with blacks. Whites supposed to be with whites. Supposed to stick with your own kind. That's what's wrong with this world today."

Customers, black and white alike, within earshot stopped to listen. Many were mortified at the hateful comments spewing from the tastefully dressed older woman. Ronnie wanted to crawl under the table and hide from embarrassment.

"Mother, you haven't changed at all. How could Daddy have married someone filled with so much hate when he loved everybody?"

"Well, your daddy ain't here no more. Is he? Guess you think he was always right, huh? Them white folks didn't do me no favors. Didn't never show my family any love. I'm the way I am because that's what I know. And I ain't gonna change for nobody! I lost my appetite. Let's go!"

Dianna marched out of the restaurant, passing by dozens of whispering strangers with her head held high, convinced she was right. Anybody who had a problem with her could kiss her ass.

Ronnie apologized to the customers for her mother's outburst. She left a generous tip on the table and ran to catch up to her mother.

"Mama, listen to me. What you said in there was absolutely awful! How can you still feel that way? See, that's why I broke contact with you all those years ago. You made me give up my child because she was half white. She was your granddaughter. Your only grandchild! Quite possibly the only one you will ever have. You didn't even bother to try and love her. Simply because of who her father was."

"Veronica, take me home. I'm tired and I don't need your lectures. You have no idea how hard my life has been. You don't know nothin' about racial prejudice. About being called a *nigger* and having adults spit on you. Don't know what it feels like to have white children throw their trash at you. What they did to my big brother. What they did to me. I hate white folks and always will."

"But Mama, what happened to your family was almost sixty years ago… Things have changed. People have changed. Barack Hussein Obama is President of the United States. And it was white people who helped put him there. Yes, I agree that those people were some sons-of-bitches who treated you and your family like that. And if you believe in the Bible as much as you say you do, you know they will get what's coming to them. For all you know, they already have."

"Be careful how you speak to me child. I am still your mother whether you care to acknowledge it or not."

Ronnie slowly exhaled under her breath and held her tongue. Why did she even try? Her mother would never change. Her prejudices and hatred were ingrained into her soul from decades before. She decided to drop her mother off and get back on the road. There was no use in trying to mend their relationship. It was too late and she was beyond tired.

"All right, you're home." She parked in front of her mother's house with the engine running.

"You're not coming in?" asked Dianna.

"No, I decided to leave early. May as well while traffic is light."

"I thought you were going to spend a couple of days with me."

"Um, well, that was my plan until your outburst in the restaurant."

"What does that have to do with you staying? I don't understand." Dianna was genuinely hurt.

There was no sense in not telling the truth. Her mother deserved to know why she changed her plans and decided to leave early. "Mama, I'm on my way to California to meet my daughter. She found me eighteen years later. After all this time my daughter came looking for me. Her name is Kiara Indigo Bradford and she's about to graduate from high school in a couple of weeks."

"W-w-what? Your daughter? My God!" She slouched down in the seat.

"Mama? Mama, are you alright? Mama?" Alarmed by her mother's apparent condition, Ronnie turned off the car, got out, and went over to the passenger's side. She opened the door and helped her mother from the car.

"Here I thought you was making a special trip to visit your mother. The mother you haven't seen in *eighteen years*. I thought I had gotten *my* daughter back." She shook her head indignantly from side to side.

"I could be in your life if you want me to, but you'll have to accept my daughter—your granddaughter, as well. I plan on building a relationship with her, if she'll have me."

Ronnie helped her mother up the crumbling concrete stairs. She held her mother steady as she put the key in the front door. Observing her trembling hands, she became more concerned about her health.

"I don't have no granddaughter! And if you ever bring that mulatto bastard into my house, may God strike you and her down! Now, you are welcome to stay here as long as you want, but no more talk about that *foolishness!*"

Ronnie looked at the old lady standing there trembling with bitterness. Just like eighteen years ago, she had drawn the line and wanted her to choose between mother and daughter. In that moment she wished her father was there. He would fix everything.

"I love you, Mama. Always have. But I can't do what you're asking me. Not this time. My daughter has found me and she wants me in her life. I will not choose between you and her. It's not fair and I can't believe you would deny your grandchild again."

"You know how I feel. Like I said, you're welcome to stay. I want you to stay, but it's up to you."

"Well then, I have to go."

"I don't understand you child, but I accept your decision. Love you too, sweetie. You drive safely."

The car was parked near the sidewalk, fully gassed up and ready to go. Ronnie wiped the tears from her face with the back of her hand. With her vision clouded, she didn't notice the missing piece of concrete on the bottom step. Her foot slipped. She reached for the railing. It was loose. She felt herself falling backwards and put her arm out to block her fall. She heard the snap before she felt it.

Dianna turned around just in time to see Ronnie fall. She quickly rushed out the door and down the steps to her daughter's side. "Veronica? Baby, are you okay?! Lord have mercy! Somebody help me! Call an ambulance!" she screamed to her neighbor who was outside watering her flowers.

The fall knocked Ronnie unconscious. When she came to, her mother was peering over the shoulder of a paramedic holding smelling salts under her nose. Her arm hurt badly—so did her head. She realized she was on a gurney looking up towards the sky. For a brief moment, she saw the bluest sky she'd seen in a very long time. She closed her eyes. The intensity of the pain caused her to pass out again. The next time she awoke, she was in the emergency room of the local hospital.

"Sweetie, how you feeling?" asked Ronnie's mother.

"My arm really hurts. Guess I should've watched my step. Huh?"

"Baby, I'm so sorry, I have been meaning to get those steps fixed for the longest. It was only a matter of time before somebody tripped and fell," she sighed loudly.

Ronnie looked at the cast on her left forearm extending past her elbow. "Guess the Lord intended for me to stick around a little longer."

Her mother laughed, "I suppose he did."

Dianna's friend drove them home. Ronnie was drugged up and feeling no pain. Her mother put her in her old room, currently being used as a guest room. Her friend retrieved Ronnie's luggage from her car, tightened the loose railing, and promised to reset the concrete steps next week.

"Hey Mama? Did you really mean it when you said you don't want to meet your granddaughter?" asked Ronnie, sitting on the sofa in a drug induced stupor.

"Veronica, don't start that mess again. Let's just enjoy this evening. Okay?"

"I'll let it go for now, but this is something we're going to have to resolve. One way or the other. You feel me?" she slurred.

"Feel you? What in heaven's name are you talking about? Girl, say what you mean."

"You understand? You get it? You know what I mean?"

"Yes, I understand. Please speak English to me. I don't understand that street slang. Anyhow, for now you need to get your rest. Give that arm time to heal. How long did the doctor say it'd take?"

"Thankfully I didn't break anything. Just popped my elbow out of the socket and got a tiny hairline fracture on my forearm. I should be able to get this cast off in a couple of weeks."

"So what you gonna do 'til then? How you gonna drive yourself to California with a cast on your arm?"

Ronnie hadn't considered that one very important fact. It was true. She couldn't drive cross-country with one arm in a cast.

Her mother had redecorated her bedroom and transformed it into a very nice guestroom. All that remained to remind Ronnie it was her old room was her little girl scribblings on the closet wall.

The full-sized bed was slightly uncomfortable. Yet still, she felt relaxed because she was home. As messed up as her relationship was with her mother, she was still home. Ronnie snuggled under the warm comforter and let the pain medication transport her to the dreams she had as a child.

When she awoke the next morning, she wrapped her body in one of her mother's extra bathrobes. She made it to the kitchen and poured a cup of coffee, spilling half of it on the countertop. Having one arm in a cast was more difficult than she imagined.

It was already after 9. She hadn't realized she slept for so long. *I must have been really worn out from yesterday.* Ronnie went outside and sat in the swing on the front porch, sipping her sugary sweet coffee. It was after 7 o'clock California time. She missed Luis's voice and needed to hear it; wanted to tell him what happened.

She dialed his cell and he answered on the first ring.

"*Hola,*" he answered.

"Good morning Luis."

"Ronnie? What a nice surprise! Where are you?"

"I made it as far as my mother's house in Oklahoma City. I was going to leave yesterday, but I had a little accident."

"What happened? Are you all right?" he asked.

"I lost my balance, tripped and fell down a few stairs. I have a hairline fracture on my forearm. It's in a cast."

"Are you in much pain?"

"Not as bad as it was—especially with the pain meds I'm on. It's more of a nuisance than anything else. Sure makes driving difficult though."

"How long do you have to wear the cast?"

"A couple of weeks." She paused. "Luis, that's one of the reasons I'm calling. Remember when you said you would fly down and ride out with me to California?"

"Yes, I remember." He wasn't going to make this easy.

"Well, since I can't drive, I was wondering if you can fly out and drive me back."

He laughed, "Oh, I see. Since you can't drive, *now* you want my help."

"Ha ha, very funny... Once you get to know me better, you'll find out that asking people for favors is not my strong suit."

"Ronnie, asking for help isn't showing weakness. It's called being human. Of course I'll come out. How soon do you need me?"

Now! "As soon as you can. In a couple of days maybe? That'll give me some time to catch up with my mother. I think somebody's trying to tell me something, it's probably why I tripped in the first place."

"Huh?"

"Nothing. Just thinking aloud."

"How about Thursday? I can make arrangements to take some time off. I think they can run the business without me for a few days."

"That's perfect."

"I'll let you know when I'll be there. Sound good?"

"Sounds great! Thank you, Luis. We'll catch up later."

"Ronnie?"

"What's up?"

"I hope you and your mother work out whatever rift you have between you. Take care now."

Ronnie glanced down the street at her old familiar neighborhood. So much had changed, yet so much remained the same. Houses, once new when they first moved in, were now showing their age. Her childhood friends were long gone and only returned for the occasional visit. The last time she was home, her father was still alive. She expected him to come out the door at any moment and sit down beside her. Engage her in stimulating conversations about friends, school, or even the state of the economy. He was not only her father, but her mentor as well. She missed him.

"Good morning, Veronica. How you doing?" shouted the neighbor from across the street.

"Good morning, Mrs. Smith! I'm doing okay... Well, except for my arm."

"I'm glad you're all right; you really scared us for a minute," she said. "Chile your momma talks about you all the time. My daughter did this, my daughter did that. Dianna's so proud of you. Yes, she is! We was starting to wonder if you were ever going to come back home."

Listening to Mrs. Smith talk about her mother's prideful boasting, Ronnie felt ashamed for staying away so long.

"Without Vernon, you're all the family she has."

"It's good to be home." She stated to her neighbor. *Mrs. Smith must be pushing 75 by now and still going strong.*

"Well, I've got to get my day started. I'll see you before you leave." Carla Smith waved and went back inside.

Dianna called out from the kitchen, "Ronnie? You hungry? Want some breakfast?"

"Yes ma'am. I'm starving." Ronnie realized her mother was trying her best to make amends.

"All right, I'll let you know when the food's ready."

"Thanks Mama."

* * *

Ronnie thought back to the last time she was home, before she was pregnant. It was almost twenty years ago, the winter break of her sophomore year. Like most sophomores, she was homesick for her family. Upon hearing of their child's melancholy, Vernon and Dianna brought her back home for the holidays. She was the first in the family to go college. Various relatives, aunts, uncles, and cousins showed up to express their love and give her encouragement to hang in there. Her family was very proud of her. Well, most were anyway.

Ronnie's Uncle Ray, Dianna's older brother, spent most of his adult life in and out of prison. Since Ray was old enough to grow hair on his chest, he was behind bars. The family referred to him as the black sheep of the family. And he lived up to that reputation every chance he got.

It just so happened Uncle Ray, who was a dead ringer for muscle-bound Ving Rhames, was released from prison the same week Ronnie was home visiting. He heard about the family get together and invited himself over. Problem was, years earlier he and Dianna had a major falling out. She was the one who called the police and got him locked up. He had stolen her diamond engagement ring right out of her home. Because of Dianna pressing charges, he was sentenced to seven years in the state penitentiary for theft.

Ray didn't even try to pretend he didn't do it. He said she owed him because of everything he'd done for her as a little girl.

He protected his sister from the white boys who used to chase her home when they were kids in Georgia, and fought off the bullies who threatened to beat her up. Ray was the one who shielded Dianna from name calling and threats. At the time, he felt it was his duty to protect his little sister.

Mostly he had a penchant for trouble. As a child, Ray got into so many fights his parents wanted to send him up north to live with relatives to keep him out of trouble. Turns out they should have because when he was only sixteen, a group of white men caught him walking alone one night, coming from a friend's house. One of the men recognized Ray and said he beat up his little brother. His "little" brother was fourteen years old. That kid, along with a group of other older boys, chased Dianna home when she was only five. She was terrified. Ray went out looking for the boys who hurt his sister. He found two.

Those men damn near beat Ray to death. They tossed him in the back of their pickup truck, and drove deep into the backwoods of the Georgia forest. Ray swore on his life had it not been for an elderly black man out walking his dog that night, he would've surely been killed. By the Grace of God, the old man happened upon the group. When he realized what was going on, he fired his shotgun into the air and told them white boys to "Git!" He carried Ray home, called his parents and told them what happened.

After that night, something in Ray changed. Those men had planted a seed of hatred in his soul which grew until it eventually took over his life. As if a beast were released from within.

He dropped out of school and straight into a life of crime. His parents always said that night ended their son's innocence. To try to get him back on the right path, they prayed for him, dragged him to church; even put him in the men's choir. There was nothing they could do that seemed to make a difference. Ray seemed destined to live a life of crime, going in and out of prison. Over and over again.

After she moved away, Dianna tried to help her older brother by offering him a place to live after his last prison stint. He was family and family watched out for each other. She felt she owed it to him. She felt guilty because she believed had it not been for Ray protecting her when they were kids, his life would've turned out differently. Vernon was opposed to Ray living with them from the very beginning. He said Ray would bring the wrong element to his home and be a bad influence on his daughter, but Dianna won out and they moved him into the basement apartment.

Things were bad from the start. Ray slept all day and was up all night. He made a mess and didn't clean up after himself. He made no financial contributions to the home. After awhile, just as Vernon had predicted, old-head thugs started hanging out in front of the house drinking and smoking. The straw that broke the camel's back arrived when Dianna's diamond rings came up missing. Immediately suspecting her brother, she called the police. They came to the house and arrested him.

Five years later, he was released from prison early for good behavior. Paroled to go back into society and make good. Not having anywhere else to go, naturally he showed up at his sister's house. It was bad enough Ray showing up unannounced during a family dinner, asking for a place to stay, but he had the audacity to bring an old broken down whore with him. He called the woman his "date".

Dianna was mortified and told him to get out of the house and to take his whore with him. Said she had enough of his mess and wasn't going to help him anymore.

Ronnie recalled their conversation as if it were yesterday...

"You supposed to be my sister. My family. If I can't come to you, who can I turn to? I always looked out for you didn't I?"

"Ray, I am sick and tired of trying to help you. We tried our best all these years to be good to you. Provided you a home, a roof over your head. We even gave you money when you didn't have any. And what did you end up doing? You stole from me!"shouted Dianna.

"I'm sorry Sis, I needed the cash. Just help me out this one last time. Please!"Ray pleaded.

"I have to say no. I don't have no more to give. Why don't you go home to that woman you were living with? What about your grown kids?"

"I ain't got no home. Don't you see? That woman and those kids don't want nothing to do with me. You're all the family I have left. Vernon, speak some sense into your wife," he pleaded to Vernon.

"Ray, my wife and I have already discussed this. We've helped you out time and time again. Nothing seems to make a difference. Now take this money, it's all I have. You're fifty two years old man! Don't you think it's time you got your life together?"

Ray looked at the money Vernon gave him. "That's it?! A measly hundred dollars?! What am I supposed to do with this?! Y'all supposed to be rich. Always bragging on your daughter and how you paying for her to go to some fancy college! And this is all you can give me?! Man, keep your damn money!" Ray balled up the five twenties and threw them at Vernon's face.

The entire room filled with relatives quietly watched the drama unfolding in front of their eyes. Why did it always have to be one family member who ruined everything? Ronnie watched her father's reaction to Ray. She'd never seen him that angry before.

Her mother tried to intervene. She picked the money from the floor. "Ray, take this money and leave. We don't want no trouble. We're just trying to have a nice evening. You're welcome to stay and have dinner with us if you act right."

Ray then turned his rage to Ronnie, "You think you something, don't you? Well, you ain't! You ain't no better than the rest of us. Going off to college and thinkin' you all that! Let me tell you something little girl, that education ain't worth a damn if you treat your family like shit! Your momma and daddy always going on about how proud they are of their precious Veronica. Ain't never tried helping my kids. Don't you think they want to go to school too? You ain't the only one who deserves an education."

Ronnie narrowed her eyes and responded in kind, "Uncle Ray, I respect you and I love you, but you have no right to speak to me or my parents that way. You don't know the sacrifices they've made to provide me a better life. I've seen them trying to help you over and over again. You've never done nothing except feel sorry for yourself. And if your kids wanted to go to college, they can. So don't go trying to make everything look like it's my parent's fault. It's not!"

"You ain't half as smart as you think you are little girl." Ray went to the table and picked up a piece of chicken. He took a bite and licked his fingers.

"Get out of my house!" shouted Vernon.

"Man, I'm leaving. But only because I want to. I can see when I'm not wanted." He looked at Dianna and continued. "Sis, you know I love you and I always will, but this is it. Not gonna bother you anymore. Y'all and your bourgeois asses. C'mon baby, let's go."

Uncle Ray walked out the house that winter's day, his hand resting on the scantily covered rear end of his whore and no one has heard from him since. His children used to come around occasionally with stories of their father's latest antics, but he refused to speak to any of his other relatives.

Later in life as an adult, Ronnie came to understand her Uncle Ray was a victim. In trying to protect his little sister, those men stole his innocence and betrayed his trust in fellow human beings. He was treated worse than an animal and unfortunately that's how he soon came to see himself. The tiniest slight, no matter how minor became an opportunity to fight. Ray vowed to never let anyone mistreat or abuse him ever again. He'd fight to the death before he would let that happen. Consequently, fighting landed him in jail too many times to count. Having a record made it difficult to find a job, not having a job caused him to steal, and stealing landed him back in jail. Uncle Ray was caught in a vicious cycle with no way out.

* * *

Her mother's high-pitched voice abruptly ended her trip down memory lane. "Veronica, food's ready! Come eat before it gets cold!"

"Okay Mama. Be right there."

Ronnie took a deep breath and exhaled. It was going to be a beautiful day. She walked into the kitchen filled with the delicious aroma of breakfast ham, scrambled eggs, and homemade buttermilk biscuits. A big bowl filled with fresh fruit salad, topped off with yogurt and bits of granola completed the spread. Both women sat at the table, blessed their food and dug in.

"How ya feeling this morning? Is the pain any better?"

"It's tolerable. Hey, what do you want to do today?"

"Um, well, usually I work out in the garden or on my crossword puzzles. I don't know…you got any ideas?"

"Yeah, I do. I heard they built up Bricktown and brought in a lot of new stores and restaurants. I'd love to see what they've done to revitalize downtown OKC."

"Uh huh, they made it real nice down there. Even got a little riverwalk. Not as big as the one in San Antonio, but it's still real, real nice. I think that's a great idea. I'm gonna ask Carla Smith from across the street if she wants to go with us. Maybe she can drive."

"Sounds good. Uh, Mama, I know you don't want to do this, but we need to talk about Kiara. About my daughter and bringing her into my life. We need to clear the air and get this mess straightened out between us."

"Veronica, I told you I don't want to get into that. Please don't ruin today with that talk…" She shook her head. "I'm a get dressed and go see Carla Smith. Put the food away, please. I'll get the dishes later."

"Mama, we need to talk. I don't want to sweep this under the rug any longer. Please!"

Dianna acquiesced. "Lawd, have mercy! Why cain't you just leave it alone? Why you got to pull that child back into your life? Don't you know sometimes you have to leave well enough alone?"

"She's my child. My daughter—your granddaughter. *Our* flesh and blood. I turned my back on her once, and I'm not going to do it again. How can you be so cruel, Mama?"

"You think I'm being cruel? Let me tell you a story. Come to the living room. Maybe after you hear what I have to say, you'll understand why you'd be better off leaving that girl where she is. In your past."

Ronnie followed her mother into the living room and took a seat. Dianna retrieved an old photo album from the bottom drawer of the stereo cabinet and sitting next to her daughter, opened it up slowly, caressing each page.

"I loved your father with all my heart and soul. When we first got married, me and your daddy made plans to have lots and lots of children. We both loved kids so much. After the first year when I didn't get pregnant, I went to see the doctor. He told us I wouldn't ever be able to have kids because of the scarring to my insides."

"What scars? What are you talking about?"

"Let me finish. My insides was scarred up because I was pregnant before; I miscarried during my fourth month. They had to scrape my insides to get everything out. It hurt like hell." Her eyes misted over at the memories.

"You and Daddy lost your first baby, I'm so sorry."

"Wasn't your daddy's child. This happened before we were married, when I was only seventeen. Me and this boy thought we was in love. Got to fooling around every chance we could. We snuck around because our parents wouldn't have approved of us dating. Didn't nobody know about us except for my best girlfriend."

"What happened? Was he an older boy?" asked Ronnie.

"Uh uh, we was the same age. He was just a boy from school." She looked away embarrassed.

"What is it Mama? Women got pregnant all the time back then. Didn't you always tell me that? Isn't that why so many people got married at young ages?"

"Yeah that's true. Me and that boy talked about getting married after we graduated high school. Planned on leaving the state of Georgia to head up north or move to California where race didn't matter as much. Once everybody found out about us, all hell broke loose. He was a white boy and that's all that mattered back then. Them white folks found us sitting together in the park. We wasn't bothering nobody, just enjoying a summer's day. They beat both of us silly. That's how I lost the baby. After I miscarried, that boy acted like he didn't know me. He wouldn't even talk to me and treated me like I was the dirty *nigger* his friends called me. He didn't take up for me. Just pretended as if he hadn't heard anything. That's what hurt more than anything. After that, I couldn't stand to be around white folks. I believed they all had evil in their souls."

Ronnie watched the tears stream down her mother's face. She understood her mother's angst. Felt how raw her pain was still, as if it happened the day before.

"Mama, I am so sorry. That must have been awful. But look, you survived. Got through it. You met Daddy and he married you. It did get better, right?"

"After my miscarriage, none of the black boys wanted anything to do with me. As if I was tainted. But not Vernon, he was my knight in shining armor. He heard about what happened and came to visit me in the hospital. He told me he always had a crush on me." She laughed.

"Daddy was a good man even back then."

"He didn't care what those other boys said. It didn't bother him that I wasn't pure no more. Vernon defended my honor, yes he did. After I got out the hospital, he used to sit with me outside on my front porch. We would talk for hours. Then he started walking me home from school. Little by little, I started having feelings for him. Fell in love. We went together for two years before we got married."

"That's sweet. Sounds just like Daddy."

"Vernon was the best thing that ever happened to me. He proposed and I accepted. We started planning our life and the first thing we did was get out of Georgia. We moved up here to Oklahoma City and settled down. We tried having kids, but when I found out I couldn't have any, both our hearts were broken. Eventually we accepted the hand fate dealt us and became content with each other. When I found out I was pregnant... Child, it was like God Himself had smiled down upon us and blessed us with you! A beautiful baby girl! Yes sir, Vernon was so happy, he spoiled you rotten. You had him wrapped around your little finger, yes you did." Dianna rocked back and forth, holding onto that photo album, remembering the good times.

Ronnie wrapped her arm around her mother's shoulder and rested her head. They sat in that position for several minutes until Dianna pulled herself together.

"Look here Veronica; I want to show you something." She turned to a class photo. "See that's me and here's that boy I got pregnant by. I wanted to burn this picture, but Vernon said not to. It was part of my childhood. He didn't blame that boy for the way he acted. Said he was weak and followed the crowd. It wasn't his fault those people were like that—filled with such hatred. Vernon encouraged me to forgive that boy and his friends. I tried, I truly did, but I hated him after that."

"Mama, that boy kinda looks like Travis, my old boyfriend."

"Uh huh, yes he does. When I saw him that day we came to visit you, all those memories of hurt and betrayal flooded back. In my mind I knew it was a different person, but he looked so familiar. My heart turned to ice thinking about that bad time. I couldn't believe that you were with a white boy."

"I didn't know. How could I know? Travis wasn't like that boy who did that to you. He loved me and I loved him."

"Me and Vernon were talking about the irony of your situation on the way home. About you ending up with a white boy who reminded me of so much pain and misery. I was a mess and he was trying to comfort me when we hit that patch of ice. Before I knew what was going on, the car went into a spin and we slid off the road. When I came to…" She paused to gather strength.

Ronnie stroked her mother's arm, patiently letting the story come forth in its own time.

"When I came to I was in the back of an ambulance. I didn't know what happened. First thing I did was ask 'em about Vernon. Where's Vernon? I kept repeating over and over again. They didn't answer me. I got to the hospital and finally one of the nurses told me that he was gone. Never told you this before, but it's all my fault Vernon died that night."

"Mama, you can't blame yourself for what happened. It's not your fault. It was an accident." Ronnie held her mother tightly, feeling the sobs wrack her slender frame.

Dianna eventually regained her composure and sat back on the sofa with her eyes shut tight. She exhaled deeply, flaring her nostrils in the process.

"If it wasn't for that white boy, I wouldn't have been so upset and Vernon could've focused on the road better. See what happens when you mess around with them folks. They bring nothin' but pain and misery."

"What happened to Daddy was nobody's fault—not yours, not mine, and certainly not Travis'. First you must forgive yourself and then let God take care of those who did you wrong. You've got to let that hatred go, Mama."

"You remind me so much of Vernon. Always finding the good in people."

"Well, neither of you taught me to hate. In fact, if I remember correctly, you were always preaching that we should try *to love thy neighbor.*"

"Yeah, but none of your neighbors was white." She joked.

"That's so awful, but true!" Ronnie joined in her laughter.

"Well, so now you know all your mother's secrets. I ain't no better than you is Veronica. I just don't want you to get hurt. That's why I did what I did. I never meant to ruin your life."

"Speaking of forgiveness... I have something to show you." Ronnie opened her purse and pulled out an envelope.

"What you got there?"

Ronnie handed her mother a stack of pictures Lexi McCray had given her. The stack included photos of Kiara which chronicled her childhood from a baby to the present. Dianna studied the images and covered her mouth in surprise.

"She is absolutely beautiful. Look, she has your Daddy's smile. And the dimple in her right cheek is just like yours." Dianna's eyes lit up with excitement. "This is really my granddaughter?"

"Yes, that's your granddaughter. Her name is Kiara Indigo Bradford. Travis raised her from a baby."

"She has your middle name? You're telling me her *father* raised her? But how? You gave her up for adoption."

Ronnie relayed the story Lexi told her, explaining that Travis didn't want to put his daughter up for adoption.

"Ain't that something? That boy went and got his child to keep her from being adopted? He actually raised her? Without you? He must've been some kind of special man," she whispered.

"Yes Mama that is exactly what Travis did. Kiara hired a private investigator to locate me because she wants to meet *me*—her mother. We spoke a few times on the phone and she sounds like a very sweet, intelligent young lady. That's why I'm on my way to California."

Dianna started crying again. "Veronica, I have a granddaughter? Praise God! Not only did you bring my daughter home, but you found my grandbaby too. Thank you, Jesus!"

"So now you're happy? Just like that? One minute you're cursing us both to damnation and the next you're thanking Jesus? What gives Mama?" asked Ronnie. She looked at her mother like she had lost their mind.

"She looks just like you when you was a baby and I see some of Vernon in her too. Seeing the family resemblance and realizing she is a part of you; part of me and your father... All that talk about forgiveness is starting to make sense. I'm an old woman, but I can learn something new. I've kept those bitter feelings in my heart for so long, it's the only way I've known how to live. You came home to remind me what I missed by holding on to foolishness. It's time to let go of hate. Your daughter found you and wants to be part of your life, despite your giving her up. If she can forgive you for that, she must be one something special. How can I turn my back on her? My, oh my! Ain't that something? I got me a granddaughter."

"Yes ma'am, and I have a daughter. Mama, you don't know how much this means to me—your coming around. I had forgotten the importance of family. I missed you all those years because I was just as stubborn as you. I held on to bitterness and let it keep me away. I'm so happy we fixed this. Now let's go check out Bricktown." Ronnie helped her mother up and returned the photo album to its resting place.

Carla Smith's husband drove a tricked out, sky blue, 1976 Buick Electra 225 with customized stainless steel rims and all. Their oldest grandson took it upon himself to lovingly restore his grandfather's car, turning the rusted out shell into a classic beauty that turned heads wherever they went. Most times it simply sat in the garage, only being driven on special occasions; usually to church and back.

Carla Smith asked her husband, "Honey, can I borrow the car today? Dianna's daughter has finally come home and we want to show her the city."

Since the restoration of the car, Mr. Smith didn't want his wife to drive. He knew her eyesight was going bad and the last thing she needed to be doing was driving on city streets.

"I don't have anything to do today, so I'll be more than honored to chauffer three beautiful women around the city," he replied.

"Alright, but behave yourself. You know how you and Dianna always get into it about nothin'."

"If she don't start no stuff, won't be no stuff."

"I'm just warning you to behave for her daughter's sake."

"C'mon woman, let's go before the traffic picks up."

Mr. Smith carefully pulled the car unto the street and waited while his wife went to get the other two. The three women piled into the spacious car. Dianna and Ronnie took their places in the back. The interior was reupholstered in luxuriously soft, cream-colored leather. The sound system was upgraded to a *Bose* system, and tuned to a local country and western radio station. Quiet strains of Toby Keith played softly from the speakers.

"Honey, can you please turn that country music to something else? We don't want to hear that mess. How about the gospel station? They should be on by now."

He tuned in a different station to hear Whitney Houston's version of *I Will Always Love You.*

"Shame what happened to Whitney. That child sure could sang. The Lord took her from us too soon," stated Dianna.

Carla Smith added, "Yes Lord, that woman had an incredible voice. It was a shame she died, but even more of a shame how she messed up her voice taking them drugs. I try to tell these kids, but none of 'em wanna listen to me. They call me a crazy old woman. At least I'm still here. Humph!"

Mr. Smith changed the station to a gospel station and let that play for a couple of songs. Anything to keep the ladies quiet.

Dianna piped up, "We don't want to hear that either. Turn on the XM station—Watercolors. I really like that contemporary jazz music."

"We got XM radio?" Carla Smith asked her husband. She fiddled with the knobs. "Oh, there it is. Yeah, that's nice. Real nice."

"Hey Carla Smith? Veronica is on her way to California. I got myself a granddaughter who's about to graduate from high school. Veronica's on her way to see her," Dianna proudly exclaimed.

"You don't say? A granddaughter? Is that right? Dianna Pierce, you got all kinds of stories to update me on. First your daughter shows up unexpectedly, and then you tell me you got a granddaughter who live in California. How come I ain't never heard about this child?" she asked.

"Girl, it's a long story. I'll tell you some other time. Let's just enjoy Veronica while she's home to visit. Okay?" Dianna didn't want to get into specifics.

"How you gonna get to California? You flying out?" asked Mr. Smith, speaking for the first time since they got in the car.

"Yeah Ronnie, how *are* you gonna drive with your arm in that cast?" asked Dianna.

"Uh, well, I have a friend who is going to fly out and do the driving. His name is Luis. Luis Duarte. I met him a while back. He'll be here in a couple of days," she replied.

"Is that right? So he gonna come all the way out here and drive you to California? Where does he live? How long you known this man?" Mr. Smith was very protective of Veronica, especially since Vernon had passed.

"He's from California and lives in a town not too far from my daughter, Kiara. I've known him long enough to know he is a good man." Embarrassed to admit to these old people she really didn't know Luis very well.

Carla Smith piped in, "Veronica, how old did you say your daughter is?" She mentally calculated dates, recalling events from years gone by.

"I didn't, but she just turned eighteen a few weeks ago," replied Ronnie.

"That mean the last time you came home, you was pregnant? Dianna, remember when I kept asking you about Veronica and how come she'd gained so much weight? You told me she got fat being off at college. I knew it was more to that story. Well that explains why you kept that child locked up in the house all that time."

"Oh shut up going on about that mess, Carla Smith. What's done is done and the past is the past. So what if she was pregnant back then? Ain't nothing I can do to change the past." Dianna pulled her purse tightly to her chest, visibly upset.

Ronnie chimed in. "Mrs. Smith, yes I had a baby and put her up for adoption. She hired a detective to locate me and now I'm going to meet her. For the first time. Look, I'm not proud of what I did back then. I gave up my child and now I'm going to get her back. My friend Luis is coming out to help drive. So nobody has to worry about anything. I've got God on my side with this one."

"Amen Veronica. Now you two old busy bodies be quiet and let's enjoy the day." Mr. Smith put his foot down and nothing further was said about Veronica's hushed pregnancy.

They drove the ten miles to the downtown area and rode past the Arthur P. Murray federal building. It was the first time she saw the somber memorial up close. Up until 9/11, it was the worst terrorist attack to happen on American soil. An American city targeted and bombed by one of its own was unthinkable until it actually happened on April 19, 1995.

In honor of the fallen, two massive gates stood opposite each other with the times of 9:01 and 9:03 etched into the dark granite, keeping watch over the shallow reflecting pool below. A field of empty chairs signified the victims who lost their lives that day. Included in the death toll were many innocent children whose lives were cut short, because of one person's senseless act. Ronnie said a silent prayer as they drove by.

Dianna pointed to a new building towering high above all others in the downtown skyline. With hometown pride in her voice she exclaimed, "That there is the new Devon Energy Center. When they finish it's going to be the tallest building here. Fifty floors high! Yes indeed, Oklahoma City is changing for the better."

184

Although the building was indeed spectacular, Ronnie thought it looked totally out of place in the surrounding skyline. It dwarfed all the other buildings by at least half the height, sticking out like a sore thumb.

Mr. Smith toured the downtown area, pointing out new attractions. "That there is the new *Bass Pro Shop*, the *Cox Convention Center*, and the *Ford Center* sports complex. That there is where our basketball team, *The Thunder* plays. We ain't the rinky dink, podunk town we used to be a few years ago; no siree!"

They parked near the Bricktown Riverwalk and piled out of the car to continue the tour on foot.

"This doesn't resemble the Oklahoma City I remember at all. They really have made a lot of improvements. Clubs, restaurants, and even a fancy new movie theater! I'm feeling kinda good about my city right about now. Who'd have thought they could pull this off?" Ronnie stopped and stared at the wall. "Hey Mama, check out this poster advertising this new up and coming band."

"What cha got there Veronica? What poster?" Dianna peered through her "going out" glasses, a fancy pair she kept conveniently hanging around her neck on a 24K gold necklace.

"This poster here. It's a promotional poster for a local group called *The Kamal's*. I read about this group in *Rolling Stones* magazine last month. They're supposed to be the opening act at the Grammy's. I can't wait to hear them play! They're supposed to be really good. Five young musicians representing Oklahoma City in a big way! You gotta give them their props."

"Props? Girl I told you not to talk that street slang. Hey ain't that Olevia's grandson?"

"Yeah, I think it might be. Yes Lord, *The Kamal's*, I think they are pretty special!" declared Ronnie.

For the next few hours, they walked about and toured the newly revitalized area. Unable to resist the sweet smell of freshly baked waffle cones, they stopped in an ice cream parlor and bought ice cream. Carla Smith and Dianna fed leftover crumbs from their ice cream cones to birds gathered in the park. They ended their day with a short ride on the boats through the canal. By the end of the day, all were exhausted and ready to head home.

On the way home, they stopped off at a BBQ shack owned by one of Mr. Smith's friends and purchased ribs, baked beans, potato salad, and greens.

"Ooo wee! I haven't had that much fun in years!" exclaimed Dianna, as they sat in her kitchen. "I sure do wish you could stay longer."

"I'm not leaving yet, Mama. Anyway, this isn't my last trip and when I get situated in California, you can come out to visit. Meet your granddaughter. Would you like that?"

"Yes, I would. Sho' nuff do want to meet my granddaughter. Kiara Indigo sure has a nice ring to it, don't it?" She absentmindedly wrung the dishtowel in her hands, expending nervous energy trying to keep busy, and keep her mind off her daughter's short stay.

"Mama, go ahead and eat. I have a few calls I need to make." Ronnie checked messages on her cell.

"All right, I'll put your plate in the oven."

"Hola Ronnie, its Luis. Sorry I missed you again. Just wanted to let you know I've made a flight reservation to Wiley Post airport and will be there Wednesday night. I hope you're having a good time. Call me." She smiled listening to the message Luis left on her voicemail.

"I will call you back in a minute, Mr. Duarte," she said to herself. She wanted to catch up with Kiara before she returned Luis's call.

"Hi Kiara, its Ronnie," she replied when Kiara answered.

"Oh, hi Ronnie. How are you?"

"Doing pretty good. Hey look, it's going to take just a little longer for me to make it out there. I hurt my arm and a friend's coming out to help me make the drive."

"Are you okay?" asked Kiara, concerned.

"I'm fine. I clumsily slipped and fell down a few steps. My arm is in a cast, but otherwise I'm well. I can't wait to see you and I promise I will be there by the time you graduate, okay?"

"Okay. Well, I'm happy that it's nothing too serious. If you can't make my graduation, I'll understand."

"No, sweetheart; that's not what I'm saying. If I have to fly or walk the rest of the way, I will be there. I promise. Nothing is going to keep me away."

"Thanks Ronnie, I really do want you to be here to see me graduate. Daddy does too."

"Kiara, I can't wait to see you. I'll call in a few days and give you an update. Stay sweet and we'll talk later."

She ended the call, wishing there was a way to make the miles disappear more quickly. Ronnie could just fly out and get the car later; that was an option and if it came down to it, that's exactly what she'd do.

Kiara mentioned Travis. That was the first time she did that. Ronnie honestly didn't know how she felt about seeing Travis again. They used to be so much in love, but that was in the past. No matter how he felt about her now, she wanted to thank him for being there for Kiara. Thank him for being such a good man and an excellent father. She owed him for holding on when she couldn't and saying thank you was the very least she could do.

She wanted to speak to Luis in private and the bedroom afforded a good barrier to keep her personal conversation private. Ronnie closed the door blocking the joyful singing coming from the kitchen. Her mother sounded happy.

"*Hola?*" answered Luis.

"Hey Luis, it's me Ronnie."

"Well, hello gorgeous."

"Oh, aren't we getting friendly?" she joked, good-naturedly.

"Don't see why I shouldn't be. It's time for us to get to know each other better anyway, don't you think? We're going to be together in your car for over a thousand miles. Aren't you curious how we're going to handle being in such close quarters for days on end?"

"Hmm, I suppose you're right. I hadn't thought about the intimate details..." She imagined they may end up sharing a hotel room. It wouldn't make sense to get two separate rooms. Yet somehow, she wasn't quite ready to make that step.

"You got quiet on me. I hope you know I *am* going to be a gentleman. I really do like you Ronnie and I'm not about to mess this up by being an asshole. You mean too much to me."

"Thank you Luis, I wasn't worried. Not really. I think I know you well enough to trust you. After all, there were lots of opportunities to do something to me while we were riding all over the Dominican Republic on that motorcycle."

"Just know that I am a very trustworthy person."

"We'll see about that," she laughed." Hey, I got your message. So you'll be here tomorrow night, huh? I'll arrange a hotel room for you close to the airport. Since I can't drive, you'll have to take a taxi to my mother's home first thing in the morning."

"You mean I have to stay in a hotel my first night in the city?"

"Uh yeah, you can't really stay here with me—in my mother's home."

"Of course, you're right. I am so used to staying with family or friends when I travel, I rarely stay in hotels."

"I understand, but my mother wouldn't." She added.

"My flight doesn't land until almost midnight, so I suppose going straight to the hotel is the wisest thing."

"See, like I said, you can take a taxi to my mother's early the next morning. She's going to love meeting you and will probably fix so much food you'll think we're having a party." Ronnie knew her mother would love Luis. *After all, what's not to love?*

"Alright, it's a breakfast date. I'll come by early, meet your mother, and then we can plan our route and get on the road. Sound good?"

"Sounds great. I've got to go. Dinner's waiting."

"Right, I remember how much you love your food," he joked.

"You got that right! Seriously Luis, I can't wait to see you. This is the beginning of my new life and I'm so happy you're going to be right by my side on this journey."

"That makes two of us. I'll see you bright and early Thursday morning."

Chapter 20

This morning would be Luis' first time seeing Ronnie outside of the DR and she wanted to look perfect for him. The downsizing of material possessions left Ronnie with very few choices of clothing, so it was difficult finding an outfit that fit over the cast. She managed to pull it off in a loose fitting, short sleeved pullover dress. Her mother helped with her hair, brushing her natural curls into a thick ponytail.

At 8 o'clock sharp, the doorbell played the first nine notes of *We Are The World*.

Ronnie took one last glance in the mirror before leaving the bathroom. She wondered, *what in the world made my parents choose that particular tune, it doesn't fit them at all.* She ran to get the door and in her haste she stubbed her little toe on the hallway bookcase. The pain radiated upwards from her pinkie, through the pit of her stomach, and into her chest. She danced around holding her foot, cursing under her breath, hoping the curses would somehow ease the pain away. She heard her mother's voice.

"Good morning. You must be Luis. I'm Ronnie's mother, Dianna. C'mon in. Ronnie is still getting dressed." She explained in a proper voice—what she called her "white folks voice".

"Good morning Mrs. Pierce, I'm Luis. I've heard so much about you. Now I see where Ronnie got her good looks."

"Oh, you're just trying to make an old woman feel good. You can put your bag over there in the corner." She blushed.

"I only say what I believe to be true. You are a very beautiful woman and so is your daughter," he said, while placing his overnight bag out of the way.

Ronnie rolled her eyes and thought, *I can't believe Luis used that tired assed line on my mother.* Apparently its intended effect worked because Dianna blushed and giggled like a school girl. The throbbing in her little toe had subsided and the pain was now tolerable. She walked into the living room.

One look at Luis and she understood her mother's reaction. A layer of wavy hair covered his previously bald head; he sported a goatee and wore trendy eyeglasses. He was dressed meticulously in a sports coat, silk shirt, and casual slacks. *Good Lord this man is fine!*

"Good morning, beautiful. It is so good to see you again." Luis stepped past Dianna and scooped Ronnie up in his arms. He hadn't realized how much he actually missed her until that very moment.

Dianna watched the couple, pleased at how happy her daughter appeared. Luis was a very nice looking man, not her type, but definitely handsome. She nodded her head in approval, smiled, and gave Veronica the thumbs up before giving them their privacy.

After the embrace, he pulled back and took another long look. Ronnie was so pretty and that cast on her arm made her vulnerable. He wanted to protect her and take care of her always. He knew it was too soon to make his true feelings known, but she was all he thought about. Day and night.

"I've missed you so much," he whispered.

"I missed you too, Luis."

He didn't say another word. Just stood their staring at her lovely face.

"I can't believe you're here—in Oklahoma City in my mother's living room. How was your flight? Was the hotel okay? Have any problems finding the house? You hungry?" Ronnie nervously fired off question after question.

"Everything was fine. And yes, I am hungry." *Hungry for you* is how he wanted to finish the sentence. He pulled her close and kissed her fully, lingering to enjoy her luscious lips, teasing her tongue with his own.

It hadn't been that long; Ronnie recognized the look of a man whose sexual needs hadn't been satisfied in a while. The look was familiar because it was the same expression she saw staring back from the mirror every day. Reluctantly the couple pulled apart.

The sound of clanging dishes came from the kitchen. Ronnie heard the back door slam followed by animated conversation. The aroma of applewood smoked bacon wafted into the living room.

Dianna chose that moment to interrupt. She stuck her head around the corner and said, "Okay you love birds. Break it up. Food's ready! Come on in here before it gets cold. I hope you don't mind that I invited Carla Smith and her husband to join us."

"No, Mama, we don't mind." Ronnie replied. "They're just like family," she whispered to Luis.

"You sure it's all right if I stay? I don't want to impose," said Luis.

"Are you kidding? My mother made enough food for eight people. Anyway, didn't you see her reaction to you? She loves you already.

190

Come on. Let's eat so we can get on the road," Ronnie said.

The group sat down at the spacious table and dug into the mountain of food.

"Mrs. Pierce that was a lovely meal. It's been quite a while since I've enjoyed a delicious hearty breakfast. Thank you so much for inviting me." Luis pushed away from the table, rubbing his full belly.

"Mama, everything was delicious." Ronnie agreed. "Can I help you clear the table?"

"Sure baby, thanks," she replied.

"Hey Luis?" Carla Smith interrupted. "You mind if I ask you something?"

He turned his attention to Carla Smith, "No, please. What is it?"

"I was just wondering... And you don't have to answer, but *what* is you exactly? You look kinda black, but you got that funny last name and you talk with an accent. Is you half Mexican or somethin'?"

"Woman, don't you have any manners? Luis is our guest, so don't you go embarrassing him like that. What's wrong with you, anyway?" asked Dianna, who wondered the same thing but was too polite to ask, while she reprimanded her friend.

Luis laughed. He was used to those questions especially coming from Black Americans. Seemed very few Americans outside of New York or Florida knew much about his country.

Ronnie was embarrassed how little Americans knew about other cultures. Even she freely admitted to Luis that until a few years ago, she didn't know anything about the DR or where it was located. *Our school system has to do better exposing us to other cultures,* she thought.

"It's alright; I get that question all the time. My family is from the Dominican Republic. It's an island nation southeast of Florida in the Caribbean Ocean. It shares its western border with Haiti," Luis explained.

"Haiti? Yeah, I remember hearing about that big earthquake down in Haiti a few years ago. Awful situation for those folks, wasn't it? All them people died and now living in tents. Shameful. I donated a few dollars through my church to help them out, but don't look like it did no good," added Dianna.

"Oh, so you're kinda like them Jamaicans? We got some of them living south of the city. Wear their hair in them nasty looking dreadful locs. When I see 'em I just wanna take my scissors and snip them ropes right off they head!" exclaimed Carla Smith.

Ronnie rolled her eyes and loudly exhaled. *Leave it to Mrs. Smith to embarrass me.*

Luis ignored Carla's last comment, "Um, no, we're not like Jamaicans. Jamaica is its own separate island. My people are a blend of African, Spanish, and the native Taino people. We speak Spanish. Haiti is predominantly French speaking and its people have mostly African ancestry from former slaves. Does that answer your question?"

Carla Smith sat at the table struggling with her dentures. Popping her top set in and out. Somehow a piece of food managed to get wedged underneath. "Uh huh. Yeah, but I still don't know *what* you is? You look Black to me, no matter where you say you come from. Don't understand why nobody wanna be black no more. Always got to pretend they something else. Wanna be more white than black. Tell me. What is wrong with being black?"

"Leave the man alone, Carla. He didn't come here to be insulted by you. Now go in the bathroom and fix your teeth." Mr. Smith scolded his wife. "Luis, I apologize for my wife. She's stuck in her ways, but she don't mean no harm. Just an old woman who don't mind saying what's on her mind."

"No need to apologize. I understand what she meant and I take no offense. To tell you the truth, most Americans see my color first and my ethnicity second. To them if your skin is dark, you're black. Most of the time I just let it go. Not worth the effort. But my family is proud of its Dominican heritage and I would never deny it for anything. Or anyone. Would you?"

"Nope, cain't say that I would. But our history is different here in the states. It's been over 400 years since slavery ended; we got ourselves a black president, and it seems like things are worse than they ever been. All them politicians talking crazy mess about returning to the good ole' days. What I want to know is what good ole' days are they talking about? Cain't seem to get them to answer that question." Mr. Smith chuckled.

"On that we can agree. Mr. Smith, I can stay here all day and talk politics with you, unfortunately we'll be leaving soon. But you know what I mean about having pride in heritage?"

"Yes, son, of course I do. Now y'all go on and finish up what you got to do."

"Mama, I'll help you put the dishes away and clean up. We need to get going soon. There's a lot of miles between here and California."

"What route y'all taking?" asked Mr. Smith.

"We haven't plotted it out yet, but I was thinking I-40 until we hit the west coast. It's pretty much a straight shot," replied Ronnie.

"That's probably the best way and it's not a bad drive. I used to drive long hauls using that route. I know it well. Roads are good and will take you through some pretty country once you get into New Mexico. Weather should be fine as well, so you two should have a nice easy drive."

"Thanks Mr. Smith. I think we are going to have a good trip. A nice journey." Luis added, while looking at Ronnie.

"Well young lady, it was very good seeing you again. Have a safe trip and I hope everything goes well with your girl. You're doing the right thing so don't worry, it'll all work out fine. Well, I've got to get going. Have some work to do down at the church. Now don't be a stranger." He hugged Ronnie and shook Luis' hand. "You take care of Vernon's little girl and get her there safely, you hear."

"Yes sir, I'll take good care of her. I promise. She's in good hands, so no need to worry." Luis shook his hand and locked eyes with the old man. They both had a vested interest in Ronnie's welfare and that handshake signified they fully understood one another.

Ronnie cleared the table and returned the dirty dishes to the kitchen. Her mother wasn't there. "Mama? Hey Mama? Where are you?" she called out.

Her mother was in her bedroom, sitting on the edge of her bed.

"Oh, there you are. I wanted to ask what you want me to do with...." Ronnie stopped speaking when she noticed her mother was crying. "Mama, what is it? What's wrong"

"Oh child it's nothing. Just me being a sentimental old woman. I'm fine." She used the back of her hand to wipe the tears away.

"So why are you crying?"

She sighed heavily, "Veronica, all these years I got used to being by myself. On my own. It took me awhile before I stopped looking for Vernon to come sit down beside me, come to bed with me, take longs walks with me, and have someone to talk to... Even got used to you not being around. But since you came back, I found out I miss having family nearby. None of my siblings come to visit me no more and I ain't got nobody to talk to. Guess I'm just lonely." She wiped another tear away.

Ronnie found a box of tissues and handed it to her. "But Mama, you're not alone anymore. I plan on coming back to visit often and I'll try to bring Kiara with me. And once I get settled, you can come visit. This is not the end, this is the beginning."

"Thanks baby. Like I said, I'm just being a sentimental old fool."

"Old woman, what in the world are you sniveling about? You got me and my husband across the street. You got your friends down at the church. Even got your man friend who comes around every now and then. Why you trying to make this child feel guilty 'bout leaving?" Carla Smith had overheard their conversation while she was in the bathroom fixing her dentures.

"I am not trying to make her feel guilty. I just want Veronica to know how happy she's made me by coming home. I'm glad we're speaking again. It's just not natural for a mother to not speak to her only child." As quickly as the words left her mouth, Dianna understood the error of her ways.

"Uh huh, you's right about that," Carla replied. "I got to go now. These doggone dentures are irritating my gums like all get out. Veronica, get to know your daughter, find out what she likes, and go from there. Take an old woman's advice; don't let nobody ever come between you and your child again. Okay? That's your flesh and blood. You take care now and come see us again soon." Carla Smith ambled over to Ronnie and gave her a surprisingly strong good-bye hug.

"Carla Smith, I'll drop by in a few hours," Dianna said.

Dianna refocused her attention to her daughter. "Come here Veronica, I want to give you something. Your father gave this to me years ago, when you was just a little baby. He called you his little angel." Dianna went to the china cabinet and pulled out a small figurine. "Take this with you and whenever you start to feel alone, pull it out to remind yourself that you're never alone. Here take it."

"Mama, I can't take this. Daddy gave it to you. It's yours."

"And now I'm giving it to you." She pushed the figurine into her daughter's hands.

Ronnie ran her fingers over the delicate porcelain figure. It was a tiny angel— a little brown girl dressed in a lime green dress. Two delicate white wings sprang from her back and a crown of springtime flowers encircled her head. It was the most precious gift she could have ever received.

"Oh Mama, it's beautiful! I'll treasure this forever. Thank you."

"You're welcome. Now go on and finish packing. I can finish cleaning up the kitchen later. Oh, here's the box to store your angel in, so it don't get broken while you're traveling."

"Is that everything?" asked Luis, placing her two large suitcases in the trunk. He threw his overnight bag in last.

"Yes, I think that's it. I didn't have much to start with—called myself traveling light."

"Are you *really* ready to leave? We can stick around for another day, if you want to. "

"No, it's alright. Just give me a moment to say good-bye again. I'll be right back." Ronnie climbed the crumbling steps she tripped on just a few days ago. A lifetime ago. She went back to see her mother one last time before she left. Her mother was in the kitchen putting away leftovers.

"Hey Mama, I need one last hug before we get on the road. I am so happy we worked this out between us. I didn't like being angry with you and holding on to all that bitterness. You're my mother and I understand you were trying to protect me the best way you knew how. I love you Mama, I really do."

Dianna stopped what she was doing and looked at her daughter. She saw a beautiful woman, inside and out. Veronica stayed away all those years because of her. "Veronica, I want to apologize for making you give up your daughter. I didn't do it for you. Didn't even do it for Vernon. I did it for me for my own selfish reasons. I was wrong. Who knows how your life would have turned out if I hadn't interfered? I am so sorry."

"Don't do that, Mama. Stop blaming yourself. It wasn't totally your fault and you didn't ruin my life. Look at me; I turned out fine. We all make mistakes. What matters now is what we do with the rest of our lives. Anyway, I came to say bye."

"Thank you for understanding your old mother."

"It's funny, but I've learned as much about myself as I have about you. I love you, Mama."

"I love you, too. Well daughter you have a safe trip. Oh, by the way, I really like Luis Duarte. He's a real gentleman and a nice guy as well. He's in love with you, you know. I can tell by the way he looks at you."

Ronnie let her mother's last comment hang in the air. She gave her a big hug and carefully descended the stairs. Luis was right there to help. She looked at this wonderful man standing in front of her with his arm extended and wondered if her mother was right. *Does he love me?* As Luis helped her into the car, Dianna stood in the doorway waving good-bye.

Chapter 21

"I think we can make it to Amarillo before we need to gas up. This is a new car, so I don't know the fuel range yet. Just don't let it get too low because we do not want to run out of gas around here, especially at night."

Ronnie surveyed the barren west Texas landscape. The recent drought left no vegetation in sight. Only dried up, reddish-brown soil and shriveled brown tumbleweeds rolling across the highway remained.

Several hours into the drive, Ronnie asked Luis, "How do you feel? You getting tired yet?"

"I'm fine, but I do need to stretch my legs. Use the men's room and such. What about you? How you doing?"

"I'm okay. I can make it to Amarillo. It's only another fifty more miles." She paused, then asked, "So what do you think about my mother? She's a bit eccentric, huh?"

"Your mother is a wonderful woman and I like her a lot. Mrs. Smith, on the other hand, is a handful. Is she always so...outspoken?"

"If that's what you want to call it. I remember my parents used to hang out with the Smiths like they were family. I thought they were when I was younger. And before I knew better, I even introduced Mr. Smith as my uncle to my friends. Those old people have been in my life for as long as I can remember. They're closer than family."

"You can choose your friends, but you can't pick your family," added Luis.

"Amen brotha!"

Every now and then Ronnie snuck a peek at Luis. *His skin isn't as dark as it was when we met. He must've had a tan back in the Dominican Republic.* His hair was wavy, thick, black, and shiny. There was a small scar on his right cheek in the shape of a tiny cross or an X. His lips were full, pouty, and dark red. *A kissable mouth.* Although his features were sharp, they belied any one particular ethnic group. He could have been African-American, South American, East Asian, Northern African or any combination.

When it came right down to it, Luis's ethnicity didn't matter—not one teensy little bit. She didn't care where he was from or who his ancestors were. Ronnie liked Luis. And he felt the same way about her.

"Penny for your thoughts?" she asked.

"I was thinking about you—your family. From where I stood, it looks like you and your mother worked out your differences. What was all that about anyway? How did you end up estranged?"

"Uh, it's a long story. I don't really feel like getting into it right now."

"I understand. You'll tell me in time. Or not. It's your call and I respect your privacy either way. However, you do know we have a lot of miles to cover and some conversation sure would be nice."

"Okay, what do you want to talk about?"

"Tell me one thing you've never told anyone. What is the one thing you've always wanted to accomplish but haven't?"

"Let me see... One thing I've always wanted to accomplish, huh? Well, it's not really a secret because I've mentioned it to a few people, but I would really like to write a novel."

"Yeah, I remember you mentioning that in the DR. So what's stopping you?"

"Life. I don't have any free time. It seems like I'm always busy with everything else, I have no time to focus on writing. But *that* is the one thing I'd really love to accomplish."

"I think you focus on what you want. So if you really wanted to write a novel, you would let nothing stand in your way. This is what I've learned; uncontrollable circumstances occur that will always provide you with millions of excuses to not reach your goal. Trust me, I know. If I had let the trivial stuff get in the way, I'd probably still be waiting tables in New York City."

Ronnie grew quiet contemplating Luis' words. She watched the cars on the opposite side of the highway zoom by.

"Hellooo? You still with me?" he teased.

"I'm sorry. My mind tends to drift sometimes and I get lost in my day dreams. You're right. I can continue to make all the excuses in the world not to write. For as long as I can remember, I've put it off due to one reason or another. Maybe this new beginning is the perfect time to refocus on what's important."

"There ya go! Since you're already risking everything by moving out to California for a fresh new beginning, why not throw writing your novel into the mix? Who knows, maybe you'll end up creating a literary masterpiece."

"Look, I have no illusions that I'm going to be a famous author. I really just want to see if I can do it and to have something for posterity."

"I totally understand and if there is anything I can do, please let me know."

"Thanks Luis. And thanks again for flying out to drive me to California. I appreciate this more than you can imagine. So tell me about *your* company. How's business?"

"Ah ha! I see you're also very sharp! Change the subject so I can talk about myself, huh? Well, let me see. I told you about a college friend inviting me out to California to get into the field of graphic design? Anyway, the business started out really small. I worked out of the living room of my one bedroom apartment. You should have seen the place... My bedroom was the only personal space I set aside just for me." He reminisced.

"The living room was equipped with a small printing press and my closets were stacked with boxes of paper in different weights. I hired students from local university art programs to help me out. They learned the intricacies of graphic design while also helping to launch my business. I paid them by how much they produced. At first we specialized in producing business cards, flyers, promotional material, brochures and such for local businesses. Business gradually picked up and I now have a full list of regular clients."

"I'm very impressed. Working for yourself, being your own boss, not having anyone tell you what to do—that's priceless."

"Speaking of jobs and working... I know your daughter is the reason you're visiting California. I get that. But why are you *moving* there? Didn't you say you've only been there once before, a long time ago?" If there was a man in her life, Luis wanted to know sooner rather than later.

"After I quit my job I honestly didn't know what I was going to do. I came to the conclusion that Hampton, Virginia was not the place for me. So I opened my heart and my soul and listened for God to send a message telling me where I'm supposed to be—point me to my purpose."

"So did you receive your message?"

"Hold on, let me finish... Shortly after I returned from the DR, that P.I. showed up and told me about my daughter. Then I spoke to Kiara on the phone... Luis, she wants me in her life. Even though she didn't say it out loud, I heard it in her unspoken words. And then to find out that you both live only miles apart, I took that as a definite sign to move to California."

"That's very sweet and touching. However, I have to say Ronnie, you know that sounds crazy. Right? People don't just pick up and move cross country on a whim. Or in your case, after supposedly receiving a message from God."

"Is that right? Well, I've got three words for you: Read your Bible."

He laughed and replied, "Touché!"

* * *

"Looks like Amarillo is up ahead. I wonder who named this place. I don't see anything remotely yellow about this city. Should've been named dust bowl..." Luis exclaimed.

"What are you talking about?" asked Ronnie, only half listening to him.

"*Amarillo* is Spanish for yellow," he started to explain, but changed his mind. "Oh, never mind. Where do you want to stop? We need gas and I need to use the restroom. You hungry?"

"Yes, I am. How about that gas station over there?" She pointed to the gas station with a Subway sandwich shop inside. The thunder rumbled loudly in the distance followed by flashes of lightning.

"Uh oh! Looks like a bad storm may be headed our way. Let's check out the weather forecast while we're eating." Luis took the next exit.

"You're right, those clouds do look ominous. We'd better keep an eye out for bad weather. You got your iPhone with you?" Ronnie recognized the angry dark clouds from her childhood—tornado weather.

"Can't use my phone, the charge is almost gone. I'll charge it when we get on the road again. How's yours?" He pulled up to the gas pump.

"It's good. I'll look up the weather channel when we get our food," replied Ronnie.

"Sounds good. I'll gas up and meet you inside."

"I'll place our order. Any preference on your sub?" she yelled over the howling wind that stirred up clouds of dust.

"No, I'll have whatever you're having and get me a cup of coffee please."

Ronnie used the restroom and when she came out, she saw Luis at the store's entrance talking to a family of five—two parents and three teenagers. They were speaking excitedly and acted as if they knew each other fairly well. He shook the man's hand then headed towards Ronnie.

"Who was that? Did you know those people?" she asked. Ronnie thought it strange for Luis to run into someone he knew way out here—in Amarillo, Texas of all places.

"Yeah, I used to work with him. He's taking his family on a cross country RV excursion. They're on their way to Houston. Hey give me a minute… I've got to use the men's room. Be right back…"

Ronnie queued up at the Subway counter, still keeping an eye on the weather outside. It had started to rain. She was next in line to order when she felt someone tap her shoulder. She turned to see the woman from the family Luis had spoken to earlier.

"Excuse me miss, I don't mean to bother you, but are you traveling with Mr. Duarte? We're friends of his from California. I saw you two together."

"Uh, yes. Why?"

"We wanted to give this to him. It's a small token of our family's appreciation for helping our daughter get into college. She's doing wonderful things with her life because of him. He is such a wonderful man. We'd stick around and wait for him, but it looks like the weather's taking a turn for the worse and we want to get back on the road. Please give this to Mr. Duarte and tell him we said thanks!" The woman pressed the object in Ronnie's hand and hurried off.

Ronnie looked at the object the woman placed in her hand. It was an old coin the size of an Eisenhower dollar; heavy, round, gold metallic, and dulled by age and use. But there was something odd about the coin. She'd never seen anything like it before. It couldn't be valuable, otherwise why would the family give it up? Maybe it was an heirloom and not a coin at all. She searched for the family to ask what the coin was, but they'd already piled back in the RV and were pulling off.

"Ma'am, excuse me? Are you ready to place your order?" asked the pimply faced teen behind the counter.

Ronnie placed the order, picked up Luis' coffee and found a booth. As she scooted to the middle of the booth, she recalled her conversation with Joie about her and Cedric's role playing and smiled. It felt like years had passed since she last spoke to her old friend.

Luis squeezed in besides her and sipped the coffee. "This has got to be the worst cup of coffee I've ever drank, but I need the caffeine.

Why aren't you eating?" He looked over to Ronnie. A confused expression was spread across her face.

"Luis, what's this?" She plopped the coin down on the table.

"I don't know. Looks expensive. Where did you get it?" He picked up the coin and studied it. "I think it's an ancient Roman Empire coin. Ronnie, where did you find this?"

"I didn't find it. That woman you were talking to earlier gave it to me to give to you. Wanted me to tell you thanks. Something to do with helping her daughter. Why would they give you something so expensive? What exactly did you do?"

He sat back in his seat and laughed, "I didn't do anything except write a letter of recommendation to help their daughter get admitted to a special program at her school. She was already accepted in the university, but the dean of the anthropology program wanted to have a personal recommendation from an upstanding citizen of the community. Her father worked for me, so naturally he asked me to write it. I knew his daughter. She was a bright kid with a promising future." He smiled. "They gave me this coin? Wish I could have thanked them personally."

"What's so special about that coin? Is it worth a lot of money?"

"Not a lot of money. Maybe a couple thousand of dollars. See, what you don't know about me is I am a coin collector. I collect coins from all over the world. He knew I've been trying to get my hands on one of these rare coins for years."

"That is really cool and very thoughtful. Think about it... Your one simple action made a huge impact on that girl's life. Writing that letter probably made all the difference in how her life turned out. You're a pretty cool person," she teased.

"Thanks, now eat your sandwich. I want to at least make it to Albuquerque tonight."

Ronnie and Luis' attention was simultaneously drawn to the front of the store. The heavy rain had changed into pellets of hail falling from the sky. Several people ran into the building trying to get out of the hailstorm. The wind whooshed through the open doors bringing in dirt and debris. Hail the size of quarters pelted those unlucky enough to be caught outside. The loudspeaker kicked on causing everyone to stop what they were doing and listen.

"Attention customers. May I have your attention please? Everyone listen up! May I have your attention please?! This is the store manager speaking. I have just been informed that this area is under an immediate tornado threat. I repeat; this area is under an immediate tornado threat. We request all customers take shelter. A tornado has been spotted on the ground less than 5 miles away and it's headed in this direction. Please take shelter in the designated shelter area near the restrooms. I repeat...."

The tornado warning sirens clicked on sending out its wavering tone to take action. Residents from the panhandle were familiar with tornadoes and knew exactly what to do—take shelter immediately! The locals and employees coaxed the out of town travelers into the small freezer. Several store managers tried to stop the many customers from running outside to get to their cars. Those who didn't want to stay didn't have to, yet it was the manager's duty to at least try to convince them they'd be safer indoors.

"Come on Luis, we've got to take shelter. Now!" Ronnie peered out the window and saw the funnel cloud headed straight towards them.

"Oh shit! Look at that thing! I've never seen a tornado up live and close! Hey, what about the car? We can probably make it and outrun the storm. I am not getting in that small room with all those people. I'm slightly claustrophobic"

"Luis, as God is my witness, I will follow you to the ends of the earth after this is over. But you have got to listen to me. I used to live in Oklahoma and I know about these storms. They are nothing to play with and can change directions on a dime. The absolutely worst place to ride out a tornado is a car or a mobile home. Claustrophobic or not, we're both going in there. Now let's go!"

Ronnie grabbed Luis' arm and literally dragged him into the shelter. With barely enough room to move or breath, the air was hot and putrid with body odor. One of the employees closed the door and bolted it shut.

The air grew still and it became eerily quiet as if the substance of the building had been sucked inside out. All of a sudden, they heard the telltale sounds of an oncoming train followed by glass breaking. The freezer shook as if it were going to break apart at any moment. Stuffed inside like sardines in a can, some cried, many prayed, and others fell silent waiting for it to end. The tornado lasted all of 30 seconds, but to the occupants sitting in that freezer, it felt like it was never going to stop.

Finally the noise subsided and they pushed open the heavy door. Broken glass, all matter of debris, and food stuff were scattered about. Part of the roof was gone revealing a twilight sky. Half the parked cars were damaged and tossed around like toys. People walked around in a daze trying to comprehend the damage from the tornado's destructive force.

"*Cogno*! I have never been through anything like that before! Ronnie are you all right? How's your arm?" He checked her for bruises.

Though Ronnie was in a state of shock, she followed behind Luis to the front entrance. Ronnie stepped over debris on the floor, trying to get outside. "I'm fine. I have an adrenaline rush, otherwise I'm good. Hey, I don't see the car. Where did you park?"

Luis tried to shake away the nervous energy. "Since we were going to stick around and eat, I didn't want to park in the 5 minute parking spots. I parked around back. Let's see if it survived. Be careful, there's a lot of broken glass about."

Ronnie said a prayer as they rounded the corner to the back of the building. All the cars parked in the rear lot were fine. With the exception of a thick layer of dirt, not a scratch was on any of the vehicles. No damage at all.

"Congratulations Luis! Your consideration for others paid off again. You are like a good luck charm. Look, the car is fine."

Ronnie's words were facetious, but in her heart she knew it was by the Grace of God the car was undamaged. She looked around at the devastation. Trees were sheared off midtop. Rooftop shingles and plywood from homes and buildings were tossed about in the field. She noticed a child's book flapping in a bush, its pages fluttering like the wings of a trapped bird.

People were running about looking for members of their families. Strangers approached each other offering assistance to the injured. Although the destruction was great, Ronnie said a silent prayer because she saw the newscasts from the May 3, 1999 tornado that hit parts of southeast Oklahoma City. In that F5 tornado, dozens of people lost their lives and thousands suffered major property damage.

She recalled trying to get information on what parts of the city were hit, and for days was unable to reach anyone. Though estranged from her mother, Dianna Pierce *was* still her mother and naturally her thoughts and prayers included her. Eventually she was able to contact a family member who let her know her mother was not affected.

"Looks like the tornado crossed the highway and jumped into the farmland over there," Luis said. "We can probably make it out of here, unless you want to stick around a bit longer. See if there's anything we can help with."

"There's nothing we can do here except get in the way. I'm not much help with one arm and it's starting to get dark. I think we should leave."

They rode in silence for several miles reliving the imagery of the devastation. Each lost in private thoughts, grateful they were spared.

"You okay?"asked Luis.

"I don't know. I feel sorta strange. Like I just woke up from a nightmare. Or left a movie set. It doesn't seem real.... It did happen, right? Luis, we survived a tornado?" she asked, realizing she was experiencing a delayed reaction. Post traumatic stress.

"Yeah, yeah, we actually survived a tornado! We walked away without so much as a scratch." Luis glanced at Ronnie's dazed expression and became more concerned. The highway sign indicated an upcoming exit for a rest stop. It wasn't much of a rest stop. Picnic tables, a few trees, and a restroom. Luis pulled off the exit and parked under a tree.

"Luis, I was so scared. I've had close calls before, but have never been in an actual tornado." The sudden onset of emotion caught her off-guard.

"Hey, come here. It's going to be all right. We're okay." He exhaled and reached for Ronnie's good hand. He stretched across the seat and held her until she stopped crying.

"Being from Oklahoma, I know how dangerous tornadoes are and I didn't want our lives to end at a truck stop in Amarillo, Texas. I have so much left to do with my life! I prayed for that tornado to spare us, to lift back up into the clouds and go away. Everyone was so quiet. Nobody said anything. You think they were doing the same thing? Praying?" She wiped her nose with a tissue she found in her purse.

"Yes, I do. I was. Ronnie, today was the first time I've experienced such a powerful force of nature."

Ronnie looked at Luis as if he had lost his mind. She thought he may have suffered a concussion because of the nonsense coming from his mouth.

"Try to look at the tornado from a different angle other than the devastation it caused. There was an unmistakable beauty to the storm.

The way the funnel dropped from the dark angry clouds and whipped around like a rope. The clouds seemed to come alive! Tornadoes don't have feelings; there's no rhyme or reason why they drop down here and not there. It's just wind and water vapor coming together to form a powerful storm. I was actually mesmerized watching it, so it was a good thing you pulled me away."

"Are you crazy? Tornadoes are horrible! Like the devil himself sends those evil things down to wipe out everything in a path of destruction. I don't see anything beautiful at all about it." Ronnie struggled to understand Luis' logic.

"I have to disagree. Tornadoes aren't good or evil, just another natural phenomenon. Sun, wind, rain—all are part of nature. All work together to keep the balance of order in check. There's a plausible explanation why tornadoes happen. Same for hurricanes, floods, fires, droughts, and other natural disasters. But we humans, in our very limited amount of understanding, try to find logic and make sense out of it. Make it fit into a nice little box. That which we don't understand we automatically label evil."

"You do make a good argument. However when you see the aftermath of the devastation, and how people's lives are changed, it's difficult to write it off as just nature acting up."

"But we're okay. No one died." He squeezed her hand tightly.

"You're right. We were spared this time. We all were. Just another reminder to live our lives fully while we're still here. I'm so glad you were here with me. I don't know what I'd have done if I were here alone. Thanks Luis."

"You're welcome. Think of it this way, now we'll have an adventure to share with others when we get to California—about how we experienced our first tornado—together."

"Luis, you are so crazy! But I'm still glad you were here to share it with me."

"Are you okay now? How about we get back on the road? Another four hours and we'll be in New Mexico," he replied.

"Yes, I'm fine. Look, if you can't make it to Albuquerque, we can stop at a motel. We can always spend the night and get an early start. How about you? You okay?" she asked.

"I'm fine, too. Feeling good with you by my side. That's all I need right now."

Ronnie stretched out and yawned. She sat back in her seat and asked, "Hey Luis, are you really claustrophobic?"

"Only in dark, confined spaces," he replied.

They both laughed, releasing some of the tension both were under.

Chapter 22

Luis was tired but he pressed on. The weariness of the day crept up on him, but he resisted the temptation to stop because he wanted to make it to Albuquerque. The rhythmic drone of the tires was hypnotizing, lulling him almost to sleep. Miles passed by without another vehicle in sight. An occasional tractor trailer whizzed by breaking up the monotony. He turned up the radio and listened to some nameless late night talk show host provide bad advice to clueless callers with ridiculous issues.

It was late when they finally arrived on the outskirts of Albuquerque. Finally he made it to the peak and saw the city laid out below. He found the hotel where he previously made reservations and parked under the overhang.

"Ronnie? Ronnie, wake up. Wake up sleeping beauty. We're in Albuquerque. I've already checked in."

Ronnie stirred to see Luis standing outside her passenger door. The bright lights hurt her eyes. "Huh? What? What's going on? Where are we?" she asked, still half asleep.

"We're at the hotel. Here's your room key; go wait inside the lobby while I park the car."

"Um, I must've fallen asleep. Sorry. What time is it anyway?" She yawned.

"A little after midnight. Now go wait inside. It's chilly out here. Be right back."

She grabbed her purse and went inside. The spacious lobby was decorated in a typical Southwestern theme with arid desert landscapes as the preferred art. Several overstuffed chairs covered in distressed leather and bordered in brass tacks, were strategically arranged around the lobby. Ronnie took a seat on a massive leather sofa and waited.

The Native American man behind the counter acknowledged her then returned to the television program he was watching. *Luis said 'my room key'. Did he get us two separate rooms? Guess I'll find out soon enough.*

"I brought both your bags up because I didn't know which one you needed. We're on the fourth floor and I got us two adjoining rooms. I wasn't sure what you thought about sharing a room, so to be on the safe side, I got two."

Guess that answers my question, she thought. "You didn't have to get two rooms. I think it would be okay to share a room. Maybe two beds though…"

"How about we take this slowly and not force the issue. We'll both know when we're comfortable sharing a room."

"Well at least let me pay for my room then." She pulled out her wallet.

"No worries, I've taken care of it. But if it'll make you feel better, you can treat me to dinner tomorrow at a very expensive restaurant. There's the elevator."

They walked halfway down the hall. "Here are our rooms. What time to you want to get together in the morning?"

"Anytime is fine. I'm in no hurry to get home. Maybe we can do some sightseeing tomorrow. See the city," he replied, knowing full well he made prior arrangements to surprise Ronnie.

"Okay, sightseeing sounds like a good idea. Make this an adventure? I like that. I'll see you in the morning." She reached over and gave him a quick kiss. Anything more and she would surely have dragged him into her room.

"Yeah, I'll see you tomorrow. Goodnight." Luis was beat. As much as he wanted to fall asleep next to Ronnie after making love, the promise of a good night's sleep was too strong to resist. He opened his door and fell straight into his bed.

Ronnie tossed and turned, twisting the top sheet around her ankles, leaving her feet uncovered—exposed. *Damn it!* She thought. *I hate it when they don't tuck in the sheets.* Sleep didn't come easily that night. Images of flying debris, people walking around like zombies with blood dripping from injuries, and that awful train whistle kept bouncing around in her head. Tried as she might, the memory of the tornado was still too fresh to push aside.

Unable to sleep, she pulled out her eReader and tried reading a new novel. It was no use. She turned on the television and flipped through the channels. At this time of night the only programs on were infomercials featuring out of work actors pushing cheap crap nobody wanted nor needed.

Her thoughts turned to sexy, handsome, wonderful Luis sleeping in the room next door. *Staying in separate rooms is tough, but it seems like Luis has enough will power for us both. I don't want to mess this up by jumping into bed too quickly and neither does he. But then again, it wouldn't hurt to just sleep together, would it? Especially since I'm still feeling traumatized after surviving that tornado.* Ronnie tiptoed to the adjoining door and pressed her ear to the door. She didn't hear a sound.

Luis awoke to a light tapping sound. He bolted upright in his bed, looked around the unfamiliar room, trying to remember where he was. The clock said it was 4:13. Faint light eased its way into the room from underneath the hallway door, barely illuminating the space. He felt disoriented. Slowly it all came back to him. He was in a hotel in Albuquerque. The light tapping continued. He switched on the lamp. He heard Ronnie calling his name through the adjoining door.

"Luis? Luis? It's me, Ronnie. You up?" She called out and knocked again on the adjoining door.

"Ronnie? What's the matter? Hold on." Still half asleep, he fumbled with the inside lock. It obviously didn't get much usage as it was difficult to open. After pushing and pulling the bolt back and forth, it finally gave. Ronnie stood before him in burgundy silk pajamas looking like a sexy angel. The sleeve above the cast was bunched up under her arm. *She is so beautiful.*

"I'm sorry to wake you, but I couldn't sleep. I kept imagining that horrible tornado... I couldn't get the images out of my head. Guess I was really traumatized by it."

"It's alright." He yawned, realizing he was still fully dressed. "You want to sleep here? Or me there? Either way, I'm fine as long as I can sleep."

"Yes, if you don't mind. I know I'm probably being silly, but I don't want to sleep alone tonight... Oh, look at you! You must've been really tired. You didn't even undress before you went to bed."

"Oh, I suppose I was. Why don't I come over there? I can get my things in the morning."

"Thanks Luis. You're such a good friend."

Luis pulled off his sports coat and tossed it on the bed. He turned off the lamp and followed Ronnie back to her room. She slipped in under the covers. He stripped down to his boxer shorts and snuggled in besides her. Within minutes, they were both sound asleep.

Chapter 23

Ronnie awoke early. Even with the stopover in Oklahoma, her body hadn't properly adjusted to the changing time zones, thus she was still on east coast time. Luis remained sound asleep, snoring slightly. She rolled over and kissed him softly on his lips. He stirred ever so slightly and wrapped his arms around her, and pulled her to him. She placed her head on his chest and went back to sleep.

Luis slid out of the bed, leaving a quietly dozing Ronnie, to return to his room. He took a quick shower and confirmed their reservation for later in the day. He heard Ronnie stir in the next room.

"Luis? You over there?" Ronnie made her way to the bathroom to brush her teeth and freshen up.

"Good morning. I didn't want to disturb you so I let you sleep. How you feeling this morning?" asked Luis, peeping his head into her room.

"I'll be right out. Got a mouthful of toothpaste." Adjusting to using only one hand was harder than she had imagined. When she was at home, her mother helped her out. Now even the simplest tasks took extra time.

"Take your time. I'm going downstairs to pick up a few sightseeing brochures and ask about the nearest restaurant. I'm starved," he said.

"Okay, I'm going to take a shower. I'll be dressed by the time you get back."

Ronnie covered her arm cast in the protective plastic cover the nurse at the hospital gave her. Taking a shower wasn't so bad, but drying off was a chore. Applying lotion with one hand was also a challenge, but she managed. When it came to hooking her bra, she held one end in her left hand and stretched the fabric behind her back with her good arm. Without much effort she managed to wiggle the bra over her breasts.

She checked the mirror. *Oh no! My hair is a hot mess!* Unruly, tangled, and sticking all over her head, there was little she could do to tame it. Combing her hair was another chore Dianna helped with. This time, unless she wanted to go out looking crazy, Luis would have to help.

She spoke aloud, "What am I going to wear? Luis didn't give me any indication about this adventure he has planned... Well, since

Albuquerque *is* in the mountains, I suppose it can't hurt to wear a light sweater." She struggled into a pair of tight jeans, zipped the zipper, and somehow got the top button buttoned. She heard the next room's door open and close. It was Luis.

"How you doing in there? Almost ready? The front desk clerk recommended a local restaurant. They're supposed to have the best food around here. Even got voted Albuquerque's best for five years running." He noticed she hadn't answered. He knocked on the adjoining door and peeked his head into the room. "Ronnie, you alright in there?"

"Yes. No," she sighed, exasperated. "Luis, I hate to ask you this, but I need help with my hair. Can you lend me a hand? Please?" She walked out the bathroom and stood before him.

Luis could barely suppress his laugher when he took one look at Ronnie. She looked so helpless standing there with hair sticking up all over her head. From the looks of things, she had unsuccessfully tried to tame it with a brush.

"Uh, sure, what do you want me to do?" He didn't know the first thing about combing a woman's hair, especially a black woman's hair. All the sisters he previously dated damn near killed him for touching their hair.

"Here, take this hair moisturizer and pour some in your hands. Smooth it throughout my hair. That'll make it easier to comb. Take this comb and start at the ends and work your way to the roots. Yeah, like that." Ronnie wanted to scream when he got the comb caught in a tangle and tried to yank it through. Instead, she persevered and took the pain like a real woman.

Luis thought to himself, *Oh my God, her hair is so thick! I can't get this comb through this stuff. Hope I don't have to do this every day.* "Okay, what do I do now? I think I got most of the tangles out."

Her scalp was on fire but she didn't let on that it hurt. "Now, take this pony tail holder. I want you to brush my hair until it all comes together, and then you're going to slip this elastic over it. Okay? It's not as hard as it looks. You've already done the hard part by combing out the kinks." Ronnie's hair looked like she stuck her finger into a light socket. It was everywhere. No way was he going to get all that hair into one little elastic band.

"Hold on, let me take off my jacket." He grunted and removed his coat. Pretended like he was going into battle. "All right, I'm ready. I'm going in," he teased her.

"You need to quit… It is not that bad. Just gather it together as you brush." Ronnie felt her head jerk from one side to the other as Luis heavy handedly brushed her hair. Finally he slipped the elastic band over the ends.

"All done… Take a look. What do you think? I'll admit it doesn't look as good as when you did it, but I think I did all right," he proudly proclaimed.

Ronnie went to the bathroom and took a look. She burst out laughing. Her hair was in a ponytail—sort of. Luis managed to wiggle the elastic over the first few inches of her hair. She looked like Don King! The rest of her hair at the roots was puffed out and the top was held together by that little band of elastic.

He joined her in the bathroom. "What? Don't you like it? Did I do something wrong?"

"Look at me! I can't go out in public looking like this." She laughed.

He joined in her laughter and said, "I guess it does need some work. Have a seat, maybe I can scrunch the band lower."

She took a seat on the closed toilet. Luis maneuvered the elastic band as close to Ronnie's scalp as possible. When he was done, it looked much better.

"Thanks Luis, it looks much better now." She kissed him on his cheek. "Hey, look at the time. It's already past noon. Let's get out of here and go get some food. I know you must be starving by now; I know I am."

"Let's go then." Luis hoped he wouldn't have to do the hair thing every morning. Although he loved helping Ronnie, doing a woman's hair was not his strong suit. He knew how to stay in his lane, and fixing her hair was so far out of that lane it wasn't even funny. In fact, it was on a different street entirely.

"So what do you have planned for us today? What kind of wild adventure do you have up your sleeve?" asked Ronnie, stuffing a forkful of *huevos rancheros* in her mouth. The egg based dish was absolutely delicious.

"First let me ask you something. Are you afraid of heights?" He sipped his coffee. "Umm, now *this* is good coffee. Nice and strong."

"Heights? As long as you don't plan on us bungee jumping off some bridge, I'm not. Why?"

"Got two options for you then. We can take a hot air balloon ride or ride the tram to the top of the Sandia Peak."

"For real? We can go on a hot air balloon ride? Seriously? How'd you swing that on such short notice?"

"I made reservations before I left California. I know a few people who pulled some strings to get us in today. So I take it that's your choice? Thought so. That's why I confirmed it this morning when I was out earlier." He sat back and smiled, proud of himself.

"Are you kidding? I'd love to do that. When do we leave?"

"The balloons can fly only at sunrise, so we'll have to stick around here for another day. You up for that?"

"I don't mind spending another day here. We do have the time, but why can't we do it now?"

"I asked the owners the same question. Apparently it's because sunrise is when the wind is the calmest. The wind speed tends to get pretty high in the valleys and it's not safe for passengers or the crew to be in a balloon during rough winds. The company will do another check of the weather tonight to confirm the conditions will be right. If so, he'll call and they'll even come pick us up at the hotel first thing in the morning."

She leaned across the table. "Come here," she whispered. "Thank you for everything." And planted a big, wet, orange juice laced kiss on his coffee flavored lips.

"Mmm delicious." He savored her kiss. "So that leaves us with an entire day to fill. I picked up a ton of tourist brochures on things to do and see in Albuquerque. Take your pick. Or we don't have to plan anything."

"I think I like the latter better. Why don't we head downtown and see what's going on. Downtown is usually the best place to pick up on a city's vibe."

* * *

City street parking was at a premium. Luis drove up one street and down the other looking for an available parking spot. Most of the parking lots were filled to capacity because there was a Science Fiction and Fantasy convention being held. The streets were crammed with people dressed as their favorite science fiction characters both past and present. Looking at the participants, youthfulness was not a prerequisite for attendance. All ranges of ages and characters were represented, including parents dressed as their favorite fantasy hero holding babies dressed as Yoda, to teenagers who had painted their skin Avatar blue, to grandparents dressed as Star Trekkies.

"What's up, Luis? Did we just enter into another world? Look at these people walking around all dressed up like this is normal. What the fuck?" She laughed.

That was the first time Luis heard Ronnie swear. *That means she is getting used to being around me—well, it's about time she let down that wall.* "Pretty weird in my book, too. But at least we know they're dressed specifically for this convention. I can't imagine this goes on every day. Look, I found a spot. You still want to hang out?"

"Of course I do. These folks don't bother me. They may be dressed weird, but I'm pretty sure they're harmless."

They walked through the downtown streets, admiring the architecture of the adobe stores and traditional Native American cultural artifacts.

"You want a cup of coffee? We can sit here and people watch, if you'd like." Luis asked as they passed a coffee house.

"A coffee break sounds good. Can you please get me a latte? I'll find a table."

"One latte coming right up. Hey, that couple is leaving; try to get that one before someone else does." He pointed to a table in the corner, closer to the street.

As soon as she sat down, her cell phone rang and Joie's name popped up on the caller I.D. She looked for Luis. He was still in line, so she accepted the call. "Hello?"

"Hey lady! Sorry it's taken so long to call, but I've been busy on my end. Anyway, I'm just calling to see how everything's going with your daughter."

"Girl, I haven't even made it to California yet. I'm sitting here in downtown Albuquerque about to have a cup of coffee."

"Whaaaat? Albuquerque? What in the world are you doing there? You should've been in California by now."

"Girlfriend, it's a long, long story, but here's the quick version. I stopped by Oklahoma City to see my mother. While I was there, I fell and fractured my left arm, so now it's in a cast. I ended up staying there for longer than expected but it worked out fine. Me and my mother cleared the air and are speaking again."

"Ronnie, that's great news! I always wondered why you two weren't speaking. But that still don't explain how you ended up in New Mexico. How are you driving with a cast on?"

"Well, of course I can't drive with one arm, so I called Luis and he offered to fly out to drive me to California."

"Luis? Is that the guy you met in the Dominican Republic?" Unfortunately, any mention of the DR made Joie shudder, but she had to get past that memory. "You telling me he flew all the way out to Oklahoma just to drive you to California? Ronnie, don't no man do that without expecting something in return."

"Yes, he's one in the same. And Luis doesn't want anything from me. He isn't like that."

"He a man ain't he? Trust me, he wants something. He's just playing it smooth and biding his time. You'll find out in due time so don't be shocked when it happens."

"Whatever girl. So let me tell you what else happened. We stopped in Amarillo to gas up. While we were sitting down having a bite to eat, the weather turned and a bad storm blew in. Would you believe we got caught in a tornado?"

"You shittin' me! Ronnie, what the hell is going on? First you tell me you done fell and broke your arm. Now you're saying you was in a tornado?!"

"Yes, me and Luis and a bunch of other people holed up in a little freezer. We took shelter and survived the storm. Girl, I was never so scared in all my life. I almost freaked out, but having Luis with me really helped."

"Anybody get hurt?" Joie asked.

"No, but the rest stop was messed up. Bunch of houses got hit, but I don't think it was as bad as it could've been."

"You sure about this moving to California notion? Seem like something trying to keep you away from there. Maybe you ought to reconsider."

"Joie, it ain't nothing but the devil trying to distract me. Well, I'm here to tell you the devil is a liar and I'm not about to believe anything he says. He can keep on putting obstacles in my path, but I got the Lord on my side. I'm doing the right thing and I won't be deterred."

"Go on with your bad self! I got your back girlfriend. One hundred percent," she stated. "Hey Ronnie?"

"What up girl?" Ronnie looked for Luis. He was at the head of the line.

"Did he give you any yet? Is it true what they say about them Latino men?"

"We haven't done anything yet. He's been a true gentleman the whole time. He even helped me comb my hair this morning, for your information."

"Oooh, now I get it. He's gay."

"The man isn't gay. He's been married before."

"Then he on the down low."

"Shut up!" Ronnie laughed. "You don't know what you're talking about. Luis is a bonafide heterosexual—as straight as they come. We're taking our time and going to let this develop slowly. Neither one of us wants to rush this and ruin a good thing by having sex too soon."

"Well, don't take too long to find out if his equipment is up to standards, if you know what I mean."

"Hell yeah, I know what you mean. I may be taking things slowly, but I'm still your girl. You feel me? But I'm not worried. It'll happen when the time is right."

Luis made his way to the table and handed Ronnie her coffee. She mouthed that she was talking to a friend.

"By the way, how's the house coming along?"

"Oh, he must be with there with you now," replied Joie.

"Yep, that's right. You get the kids settled in?" asked Ronnie.

"You know I love your house. Always have. And the twins have settled into their own rooms nicely. Girl, you know Maya had to have your purple room. She didn't want to change a thing. But Trey, he said he didn't like whatever color the spare bedroom was painted… Think it was some kind of green, so we went to the store and he picked out his favorite color."

"That's good you're getting settled. Any more news from Cedric?"

She held her up a finger to Luis to indicate she was almost finished in her conversation.

"Cedric stopped by and dropped off the kids stuff. He'll call occasionally when he wants to see the kids. I got the divorce papers a few days ago. We're waiting for them to be finalized."

"Joie, I'm sorry. Stay strong girlfriend and keep your head up. It'll get easier as time goes on."

"I know, but right about now don't nothin' seem easy. Oh yeah, your neighbor, the old woman, stopped by with a house warming gift. Girl, she brought in a bunch of dried herbs and lit 'em straight up. She walked to every room praying in some language I never heard before. Said she wanted to get rid of any evil spirits that may have drifted in after you moved out—wanted to smoke 'em out. She said your house was always filled with love, even when you was the only one who lived here. I told her that's because the love resided within you and not just the walls of the house."

Ronnie's eyes teared up when she heard Joie express her thoughts. "Thank you Joie, you are sweet. I know that as long as you and the kids are there, it will continue to be filled with love. You take care girlfriend, Luis is here and we have lots of plans to make. I'll catch up with you when I get to my final destination."

"You be careful and enjoy your new life. And you're right about not letting those obstacles block your path. They can be a bitch to get out of your life once you let 'em get hold of you. Okay girlfriend, we'll catch up later. Love you! Bye."

"Bye Joie. Love you too. Take care."

"Everything all right?" he asked. Luis sat opposite Ronnie and offered her a *sopapilla* drizzled with powdered sugar and honey. She picked off a piece of the delicate pastry and popped it into her mouth.

"Yes, everything's fine. That was Joie; she hadn't heard from me and was just checking in. I told her about my mishaps and she wondered if I was doing the right thing by moving out here."

"What do you think? You having second thoughts about moving?" he asked.

"Not at all. I have no doubts about what I'm doing. I'm on a journey that is taking me to my predetermined destiny. So what if I have to go through a few obstacles to get there? No one said this journey called life was going to be easy. Anyway, easy is for those who aren't willing to go through the pain, hurt, betrayal, agony—the stuff you have to go through to get *to* the other side."

"Preach sister," stated a young man sitting behind them.

Luis turned towards the young man. The young brother was in his mid-20's and wore his hair in dreadlocks that extended down his back. Dressed professionally in a silk shirt, bowtie, nice slacks, and expensive shoes, one would think he was perhaps a law student.

"Excuse me young brother," Luis made eye contact with the young man. "You know what my woman is talking about? You know something about predetermined destiny?"

"Pardon me... I wasn't eavesdropping on your conversation... And I don't claim to be an expert or anything, but I do believe in

Patricia Hopkins

predetermined destiny. If you have the time, I'll share my story with you."

Luis looked at Ronnie. She shrugged, interested in what this young man had to say. Interested even more because Luis referred to her as his woman.

"Hi, my name is Lamar." He extended his hand to them both.

"Pleased to meet you Lamar. I'm Luis and this is Ronnie."

"Pleasure's all mine. Well, I'm 26 years old and for 5 years of my life, I lived on the streets. I was homeless. It's not what you think, my parents weren't drug addicts and we weren't poor. We were an average middle-class family; two well-educated parents of three very intelligent children. Although we attended church regularly, we weren't Bible thumpers. You know what I mean? Well, when I was fifteen, I got involved with the wrong element and started hanging out on the streets. I tried to be tough and ended up joining a gang. The homeboys became my family and I treated them better than I treated my own."'

"I can only imagine your parent's pain. They must have felt like failures," Ronnie added.

"Yes, I hurt my parents pretty badly. I started stealing from them. Man, I sold my family's stuff on the street to buy drugs—to build up my stash. I didn't use, thank God. Just sold. Surprised I never got arrested. I foolishly called myself a businessman."

"In some ways you were a businessman," added Luis.

"So one day I was out on the corner in my usual spot dealing, selling, making money, when up walks this old white preacher. I knew he was a preacher because of the white collar. At first it kinda messed me up. I just knew this supposed man of God wasn't about to ask me to sell him no dope. On the real side though, in that line of work you meet people from all walks of life. I asked him what he wanted.... Weed, dope, smack, crack, I even sold scripts."

Lamar continued, "He messed me up when he told me he was sent by God to deliver a message. He told me and I'll never forget, "Son, God loves you. When you discover your predetermined destiny, you shall never want for anything ever again." And he walked away. Just like that. When I turned around he was gone. I ran up and down the street, asking people if anyone had seen that old man. No one saw anything. Said I must've been hallucinating."

"Not a hallucination... What you had was an epiphany," stated Ronnie.

"I guess I did. I stopped selling drugs, quit the gang, and turned my life around. I went back to school and got my GED. I managed to snag a partial scholarship in the engineering department at the University of New Mexico, so I moved out here to Albuquerque. I discovered I love this city and it loves me in return. I made a few influential contacts in the business community and with their mentorship; I ended up opening my own engineering firm. We develop plans, designs, and coordinate construction for several contractors. I also married a wonderful woman who just gave birth to our first child. In my free time, I volunteer at the local chapter of 100 Black men. I can honestly say that I love my life."

"Man, I think that's a great story!" Luis exclaimed.

"Yes, I followed the path I was meant to pursue and stopped doing the things I knew were wrong. When I let go of all that negativity, it seemed like the gates opened and the path became clear. I discovered what I was put here to do. I found my predetermined destiny. My life is full and I am content. What more can I ask for?"

"Seems like you have it all together. Let me ask you a question. What do you believe would have happened had that priest not stopped by?" asked Ronnie.

"See, that's the weird part. I'm not sure he actually did. What I mean is; I'll never know if that was a real man or if God sent a messenger. In the end, I suppose it doesn't matter."

"You're right. Doesn't matter how you get the message as long as you did. Thanks for sharing the blessing," said Ronnie.

"Hey young brother, I'm going to give you my business card. If you're ever out my way, look me up," replied Luis. He removed a silver case from his inside pocket, withdrew a glossy business card, and handed it to Lamar.

"Thank you Luis," he said reading the card. "Ma'am, I just hope I can help somebody out the same way He helped me. I hope you guys enjoy your stay in the Que. Take care, now." Lamar pulled out his wallet and handed his business card to Luis. He gave a quick wave and went along his way.

Ronnie sat back in her chair and stated, "That was a testimonial if ever I heard one. You don't hear stories like that too often. Usually those young brothers end up in prison, or worse, dead. Gotta hand it to him, he pulled his life together and I pray he continues doing the right thing." She finished her remaining coffee.

"Very impressive young man. His card says his name is Lamar Robinson, P.E., Certified Structural Engineer, Owner LR Engineering, Inc.. Maybe we can do business sometimes. You never know. Well Ms. Pierce, you ready to get going?"

Ronnie turned and watched Lamar leave. As she swiveled around in her chair, a sign in the window across the street caught her attention. *African Braids. Walk-ins are welcome.*

"Luis, do you remember how much fun it was combing my hair this morning?" she asked.

"Oh yeah, I remember. Lots of fun that was. Can't wait to do it again tomorrow," he teased.

"Hey, it wasn't easy for me either, but I think I have a solution to both our problems. Look at that shop across the street. They braid hair."

"You want to get your hair braided? Don't you have to have an appointment?" Luis wasn't upset, just surprised.

"I don't *want* to get my hair braided, but I don't have much of a choice. I can't comb it with one hand. You have a hard time with two, and it's only going to get worse the longer I go without really combing it. Braids are the perfect solution. Almost no maintenance required."

"Okay, you talked me into it. If I can get out of yanking your brains out, I'm all for it. Let's go check it out. See if they have any openings." He picked up the empty coffee cups and tossed them in the trash can.

"Six hours?! You're telling me it takes six hours to braid her hair? Are you kidding me? Ronnie, is she kidding me? Who sits in a beauty salon for six hours? What are you going to do? Grow it for her?" he joked.

Ronnie noticed the reactions of the hairdressers to Luis' obnoxious comments and incessant questions. They rolled their eyes and smacked their lips in succession. Simply put, they were not amused. She pulled him aside.

"Luis, that's the amount of time they need. I've had my hair braided before and it's taken twice as long. Stop your ranting, you're embarrassing me. If you don't want me to do it, I won't get it done, but you're going to have to do my hair every time we go anywhere. Your choice."

"Okay, okay, I'll hang out by myself and come back to pick you up later. I hope it's worth it. Six hours? That's incredible." He chuckled.

"Well, you have my number so call if you're done sooner. Good-bye ladies." He waved at the women and planted a kiss on Ronnie's cheek before he left.

* * *

Luis had six hours to hang out in a city he knew nothing about. He picked up the brochures and leafed through the stack. He didn't want to see the Cowboy Boot Hall of Fame. Nope, he wasn't interested in seeing an enormous ball of yarn. The world's largest cactus didn't catch his interest, either. He eliminated all malls, shopping centers, amusement parks, and the zoo. He was down to two brochures. One for the Native American Art museum or Ripley's Believe It or Not. Or as a last resort, he could always return to the hotel and watch television.

Twenty minutes later, he found himself in the parking lot of the Albuquerque Native American Art museum. He expected the museum would be housed in a nondescript one story building and take all of five minutes to tour, but he was pleasantly surprised. This contemporary museum rivaled art museums found in many larger cities. Three floors and multiple wings housed a huge treasure trove of Native American art from all over the United States.

He paid the small admission fee, got a set of audio headphones and set about passing a few hours until Ronnie called. Halfway through the tour, he noticed a woman watching him. He acknowledged her, smiled and continued on his self-paced tour. He took notice of her following closely behind.

"I love this artist's style of painting. Look at his brush strokes. Nice and long..." The woman smiled, displaying a perfect set of bleached white teeth.

"Excuse me miss, are you speaking to me?" Luis turned to face the woman and pulled the earplugs from his ears. His eyes were drawn to her more than ample bosom proudly on display for all to see. A tiny charm rested in the crevice of those 40DD's.

The woman coughed, obviously noting where his eyes rested, to deflect his attention. "Yes, the artist. I was referring to the painting you were admiring. I like the artist's style. I'm Alexis by the way." She offered her hand.

Luis cleared his throat, embarrassed he'd been caught leering at her breasts. "I'm Luis, nice to meet you."

"Oh, I hear you have an accent. Not from around here, are you? Where's home?"

"I live in California. Just passing through." He continued on his tour, trying very hard to only admire the art on the walls, and not the piece of work standing in front of him.

"Mind if I join you? Looks like you're here alone."

"Suit yourself." He replied. Luis recognized her type immediately. A single woman over 40, looking for an eligible man—any man, who could satisfy her needs for the night, or hopefully for the next forty or so years. They dressed to the nines, kept every hair in place, and worked out like a madwoman to maintain a slammin' body so she could trap some poor innocent defenseless man. The minute she got hold of them, she let herself go. Yes, he knew her type all too well.

"I love that shirt. Most men can't wear pink, but it looks fabulous on you." She smiled and twirled her bleached blonde hair around her fingers.

"Thanks." He was trying to be polite.

"Oh man… I think the heel on my shoe is loose." She gazed over to Luis and asked, "Can I lean on you for a moment to check?"

"Of course." Luis held out his arm for the woman to steady herself. She bent over revealing the fullness of her breasts. He swallowed nervously. She wiggled her shoe around causing the material on her dress to gap open. She wasn't wearing a bra.

Alexis giggled. "Oh silly me, this is a new dress and I'm still trying to get this thing to fit right. Guess I should have worn a bra. I'm sorry. My shoe is fine. The strap is a little loose though." She knew her flirtations were working when she "accidently" provided Luis a glimpse of her full breasts. She noticed his erection and smiled.

"Uh, do you need help getting to that bench over there? To fix your shoe?" Luis pointed to a bench near the window.

"Yes, if you don't mind. Thanks." He helped her limp over to the bench. Although she adjusted her dress and pulled it taut, her nipple continued to make an impromptu appearance.

"There you go. You should be alright now." He wanted to leave before he got in over his head.

"You sure are handsome. I'll bet you have all kinds of women out there in California climbing all over themselves to get to you. Before you go, can you please help me undo the strap on my shoe? If I bend over, my dress is so loose… Well, you get the picture…" she said in low, husky sexy voice.

"Yeah, I'll help you with your strap, but after that I've got to go. My girlfriend is waiting for me." Luis got down on his knee and struggled with the woman's shoe strap.

"Where is she? If you were my man, I wouldn't ever leave you alone. There's no telling the trouble you'd get into out on your own." She uncrossed her legs and pulled her dress aside to reveal she was also pantiless.

Luis couldn't help but to look, partly out of shock, but mostly at her nerve. He stared at the woman's clean shaven pubic region. She placed her hand between her legs and began to masturbate right there in the museum for all to see. He looked around. They were the only ones there.

"Uh, what are you doing?" Luis felt his erection grow until he was about to burst.

"You want some of this? I'll give it to you. Free. No charge. We can go back to my place and fuck until you need to return to your girlfriend. I won't tell." She said in a deep husky voice and continued to masturbate so intensely, she almost climaxed on the bench.

They heard steps approaching. Alexis pulled her dress taut and stood up. Her face was flushed and she appeared momentarily embarrassed. The guard glanced in their direction and continued on his way, making his rounds.

Luis looked away from the woman, feeling guilty at the thoughts that swirled in his head. For a moment, he considered taking her up on her offer. She wanted it and he needed the release. What could it hurt? He and Ronnie were only friends. And yet, in his heart he knew he couldn't do anything with this woman. Because if Ronnie ever found out, any chances of being with her were would be ruined.

"Lady, I've got to go. Good luck with the next one though. You're good. Really good. And you shouldn't have any problems trapping the next guy. Only next time, you might want to leave something to the imagination."

Luis sat in the car and laughed so hard he almost cried. "Where in the world do these people come from? All I wanted to do was pass the time until Ronnie was ready. I never imagined I would be propositioned in a museum. It is a crazy world filled with crazy people!"

Instead of chancing any more crazy encounters with sexually deprived women, Luis returned to the coffee shop across the street from the beauty salon and picked up a mindless magazine to read. He spied a well-worn paperback novel titled *More Than A Notion* left by another customer. He picked it up and started to read. It was a new novel by an unknown independent author. The premise was good so he dove straight in, becoming intrigued after reading the first page.

A very used sofa beckoned him to make himself comfortable. He sat down, sent Ronnie a text of where he was, propped his feet up on the coffee table, and engrossed himself in the dog eared novel. He felt safe in the coffee shop. Ronnie was across the street, which was comforting in itself. Three hours down, three more to go.

Two and a half hours later, Ronnie sent Luis a text. "Come on over," it read. He dropped the novel, noting the author's name and made his way across the busy intersection. The streets were teeming with aliens, space creatures, and Japanese anime cartoon characters. It soon became obvious the science fiction and fantasy convention was ending for the evening or on a dinner break.

"Wow!" exclaimed Luis upon seeing her. Ronnie's braids extended down to the middle of her back. She didn't look her age to begin with, but somehow that hairstyle took ten years off her.

"So, what do you think? You like?" She tossed her braids to the side and looked up at him as if some sexy, sultry vixen replaced the old Ronnie.

"Yes, surprisingly I do. On you they look great. Gotta admit I've never been a big fan of braids. Depending on who wears them, they tend to look....well, *ghetto*."

"Ghetto huh? For your information, I know lots of professional sisters who wear braids and ain't nothing ghetto about them. I think you've been watching too many hoochie mama videos, or either you've been up in the 'hood one too many times. All you men just alike. You want a hood rat freak in the bedroom, but a lady in the street."

"Hey, hold on a minute. I didn't say you were ghetto. And I know what I want. Don't get it twisted Ronnie, I'm just saying most of the women I've seen wearing braids are from the 'hood and usually have a bunch of children running up behind her."

Ronnie did not hesitate to hide her annoyance with his arrogance. With her mouth twisted to the side, she pulled a bunch of bills from her purse, thanked the women profusely for doing such a great job, and walked out the door with Luis trailing behind her.

"Ronnie? Wait….I didn't mean to insult you. Your hair looks great! You look great! And I didn't call you ghetto!" he shouted. "Hold up woman, I am not going to chase after you. Stop walking!" He stood in the middle of the sidewalk with his hands held up in frustration. He watched a half naked couple covered in multicolor body paint pass by. "Ronnie, I'm sorry!" he screamed.

She stopped walking, crossed her arms, and stood tapping her foot without turning around. Her feelings were hurt. She thought, *who does he think he is calling my hairstyle ghetto?* She experienced enough of those sentiments from white people. She sure as hell didn't need it from him. *Oh no!* She realized. *I sound just like my mother!*

Ronnie uncrossed her arms, turned around and took a long hard look at Luis. She took in the scenery of the city street and exhaled. There was no malice intended by his comments. In his world, women probably didn't wear braids. She recognized her anger wasn't about braids and hair had nothing to do with it.

Suddenly all the hurt feelings of betrayal surfaced. She wasn't angry at Luis. It was Derek she was pissed off at; first for divorcing her, then for dying. Her daddy left her at a time when she needed him the most. So did Ike by returning to his ex. Every significant man in her life had betrayed, walked out, or died on her. The pain in her heart was from the loss of love, yet love stood right before her eyes, waiting for her to embrace it.

Luis didn't know what to do. He didn't know why she was upset, after all he was just joking. The hairstyle was essential only because of her arm being in a cast. It wasn't even permanent and if it were, he didn't care one way or the other how she styled her hair. Standing there feeling like an asshole he called out again, "Sweetheart, I'm sorry! Please forgive me. I didn't mean it."

As she listened to his apology, her feet began to move on their own, faster and faster, weaving through the cartoonish figures blocking her path. This man, this handsome, lovable, charming, wonderful man was there only for her. He even put his life on hold to drive cross country with her. Before she realized what she was doing, Ronnie ended up in Luis' arms kissing him like she'd never kissed a man before. Kissed him as if her life depended on it.

"Get a room!" "Somebody's getting lucking tonight!" "Need some help with your lady, man?" "They're such a nice looking couple." "Why don't we kiss like that anymore…?" The unsolicited remarks came nonstop from the crowd, as they passed by the couple locked in a passionate kiss as if they were the only people on that sidewalk.

When they pulled apart Luis tenderly touched Ronnie's cheek and apologized. "I'm sorry. I didn't mean to hurt your feelings," he said. His hand traveled down the long intricate braids. He studied the hundreds of tiny braids piled upon each other and thought her hairstyle could be considered as its own work of art.

"I'm the one who should apologize. I was being silly. I'm sorry, too." She played with her hair continuing to feel self-conscious. "Do you really think I look ghetto?"

"I think you're absolutely gorgeous. But the most important part about all of this is I don't have to do your hair tomorrow morning!" he laughed.

"You are soooo crazy! C'mon, let's get something to eat, I'm starved," Ronnie said.

"Me too. How about steaks? I drove by a steakhouse on the way back from the museum. It smelled delicious."

"Museum? You went to a museum? I thought you were across the street all that time—in the coffee house." Ronnie accepted Luis' holding her hand while they walked. It felt good and something she hadn't done with anyone else. Not even Derek.

Luis was hit with the dilemma of telling Ronnie about the woman in the museum who so blatantly exposed her genitals as a proposition for more, or keeping his mouth shut. He imagined the news would send her into another funk. For now, he'd keep that experience to himself. In time perhaps he would tell Ronnie, but then again maybe not. After all, it's not like he cheated.

"Yeah, I found a brochure for the Native American Art museum.

It was a good sized building and took a few hours to tour. It was very interesting. Very interesting..." He repeated.

"Is that right? Well you'll have to tell me all about it. I love art."

"Okay, so do you want steak or something else? I'm literally about to pass out from lack of food," he joked.

"The steakhouse sounds fine. Is it far?"

"Nope, only fifteen minutes away."

Before being seated, the waitress provided the option of selecting their steaks from a display window near the entrance. Ronnie chose a ribeye. Luis selected a porterhouse. The aroma of charbroiled steaks made their mouths water and stomachs growl. A very busy waitress brought out a bucket of peanuts and two beers to tide them over until their meals were ready.

"I hope the food tastes as good as it smells," said Ronnie, diving into the peanuts.

"The local paper rated this as one of the top steakhouses in the city, so it should be okay. Plus, look at the crowd waiting to get in. That's always a good sign."

"It *is* very crowded." She looked around and inhaled the aroma again. "You ever wonder how food would taste if you couldn't smell it? I mean, isn't the ability to smell as important as tasting it?"

"I suppose so. But which sense is most important? Sight, hearing, taste, smell, touch? I would think humans require all to have the fullest sensation. Why do you think they put on this show with choosing your steak and allowing diners to see inside the kitchen? It's all part of the experience."

"I just mean that it must suck to not be able to smell what you're eating. Then again, not being able to taste your food would probably be just as awful. By the way, I'm about sick of these salty peanuts."

"They say that when you lose one of your senses, the other ones kick in to compensate for the loss. *Senorita*, I'm just happy I am able to see, so I can marvel at your beauty." He smiled and playfully tossed a peanut her way.

"Thank you, you're so kind, sir." She laughed along, tossing a peanut back at him.

Just when Ronnie thought she couldn't eat another salty peanut, the waitress brought out two sizzling hot plates of delectable grilled steaks with all the delicious sides.

"Here you guys go. Be careful...these plates are hot," said the waitress, placing the food in front of them.

"Well it's about time; I'm starved!" Ronnie exclaimed to Luis.

"Thank you, miss. It all looks delicious," he said to the waitress.

"If y'all need anything, just holler. Be back to check on you in a few," said the waitress.

They enthusiastically ate their meals, periodically stopping to express how delicious the food was.

"Mmm, that was excellent. I can't believe I ate that entire steak. I am so stuffed." Ronnie turned up her glass and sipped the remaining red wine to wash down the meal.

"I agree. It was very good. I am done, too. Can't eat anymore. This cut must have been almost two pounds." Luis sat back and rubbed his full belly.

The waitress stopped by with the dessert menu. As she reviewed the decadent house specialties and went over the twelve different kinds of cheesecake with Ronnie, Luis spied a familiar face. *Oh shit!* he thought. *It's that crazy bitch from earlier today.*

"Hey, why don't we leave now? You just said you were full. Won't cheesecake be too heavy sitting on your stomach this late? Waitress, please bring the check." Luis wanted to leave before the woman made a scene.

"I'll be fine. I'll get it to go and by the time we get back to the hotel, I'll have room in my stomach." She returned her attention to the waitress, "I think I'll have the turtle cheesecake, no wait a minute. Maybe the key lime would be better, it's not as heavy. Hold on, I changed my mind. I'll take the white chocolate with raspberry filling. Yeah, that's the one I want. Thanks."

Luis' mind was anywhere but on dessert. Of all the people to run into that evening, it had to be that freaky nympho from the museum. Alexis saw him in the same moment he saw her. She wore a different version of the same wraparound dress. Luis' thoughts drifted to the delicacies hidden from view underneath the thin silky material. He took a good look at Alexis. Not a bad looking woman. Her hair was bleached platinum blonde. Face was okay—though she wouldn't win any beauty contests, she was attractive. Of course, her big boobs and long tanned legs that went on forever would make any man happy to have them wrapped around his back. He felt his erection stiffen.

"Hellooo? You still with me? Who are you staring at? I'll bet you haven't heard a word I've said, have you?" Ronnie's gaze followed to the object of Luis's attention. "Do you know *her?*" she asked, perturbed at his audacity.

"Yes," his voice squeaked. "I mean no, I met her at the museum earlier today. He squirmed uncomfortably in his seat trying to think of anything but Alexis masturbating. Seeing her fingers slip in and out. In and out. In and out. He could not get the images from his mind. But the truth was, as much as Alexis tantalized him with her very explicit display, it was not she he wanted. He wanted Ronnie, the woman sitting across from him. Wanted to make love to her and express how he felt. Alexis was nothing but a distraction.

Alexis boldly walked past their table, her date trailed behind looking like he'd hit the jackpot. Too bad his jackpot had been hit by more than he could ever know. She glanced over her shoulder and winked at Luis, then puckered her ruby red lips and blew him a kiss.

Ronnie damn near lost her mind. "Who is that? Is there something you want to tell me Luis?" She waved the waitress off to fully focus her attention on Luis.

Without responding, he dropped enough money to cover the meal and left a generous tip. "Come on, let's get out of here." He stood and reached for Ronnie's hand.

"Uh unh...Before we go anywhere, you need to tell me what the hell is going on." She planted her butt further into the chair and wouldn't budge.

"I am not going to do this here. Not like this. Please Ronnie, believe me. Nothing happened. Trust me. Let's go." His displeasure with the situation was evident on his face.

She cut her eyes over to the booth where the blonde and her date sat—groping each other. Both were so engrossed in whatever naughtiness was happening underneath the table that neither paid much attention to her or Luis. The woman's date reminded her of the men on that television show; the one where they caught child molesters on camera. And the woman was about as fake as they come. Fake hair, boob implants, artificial nails, and an orange glow tan, topped off by an expressionless face courtesy of *Botox*. No way Luis could ever be interested in that.

"All right, but something's up. Don't no woman blow kisses to a stranger; I do know that much."

They walked to the car in silence. Ronnie held her tongue waiting to see what Luis would do. He waited until they were a few miles from the restaurant before he spoke. Not knowing how she would react to his explanation, he didn't want to chance Ronnie going crazy on him or that woman in the restaurant.

"Don't be mad. I told you I met her at the museum. Well, that *is* the truth."

"Go on," she said.

"I only went to the art museum because I needed to fill the time you needed to get your hair braided. Anyway, the audio tour said it would take about two hours to see the art collection properly. That's exactly what I was doing when that woman approached me. In fact, she trailed behind me for several minutes before walking up and introducing herself. We talked for a few moments and I told her I was passing time until you were ready." They were almost at the hotel.

"So what was her throwing a kiss at you about?"

"I don't know. Maybe she was trying to upset you off to get back at me. Ronnie, the woman pushed up on me and propositioned me like a pro. I didn't take the bait. I left her at the museum feeling foolish and embarrassed."

"Embarrassed by what? Because you turned her down? You may be fine and everything, but come on…" She laughed.

"Oh, so you don't think I have that effect on women?" he asked, parking the car near the closest entrance. He removed the hotel key from his wallet.

Ronnie looked at him with those big brown eyes that went straight to his soul and asked, "Is there anything else you want to tell me?"

Luis weighed his options. Tell her the truth and see how she handles it, or lie and risk it coming out eventually through a careless slip of the tongue. "No, that's not it. She pretended the heel of her shoe was broken. I helped her to a bench to fix the strap."

Here it comes, she thought. The protective defensive wall automatically went up to shield her heart from whatever he was about to say. She steadied herself and listened.

"When I was bent over to help with the strap, her dress slipped open. She wasn't wearing underwear." Luis gulped and glanced over at Ronnie. She stared ahead silently.

"Friggin' slut! She showed you her *cootchie*? What did you do then?" she whispered in an amazingly controlled voice.

"I'm a man. I couldn't help it. I watched. I tried to look away, but I couldn't believe my eyes. She literally began to masturbate! Right in front of me!"

Ronnie rolled her eyes and laughed, "You're telling me she started masturbating right in front of you and you didn't do anything? What do I look like? A fool?"

"I admit it was erotic in a slutty sort of way. But I didn't want her and more importantly, I didn't desire her. She was simply a live sex show. That's all. I said a few choice words and walked away. That's the end of the story. I promise. All I could think about was getting back to you."

"You know what Luis?" she asked.

"What Ronnie?" he asked, weary from the day's events.

"I believe you. I believe you because nobody could make up a story as wild as that. And after seeing her with that man in the restaurant, I can imagine someone like that pushing up on you. After all, you are a very sexy, handsome man. If I didn't know you, I'd proposition you too." She felt the wall around her heart retreat.

"Mmm, is that a promise?"

"Yeah, it is. And one day I'll show you what I mean."

"*Cogno!* So *one day* doesn't mean today?"

"Yeah. Sorry, afraid not," she replied.

Luis shrugged, "Can't blame a man for trying." He teased.

Shortly after entering his hotel room, the balloon company called and confirmed the next morning's flight. He provided Luis with the address to meet and told him to dress comfortably.

Because of Ronnie's inability to sleep the previous night, they decided to sleep in their separate rooms and leave the adjoining door open.

* * *

"Beep, beep, beep, beep….." Luis's alarm clock clicked on at 5:30. He pushed himself from the comfort of the warm bed and made it to the bathroom. The coolness of the tile floor helped chase away the drowsiness.

"Ronnie? Ronnie my sweet, time to wake up." He called out before jumping into the shower. Five minutes later, he was finished.

Noticing her room was still dark, he called out again, "Ronnie, time to get up. We don't want to be late."

She turned over in her bed and muttered to herself, "Is it time to get up already? "Okay, okay… I'm up. Sort of." She reached for the bedside lamp, found the on switch, and rolled out of bed. Half asleep she managed to turn on the shower and step in. At least she didn't have to worry about her hair.

* * *

Along the way to the meeting point, they stopped at a tourist shop and purchased two oversized sweatshirts and a couple of baseball caps, because there was a slight chill in the morning air. The meeting point was basically just an open field. Several men were gathered around a truck hitched up to a long trailer. A huge semi inflated, colorful balloon seemed to be weighted down by several sandbags.

The owner, a barrel-chested man in his mid to late 40's, greeted them. His deeply tanned skin resembled worn leather, indicating he spent a great deal of his time in the sun. He introduced himself, provided a quick yet detailed safety briefing, and took them to the balloon. Two other men walked around the balloon, doing safety checks and preflight preparations.

Ronnie held tightly onto Luis' hand as she watched the men inflate the balloon. The operator manipulated the gas tanks to send intermittent bursts of flames shooting upwards into the hot air balloon. Ever so slowly it rose from the ground. While they were waiting, another two couples joined the group for the ride. When the balloon was fully inflated, all six passengers and the tour guide climbed into the basket, acknowledging each other, before claiming an open spot along one of the sides.

One of the men on the ground shouted, "Clear!" He simultaneously released the ropes from the basket. The giant balloon rose slowly, gently, gracefully until it was high above the ground.

Ronnie gushed at the breathtaking sight unfolding before her eyes. "It's so beautiful up here. Hey look, the sun is beginning to rise over the mountains."

Luis wrapped his arm around her waist and pulled her closer. Yes, he loved how she got excited about those small things, the way she took joy in the ordinary. "You're enjoying this, aren't you?"

She nodded.

"This is the first time I've done anything like this. I must admit, I'm enjoying myself, as well."

"It's so romantic flying high above the city first thing in the morning. I can't believe how quiet and peaceful it is up here. I feel like we should whisper to not break this magical spell." She snuggled closer to Luis. *Umm, I love having his strong arms wrapped around me. I feel safe and protected in his embrace.*

"I know what you mean, listen to the silence. Never heard silence as loud as this before. Ronnie, I am so happy you wanted to take this ride. I am really digging this. Woman…what are you doing to me?"

"Don't know what I'm doing to you. Don't know what I'm doing to myself. This ain't me. I used to be Miss "By the book". In this moment, I feel free—freer than I have ever been. Is this what it means to live in the offbeat?" Ronnie appreciated Luis' open outlook on life. How he was willing to explore—do things out of the ordinary. Not the same old stuff like the rest of the guys she dated.

"Yeah, I think it does. But one thing's for sure. I'm glad we're in this offbeat together," replied Luis.

In between telling bad jokes, the tour guide pointed out natural landmarks and provided an abbreviated New Mexico history lesson. For a little over an hour, they floated over the Rio Grande river snaking through the valley below. Since neither one had the foresight to bring a camera, the tour guide snapped a commemorative photo and said it would be ready to pick up later in the afternoon.

The wind began to die down and the hot air balloon started its gradual descent. The operator carefully navigated the craft to a large open field and landed. The two men who helped raise the balloon met the group and directed all to an eight passenger van. Another truck pulling a large white trailer, advertising the hot air balloon company, pulled up beside them.

Full of wonderment and still beaming from the inspiring sights they'd just seen, all the passengers were elated. They piled into the van for the thirty minute ride back to the origination site. It was still early— not even eight o'clock yet.

"Oh my goodness! That ride just about topped about everything I've ever done in my life. Thank you for bringing me here, Luis. It was amazing, absolutely amazing," she replied with unrestrained enthusiasm as they approached the car.

Luis loved how excited she was, and in that moment, she was beyond beautiful. She turned around and smiled. He stopped walking and admired her beauty. It was as if all the angels in Heaven above were smiling upon her.

Ronnie stopped walking when she noticed Luis was no longer at her side. "Hey, where'd you go?" She looked over her shoulder. What she saw nearly brought her to her knees. Luis stood with his hands in his pockets. His face was covered with an expression she'd never witnessed on anyone's before. It was as if all the goodness in the world was coming through the pores of his skin. He radiated pure love.

They started walking towards one another and stopped within several inches of each other. No words could capture the essence of the moment. Both felt it at the same time. An imperceptible shift had taken place in the universe to bring them together in a moment of absolute perfection. For a mere fraction of a second the earth stopped spinning, the wind ceased to blow, and all of God's creatures fell silent to observe the transformation occurring in Ronnie and Luis. And that is when they knew they were destined to be together.

Luis gently stroked her face, wiping away a tear trailing down her lovely cheek. He touched her chin and kissed her top lip, followed by the lower. His heart felt like it was going to burst open. He loved this woman. Loved her with heart, body, and soul.

Ronnie didn't know why she wept, but she felt blissfully happy, content, and loved. Finally! This man God put in front of her was who she had searched for all her life. When Luis touched her face and wiped away her tears, she closed her eyes and prayed a silent, *Thank you Lord.* And when he kissed her, her heart opened, releasing all the anger, hurt, and bitterness that made its way in and lived for years.

"Y'all alright over there?" asked one of the men from the group.

With those words, the magical spell was broken and the earth started to spin once more.

"Yes, thanks, we're fine," replied Luis to the man.

Ronnie laughed nervously. "I don't know what just happened, but it sure feels good."

"I felt it too," Luis said. "You're right, this does feel really good." He draped his arm over her shoulder and walked to the car. The passenger door's window reflected back the bright morning sun. He fished inside his pocket for his sunglasses as the world returned back to normal.

Chapter 24

"Luis, we have over 900 miles to get to California. What do you say we head out after breakfast?" Ronnie felt lightheaded.

"I was just thinking the same thing. Maybe we can make it as far as Las Vegas. Spend the night there and head out the next day. What do you think about that?"

"Okay, sounds good. Hey you hungry? I'm starting to feel faint."

"It's probably the high altitude. Let's get some food and water inside you. Can't have you passing out on me."

They checked out of the hotel and hit the road. Las Vegas was about an eight hour drive away.

"We'll make it there just before nightfall. Maybe we'll hangout and hit a few tables. You gamble?" Luis turned his head partially to focus on Ronnie.

"Um, not really. Never got the hang of it. I'll play the slots, but that's about it. How about you?"

"I primarily stick to black jack because I'm not much of a gambler either," he replied. "Ronnie, can I ask you something?"

"Sure. What's up?" Ronnie was distracted by the desert landscape. Mountains soared high into the sky still covered with snow in stark contrast to the scorched earth below. Cacti of all shapes and sizes became more plentiful the closer they got to Arizona.

"When we first met in the Dominican Republic, you said you were just getting out of a relationship. Well, a lot has happened to you—to us, since then. I was wondering if you still think it's too soon for us to become involved."

Ronnie pondered his question and reflected back to the past month about how much her life had changed. She was a different person than who she was just a couple of weeks ago. What was once important, no longer was. Material possessions no longer mattered. Keeping up with the Joneses and maintaining an illusion of wealth were no longer central in her life. Her daughter was now the primary focus. Yet, the promise of being with Luis felt so right.

"That trip to the DR feels like it happened years ago. You and me together? I think I'd like that very much," she answered.

He reached over and squeezed the fingers of her good hand. "Good, I hoped you would say that. I want to share something with you. Don't think I'm crazy when I tell you this, but when we got off the balloon ride and were on our way back to the car, I felt something strange."

"Strange?" she wondered. "What do you mean?" She wanted to hear the words from his mouth first.

"I felt this odd sensation as if we've known each other longer than a month. Like we're connected on a much deeper spiritual level. As if you and I are supposed to be together—like we've always been together. Maybe you *are* my soul mate, if I were to believe in such a thing. I don't know. It was a weird feeling. Sort of like that kid we met yesterday when he spoke of predetermined destiny and all..."

She turned to look at him and asked, "When did you say you felt this strange sensation?"

"Uh, when we were on the way to the car. Right before we kissed."

"Hmm... Yes, I felt something strange right about the same time. Do you think it was the high altitude?" she asked and continued. "Maybe the thin air hit us both at the same time." She nervously twirled a braid around her finger.

"No, it wasn't the thin air. When I looked at you, you seemed so... happy. That's when I saw your beautiful, loving, generous heart. In that moment, I knew I wanted to spend the rest of my life with you."

"Luis, I understand how you feel because I felt the same thing. I prayed that God would send someone for me to love. Someone who loved me unconditionally! A man who would shower me with love and affection and allow me to fully love him in return. After my marriage was over, I gave up on finding that elusive thing called love. Used to think it was the stuff of fairy tales. You know, the Princess meets her Prince Charming and they fall in love and live happily ever after. I thought falling in love was made for fairy tales designed to hook little girls into believing in make believe," she explained.

"I know what you mean. I've dated several women since my divorce, but none of them made me want to pursue a relationship. I knew you were someone very special when you pulled me out of the ocean. You didn't panic or start screaming for help; just calmly offered me your lovely hand and helped me out. Veronica Pierce, you are a smart, beautiful woman with a heart of gold," he sighed.

"That's sweet of you to say that about me. I'll let you in on a little secret. That evening when you came up to me in the dining room and asked if anyone was sitting in that empty chair, I thought you were interested in me. I was thrilled because I was attracted to you. Oh my God, I was soooo embarrassed when you said you needed it for your group." She laughed.

"Sorry about that. My nieces and nephews are a handful and I really didn't have much time to focus on you. But I did notice you were a pretty lady sitting alone."

"Yeah, me and my *empty* chair. It took a lot of courage to sit in that dining room alone. I should've been with someone—a husband or at least a boyfriend. I hope I haven't gotten jaded, but I've known very few couples that have survived and thrived in a marriage. Most end in divorce. Look at us. Two divorces between us. I gave up on love a long time ago."

"Aren't you being a bit cynical? You're much too kind to have given up on love totally."

"Maybe I am a bit jaded."

"Try not to be; you haven't given me a shot yet. Maybe I will be your Prince Charming—the man who sweeps you off your feet."

She laughed and replied, "Why not? Maybe you *can* be my Dominican prince charming, my *Príncipe Encantador.*"

"So I see you know some *Español?* Stick with me and you'll be fluent in no time at all."

"All right, it's a deal." She started playing with the radio. "Hey, you want to listen to music or an audio book? I also have XM radio; I started to get rid of it when I downsized my car, but I'm glad I didn't," she added.

"Anything is fine with me…"

"Hey, Luis can you pull over for a minute?"

"What's wrong? You feeling sick?"

"No, I feel fine. I saw something over there in that field of desert flowers. Look over there. What is that?"

A blanket of purple rose and fell. Lifted high in the air, then rose and fell again.

"I don't know, but you sure you want to stop and look?" he asked, skeptically.

"Can't hurt us. Slow down, please. I'll leave the windows up until we can tell what it is."

Luis pulled safely to the side of the road, far away from the cars whizzing past, some going as fast as ninety miles per hour. "Can you still see it?"

"Wait a minute. I think… I think those are butterflies!" she exclaimed.

"What in the world? Purple butterflies? Is that normal for way out here?" Luis shielded his eyes from the sun to better observe the natural phenomena.

Each creature flew in perfect synchronicity to the other, as if they all shared one brain. He observed the same behavior in schools of fish and flocks of birds.

"I don't know. The last time I saw a purple butterfly was in Virginia." She suddenly recalled the conversation with old Sam in the parking lot.

"My father loved purple butterflies. Whenever I see them now, I think about his love. Daddy told me butterflies are tiny messages of love sent from God. Don't think I'm crazy, but I think my father is trying to tell me something. About you. About us. I think he approves of you." As she spoke, a lone butterfly flitted outside her window then went to Luis's side.

"Would you look at that? Is it checking us out? If I didn't know better I'd say it was. Now *that* is weird."

"Not weird. Consider it as a good omen. Look, it's returning to the others."

They watched the butterfly until they could no longer distinguish it out from the group.

"That was beautiful—what you said about your father. I'm glad we stopped." He brought her hand to his lips and kissed. He carefully pulled back into traffic.

"Do you think I'm silly for believing in stuff like that? About the butterflies being messages from God? Or being sent from my father?"

"No, I don't. You seem to be a very spiritual person with an amazing sense of self-awareness. You get that we're all connected. Not just to other people, but to all living things. I think that one small change in the world eventually touches all our lives in some small way. Nothing happens in this universe without affecting something else. Kind of what happens when you drop a pebble in a pond; the resulting ripple touches everything in its path as it makes its way across."

"Hmm, I never thought of it that way. See, that's why I love talking to you. You have a very open mind that's receptive to new ideas. "

"I am trying to be more open minded. It's kind of difficult when you're raised with a very strict upbringing, but I'll get there eventually." He winked and took a swig of water. "Hey, you mentioned earlier you got rid of your car. Why? Was there something wrong with it?" He noticed they'd crossed the New Mexico, Arizona border.

"Nothing was wrong with the car. I got rid of it because it was part of minimizing my life. Getting rid of the excess stuff I didn't need. I loved that *Infiniti*, but without a steady income, I couldn't afford it. It was a status symbol plain and simple. So I traded it in and bought this off the lot. Cash on the spot."

"So let me ask you something; did you consider yourself high maintenance before you got rid of the excess?"

Ronnie measured her words carefully, recalling the conversation about his high maintenance ex-wife. "Tell you the truth, I used to be, but since I paid for my own upkeep, I didn't see anything wrong with looking good and having nice things. Sure, I'd like to be able to live a champagne and caviar lifestyle, but for now that's not my goal. My goal is to get to California, meet my daughter, and begin a new life. My purpose lies somewhere out there and I'm going to find it, no matter what it takes."

"I'm happy to see you're not afraid to work for what you want. Any idea of what you're searching for? And what makes you so certain it's in California?" He passed a slow moving RV pulling a mid-sized sedan.

"Past getting reacquainted with my daughter, I'm not sure what I'm searching for. Maybe when I finally see Kiara, things will become clearer. Start coming together."

"How about her father? Do you have any unresolved feelings about him?"

"Where did that come from? Actually, I haven't thought much about Travis, except how grateful I am he kept our daughter. Our relationship was—is part of the past. Can't say I feel one way or the other about him. Why?" She wiggled a pencil under the cast trying to scratch an itch. It didn't work.

"Just wondering about my competition. Once a child is involved, you're joined to that other person for life. Since you were in love with him, perhaps there are some leftover emotions that need to be fleshed out."

"No, it's nothing like that. Like I said, I'll always be grateful for how he stepped in and raised Kiara. If it weren't for Travis, she probably would never have found me. What about you? Are you satisfied with your life?"

"Yes, I am very satisfied with my life. I'm living my dream and doing what I love. There's no greater satisfaction in life than being content in your own skin. After my wife moved out, I put that house up for sale and bought the one I always wanted. Now it's just me and my dogs. I'm extremely happy. And now that I have you in my life, what more can I ask for?"

"Doing what you love? Being content in your own skin? Now that has to be a great feeling."

"It is. I started my business because I wanted to have the freedom to make my own decisions about how I wanted my graphic designs to look. They aren't the typical commercial fare most people think of because I put a Latino spin on my work. When you work for someone else, you have to follow their vision and that's alright if that is your choice. Or if you have no other options. I started my own business because I had nothing to lose and everything to gain. Following my passion led to my success."

"I hope one day to be able to say that as well…" she sighed.

"Okay, I have another question, if you don't mind."

"Go ahead. I've developed an appreciation for your thought-provoking questions," she replied sarcastically and smiled.

"What are your plans when you get to Santa Elena? Do you have a place to stay?"

"Sort of. I rented an efficiency apartment near the downtown area for now. I'll look for a permanent place after I become more familiar with the area."

"Listen, I'm going to make you an offer…only as a friend." Ronnie was about to protest, but Luis hushed her. "Hear me out first. I have a small apartment on the back of my property. The people who owned the house before me used to rent it out as rental property. I haven't done anything with it, and it's not much, but it's yours until you get settled."

"Thanks Luis, I appreciate the offer and depending upon how it all works out, I may just take you up on it. Of course, I'll pay you rent. I don't want to take advantage of our friendship."

"Whatever makes you happy. Just know the offer comes with no strings attached," he added.

She turned and smiled content in the knowledge of having at least one good friend in her corner.

* * *

The Vegas strip was really jumping for a weekday night. Then again, it didn't matter what day it was because every day was the weekend in Vegas.

The bumper-to-bumper traffic made a slow progression down the artificially illuminated strip, lined with casinos, restaurants, nightclubs, and tourist traps. The crowd consisted of thousands of tourists struggling to navigate the sidewalks and bypass dozens of illegal Mexicans handing out advertisements for strip clubs. Postcards with photos of topless women were shoved in the hands of anyone appearing to be of legal age—and some who didn't. The street lay littered with layers of postcards, discarded as soon as tourists realized what they held in their hands.

"Do you want to go straight to the hotel? Or do you need to stop anywhere else?" asked Luis, trying to concentrate on not getting hit by an impatient driver trying to cut into traffic.

"Whatever you think is best. This is my first time here so I have no idea where to even begin. Man, the strip looks just like it does on television."

Ronnie took in the magnificence of the brilliantly lit-up marquees that lined the seemingly never ending Vegas strip. The owners of the casinos used the billboards to compete with each other, thus they continued to become more extravagant the closer they got to the high dollar hotels. She heard the music from the *Bellagio's* famous water fountain dance before she saw the crowds lining up for a better view. Further down the strip, pirates battled one another on a life-sized replica of a pirate ship. The Eiffel tower and a hot air balloon were not to be outdone by the *Venetian* hotel and its authentic canals.

"Well, I've only been a few times. Vegas doesn't change much; just gets brighter, more congested, and noisier."

"How about we find the hotel and then go from there? How do you feel? You tired?" She noticed him stifle a yawn. She checked the clock on the dashboard. It was almost ten o'clock.

"I'll be fine once I take a nice hot shower. Don't you worry about me." He found the hotel and pulled the car into the parking garage.

On the way to the reservation desk, Luis asked, "One room or two? Either is fine with me, because I plan on being a perfect gentleman. Understand?" He raised one eyebrow to emphasis his point.

241

"One room with two beds is okay with me." She shrugged.

Luis approached the hotel desk clerk, "I need a suite with two double beds please."

"Please wait one moment sir while I check our availability." The desk clerk started to type on the keyboard. Then he typed some more, followed by more typing.

Ronnie wandered around the luxurious cavernous lobby. A directory in the middle of the floor may as well have been in a shopping mall. The hotel, casino, restaurant, shopping center, were all contained in one massive building.

Luis returned to her side, "Sorry, the only rooms available were the penthouse suite and a few king-sized rooms. I didn't want to drop several thousand for the penthouse, so I went with the king size suite. We can go somewhere else and see if they have availability if you want." He stifled another yawn.

"No, a king-sized room will be fine."

"Oh, I also ordered a New York style pepperoni pizza from room service and a couple of beers. I am so hungry I could eat a horse. They'll deliver it in about thirty minutes. When we go out later, we'll have a real meal. Okay?"

"Sure, that's fine with me. I know you're beat from all that driving. Anyway, I trust you to stay in the same room. Do you trust me?" she asked, sensuously chewing on her bottom lip.

"Ronnie, don't play games and start something you can't finish. We both agreed we were going to be friends first. Let's try to stick to the plan. If all goes well, we'll have the rest of our lives to make love." *I desire Ronnie so much. Seeing her lying naked in my bed, squirming underneath me while I love her up and down. And she looks so sexy standing there with those long braids swept atop her head.* He exhaled and tried to push the sexy thoughts from his mind.

"You're right. I'll be good." *Or at least I'll try to be.* Ronnie replied.

The bellboy brought their bags to the suite. Instead of walking into a typical nondescript hotel room with the bathroom right off the door, this suite opened into a formal foyer. A bouquet of freshly cut flowers rested in a vase atop an antique table. The suite resembled a small apartment; including a living area, a mini kitchenette, and a separate bedroom containing an oversized California king bed. The bathroom was exquisite as well.

Luis generously tipped the bellboy and shut the door. "Is this room suitable to your tastes, my dear?" he asked looking extremely pleased with himself.

"This can't be a standard room?" she gasped. "Luis, how much did this suite cost?"

"Don't worry about it. I'll write it off as a business expense." He shrugged his shoulders as if it were nothing.

"Is that right? Well mister I'll-write-it-off, I hope you don't get into trouble for this, because I absolutely love this room! Take a look; we have a great view of the strip."

Luis stepped next to Ronnie. She was right. It was a great view. Being near her was as close to torture as he could imagine. He kissed her hand as they stood taking in the view.

"I've got to hit the shower. You want to go get a bite to eat and maybe do some gambling?"

She hesitated. At this point, she didn't want to leave the room. It was so romantic—this suite. Being so close to him. Her eyes traveled to the bedroom, then to the bed. She imagined they could make really good use of that king-sized bed. Plenty of room to stretch out, roll around, jump up and down.

"Yeah, okay. Food sounds good. I'll shower after you."

Luis let the cool water wash away his sexual urges. In the midst of experiencing a massive erection, he refused to relieve himself in the shower. *I promised her I would wait. Don't want to rush anything, but damn I'm horny!* When it was safe to leave the bathroom, he wrapped a towel around his waist and called out, "I'm coming out. Your turn."

Ronnie tried to avert her eyes when Luis stepped out of the bathroom. Beads of water rolled down his chest and became trapped in his chest hair. The temptation of running her hands over his body was strong. Very strong. She fought the urge by looking away. Her gaze ended up on the towel loosely wrapped around his waist. With all her might she willed it to fall.

Luis was aware of her stare and tried to ignore it. The sexual tension grew more pronounced as time went on. Her prolonged stare didn't bother him. On the contrary, he relished knowing his desire for her was mutual.

"Hey, I'm going to get dressed in the bedroom. The bathroom's all yours. Take your time," he said as he strutted into the other room.

Goodness, he is too fine, she thought. *All I want to do is go in there and throw myself on top of that man and let him take me right here in this beautiful Las Vegas suite. Forget about waiting.* She fantasized about making love to Luis. Wondered how it would feel to physically connect and become one. "Okay, I shouldn't be long," she answered.

By the time Ronnie finished showering and was almost dressed, she heard a soft knock at the door. "Luis, get the door will you?" she shouted. She heard the knock again. "Hey Luis, will you please get the door?" she asked again. When she didn't get a response, she peeked into the bedroom. Luis was knocked out—sprawled out sound asleep on top of the bed. She smiled and went to let room service in.

"I'm sorry, but I don't have any change for a tip," she said to the waiter.

"Mr. Duarte has already taken care of it, ma'am," he replied. "Where would you like me to place your pie?"

She pointed to the kitchenette's counter. He sat the pizza and the ice filled canister containing two cold beers on the small counter and quietly left. Ronnie locked the door behind him and went into the bedroom.

He must've been really tired because he hadn't bothered to get dressed. Luis was sprawled on his back, still wearing the damp towel. Although he wasn't snoring, she could tell he was in a deep sleep.

She quietly crept to his side and softly called out his name, "Luis? Luis the pizza's here." He didn't move a muscle. She watched his chest rise and fall, wanting to rest her head against his chest again, listening to his strong heartbeat. Getting caught up in between his beats.

The age old battle between good and evil raged inside her mind and invaded her thoughts. The urge to look underneath the towel to check out his "equipment" grew stronger the longer she stared. *What would it hurt to take a little peek?* She rationalized. *I've seen everything else, so why not take a look?* As she hovered over him, she listened for any change in his breathing pattern. There was none. With her good hand, she carefully took hold of the towel and started to gently move it over.

All of a sudden Luis grabbed her hand and asked slyly, "Woman, what in the world do you think you're doing?"

Ronnie was stone cold busted. She stood upright and stammered, "Uh, uh, well, I uh, I was just trying to get this wet towel off you. It's kinda chilly in here and I uh...." She replied, blushing in obvious embarrassment.

Luis sat up and repositioned the towel to cover his nakedness. In spite of himself, he started to laugh uncontrollably. He noticed how embarrassed she seemed, which only made his laughter increase.

"Are you trying to see what I have under this towel? Really? Ronnie, you don't have to sneak a peek, I'll show you if that's what you want."

"Luis, I am so sorry, truly I am. I am so embarrassed. I couldn't help myself. I came in to tell you the pizza was here. Then I saw you lying on the bed undressed and something made me want to look. I am soooooo sorry." She hung her head in shame, apologizing profusely.

"And what were you checking for exactly? You want to see how big I am? Or how small? Does it really matter? Do you have a preference for a particular size or shape? What if I don't meet your expectations? Then what?" Luis was no longer laughing.

"No, I don't have any preference. My curiosity got the best of me, that's all. The size of your penis doesn't matter as long as it works. C'mon haven't you heard the expression? 'It's not the size of the ship, but the motion of the ocean?' Truly, I do not have a preference. Look, I really, really like you Luis and your penis size has nothing to do with that. And that's the truth."

Luis contemplated her explanation. She seemed sincere in her apology, although truth be known, he also wanted to see her fully naked and explore all she had to offer. Without any further hesitation, he whipped that towel off and stood fully exposed in all his glory.

Ronnie's eyes bugged out of her head upon seeing Luis fully naked. She was pleasantly surprised, enjoying a full range of emotions.

"Okay?" he asked.

"More than okay," she replied in satisfaction.

He shook his head in mock disbelief. He pulled on a pair of boxers and continued to get dressed. Every now and then he laughed at Ronnie's boldness.

"This is really good pizza. Good idea preordering it so we wouldn't have to wait."

Luis folded his in half New York style and bit into it. "Umm, it's pretty close to the real thing. I can't find good pizza in California. Who ever heard of pizza with barbecued chicken or macaroni and cheese? Yes sir, there's nothing like a good old fashioned New York slice."

"So you want to do some gambling while we're here? Slots, blackjack, craps?" The cold beer felt good chasing down the hot pizza.

"Yeah, okay. Whatever you like. I really needed that nap. Couldn't believe how exhausted I was. Driving takes a lot out of you."

"I know and I want to say thanks again for doing this. I don't know what I would've done without you." She raised the bottle of beer, tipping it towards him in a toast.

"My pleasure, I'm enjoying my time with you. You know we'll be in California tomorrow. Wish it didn't have to end so soon."

"I know. That reminds me, I should call Kiara tomorrow and set up a place and time to meet. But this isn't the end of us, it's the beginning. You'll see."

* * *

After an hour sitting at the slot machine watching her initial $100 of mad money continuously decrease to $28.75, Ronnie had enough. She went over to the blackjack table where Luis sat. A stack of colorful chips lay neatly stacked at his hands. He signaled for another card as the dealer made his rounds. When all was said and done, the hand was his.

"Looks like you're doing pretty good. I was going to suggest we leave, but since you're on a roll, I'll be back later." She leaned over and kissed him.

He picked up his complimentary drink and sipped. "Yeah, I'm up. Give me a bit more time because I'm going to ride this for a little longer." He tapped her on the ass and returned to the game.

Ronnie wandered the floor in search of another slot machine that looked promising. As she sat down and inserted her casino card to start playing the dollar slots, her cell phone vibrated. She'd forgotten the cell phone was in the clutch purse she always kept by her side. It was her mother.

"Hello?" she yelled into the phone.

"Hi Veronica, it's your mother," Dianna replied.

"Hey Mama, how you doing?" she asked and noted the time. It was the middle of the night in Oklahoma City.

"I'm doing alright. I couldn't sleep because I've been worried about you. I haven't heard from you and I was wondering how everything is going."

"Mama, it's after 2 o'clock in the morning." She balanced the phone on her shoulder while pushing buttons on the slot machine.

"Child, I don't sleep much anymore. Anyway, how you been doing? You seen Kiara yet?"

"No, I haven't made it there yet. I'm in Vegas. Me and Luis decided to take our time driving to California. We spent a couple of days in New Mexico and will spend the night here. I plan on seeing her tomorrow or the next day."

"Oh really? So you two are getting along then? He seemed like such a nice young man."

"Yes, we're getting along very well. Hey Mama, I can barely hear you over the machines. I'll give you a call when I get settled in."

"Hey listen, before you go, can I give you a few words of advice? As a woman and as your mother?"

"Yes, what is it?"

"When you first meet your child—Kiara. Don't expect much right off the bat. While it is true you gave birth to her, you're basically a stranger. You don't know anything about her. Don't know if she was raised by another woman or not. And you have no idea what that child has gone through. I'm telling you this so you won't be hurt or disappointed if you don't get the reception you expect. She may not welcome you back into her life with open arms right away. That's all I'm saying."

"Thanks Mama, I understand and I appreciate your advice. I am getting more and more nervous the closer I get to meeting her. I know I shouldn't expect much, but I'm hoping for the best. I'll just have to take it slow. One day at a time." Her eyes teared up from her mother's concern.

"All right, that's all I have to say. Tell Luis I called and said "hi". Veronica? One more thing…"

"Yes, Mama?" She hit the roll button and watched the numbers settle.

"I love you."

"I love you, too," she replied.

Ronnie couldn't believe her eyes. She watched all four sevens on the screen line up perfectly. *I hit the jackpot?!* She screamed into the phone. "Mama! I just hit the jackpot! I just won five thousand dollars!" she shouted jumping up and down. She accidently dropped the cell on the floor.

A very obese woman rushing over to see the excitement stepped on Ronnie's phone, breaking it into several pieces. She looked at the phone, then at Ronnie.

"What? Veronica, what's that you say?!" Dianna reluctantly hung up. That last thing she heard was something about a jackpot.

"You have got to be kidding me!" Ronnie looked down to see her cell phone lying shattered underneath the fat woman's foot.

"I'm sorry; I didn't see your phone. Can you still use it?" She huffed and puffed bending down to retrieve the phone. She handed it over to Ronnie.

"Well, it is definitely broken. Don't worry about it. Really," she said to the woman.

Ronnie took the broken phone from the woman's puffy fingers and refocused her attention on the attendant making his way over. She dismissed the woman and greeted the attendant. He verified that the jackpot win was legitimate and stamped the ticket with his magic stamp of approval. He pointed to the cashier's window where she could pick up her winnings.

She ran over to the blackjack table where Luis still sat. "Luis! I hit the jackpot for five thousand dollars!"

Luis swiveled around in his chair. He was also smiling and gathering up a pile of chips. "That's great! I guess we're both a couple of winners tonight. You ready to leave while we're ahead?" he asked, slightly slurring his speech.

Ronnie noticed a scantily clad waitress offering him another drink. She waved her off. "I think you've had enough for tonight. By the way, how many have you had?" She accepted a small plastic bucket from the dealer and helped Luis scoop the chips inside.

"I don't know. I lost count. That waitress kept bringing them out one after another. Guess I had more than I realized." He stumbled as he tried to stand. "C'mon sexy. Let's cash these chips in and head up to the room."

All together, Luis won a few thousand dollars playing the five dollar blackjack tables. Management offered a complimentary night in the hotel if they wanted to stick around another day. Ronnie knew what that was about. If they stayed an extra day, chances were they would put all their winnings right back into the casino and leave with less than they came with. Leave broke like most people who came to Vegas did.

When they returned to their suite, neither was in any mood to do anything but sleep. Luis basically passed out in the bed as soon as they hit the door. Ronnie removed the broken phone from her purse and sighed. Now how was she going to contact Kiara? The damned thing wouldn't even turn on.

She climbed in alongside Luis listening to him breath. The rhythmic sounds of his restful sleep relaxed her. Lying in that bed next to Luis is where she belonged, listening to the peaceful pauses between his every breath. The melodic sound of his heart seemed to play out a song made especially for her. With this realization, she knew that she was finally at home.

Chapter 25

"Luis, what am I going to do about my cell phone? All my contacts were stored there. I stopped memorizing phone numbers long ago, so I don't know anyone's number by heart. Not even yours. How am I going to get all those numbers back?" she fretted.

"We can take care of it when we get into town. You can buy a new phone and they'll even transfer the data from the SIM card. Shouldn't take more than a few minutes. Now your pictures are a different story... Were they stored on a cloud?"

"Huh, a cloud? What's a cloud?" Ronnie freely admitted she was not technologically savvy. As long as the phone came on when she hit dial, she was good.

"Don't worry about it. The store techs will explain it all. For the meantime, sit back and relax. We'll be in Santa Elena in no time at all. This highway can get pretty busy on the weekends, especially going from LA to Vegas. Since we're traveling the opposite direction, we should have no problems at all.

"Okay, I just hope that SIN card wasn't destroyed. The lady who stepped on my phone was a pretty big girl," she laughed. "You should have seen her face. I don't know if she was more excited about me hitting the jackpot or nervous about breaking my phone. I was right in the middle of talking to my mother."

"It's called a SIM card... Oh, never mind. You were saying you spoke to your mother last night? When?"

"She called right before I hit the jackpot on the slot machine. Can you believe she wanted to provide parental advice about meeting Kiara? By the way, she also said to tell you 'hello'." Ronnie laughed.

"Cool. I like you mother. Advice huh? Did she offer anything worthwhile?"

"Yes, actually she did. You know it felt good talking to my mother and knowing she was concerned about me. I didn't know how much I missed that. You talk to your family often?"

"If I don't call home at least once a week, my mother starts to panic and my father has to calm her down. She says if I were a good son, I would never forget to call. She tends to be on the overprotective side, but hey... she is my mother. I respect her wishes up to a point, but I have my own life to live, which doesn't always lend itself to continuously keeping in touch."

"What about brothers and sisters? Besides the one I saw in the DR, how many do you have?"

"Four of us total; two girls and two boys. Both of my sisters live in Santo Domingo with their families. My oldest brother moved to New York City shortly after I did."

"Must be nice to have siblings. I'm an only child. I always wanted to be part of a large family. My mother and father called me their miracle baby because she thought she wasn't able to have any." The memory of her mother's awful story came back with a vengeance. She shed a tear for her mother's tragic childhood and quickly wiped it away before Luis noticed.

"I admit I do like knowing there's someone out there who shares my genes. And no matter what happens to me, my family will always have my back."

"Luis, can I ask you something? I want your honest answer."

"I'm listening," he replied.

"When we first met, you mentioned you wanted to get married, have children and move back to the Dominican Republic; return and start your own company. Are those still your plans?"

Luis knew what she was getting at. She needed to know where she fit in his plans, if at all. He sighed, "Yes, I do still want that. I love children. I'm a terrific uncle and I could be a really good father. Look, I know we're just starting out and this is a bit premature….so let's see where this path leads us."

"I'm already 41, so my childbearing years are coming to an end. I'm no spring chicken anymore. "

"So what does that mean? You're in great shape."

"Stating the facts, that's all. Just stating the facts…."

Chapter 26

"You sure you want to stay here?" Luis scoped out the area for drug dealers or murder victims.

The retaining wall behind the apartment was tagged by gang bangers intent on marking their territory. Even Santa Elena, the city of glitz, glamour, and weekend getaways for movie stars, had its undesirable areas. The duplex Ronnie rented, sight unseen, had seen better days, yet it was the least expensive option she could afford.

"I'll be fine; I have your number in case I need to call. Don't worry, I'll be okay," she said while waving her new phone, attempting to convince herself as well as Luis.

"Alright, but at least let me check this place out first. Make sure it's secure."

Luis did a thorough walk-through inspection. He checked the front door and tested the bolt lock. He opened and closed all windows, ensuring they were locked and secure. He also confirmed the outside light was operating properly.

"Are you always so protective of women?" She joked.

"Only the ones I care about. Well, everything seems to be in order. It's not so bad inside—pretty clean. Furniture isn't new but it's functional. Hey listen, my ride is here to pick me up," he said checking his phone. "If you need anything, anything at all you call me. I don't care what time of day or night it is. Promise?"

"I promise. Thanks again for everything, especially for getting me out here safely. I'm going to turn in after I call Kiara. See when she's free to meet tomorrow." Ronnie walked him to the door.

"Call me tomorrow. I understand you'll be tied up with your daughter, but I want to see you again soon. Lock the door behind me." He waited until he heard the bolt lock securely into place. As he left the complex, he saw no obvious signs of danger, but one could never be too sure.

Ronnie surveyed the small efficiency. It was sparse. No frills at all. The manager made sure the unit was functional, but that was about it. She opened the kitchen cabinets and surveyed the contents. The online description did indicate a fully stocked kitchen, however she expected more than cheap plastic dinnerware. The cutlery drawer was filled with eating utensils from years past. Pots and pans were old, well used and covered in scratched up, peeling off Teflon. The refrigerator barely worked, humming noisily trying to keep the correct temperature. The bathroom was clean but also very old.

A well-used shower curtain hung limply from pieces of string tied to the bar. A previous tenant had spray-painted the bathroom window white in an attempt for privacy. She sat on the worn out sofa sleeper. A spring poked her leg as she tried to get comfortable.

She accepted the fact that her surroundings were temporary and simply the price she must pay to get to know her child. She dialed Kiara's number.

"Hello?" she answered in a little girl's voice.

"Kiara? Hi, it's Ronnie. Well, I'm here—in Santa Elena." She held her breath, awaiting her daughter's response.

"You made it? Really? When can I see you? Can you like stop by tonight? Where are you staying? Daddy can send a car for you," she gushed, excitedly.

"Yes, I finally made it. How about we get together tomorrow since it's so late? Maybe have brunch or something?"

"Oh, okay. Guess it is late, but I was like hoping I could see you tonight. I am so excited I'm finally going to meet you. I know the perfect place to meet. How about the Santa Elena Pier? They have a cool seafood shack and it's like my favorite place to hang out." The initial disappointment in her voice was evident, but she quickly recovered.

"Yeah, that sounds like fun. How about noon? That'll give us time to sleep in."

"You're right, tomorrow *is* Saturday. Do you know where the pier is?" asked Kiara.

"I'll find it. Hey Kiara, I can't wait to meet you," she added.

"Me too. Wait until I tell Daddy, he's going to be so excited. I'll see you tomorrow. Bye."

Wait a minute. Did she say Daddy? Travis is also going to be there? "Okay Kiara, I'll see you then. Goodnight." Ronnie hung up the phone and paced the floor. "Of course Travis is going to be there. He wants to protect Kiara, but I wonder what he has to say to me?"

With this revelation, she knew she wouldn't get a wink of sleep even if the sofa sleeper were comfortable. Ronnie tossed the worn sofa cushions aside. With one foot steadying her balance and the other propped on the edge to provide leverage, she used her good hand to pull the full size sleeper open. The mattress was old, lumpy, and covered in unmentionable stains. She wrinkled her nose in disgust. Unfortunately, it would have to do.

The complimentary bed linens were stored in the hallway closet along with a few threadbare towels. She managed to make up the bed with one hand. By the time she was finished, she collapsed on the bed from exhaustion. Luckily, the television worked so she turned it on for company. After taking a quick shower, she climbed beneath the light bedspread.

She lay in the bed, trying unsuccessfully to turn her mind off of tomorrow's events. *Travis Mitchell Bradford. It's going to be very interesting seeing him after all these years. He was once the love of my life, the man I wanted to raise a family with and spend eternity as his wife. But he's also the father of the child I put up for adoption.* She wondered what *he* thought about her meeting Kiara. Tomorrow would come too soon. Yet at the same time, not soon enough.

Somewhere in between nighttime advertisements of "how to clean bathroom grout without scrubbing" and another one promising "you'll never have to blow dry your hair again", sleep finally found her.

*   *   *

When she awoke the next morning, every muscle in her body ached from sleeping on the uncomfortable bed. She checked the time; it was a little past nine. She realized she had no food and more importantly, no coffee. There was plenty of time to get showered and locate a café. After all, this was Santa Elena, and there was bound to be a coffee house on every corner.

Ronnie *googled* the location of the nearest café. Since it was a beautiful morning, she decided to walk the couple of blocks to get breakfast. As she strolled down the sidewalk of the main thoroughfare, she was struck by the absolute beauty of the city. When they arrived yesterday it was already nightfall, but this morning, the sun sparkled brightly off the tall palm trees.

Upon locating the café, she was delightfully surprised at the décor and the menu. The café resembled an authentic Italian *trattoria* or a French *bistro*—very chic and very European. Ronnie perused the menu, while the very helpful staff provided directions to the Santa Elena Pier. She ordered a large coffee and a breakfast sandwich—just enough to tide her over until lunch. Then again, once she was with Kiara and Travis, her nerves would most likely prevent any food from making its way into her stomach.

Shortly after leaving Vegas, she made up her mind to send her jackpot winnings to her mother. The post office was on the way, so she transferred the cashier's check from her name to Dianna's and sent the money overnight. *Now Mama can afford to fix some of those costly repairs around her house, especially those rickety stairs.* She thought. Dropping that envelope in the mail to help out her mother made her feel like a million bucks.

"Good morning. How you doing?" She waved to one of her new neighbors before going inside the apartment.

"Morning. You in the apartment downstairs?" asked the young man, carrying a laundry basket down the stairs.

"Yes, just got here last night."

"Well, welcome. Name's Taj. I'm upstairs at the end. Feel free to knock on the door anytime you need something. All the neighbors are pretty close around here and look out for each other."

"Nice meeting you Taj, I'm Ronnie. Thanks, I'll keep that in mind," she replied before going inside.

The clock seemed to speed up and before she knew it, it was half past eleven. Time to go. After one last check in the mirror, she locked up the apartment and headed out.

Despite the difficulty of driving with one arm in a cast, she maneuvered the car quite well. Locating the Santa Elena Pier was also easy, because it was one of the prime tourist spots in the area, and there were signs pointing to it from all directions. She pulled into the parking lot. It took a few tries and a couple of people impatiently honking their horns before she was able to park the car in between the lines.

Ronnie gathered all the strength she could muster and prayed her meeting would go well. Her legs carried her down the long wooden pier that seemed to go on forever. She felt her heart beat loudly in her chest and wondered if others noticed. Of course they couldn't, yet she imagined her shirt rising and falling. Rising and falling. Rising and falling in a perfect harmonious beat. Between the beats, she breathed deeply and willed the nervousness to go away.

The seafood shack was less than fifty feet away. She stopped dead in her tracks when she saw the young woman from the photos. Kiara leaned over the pier, staring into the water below. Lexi McCray was at her side.

Her daughter stood about five foot nine with a feminine athletic build. She moved gracefully, stretching upwards like a long lean cat. Her honey brown chin length hair was left unprocessed, hanging loosely in natural curls around her beige face. She wore a Bohemian type skirt, a white t-shirt, and a brightly colored vest on top. Ronnie noticed a striking resemblance to her younger self when she looked at Kiara, for her features were a perfect blend of hers and Travis'.

Lexi noticed the familiar looking woman watching them. It was Veronica Pierce. She waved enthusiastically, calling out, "Veronica! Over here…" Lexi headed in her direction with Kiara trailing behind.

"Hi," Ronnie managed to say to the two women as they got closer.

"Veronica Pierce, I'd like to introduce you to your daughter, Kiara Indigo Bradford," Lexi said with a huge grin spread across her face.

"Hey," answered Kiara. She looked at the older, darker version of herself. *Not bad*, she thought, *I've got good genes in me.* "Pleased to meet you. Um, my Daddy's waiting in the restaurant. You wanna go say hi?" she asked shyly.

"Kiara, you are absolutely beautiful!" Ronnie tried to hold it all together. "May I?" she asked with outstretched arms.

"Sure, okay." Kiara let Ronnie embrace her. After a few moments, Kiara relaxed in Ronnie's arms and felt an immediate connection between mother and daughter.

Ronnie released her. By this time, they were all crying tears of joy. Lexi, used to these emotional reunions, produced two handkerchiefs and gave one to each woman.

"Thanks Lexi. Thank you so much for finding me," she stated, looking at Kiara, admiring her child's poise.

"It was my pleasure. By the way, what happened to your arm?" asked Lexi.

"I broke it trying to catch myself from falling. It's fine. I should be able to get this cast off in another week or so."

"C'mon Ronnie, Daddy's probably crazy by now wondering where we are." Kiara led the way.

Ronnie followed the two women into the restaurant. She searched the crowd looking for Travis. Wanted to see if she'd recognize him, if he'd changed at all. She was surprised at her nervousness and how her heart beat wildly in anticipation of seeing him again. Kiara passed all the tables and went out to the patio.

Travis sat on the far side of a table facing the door. Ronnie recognized him immediately. He had a full head of hair, though it was now more silver than black. And the smile she fell for so many years ago was the same. He was just as handsome as she remembered; only now he appeared more distinguished. The years were kind to Travis. She went to give him a hug. When he didn't stand to greet her, she paused. As she got closer, she suddenly understood. Travis was in a wheelchair.

"Daddy, here she is! And you were right... I do look like my mother." Kiara brimmed over with excitement.

Ronnie regained her composure and bent over to give him a hug. "Hi Travis...You look great. I see you got rid of your glasses," she said, hoping the initial shock she felt inside didn't make its way to her face.

"Ronnie Pierce, it's been a long time. You look great yourself. Yeah, I had the LASIK surgery a few years ago. Have a seat. We were just about to order." He motioned to the chair across from Kiara. Lexi joined the trio and sat opposite Travis.

"Daddy, I'll take my usual. Ronnie, I always get like the same thing every time we eat here. Aunt Lexi encourages me to try like other dishes, but the way I feel is if I really enjoy the food, then why should I change?"

Ronnie looked over at Lexi. "You're related? How?"

"Lexi is my sister-in-law. She's married to my younger brother and has been a God send to both me and Kiara ever since the accident," replied Travis.

"I kept my maiden name. In my profession, somehow Lexi McCray has a better ring to it than Lexi Bradford." She laughed.

No one bothered to elaborate any further on the accident, so Ronnie felt it best to leave that conversation alone until another time.

"Santa Elena is such a pretty town and I love this pier," Ronnie tried to ease away the tension.

"Yeah, I love it so much I'm going to like stay here the rest of my life. I've already been accepted at UC Santa Elena. I'm going to be a graphic artist. I'll move on campus in the dormitory and still be able to visit Daddy whenever he needs me."

"That's right angel, but you know I don't want you staying here because of me. I want you to go out and explore the world."

"I know, but I want to stay *here*. Why would I want to live anywhere else?" asked Kiara.

"Honey, it's not too late to change your mind about the University of Illinois. That's where both Ronnie and I went…"

"Oh Daddy, I told you I want to stay here. Move to Illinois? Nah, I think I'll pass."

Travis returned his attention to Ronnie. "So, how was your trip? Did you drive all the way here? I heard Lexi found you in Virginia."

"Well to tell you the truth, it took a little longer than I expected. After I left Virginia, I stopped in Oklahoma City to visit my mother. I fell and ended up with a hairline fracture on my forearm. So a very dear friend flew out and helped me drive the rest of the way," she explained.

"That was very thoughtful. Is your friend from around here?" asked Travis nonchalantly, as he studied the menu. "Oh, how are your parents by the way?"

"Luis, that's my friend, actually lives in Montverde. My mother's fine. Remember my father passed years ago." She was surprised that Travis had forgotten about her father's misfortunate accident.

"Oh, I'm sorry. Yes, now I remember," he replied, embarrassed. He was grateful for the diversion the waitress provided by coming to take their orders. *How could I forget her father died?* He thought.

"It's alright. It happened a long time ago." Ronnie focused on the menu. Her appetite had all but disappeared. "I think I'll have the clam chowder in the bread bowl and a glass of iced tea. Sweet if you have it," she added.

"I'm sorry, all our tea is unsweetened, but there's sugar on the table if you need it," replied the waitress.

Travis laughed. "Sweet tea? That must be a southern thing," he said, trying not to appear condescending. He placed both his and Kiara's orders. "Out here in California they serve hundreds of variations of tea, but *sweet* isn't on the menu."

"You're right. I forgot I'm not in Virginia anymore. I'll take the unsweetened, please," she replied to the waitress.

"Ronnie, are you going to make it to my graduation? It's like next week on Friday. It's going to be outside in the Santa Elena Bowl."

"Yes, I'll be there." Ronnie smiled. "I'm really looking forward to it."

"Awesome! I am so hyped to be like graduating. And Daddy is throwing me this really cool party afterwards. You can come to my party too. Right Daddy?"

"Yes, of course Ronnie is invited."

A million questions trickled through Travis' mind, though none were appropriate to ask in front of Kiara or Lexi. Eventually, he glanced at his sister-in-law, pleading with his eyes for her to give him and Ronnie a private moment. Thankfully, she took her queue to leave with Kiara.

"Daddy, if you and Ronnie don't mind, Aunt Lexi is going to take me home. She thinks you guys need to have time to like talk or something." Kiara rolled her eyes in Lexi's direction.

"Thanks Lexi. I'll send for my driver when I'm ready to leave." Travis paid the dinner tab.

Kiara whispered to her mother, "Maybe we can get together, like just the two of us, and do something later?"

"Sure, I'd really like that. I'll give you a call," replied Ronnie.

"We'll see you guys later." Lexi bent over to give Travis a kiss on the cheek. She turned to Ronnie and said, "I can't tell you how happy we are to have you here. Your presence has made so many people very, very happy."

"I appreciate your saying that Lexi. I'll see you soon." Ronnie watched the two women who could have passed for models walk away, their heads bent together in deep conversation. She envied Lexi for the closeness to her daughter.

"You want to go for a walk?" asked Travis. "It's okay. The wheelchair is motorized."

"Okay. Where?"

"Follow me, there's a park along the boardwalk with a great view of the ocean." He backed away from the table and maneuvered his chair through the restaurant and on to the pier. The wooden planks caused the chair to bounce every couple of inches. Travis took it all in stride.

"Travis, you haven't changed a bit. You look really good. You work out?"

"Thank you for noticing. I try to stay in shape by working out my upper body every day. Without the use of my legs, I have to compensate by keeping my arms really strong," he explained.

"Whatever you're doing, it's working. Your arms are massive." She gripped his muscle with her good hand. Ronnie also had many questions to ask Travis, but she waited until they were in the park. He wheeled his chair next to an empty bench.

"Have a seat. I have so many questions, I can't even think of where to begin." He looked exasperated. "When Kiara was about to turn eighteen, she said the only present she wanted was to find her birthmother. I had no clue where you were. I didn't even know where your parents lived. All I had was your name."

"I'm sorry, Travis. How could I know you raised her? When I left the hospital that day eighteen years ago, I thought I'd never see my child again. We both signed the adoption papers. I'm sorry, I didn't know."

"How *could* you know? The only way I found out she was born was because the adoption agency called to verify and confirm that I still wanted to go through with the adoption. The caseworker said I had three days to change my mind, my being the natural father and all. As soon as I found out where she was, I was on the first plane to Oklahoma City. My mother flew out and met me." His eyes misted over.

Ronnie remembered that day very well. If what Travis said was true, she was still in the hospital waiting in the maternity ward to go home when he was picking up Kiara.

"As soon as I saw that perfect little face, I fell in love. She didn't even cry. Just wrapped her tiny hand around my finger like she knew who I was. And from the very first moment I held her in my arms, she's been my whole world. I was so angry at you. I often wondered how you could give up our child. Our beautiful daughter."

"You have no idea how much I regretted that decision. It haunted me every single day of my life." She sniffed and continued. "So you took her back to California?"

"Not at first. She was too young to fly on an airplane so we spent a couple of weeks in Oklahoma City. We got a hotel room and took care of her until the doctors cleared her to fly. I missed my finals and the graduation because I was in Oklahoma. Luckily, the dean allowed me to finish course finals online. Anyway, my mother setup a nursery in my old room and I slept on a cot. I never left Kiara's side."

"That must have been difficult for you."

"Yes, I'll admit it was. I was only twenty-three and didn't know anything about babies. Thank God for my mother. She loved her granddaughter. Both of my parents did. If it weren't for them, I don't know what I would have done."

"Travis, I know this won't make any difference now, but let me try to explain why I did what I did." She relayed the entire story about her mother, the boy her mother got pregnant by and Travis's resemblance to him. She reminded him about the last promise she made to her deceased father.

"Ronnie, we loved each other. We made plans for a future together. How could you let your parent's racism come between us? Let your mother convince you to give away our child?" He stared off into the distance, remembering how crushed he was the day she moved out.

"I was wrong. I did not mean to hurt you. I'm sorry," she said.

"So what *did* you do after Kiara was born? Where did you end up after graduation?" he asked, trying to get away from the memory that haunted him.

"Believe it or not, I was in Oklahoma City for the first few months until I found a job in Virginia. I was so angry at my mother and blamed her for making me give up my baby. When I moved, I cut all ties with her. This trip out here is the first time in eighteen years we've seen one another."

He thought *at least she suffered some heartache from giving up Kiara.* "Being a single parent was harder than I could have ever imagined. It was up to me to be both mother and father to Kiara. Most of the time I didn't know what I was doing. My parents stepped in sometimes, but mostly I parented by trial and error. I learned how to comb her hair. I explained things about her body; about why her skin was darker than mine. She was the only girl in her class without a mother. I comforted her when she came home crying after the kids teased her about it." He clenched his fist and pounded his frail legs, angry with himself for the pain his child had to endure.

"That must have been hard for both of you, especially for Kiara. I know how mean kids can be sometimes. I feel awful…" Ronnie replied in a weak voice.

"I eventually found a decent job and Kiara and I moved into our own apartment. That little girl was so happy to have her own room. She was such an inquisitive child. Smart as a whip. She always brought home good grades. In many ways, she reminded me of you." He smiled.

Ronnie sighed wearily and continued listening, for she had nothing valuable to add—nothing but guilty feelings.

"For several years, it was just the two of us. When Kiara was eight, I married a wonderful, very special lady named Janelle. She was a beautiful black woman, as regal and elegant as they come. Yes sir, we were finally a real family."

"Good for you! I'd love to meet her sometime."

Travis looked away. He swallowed hard, trying to hold back the flow of emotions threatening to come forth. He cleared his throat and it took several moments before he was able to speak again.

She had no idea his life was so difficult. The guilt of her selfishness washed over her like an ocean wave.

"A couple years into our marriage, Janelle and I were headed up to Sonoma for a weekend getaway to a wine tasting tour. It was raining and the roads were slick. It happened so quickly. She was driving because I had a tough day at work and didn't want to fall asleep behind the wheel. We got hit head on by a long hauler. Janelle was killed instantly and I became a paraplegic. My spinal cord was damaged beyond repair, so I'll be in this wheelchair for the rest of my life. Doctors say I'll never walk again."

"Oh my God... Travis, I am so sorry," she whispered with compassion.

"For the longest time I blamed myself. I fell into a really bad depression because I didn't want to live like this. Lexi and my brother stepped in to take care of Kiara while I recuperated. I ended up back in my parent's home."

Ronnie could offer no words of comfort; mere words seemed so inadequate.

"Turned out the driver had been drinking. He walked away without a scratch. I eventually sued and was awarded a very large settlement. It was enough money to make a comfortable life for me and my daughter."

She shook her head. "I wonder why it always seems like the drunks never get hurt..."

"After awhile, I needed to do something besides sit around feeling sorry for myself. So I started going to a support group for disabled people—those wheelchair bound like I am. I discovered how few places offered the special rehabilitation services we require, so I started a physical therapy center for people with spinal cord injuries with some of the money I received from the settlement. We've been in business for over seven years now and have successfully helped hundreds of patients. The *J. Bradford Rehabilitation Center* is considered to be the best on the west coast. We're also partnered with research doctors searching for a cure to repair spinal cord injuries. One day we're going to discover a cure for this. I'm going to beat this and walk again. Just you wait and see."

"Travis, with your persistence, I have every confidence that you will."

"Thanks, but that's not all I do to keep busy. I'm also a part-time professor at UCSE. I teach creative writing classes in the morning, so I'm home when Kiara gets out of school."

"You've been through a lot Travis, but it looks like everything is going alright. I think it's great that you're keeping yourself busy. Maybe I'll sit in on one of your classes. *This cannot be a coincidence that Travis teaches creative writing. Maybe he can offer a few tips on my novel...* Look Travis, I want to express my gratitude for the wonderful job you've done raising Kiara. You stepped in when I wasn't there and I will forever be grateful."

He nodded and said, "No need to thank me, it was my pleasure as well as my responsibility to raise my daughter. By the way, how long you staying?"

"Actually, I'm moving here, so I plan on being here indefinitely."

"*You're* moving to Santa Elena? Why?" Travis asked with obvious suspicion.

"Up until a few weeks ago I was an assistant to a sports manager. We drafted contracts for kids who played professional sports. I made a pretty good living at it, but it left me unfulfilled. I hated the job and the people I worked for. That job was sucking the life out of me. One day, something inside me changed and I knew I needed to find my purpose."

"I'm with you so far..."

"I visited the Dominican Republic for a couple of weeks of vacation. I took the time off to clear my head. When I came back, there was a message from Lexi about Kiara on my answering machine. I took her visit as an indication to change my life. I quit my job, sold my house, gave away most of my material possessions, and came on this road trip. To tell you the truth, I really don't have a good explanation about why I moved other than it just feels right."

"That doesn't sound like the Ronnie I know. You were always so by-the-book."

"You mean anal retentive?" She laughed.

"Your words, not mine." Travis joined in her laughter. It felt good.

"No really, I wanted to come out here and meet my daughter. I missed the first eighteen years of her life. If she wants me involved in her life now, I'm not going to make that mistake again. How do *you* feel about my moving out here?" She turned to face him and saw the young man she fell in love with years ago. Despite their history, she realized sometimes it's best to let the past remain where it is. Thus, she focused only on Kiara's welfare.

Travis considered how Ronnie's presence would affect everyone and carefully measured his response. Kiara needed her mother in her life and having her near would be wonderful. After all, Ronnie was her flesh and blood. On the other hand, he couldn't imagine having another significant person in his daughter's life. In the end, he did what he thought was best.

"I think it'll be alright. Kiara will have an opportunity to get to know you and learn about the other side of her family. She'll love it. Have you told her you're staying?" he asked.

"Not yet, I wanted to talk to you about it first. I rented out an inexpensive apartment on the lower east side. It's only temporary until I find a permanent job and can afford something better." She shrugged. "I don't mind. It's just me."

"So you never married? No other children?"

"I was married. Got divorced about five years ago. Nope, no other children."

His wheelchair was equipped with all the latest gizmos, yet he manually backed himself away from the bench and faced her. He stared at her intensely remembering the past and quietly spoke. "I used to dream of about you coming back for your baby. I fantasized about how we would get married and the three of us would become a real family. I wanted it so badly I thought I was going to lose my mind. After the first couple of years went by and I realized you were never coming for her—or for me, it broke my heart. You walked away without any explanation and for years I was bitter. But all that is in the past, I've moved on with my life. Kiara and I are doing fine. I'm not sure what you hope to accomplish or what your motives are, but I will not let hurt my daughter."

"Travis, I'm not trying to take Kiara away from you and I didn't move out here hoping to get back together. We're both very different people now. I'm here to get to know my daughter. That is it. I don't want anything from you other than your support. Okay?"

"Okay, I needed to make sure we're on the same page. Now that we've got that settled, how about you come by the house later this evening? I'll give you a tour of the center first. We can throw a few steaks on the grill and you and Kiara can catch up."

Ronnie studied Travis and saw the protective nature of a loving father. She'd seen that look on her father's face many times, so she totally understood where he was coming from. She may be Kiara's biological mother, but that's all she was. Kiara's allegiance lied with her father and his with her.

"Travis, I understand. I just want to be here for Kiara when she needs me. I can't make up for those lost years; I can only begin from where we are today."

"In all seriousness, I'm glad you're here because you've made our daughter extremely happy. She really wants you to be at her graduation." He checked his watch. "I'm sorry, it's getting late and I have a meeting with a family considering our center. Kid's only sixteen. He broke his neck jumping headfirst into a lake and now he's a quadriplegic. It's a goddamn shame, that's what it is." He retrieved the cell phone from his inside pocket and dialed his chauffer. "You need a ride anywhere? We can drop you off."

"No, I'm fine. My car's over there in the public parking lot."

"Well, then, I'd better be going. If you need anything give me a call."

"Thanks Travis, I'll see you later this evening." She bent over and hugged him. He hugged her back. Once again, they were friends.

* * *

"I'm fine. Really, I am. It went very well. Travis even invited me to dinner to give me and Kiara time to get to know one another," she explained to Luis.

"That sounds cozy. Just the three of you, huh? Sounds like quite the little family reunion."

"Do I detect a note of jealousy?" she asked, noting the sarcasm in his voice.

"You *are* reuniting with the man who fathered your only child. It wouldn't be unusual to have unresolved feelings for him and vice versa. So possibly I am jealous."

"You have absolutely no need to be jealous. My thoughts are only for Kiara. The relationship between Travis and me is in the past. There's nothing between us now."

"Alright, but I want to see you tomorrow. No more of this over the phone stuff."

"Of course, I'd love that. I'll call you in the morning. Bye."

*   *   *

Ronnie drove to the address Travis provided her with earlier. Driving down the private street, she double-checked the address, then triple-checked it. *This can't be the right place!* she thought. *This doesn't look like any physical therapy center I've ever seen!* An impressive looking building loomed in the foreground of a beautifully landscaped estate.

Her initial impression led her to believe she had stumbled upon a luxurious spa or maybe an artist's retreat, but she was at the right place. A small bronzed nondescript plaque inscribed with *J. Bradford Rehabilitative Center* was strategically placed high above the gate. The driveway to the center was blocked by a twelve foot wrought iron fence.

A speaker mounted to the gate post with the words, *Push for Assistance*, was there for anyone who didn't have the access key code. She pushed the red button below the brightly lit keypad.

"Yes, may I help you?" asked the unseen voice of a man hidden deep within the building structure. *Must be the security guard.*

She looked up at the camera aimed down on her, surveying surroundings for anything suspicious. "I'm here to see Travis Bradford. My name is Ronnie. Ronnie Pierce," she replied to the camera.

"Let's see. Ronnie Pierce? I have a Veronica Pierce. Is that you?" asked the guard.

"Yeah, I'm Veronica. I go by Ronnie though; Travis should be expecting me."

"Right. Please drive through, park in one of the visitor spots, and come in the main entrance. The receptionist will provide further directions. Have a nice day ma'am." The large gate slowly opened allowing her to enter.

Ronnie surveyed the grounds as she followed the drive and parked. She located the main entrance and went it.

"Hi, my name is Veronica Pierce and I'm here to see Mr. Travis Bradford," she said to the perky receptionist studying her *iPad*.

"Take a right at the double doors, his office is down the hallway on the left." She handed Ronnie a tag with her name written in permanent marker. She pasted the white sticky over her t-shirt and wandered through the maze of doors and hallways. Finally she came upon Travis's office and knocked.

"Come in," he replied.

"Hey Travis, it's me coming for my official tour," she said.

"Ronnie, come on in. So what do you think about the place so far?"

"Gotta admit, from the outside this place is great. I love the spa-like atmosphere. Very relaxing with a Zen-like quality. This is pretty cool, Travis. I always knew you were going to be successful!"

"Thanks. I find the less our patients are reminded they are in a rehab center, the better they feel about being here. Now don't get me wrong, we have a state of the art physical therapy center on the grounds and when patients are there working out, they know this isn't a spa."

"Even so, this place looks wonderful. I love the serene landscaping. You should be very proud."

"C'mon, let me show you around so you'll have a better understanding of what we're trying to accomplish here."

Ronnie trailed behind Travis listening to the whir of his motorized wheel chair as he gave a private tour of the facility. He explained how they used cutting edge technology to provide patients with the best supportive care possible. The mission of the center was simple: *To provide physical therapy and therapeutic support to those suffering from spinal cord injuries.* After about forty minutes or so, he arrived back in the office. She noted his desk was a mess.

"I am so impressed. Everything seems to be so well organized, well, except for this office." She looked at the papers and file folders strewn about.

"Yeah, I know. My business manager just quit to move to Hawaii with her boyfriend. I've been trying to decipher these documents and look for someone to fill this position at the same time. So far, no luck on either front." He rubbed his chin in frustration.

"You mind if I take a look?" she asked, picking through the files.

"No, please go right ahead. Maybe you can make sense out of this mess."

Ronnie poured over the documents. She arranged the files according to inpatient, outpatient, and discharged patient, and then reconciled the outstanding accounts. Any files with missing documentation, she annotated the record and entered the data into a spreadsheet. She reviewed several grant requests, revised a few paragraphs, and added in the necessary verbiage required to help get the grant. After all was said and done, she presented a neat bundle to Travis and prepared a backup disk to boot.

"You're finished already? I've been working on this for the past week trying to get this mess straightened out. Ronnie, you're a God send!" he exclaimed.

That's when it hit her. She *had* been sent by God to help Travis. Part of His plan was for her to offer her vast business knowledge to assist in his very important mission of helping people who faced the most tragic of circumstances. She took a step back and exhaled.

"Yeah, it was easy. I could've done this with my eyes closed. This is what I've been doing for the past decade, only then it was to help make money for greedy sport managers. Helping you clean up this mess felt good. Like I was helping your patients by helping you. Straightening up your files made me feel like I have a real purpose." She couldn't wait to share her revelation with Luis.

Travis sat back in his wheelchair in deep thought. He spoke softly, "Ronnie, I know you just got here and haven't had time to adjust yet, but you've done such an amazing job with these files, I would like to offer you a job. You won't be working for me directly, but will be over in the business department. The woman who's there now isn't very knowledgeable, but she's a very hard worker who simply needs to be pointed in the right direction. I think you'd be perfect for this position."

She couldn't believe her ears. Or her luck. Work at this beautiful center whose only mission is to help people recover from life-shattering disabilities? "Travis, I'd love to. I can't think of a better place for me. Thank you I'll let you know my decision," she said and went over to hug him.

"You're very welcome. You ready to go? Kiara's at home helping to make dinner. She's not a very good cook, but she's learning." He switched off the light and closed the door behind them.

* * *

Travis and Kiara lived in a modest house towards the back of the center grounds. If you didn't know the house was there, you would never find it.

Travis steered his way towards the house and Ronnie trailed along beside him.

"I installed this track so I don't have to rely on anyone to get me back and forth to work. Convenient huh?"

"Yeah, great idea." She observed the natural beauty of their home environment and was pleased to know this is where Kiara lived her life.

"Kiara? We're here!" shouted Travis.

"Hey, you made it." She gave Ronnie a hug. "Hi Daddy."

"Yep, I said I would. So what are you doing?" asked Ronnie, noticing bits and pieces of food stuck to her shirt.

"I made an arugula salad and chopped up vegetables to put on the grill. Daddy usually cooks the steaks," she said to Ronnie. "You want to help?"

"That's all right sweetheart, I'll take over from here. Why don't you show Ronnie the rest of the grounds? Go for a nice walk and take your time."

"Okay Daddy, I can take a hint. We'll be back." Kiara kissed her father's cheek. "Ronnie, can I get you a bottle of water or something?"

"Sure, water will be fine," Ronnie answered.

"Be right back."

"Thanks Travis. I'm not sure what questions she's going to ask, but I want to be as honest as possible. She deserves the truth."

Travis nodded. "I understand, but remember she's been through a lot. I don't want to see her hurt anymore than what's necessary."

"Here you go. I brought two. It can get kinda hot walking out here in the woods. See you later Daddy."

He waved and wheeled himself inside, watching the two women who favored one another go off into the woods. He thought *Kiara is so excited. Despite everything I have done for her, giving her a mother is the one area I failed. Maybe it's not too late. Kiara is eighteen. I wonder if Ronnie has already missed out on the most important phases of her life. Or will her influence and guidance be most critical at this stage when she's embarking upon adulthood? Only time will tell, but I must admit, I sure am happy to have her here.*

The women followed a path through the trees to a clearing overlooking the ocean. It was high tide and the waves pounded against the rocky shore of the secluded beach. A couple of weather worn Adirondack chairs sat facing the water.

"What is this place Kiara?" Ronnie thought it was the perfect spot to reconnect with one's soul.

"I come here sometimes when I like need to think. Daddy tends to hover at times. You've probably noticed he's a bit overprotective." She kicked loose rocks with her flip-flop covered feet.

"Yeah, but I understand. He loves you and only wants the best for you. You're his little girl and that's what fathers do. I know mine used to."

"Used to? Is he dead?" she asked.

"Yes, my father died a long time ago. All I have now is my mother."

"Tell me about your family. I mean *our* family."

Ronnie filled her in on as many relatives as she could remember. She gave her the sanitized version of her grandmother Dianna and her hometown of Oklahoma City. She spoke about her father Vernon with a reverence at his memory and confided how much he would have loved his granddaughter. Her eyes widened in awe listening to the stories filling in the gaps of her history.

"So you're an only child like I am? I always wanted to have a little brother or sister, but when Daddy got into that accident..." She sniffled and wiped away the tears. "Anyway, I was just happy he didn't die. I was so scared. Aunt Lexi helped me out a lot. She took me to see Daddy everyday and we'd just sit there and read to him. Or I'd tell him about my day."

"She really cares about you. Does she have any children of her own?" Ronnie asked.

"No, she says I was more than enough. But now that I'm about to leave home for college, maybe she can start living her life," she said, acknowledging the sacrifice her aunt made for her. "Tell me Ronnie, how did you and my dad meet? He doesn't like to talk about it...says the memories hurt too much."

Ouch, that stung. "Travis and I met during our first year of college….." She relayed the story, leaving out the ugly details that led to their breakup. "We were two kids wildly in love, but it didn't work out the way we expected."

"That sounds so romantic. Ronnie, if you guys loved each other so much, why did you break up?"

"I really don't have a good answer other than sometimes things just happen." Ronnie anticipated the next question. Knew it was going to come and when it did, she still wasn't prepared for it.

"Can I ask you another question?" Kiara asked timidly.

Ronnie braced herself for the inevitable. Here it comes.

"Why did you give me away? Didn't you love me?"

It was the same question she asked herself since that fateful day eighteen years ago. Whenever she wiped a tear from one of Derek's children's eyes, she hoped a mother was there to wipe her child's tears away. She prayed for her child with every bubble bath she drew; all the trips dropping Derek's children off to school; making a special birthday cake for his kids—with each task she prayed someone was doing the same for her child. Prayed her child was loved. Hoped she was told often how special she was.

"Kiara, no matter what I tell you, it will never be the right answer. I was young. I was scared. I didn't know what to do with a baby. I wanted you to have a better life than I could provide. Yes, I loved you. That's why I gave you away. I know it doesn't make any sense, but that's the truth."

"I don't understand. Why did Daddy come for me and you didn't? Wasn't it harder for him? He's a man and he didn't know the first thing about girls! But *he* took care of me!" she yelled.

"I didn't know Travis was raising you. We both signed the adoption papers. Had I known, things would have probably turned out differently. I don't know what more to say except I'm sorry. I am so sorry. Won't you please forgive me?" pleaded Ronnie.

Kiara sighed, "You want to hear something funny? When I was younger, I didn't know I was half black. I thought I just tanned easily. Daddy never told me. I didn't find out I wasn't one hundred percent white until I went to school. There was a little girl in my first grade class with the same color skin as mine. Her hair was thick and curly like mine and we looked more like sisters than classmates. I remember the first time I saw her parents. They were both black. I remember going home crying because I was so confused."

Ronnie could only imagine the pain her child must've gone through.

"That little girl used to tease me and say I was adopted because my father was white. When I asked Daddy if he was my real father, he told me about you. I asked him all time to go find you so I could have a mother too." The tears ran freely now. She wiped them away with the bottom of her shirt.

"Oh Kiara. That's awful you experienced so much pain as a child. I'm so sorry you went through that, but if there is anything I can do now to help, please come to me." Her words sounded pitiful and hollow, even to her own ears.

"Daddy married Janelle when I was eight. She was awesome. Her skin was the color of mine and she showed me how to comb my hair the right way. We were finally a family and we were so happy. I loved her even though she wasn't my real mother."

The words stung more than she realized, but it was true. Ronnie had let her daughter down.

"The day of the horrible accident, Aunt Lexi came into my room and told me we needed to go to the hospital. Daddy was injured so badly I didn't recognize him and when I found out Janelle was gone, I thought God was punishing me." Sobs wracked her body.

Ronnie went to her child and held her head to her breast until she cried no more. Held her until Kiara heard the strong heartbeat of a mother who loved her dearly—the same heartbeat she first heard in the womb. Stroking her hair, Ronnie whispered everything was going to be alright. And lo and behold, she became her mother again.

"Kiara, I am here for you and I promise I will always be here for you. You need to know I have always loved you. I never stopped, not even for a moment. You will never be without a mother again. I was going to tell you later, but might as well tell you now. I'm moving here, I'm not just visiting."

She pulled back and sat up in her chair. "You're really moving to Santa Elena? Does Daddy know?"

Ronnie nodded. "He knows and he's okay with it. I'm going to get a real nice place—fix up a guest room real nice so you can visit. And that's not all," she said.

Kiara wiped the tears from her eyes. "What else could there possibly be?" She smiled through her tender emotions.

"Well, I have some more good news. Travis offered me a job at the center and I'm thinking about accepting. What do you think about that?"

"This is so cool! Oh my God! I cannot wait to tell Auntie Lexi. She is going to freak!" She jumped up and hugged her newly found mother.

Chapter 27

The owner of the café recognized Ronnie from yesterday. "Hello miss, you've come back for another breakfast sandwich? I tell everyone we make the best breakfasts in these parts. I must warn you, the coffee here is addictive, as well," replied the woman with a wink and a huge smile.

"This *is* really good," Ronnie replied, nibbling on the rustic bread. "Thank you so much for suggesting it." Ronnie found an empty table outside for privacy. First person she called was Luis.

"Hey Luis," she replied when he picked up. "Last night turned out better than I could've ever hoped for. Kiara was thrilled when I told her I'm staying."

"Good morning," he laughed at her enthusiastic outburst. "I knew everything was going to be alright. How did her father take the news?"

"Travis? Well, at first he wasn't sure, but after I let him know this was only about being with Kiara, he was fine. He even offered me a job."

"He did? Doing what?"

"To help out in his business department. I don't have an official title, but it doesn't matter. After taking a tour of that place, I knew it was where I am supposed to be." She sipped the coffee and took another bite.

"That's great. Maybe this is the purpose you were searching for? The reason why you came out? So what's the name of his company?"

"I'm sorry, that's the most significant part of this. He runs the *J. Bradford Rehabilitative Center*. It's a nonprofit agency that treats people with spinal cord injuries. I don't think I mentioned it, but Travis is a paraplegic—a result of a very bad car accident several years ago."

"Wait a minute... Are you talking about *Travis Bradford*? White guy, early 40's, nice looking cat...?"

"Yes, why?"

"Travis Bradford is Kiara's father?! Ronnie, I know him! He's one of my major clients. His daughter provided some really good suggestions to help personalize their logo. It truly is a small world."

Ronnie almost choked on her coffee. "What? You and Travis are business partners? And you know Kiara? That's incredible!"

274

"Yes, I do. Who would have thought the daughter you've traveled all this way to meet is part of the Bradford family. Well I'll be…"

"I don't know what to say other than God *does* work in mysterious ways. Meeting you in the DR, my coming out here to California… This was all part of His plan. We were linked together without even knowing it. This is totally blowing my mind!"

"Hey, I have an idea… Why don't I pick you up and show you around town? It'll give us another chance to compare notes on our coincidences."

"Sounds like a great idea. What time?" She checked her watch. It was almost eleven.

"I can be there in an hour. That enough time?" he asked.

"Perfect. I'll see you at noon." She thought, *all this time, there has been a plan for my life and I was too busy to see it. All I had to do was open my eyes and be faithful. Wow!* She shook her head in amazement at the powerful blessings she was given.

* * *

Ronnie made good use of the walk back to the apartment. She hit speed dial and waited for the call to pick up.

"Hey girlfriend, what's up?"

"Ronnie? Girl, is that you?"

"Of course it's me… What other woman calls you *girlfriend?*" She laughed.

"Whats up, Ronnie? Are you in Cali yet?" Joie's enthusiasm overflowed through the phone lines.

"Yeah, girl I finally made it and met my wonderful daughter. Even saw Travis. And I'm hooking up with Luis in an hour. Life is good and I am blessed."

"That's good news Ronnie, I'm really happy for you. Tell me about it," she replied sincerely. Her friend sounded so excited, happier than she'd been in a long time. Leaving her old life behind, starting over in a new place with family and friends was exactly what she needed. Joie admired Ronnie's bravery to walk away from a life that so many envied. The two friends had their issues, but when all was said and done, deep down they were girlfriends. Through thick and thin.

"Thanks Joie, I have to admit the journey out here and all the drama I went through made me pause. But like I told you back then, I wasn't about to let anything stand in my way. God put me on this path, told me where to go and what to do; I was obedient and look what happened."

"You deserve to be happy. Girlfriend, you should use your life as a testimony to what happens when you do God's will." She hesitated and asked, "Does this mean you forgive me? Are we good now?"

The rift between the two women was all but a distant memory. So much joy now filled her heart there was no room for bitterness. No room for anything but forgiveness. The pain from betrayals, lies, and deceit slowly evaporated away.

"Yes Joie, I told you when I was still in Virginia that I forgive you."

"Thank you Ronnie. Just checking. That means a lot, not only for me, but to Trey and Maya as well. My kids don't have many relatives at the moment. Derek's family hasn't reached out to me. In time I will make contact with his parents and siblings, but for now it's probably all too fresh for them to deal with me."

"Give them time. Derek's parents have big hearts and they love all their grandchildren. Considering they didn't know about you, your showing up with the twins at their son's funeral must have been a huge shock. I know them and they will do the right thing. You just keep on loving your kids and don't worry about nobody else loving them."

"Thanks girl. Raising kids on my own is more than a notion." She laughed.

"I can only imagine," she replied, thinking about Travis. "But hang in there, you can do it. You heard anything more from Cedric?"

"He stops by to see the twins, sometimes he'll take them for the weekend, stuff like that. But I expect his visits to trickle down to nothing once the divorce papers are signed. Girl, he even petitioned the court to have their DNA officially tested again. Told me, he is not going to get stuck paying child support for the next thirteen years when Derek's estate should be doing it. He told me to go file for social security support for the kids."

"I'm sorry Joie. That's gotta be tough, but it makes sense. If what you say is true about Trey and Maya being Derek's children, they should be able to get social security and whatever else they're entitled to."

"I know. I just don't want to deal with it right now. Girl, with Tequila's two kids and his other three, Trey and Maya make seven. That man didn't make that much money to take care of all these children."

"Joie, three are grown and he's finished supporting them. Anyway, it should have always been his responsibility to take care of his children, not Cedric's. After all, he made them. Now had you two stayed together, I'd be singing a different tune…"

"Damn Ronnie, cut a sistah a break. But you're right. I'm not gonna stress about it. I make enough money on my own so I really don't have to rely on the government, not like that Tequila."

"Okay, I'll back down." She laughed. "I think you intentionally like to get that girl's name wrong. It's Tequitta! Girlfriend, you'll be alright. What you need to do is find Jesus and let him lead you the right way. Trust me it works."

"I ain't trying to hear about no Jesus, so don't you start preaching to me again. I'ma be alright."

"Okay, okay, I'm just saying when your life isn't going right, there's always a reason."

"Yeah, whatever. Hey, I gotta go, the twins are up and I'm taking them to the amusement park. Let me know when you get settled. Summer is coming up and I *really* need a vacation. Since you in Cali now, I was thinking about us coming out for a visit."

"Sound great! I'll keep you updated and I can't wait to see you guys. You take care and keep your chin up!"

"Thanks, we'll talk soon. Bye."

* * *

Luis showed up promptly at noon in a Jeep. When Ronnie answered the door, he pulled her into his arms and kissed her as if he hadn't seen her in years. "You ready for your tour of the town?" he asked, presenting a bouquet of freshly cut flowers.

"Umm, that was nice." She pulled away, admiring his boldness. She felt her heartbeat speed up when his warm lips touched her own. "Thank you for the flowers. They're lovely. Come in and let me see if there's vase to put them in." Ronnie opened all the cabinets searching for suitable container for the flowers. She was unsuccessful, but what did catch her eye was a large cockroach scurrying across the dishes.

"Looks like they need an exterminator." Luis used a napkin to knock the pesky roach on the floor and promptly stepped on it.

"Ewww! I can't stand cockroaches! And seeing that nasty thing crawling over my dishes..." She shuddered.

"Don't worry about it. Let's go!" Observing her reaction to that cockroach helped Luis make his mind up on what needed to be done. *I am not going to let Ronnie live in these deplorable conditions. I'm going to rectify this situation as soon as possible.*

Ronnie dropped the flowers on the table, grabbed a light sweater, and followed Luis out the door. "What in the world? You have a Jeep? Okay, this is different..." She hopped in and sat down to enjoy the ride.

"It's such a nice day it would be a shame to be stuck inside the car. You'll get a much better experience riding in the Jeep."

Luis drove up and down the streets of Santa Elena, pointing out landmarks and tourist sites, such as the popular State Street, the famous Four Seasons resort, several of the Old Missions renovated into museums, the historic beautifully restored Arlington Theatre, and finally ending up at the beach that so many called the California Riviera.

"Luis, this has got to be the most beautiful city in the world. Well, at least in the United States. I love the architecture. What is it, Mediterranean?"

"Actually there is a heavy Spanish influence in Santa Elena. That and old world Mexico. I think that's why it feels so special. Kinda reminds me of home, but on a more upscale level."

"It must also be very expensive to live here," she stated, noting the numerous homeless people lying on the street.

"Yes, it can be very expensive to live in Santa Elena, but as you can see, the cost of living doesn't discourage people from wanting to move here. The entire area is highly desirable because it is so unique. Many want to come; very few can afford to stay. Unfortunately, some discover too late what the real costs are and end up homeless. Living on the street."

Ronnie took his words with a grain of salt and swore she would never wind up living on anybody's street.

Luis jumped on the highway landing in bumper-to-bumper traffic. The noonday sun reflecting off the asphalt raised the temperature in the Jeep considerably. Ronnie turned on the A/C which offered very little relief.

"Not much further," he said.

"Where are we going anyway?" she asked, fanning herself.

"I'm going to show you where I work." He looked over and grinned. "Thought I'd surprise you before heading back."

"I hope it's not much further; all this bright sunshine is killing my eyesight. Why does it seem brighter in California?" She looked west to the ocean. The water appeared to sparkle as if it were a sea of diamonds.

"Here's our exit." Luis drove another few miles through an office park and pulled in a parking spot reserved for the CEO.

Ronnie's mouth dropped open in surprise. When Luis told her he owned his own graphics design firm, she envisioned a storefront office in a strip mall. *L. Duarte Graphics* was housed in a large two story building. His office was located in the administrative section of the warehouse, co-located on the same property.

"Is *this* all you?" she asked.

"All mine," he replied, proudly. He took her on an extended tour of the building, explaining the processes and showing her the equipment. A small weekend crew was busily working the presses, making sure all went smoothly.

A guy wearing a ball cap yelled out, "Hey boss? Whatcha doing here on this beautiful Saturday afternoon?"

"*Buenos dias,* Julio, I'm giving my friend a tour of the building. How long do you guys plan on being here today?"

"*Hola senora,*" he acknowledged Ronnie. "We'll leave when the job is done, sir. This was an urgent last minute order which shouldn't take more than a couple of hours."

"Sounds good. I'll see you on Monday." He waved goodbye. "That was Julio, one of the shift supervisors. He's a good man and a great worker."

"Luis, I'm impressed. When you told me about your business, it never occurred to me how successful you are. And you actually started all this in a one bedroom apartment?"

Luis shook his head modestly and replied, "On a shoe string budget."

They hopped back on the freeway heading south. After a few miles he exited and pulled into a very busy hamburger joint. It wasn't even a restaurant, just a walk up window to place "to go" orders.

"Ronnie you've got to try these burgers. They are so delicious, one bite will instantly turn a vegetarian back into a meat lover."

"Umm, you know how much I love a good burger. By the length of the line, I'll take your word for it. C'mon, let's go. I'm starved."

On the way back to Ronnie's apartment, they noticed a commotion. Dozens of people were gathered in the street watching the latest neighborhood tragedy unfold. Half a dozen police cars and an ambulance blocked the street and a policeman directed traffic away from the area. Yellow crime scene tape blocked the crowd's view, effectively preventing those with camera phones from videoing the murder scene and uploading to *YouTube* later.

"Yo man? What's up?" Luis asked a group of guys hanging back from the others.

"Homie got shot. Must've been a drive-by," replied a teenaged Mexican boy with a hairnet tied on top of his head. The knot rested high on his forehead causing him to resemble a short order cook. Or a gangbanger wannabe. He was stereotypically dressed in a white wife beater t-shirt and short khaki pants that rested well below his ass.

"Okay, thanks man." Luis turned the car in direction of the detour. He drove the alternate route to Ronnie's apartment and parked.

"Did he say a drive-by? Ain't that a trip? You can live in the most beautiful of cities in the United States, and still have this shit happen. We live in a really messed up world."

Luis didn't say a word until they were inside Ronnie's apartment. When she turned the light on, another cockroach scurried across the floor.

"That's it! Pack your bags. I'm getting you out of here tonight."

"I'll be all right here. Look around. There are families living in this building—in this neighborhood. They're not running away. I can deal with this until I can find something better."

As quickly as her words found space in the decrepit apartment, an unexpected loud noise came from next door followed by shrill voices. Angry voices shouting hateful words. Luis looked at Ronnie. Ronnie looked at Luis. She hunched her shoulders and threw her hands up in defeat.

Five minutes later, without uttering a sound she repacked her suitcases and fled. They were back on the road in record time.

"Now where are you taking me?" Ronnie felt helpless and at the mercy of Luis. It was a role she was quickly getting comfortable with.

"I'll send someone over to get your car tomorrow morning. Ronnie, there was no way in hell I was going to leave you at that apartment again tonight. Considering what we just saw? And the potential domestic situation going on next door? Come on... I know you're stubborn, but this time I win. After I saw the state of your apartment, I made arrangements to have the rental apartment cleaned up for you. It's not much, but you will be safe *and* it's clean and cockroach free. I think you'll like it."

Ronnie began to protest. "Luis, I can't let you do this. You've already helped me so much already."

"Too late. It's already done. Like I told you before, you can pay rent if it helps you feel any better. You are not obligated to me and I don't want you to feel that you are."

"Thanks Luis." Ronnie felt her heart open fully to Luis. In that open space, love replaced any doubt she had about this man. He proved over and over again that he would and could take care of her. With him, she was safe.

Luis pulled the Jeep into a private driveway off the main drag of downtown Montverde. From the look of things, Montverde was where the rich and famous lived and shopped. Ronnie saw enough Mercedes-Benzs, Bentleys, and Aston Martins parked in front of a shopping center to last a lifetime. He drove another few hundred feet on the road before stopping in front of a rather modest country cottage. A mid-height, white picket fence added enough charm to make the cottage welcoming. The grounds were impeccably landscaped in native plants and flowers.

"Here let me help you down," he said. "I'll give you a tour of the house first, and then I'll show you the apartment."

The stone pathway led them underneath a trellis covered by a climbing rose vine from the driveway up to the front entrance.

Ronnie knew before she stepped through the door that she was going to love his home. And she did. It was as if she had decorated the place herself. The living room was bright, airy and inviting. Ethnic artwork from Dominican artists dominated the colorfully painted walls. Live plants gave the space an indoor outdoor feel that provided an overall comfortable atmosphere. Two large brown Boxers bounded to the front door and began licking Luis' face.

"Bruno! Ariel! Get down!" He ruffled the dogs behind their ears and sent them on their way.

Ronnie stepped aside to let the dogs pass. "Your dogs, I presume?"

"Yes, they're like my children. Don't worry, they're very gentle. Most of the time, I keep them in a separate area of the house."

"Okay, if you say so. By the way, I love your house. Did you decorate this on your own?"

"Ronnie, you must have forgotten I am a graphic designer. Artistic design and colors are my specialty and I have an eye for art. So to answer your question, yes I decorated this all on my own."

She ran her hands over the furniture imported from his island. Somehow he succeeded in bringing elements of the DR into his home in California. The shiny metal objects sitting in the china cabinet caught her eye. Displayed in a sealed glass case was his international collection of coins in all shapes, sizes, and ages. She recognized the coin from their encounter in Amarillo and smiled at the memory.

Luis picked up one of many remotes and clicked on the stereo. Soft mellow jazz immediately filled the room. He opened a bottle of wine and offered a glass to Ronnie.

"Mmm, this is good. Is it local?" She read the label on the bottle.

"Yeah, one of my good friends owns a vineyard about an hour away. He comps me with a case of wine and I design his wine bottle labels."

"Ronnie, let's cut out the small talk. We've been dancing around this issue all day long. Neither of us has brought it up, but we need to talk about *us*." He motioned for her to have a seat on the sofa.

"I know. You're right. I've been putting you off because I was focused solely on Kiara. Wondering and worrying on how that was going to work out."

"I understand how meeting your daughter for the first time is pretty significant. But you had nothing to worry about. I know Kiara pretty well and she is a very mature, thoughtful, intelligent young lady. Travis did a very good job with her."

Ronnie watched Luis speak. She loved how his eyes crinkled around the edges when he laughed and he had a way of tilting his head when a topic proved to be thought provoking. She found his mannerisms absolutely adorable.

"Luis, from the first day I met you in that restaurant in Puerto Azul, I have loved you. I realized it little by little every time we were together. I felt it when we spent days touring your country on the back of that motorcycle. I accepted it when you flew to Oklahoma and drove me halfway across the country. I embraced it when you didn't let me stay at that fleabag apartment. No man has ever treated me the way you have. No man has ever loved me the way you do. I fell in love with you after I already loved you. Does that make sense?"

He placed his wine glass on the table and removed hers from her good hand. "I love you too," he uttered breathlessly, happily, joyfully.

Their mutual declaration of love was a welcomed relief for both. Individually they felt it, yet neither wanted to admit it for fear of scaring off the other.

"I was hesitant to express my true feelings for you when we were in the DR. The night we kissed, I knew I loved you then. I wanted to tell you so badly, but you were focused on the issues consuming your life. I did not want my love to be a burden."

"You're a pretty great guy. You gave me space that allowed me to realize what we have. Your patience and understanding let our love blossom and develop at its own pace. Thank you."

He sighed heavily, happy to know his love would not go unrequited. With another sip of wine, he picked up the remote and switched it to *merengue* music and turned it up loud. "Hey pretty lady, you want to dance?" he asked.

"Of course, but you'll have to show me how to move my hips again," she replied demurely.

"That will be my pleasure."

Luis was warm not only from the wine coursing through his body, but from the love emanating from the lovely woman swaying her hips in front of him. Ronnie was positively gorgeous from the top of her braided hair to the tips of her French-tipped manicured toes.

Embracing the joy of their love; listening to the music; holding her closely; feeling their hearts beat in time—in perfect harmony to the offbeat of his native music, two became one. He could no longer resist the temptation. Neither could she.

Ronnie took Luis by the hand and guided him to the bedroom. The bedroom she discovered merely minutes before, yet none of that mattered. The king-sized bed beckoned the two lovers to fully express their love.

Standing beside the bed, they kissed passionately, exploring each other's unique flavors. Luis unbuttoned her blouse and carefully pulled it past the cast on her arm. He helped her out of her shorts then pulled off his pants. He wore no underwear. She stood before him in sexy matching lingerie. His erection grew stronger and firmer as he took in her natural beauty.

Oh my! Ronnie thought. *And I was worried about what he had to offer.* She stepped towards him and unbuttoned his shirt with one hand. She rubbed his chest, fingering the curly hairs. His nipples were erect as well, so she took one in her mouth. He moaned in ecstasy.

Luis helped remove her underwear fully exposing her body for his viewing pleasure. He loved her body, for it was absolutely perfect. She was fit, just the way he imagined she would be. He gently massaged her luscious breasts whose two erect nipples served as an invitation for his enjoyment.

Ronnie climbed atop the bed, maneuvering her body next to his. He pulled her on top and whispered, "Veronica Indigo Pierce, I love you."

"Luis Eduardo Duarte, I love you, too." She smiled with love in her eyes and her heart.

One by one, she kissed each of his fingers and explained, "I love you because you are: Loving. Caring. Passionate. Thoughtful. Intelligent. Honest. Extremely Sexy. Loyal. Funny. Dependable." She kissed the tip of his penis and said, "I love this, because it's for me."

He reciprocated and kissed every inch of her body beginning with the nape of her neck, down her stomach, and ending at the sweet, sweet spot hidden deep between her legs, waiting to be discovered by his eager tongue. She arched her back as Luis brought her to orgasm over and over again.

And when he finally entered her, the rest of the world melted away. Nothing else mattered. As their bodies joined and became one, they fell headfirst into the beautiful infinite space reserved exclusively for their love. The space residing in between the beat of their hearts. The space in the offbeat.

"Um, I feel so gooood!" Ronnie moaned. Although physically Luis was a magnificent lover, her contentment resided in knowing she shared a powerful love with a man who loved her back.

"I could get used to this," Luis thought aloud.

"You could get used to what, my love?" Ronnie asked, turning on her side to face him.

"You. Us. This. Loving you, that's what. What do you think about that?"

Ronnie contemplated his words, turned them upside down, played with the idea for a moment, and viewed the relationship from several angles. She replied, "Know what? So could I."

"Here's a bottle of water. I don't know what you did woman, but for some odd reason, I seem to be dehydrated." He laughed.

"Maybe it's because you came twice."

"Hmm, now that you mention it….maybe you're right." He took a swig of water and returned to bed.

Lying there next to Luis, Ronnie imagined this is how her life was supposed to be. She closed her eyes and prayed, *"Thank you Lord for bringing me to this place; introducing this wonderful man into my life; leading me to Kiara. Thank you for showing me your will and giving me the tools to follow. I believe, deep within my soul, everything I have done thus far in my life has led me here. I know my work is only beginning and I vow to make good and live my life as you would have me. Thank you for removing the blinders I wore against my mother. I am thankful for all the blessings you have bestowed upon me. You have given me so much and for that I shall be forever grateful. Amen, amen, amen."*

"I love you so much," he whispered. He kissed away the tears streaming down her face. Taking her in his arms, they made love once more. He kissed the top of Ronnie's head, resting quietly on his chest. Sleep quickly came, carrying them both away.

Chapter 28

"Good morning sweetheart," Luis greeted Ronnie coming from the bathroom. "I have a ton of things to take care of this morning, but I wanted to show you the apartment and give you a quick tour of the grounds since we never got around to it last night." He smiled mischievously.

"Oh, alright... My suitcases are still in the Jeep..." She wore only a t-shirt pulled from his chest-of-drawers.

"Nope, I brought your suitcases in this morning. Check the closet. I'll be back in a minute."

She showered and quickly changed. Luis was in the kitchen making breakfast. *Merengue* music played quietly in the background. He seemed so happy. *Oh look at him... Why does he have to be so handsome?*

"I poured your coffee. Cream and sugar are on the counter. I've got to get going in about thirty minutes, so please make yourself comfortable. Like I said, I want to show you around and let you take a look at the apartment out back. It'll only take a few minutes."

"You sure are perky this morning." She sipped her coffee, holding the cup to warm her cold hands.

"I have good reason to be. That's what the love of a good woman does to a man. Cheers him right up!" he exclaimed. "I'll put breakfast in the oven to stay warm. Follow me."

The morning was warm and sunny. Ronnie grabbed the mug of coffee and padded after Luis. His two dogs trailed closely behind, apparently curious of their master's new friend. The yard was beautifully landscaped with a large swimming pool in the backyard. They followed the stone path towards the back of the property which led to the apartment which resembled a small cottage. *My goodness! Luis must be loaded!* The knowledge of his wealth made her slightly uncomfortable. She did not want him to think she was a gold digger.

"Go on, take a look inside." He pushed open the door.

The outside of the apartment gave the impression the space was small. However, after stepping inside she realized the one bedroom apartment was quite large. As was his house, the area was beautifully decorated in Caribbean style.

"Luis, this is exactly what I need!" she exclaimed. "My furniture should fit perfectly. *I gave most of it away, but what I have left will fit the space well.* I love it! You know you can probably get anything you want for this apartment, especially considering all the upgrades in the kitchen and bath, right?" She noticed a closed door with a huge purple ribbon mounted across the frame. "What is this?"

"It's a surprise. Look inside." He grinned.

Ronnie opened the door and gasped. "What did you do?"

The small room contained an antique table and a black ergonomic chair. A laptop with a large monitor sat atop the table and a printer rested on a stand in a corner. An overstuffed, oversized chair and ottoman done up in antique rose print, were situated across from a large window overlooking the gardens. Soft music played in the background.

"It's for you. Your writing studio. Before you get caught up in life again, I wanted to give you an opportunity to write that novel you've spoken about. Do you like it?"

"I love it. Thank you so much!" She wrapped her arms around his neck in a display of gratitude and love, planting kisses all over his neck.

"You're so welcome, my love. Just remember me when you become rich and famous. And I want an autographed copy of your first book. Deal?"

"Deal!" She took a seat in the chair and exhaled.

"I'm happy to hear you like the apartment. You can use it for as long as you need to because I have no intention of ever renting it out. I'm not very fond of having a stranger living so close to me."

Not wanting to take advantage of Luis, she wanted to pay her way. "How much is the rent by the way?"

"The rent is whatever you can afford to pay. How about a token amount of one hundred dollars a month?"

"A hundred dollars? Do you realize how much I'm paying for that piece of crap apartment? Fifteen hundred a month, that's what! And you're willing to let this go for a pittance?" Ronnie appreciated his generosity, yet the feelings of obligation were kicking in.

"First of all, I don't need the money. And secondly, I'm doing a friend a favor. I do not want you feeling obligated to me. I will respect the boundaries of our relationship and let it grow naturally, and if you feel uncomfortable, we can discuss other options."

Luis approached her and said, "I just want you to be happy and if there is anything I can do to help that along, I'm going to do it. I love you Ronnie Pierce. If you want to move into my house and make it our home, I'm all for that too. But I suspect you need to have your own space at the moment. You need time to get acclimated and bond with your daughter. I get it. I'm simply offering you a place to stay—a safe place, until you are ready for *us.*"

She threw her arms around him and whispered, "You really are a Godsend. Thank you so much. Thanks for everything."

"Well, I've got to get going. I left your breakfast in the oven. I should be home in a few hours. Make yourself at home. Relax. Oh, by the way, one of my partners is going to get your car and bring it back to you this morning, so I'll need your keys."

As Ronnie and Luis were returning to the main house, a single purple butterfly flitted from flower to flower. It flew towards her then quickly flew away.

She sighed in contentment. She *was* really home.

Ronnie walked Luis to the door then returned to the kitchen to have breakfast. She hummed softly as she recalled their lovemaking. *Umph! Luis has exquisite taste in art.* She thought as she surveyed his living space.

Her purse remained on the couch from last night; the unmistakable simultaneous ring and vibration of her cell phone reverberated from inside. She refilled her cup with coffee, anticipating a long conversation with whoever was calling at this time of the morning. Must be someone on the east coast.

"Hello?" she answered.

"Hi Veronica, it's your mother."

"Oh hey, Mama? How are you?"

"I'm fine. Are you in California yet? Last time I heard from you, you was in Vegas."

"Oh yes, I'm here. Sorry I didn't call you back. Some woman stepped on my phone and broke it and since I've been here, I've been very busy," she explained.

"I see. So tell me, how was the meeting with Kiara? Did it turn out okay?"

"Our meeting turned out better than okay. She is as intelligent as she is beautiful," gushed Ronnie.

"I'm so happy for you both. Well, I just called to say thank you. I got the check today. Child, you didn't have to send me all this money."

"I won it in Vegas, so I won't miss it. It was unexpected free money I didn't plan on having so it was nothing to send it to you. Plus, you can use it to fix up the house and buy yourself something nice."

"I sure do appreciate it and will put it to good use. Thank you," she hesitated then added. "Veronica, I want to ask you a favor."

"Sure Mama, what is it?"

"Uh, you mentioned your daughter—Kiara, is graduating from high school this week."

"Yeah, the graduation is this Friday. Why do you ask?"

"I was thinking how nice it would be to see my only grandchild graduate from high school. I was wondering if it's possible to fly out there for a few days? If I can attend the graduation ceremony?"

You actually want to see the granddaughter you wouldn't acknowledge for her entire life graduate? Meet the child you made me put up for adoption? "Uh, I think that would be okay. Mama, you do know Travis is also going to be there? He *is* still her father. I don't know how you feel about him now, but you need to also take that into consideration."

"I know he is that child's father. And I expect him to be there," she sighed. "Since your visit, I've been praying a lot and asking the Lord to remove that seed of hatred from my heart. I talked to Pastor and he told me this is something I must do to let go of my past. I've got to face what's troubling me head on. Plus, I really want to meet my granddaughter."

"Okay, I'll make the arrangements and will let you know about the ticket. I've found a nice little apartment and you can stay with me."

"Thank you Veronica. This means the world to me."

"Me too, Mama. I'll talk to you soon. Love you."

"Love you too, daughter. Bye now."

* * *

Upon discovering Travis Bradford was the father of Ronnie's daughter, Luis knew he needed to make a personal visit. So that morning while Ronnie was still fast asleep, he phoned Travis and asked if they could meet. Said there was an important issue they needed to discuss. Travis agreed to the meeting and asked Luis to be at the center at nine o'clock.

"Luis, what a nice surprise. Come in and have a seat." He offered his handshake and motioned to an empty chair.

"Travis, my man! Yes, it has been quite a while. How's the business going?" asked Luis as he took a seat in Travis's office.

"You know. Keeping busy. Can't complain." Travis wondered where this was going. Not one for small talk, he asked outright, "Luis, you said you have an important issue to discuss. What's going on?"

Luis cleared his throat and said, "Travis, this meeting has nothing to do with business. It's strictly personal. But I needed to speak with you man to man."

"You have my attention. Go on..."

"Okay. Well, do you know a Veronica Pierce?"

"Yes, I know Ronnie. Why?" Travis's interest piqued upon hearing Ronnie's name.

"I met her when I went home to the Dominican Republic last month. She was there vacationing. We hit it off and have kept in touch."

"So what does that have to do with me?"

"Travis, Ronnie and I are *involved*. I drove her out here and she's staying at my place. In the apartment." Luis watched carefully for any display of emotion. Any hint of unresolved feelings he may still hold for his old girlfriend. He needed to know where Travis's head and heart were in relation to Ronnie.

Travis sat back in his chair and studied Luis. "*You're* the guy who drove her?" He laughed at the irony. "She told me a friend helped her out. But never in a million years did I expect it to be you. We've known each other, what... about six years?"

"Yes, going on seven. It tripped me out too when I found out. She told me her daughter's name was Kiara, but I didn't associate *your* Kiara with *hers*."

"Why, because I'm a white guy?" He smirked.

Luis nodded. "Maybe... What are the chances of my meeting a woman who is the mother of your child? Think about it."

"You're right. The chances are astronomical." He leaned forward. "Luis, do you believe in fate?"

"More and more every day." He exhaled.

"Well I do. Since my accident, I've had lots of time to think about life and how one person's actions can affect so many others. That man who decided to drink and get behind the wheel of that truck had no inkling how his one careless decision would affect my life. And my daughter's life. That he would end Janelle's."

"You're right. It's the law of *Cause and Effect*—we are all connected and anything a person does impacts someone else's life."

"Right. I say I believe in fate, because had it not been for that man drinking, I would not have been paralyzed, and I would not have started this center to help other paralyzed individuals. My life was changed so I could help others. I have accepted *this* as my fate. It was my destiny to end up here, in this place, doing what I am doing. If I were to believe it was just a senseless accident, I would lose my mind," Travis said.

Luis, clasped his fingers together and said, "I don't have a rational explanation for why Ronnie and I met in the DR. After she left, I really didn't expect to hear from her again. We talked a few times over the phone and she kept me abreast of her changing situation. I made an off-hand comment that I'd love to ride with her to California since it was a long drive. She turned down my offer—wanted to do it on her own. I let it go at that. But then she called and said she needed a driver to get to California to meet her daughter and make it in time for the graduation."

"Ronnie always was an independent woman. Never asked for help until she was backed into a corner." Travis smiled, remembering her in younger days. "I hear you though. Often times, there is no reasonable explanation for what happens. None we can make sense of anyway."

"Travis, I consider you as a good friend. I've known both you and Kiara for many, many years, yet you never mentioned anything about her mother and it wasn't my place to ask. But now I have to. I love this woman and I need to know if there are going to be any problems between us because of Ronnie." Luis nervously awaited his response.

Travis looked at the picture of him, Janelle and Kiara, sitting on his desk. Ten years ago, he may have answered the question differently. Today he was able to provide Luis with peace of mind in knowing Ronnie was nothing more to him than a dear friend and the mother of his daughter.

Luis, you have nothing to worry about. Whatever feelings I had for Ronnie ended years ago. The only thing we have in common now is our mutual love for our daughter. We've both moved on with our lives and are not the same people we were in our 20's."

"Thank you, Travis. Please understand… I had to know."

"You're welcome, but you should also know that I offered Ronnie a position at the center. That woman is a whiz in business. She is really going to make a difference here if she accepts the job. What took weeks for me to figure out, she did in about an hour, and that was coming in cold, fresh off the street!"

"She is a very smart lady; of that I can agree." He stood to leave and said, "Travis, if there is anything I can do please give me a call. Business or personal. We're all in this together now."

"Thanks man. Hey, you coming to Kiara's graduation? It's going to be at the Santa Elena Bowl this Friday."

"Wouldn't miss it for the world," Luis replied.

"Great! Then I'll see you there. Take it easy brother."

Chapter 29

The remainder of the week went by fairly quickly. Ronnie found a local doctor who suggested removing the hard cast in favor of a soft one. Getting that cast taken off was a welcome relief. Although she didn't have full use of her arm yet, at least she could scratch the ever present itch.

Because Kiara was busy with finals and graduation preparation, she and Ronnie didn't have much quality time to spend together. However, Ronnie promised to take Kiara to a beauty salon she recently discovered through the "sistah hotline". Kiara was going to have her hair flat-ironed. Her daughter's excitement of going to a black beautician for the first time was troubling to Ronnie. With a realization of how sheltered her daughter was raised, she vowed to rectify the situation immediately. It was her mission to introduce this child to her roots.

When Ronnie told Luis her mother was flying in for a visit, he admitted he was very surprised. He agreed to let Dianna stay in the apartment while Ronnie resided in the house with him. Although the two women had only recently mended fences, they now seemed to be thick as thieves. Women! He would never understand them.

He loved having Ronnie in his house. Used to be when he came home, he'd turn on the television just for white noise. Used it as a means to erase the amazingly loud silence of living alone. For the last two days, he was greeted by the delicious aroma of Dominican food. Ronnie had recently discovered his vast collection of cook books and took it upon herself to learn to cook his favorite meals. Although her version of rice and beans wasn't quite there yet, he appreciated her enthusiasm and effort to make an authentic meal. He was convinced Ronnie Pierce was the right woman for him.

* * *

Ronnie, Kiara and Dianna spent the day together getting manicures, pedicures and Kiara's hair done. The bonding between three generations of Pierce women went extremely well.

"Ronnie, I love my hair. It's longer than I imagined and I love the way it swings in the breeze. But after today, I think I'll return to my big curly hair. It's more my style." She admired her reflection in the mirror.

The beautician who had just spent nearly two hours flat-ironing Kiara's hair, rolled her eyes in silent protest to letting this girl with all that hair return to that wild child look.

"You look beautiful. It's nice to have the flexibility, whatever you eventually decide," replied Ronnie, looking at the beautician standing there with her arms crossed.

"For sure." She tossed her hair again. "Hey, you guys hungry? I'm like starved. You guys like Mexican food? There's a good Mexican restaurant a few blocks from here."

"It's alright with me. How about you, Mama?"

"As long as I don't hafta eat none of that refried beans mess, I'm good," replied Dianna.

The women walked the few blocks to the restaurant with Kiara pointing out her favorite stores along the way. She was excited to share her city with her mother and grandmother. They arrived at the Mexican restaurant, went inside and were immediately seated.

While reviewing the menu to decide upon what to eat, Dianna pulled a large book from her huge purse.

Ronnie teased, "Mama, you are going to throw your back out carrying around such a heavy bag."

Dianna ignored Ronnie's comment and focused on her granddaughter. She said, "Kiara dear, I want to give you a graduation gift. It ain't much, but I started working on this as soon as your mother left. My gift to you is your history. This book will fill in the blanks and tell you something about this side of the family. The Pierce's—me and your grandfather, Vernon. I made this scrapbook and included pictures, newspaper clippings, and personal notes about who these people are and how they're related to you."

"Dianna, it's beautiful! You put this together yourself? The leather cover is absolutely gorgeous. And you had my name inscribed on it. Thank you. Thank you so much!" Kiara hugged Dianna and browsed through the pages of her history.

"Mama, that was really a very thoughtful gift... You keep surprising me more and more every day." Ronnie sat back and wondered if an alien had taken over her mother.

Dianna smiled, content in knowing that she had finally done the right thing. "Every child deserves to know their history. Better late than never, I always say."

Chapter 30

The Santa Elena Bowl was packed with excitement as nervous graduates mingled with proud parents and friends. Comments reverberated throughout the crowd. "Congratulations!" "You did it!" "I can't believe you made it!" "We're so proud of you!"

The announcer's voice came over the state-of-the-art sound system and instructed all to find their seats and for graduates to report to their designated areas.

"I am so proud of you, honey," Travis said to Kiara. His voice cracked as he unsuccessfully tried to hide his emotions.

"Thanks, Daddy. I love you." She bent over and kissed him, wiping her happy tears away.

"Kiara, thank you for sharing one of the most important days in your life with me. I can't tell you how happy I am to be here." Ronnie stroked her child's face.

"You sure are a lovely young lady," said Dianna. "Look just like your Momma did when she was 'bout your age."

"Thank you both for being here. I've got like my whole family with me now. This is so awesome! Well, I've got to go. Wish me luck guys!"

"Good luck!" They all cried out in unison.

"Hello Mrs. Pierce. You're looking well. Good to see you again," Travis said to Dianna.

"Good to see you too," she replied. *Ronnie didn't mention Travis was in a wheelchair.*

"How was your flight out?" he asked.

"Not bad. A bit bumpy over the mountains, but I survived." She inhaled. "Look Travis, I want to explain something to you about the first time we met…"

Travis held up his hand and shook his head. "No need to explain Mrs. Pierce, Ronnie already told me about that day. She told me about everything and all of that is in the past. Let's start over with today. What do you say?" He offered his hand.

"Well then, here's to letting bygones be bygones. You're alright Travis. Yes you are." She accepted his handshake and bent over to give him a big hug.

The handicapped seating area was reserved on the floor near the stage. Because Travis required special seating, the entire family sat in the designated reserved row with him. Lexi and her husband sat next to Travis.

"Hi Lexi," said Ronnie.

"Veronica, glad you could make it." She looked at Luis curiously, "Hey Luis, how you doing?" Her facial expressions asked a million questions, but none made it to her mouth.

"Lexi, good to see you again. I'm doing well. Hard to believe little Kiara is all grown up," Luis replied and also acknowledged Lexi's husband.

Lexi turned and whispered to Travis. He said something causing her to gasp. She turned and looked at Luis and Ronnie and smiled.

Ronnie opened the graduation program. "Look guys, Kiara is the Valedictorian! She's addressing the graduation class!" Ronnie couldn't hide her excitement.

"That's my granddaughter! Smart as a whip… just like her Momma. Vernon would have been so proud. Yes indeed!" Dianna proudly proclaimed.

"Ladies and gentlemen! Please help me in welcoming the class of 2012!" shouted the young student making the introductions.

Five hundred graduating seniors marched into the stadium with wide, proud smiles plastered across their faces. *Pomp and Circumstance* played on in the background in one continuous loop until all graduates were on stage.

"Please remain standing for the playing of the national anthem," instructed the proctor into the microphone.

A young girl tentatively walked across the stage holding a microphone in her hand. To everyone's surprise, she belted out a very powerful rendition of the *Star Spangled Banner* in a voice that contradicted her small stature. As she sang the last note, the crowd's applause was directly in proportion to her great performance. She quickly bowed, waved, and left the stage to return to her proud parents. After everyone took their seats, the proctor announced each graduate, calling out their names in alphabetical order. The more popular students received loud shout-outs from the crowd.

When the announcer called out, "Kiara Indigo Bradford, 2012 class valedictorian!" The stadium went wild. Cheers, air horns, and the ringing of cowbells were all in support of Kiara. It seemed that many people in the community knew and loved the Bradford family.

Ronnie's heart swelled with both pride and shame. She was proud of her daughter's accomplishments. Despite the hardships Kiara experienced, with the love and guidance of Travis and his family, she persevered and did extremely well. Ronnie felt ashamed because she played no part in her daughter's success. So holding back the lump in her throat, she stood and shouted out with the rest of the crowd. She looked over at Travis. He looked in her direction with a huge, happy smile on his face. He nodded his head in satisfaction of a job well done.

When it was time to deliver her speech, Kiara walked up on that stage with a grace and dignity that belied her eighteen years. Her persona portrayed a person who addressed a crowd this size on a regular basis. She smiled and spoke clearly into the microphone. The crowd finally settled down and grew quiet.

"Congratulations Santa Elena class of 2012! We did it!" she shouted out loudly to the students seated behind her. The class went wild for another five minutes.

"All right, all right, settle down, settle down," she calmly quieted the class.

"We want to thank all our family and friends for coming. Your presence is very important to us all. I also want to send a special shout out to my father, Travis Mitchell Bradford." She paused to let the crowd's excitement die down again. "Daddy, I love you. I am here today because of your never ending love and commitment. Without you, I wouldn't be the person I am today. For everything you have ever done for me, I am grateful. Thank you. I also want to thank my Aunt Lexi for being there for me always. You are my best friend and I love you so much."

Ronnie looked over and smiled at both Travis and Lexi, acknowledging their accomplishment at raising a wonderful young lady.

"But there is also someone else I'd like to acknowledge today and that is my mother, Veronica Indigo Pierce. You see, my mother gave me up for adoption at birth. She wasn't much older than we are today. It's only been recently that she's come back into my life." Kiara looked directly at Ronnie as she spoke.

Luis put his arm protectively around Ronnie's shoulder and gave her arm a gentle squeeze. Kiara's speech was totally unexpected and he worried how her words would affect Ronnie.

As Kiara spoke, Ronnie tensed up. She was caught off guard and felt put on the spot. *On my God! Kiara is talking about me! Speaking to me! I've got to get out of here! Oh good, Luis has my back. He always does. I can do this. I can get through this. What in the world is she going to say? Is she going to publicly humiliate me and tell the world how terrible a mother I was? Lord please let this be over quickly…* Ronnie pasted a smile on her face, praying this would be over soon and that whatever was said wouldn't hurt too badly.

"I want to talk to you today about actions and consequences. Graduates, there will come times in your lives when you will encounter difficult situations. In those situations you have to make tough choices. Life or death decisions that may profoundly change your life and the lives of those you love. The reason I am telling you this is you must be able to *live* with the consequences of your actions. All too often, we make careless decisions not worrying about what's going to happen tomorrow. We get caught up in the trap of living for today and letting tomorrow take care of itself."

The crowd was silent as all listened intently to the words of wisdom spoken by someone so young. Kiara had everyone enthralled with her speech.

"I'm here to tell you to be mindful of the decisions you make. Think before you act! Consider the consequences down the road. Mull over what may happen in a few years because of what you did today. If you are unable to live with those consequences, then you'd better make a different decision. Because once that ball gets rolling, it's very hard to stop it. You don't want to one day wake up and find out you messed up because then it will be too late." She smiled at her father and Lexi.

"Class of 2012, I challenge you to find that special place where you belong. Follow your passions, your hopes, your dreams! Listen to your heart when it tells you what is right and true. Don't get stuck following the crowd. I challenge you to let your passion guide you to your purpose. My fellow classmates… please live your life on purpose every single day because tomorrow is not guaranteed." Her voice cracked for a moment before she regained her composure.

The crowd cheered, providing their support for her to continue. Dianna looked over at Ronnie with tears streaming down her face. She used one of her favorite handkerchiefs Vernon had given her years ago to wipe her face.

"My mother chose to put me up for adoption because she wanted me to have a better life than she was capable of providing. She loved me so much she sacrificed being a mother so another family who wanted a baby girl would have the opportunity. And you know what? Veronica Pierce made the right decision. I was raised in a loving family by a father who loved me to the ends of this earth. So I want to say thank you to my mother for making a tough decision. I love you and I turned out okay." Tears streamed down her face as she spoke.

Ronnie wiped her eyes, stood, and blew several kisses to Kiara. Her heart swelled with love.

By the time Kiara's speech was finished, there wasn't a dry eye in the stadium. The crowd stood and applauded for at least five minutes. Seemed there were quite a few adults who also needed to hear the message she delivered to her mother.

Ronnie looked over to see Luis and Lexi's husband helping Travis stand in honor of his daughter. She broke down in tears and joined the trio. Today they all celebrated the life of a young lady who had the world at her feet. Celebrated her finding her place and making it her own. At eighteen years of age, Kiara had already understood the meaning of living in the offbeat.

The principal took the stage, dabbing her eyes dry along the way. She embraced Kiara in a celebratory hug. Kiara waved at her family, and then took her seat amongst her classmates.

With a booming voice the principal shouted out, "Thank you all for coming! Class of 2012! Congratulations and welcome to adulthood! Time to party!"

The End

Loving In The Offbeat
coming in the Summer of 2013

About the Author

Patricia Hopkins is originally from St. Louis, Missouri. She loves traveling, cooking, reading, and writing. She started writing short stories when she was just a teenager, and has since expanded her hobby into writing creative fiction.

This novel includes a reference to "The Kamal's", an Oklahoma City based band. Her son Zak and his four friends make up this popular local group. For more information about The Kamal's visit *YouTube* or join them on *facebook*.